PRAISE FOR *THE SECOND CHANCE YEAR*

"A touch of magic and a heap of self-growth animate this sparkling and sophisticated rom-com."

—*Publishers Weekly*, starred review

"A swoony romance with a subplot about harassment and sexism in the workplace, Wiesner's latest will resonate with every reader who's wondered, 'What if?'"

—*Booklist*, starred review

"A self-aware, flawed, quirky heroine—with a slow-burning, opposites-attract romance—makes for a delightful serio-comic read that dynamically explores the what-ifs of life."

—Shelf Awareness

"An ambitious woman finding her way in the world and the heart-meltingly caring man who loves her for who she is combine to make this a charming romance."

—*Library Journal*

"Tough themes with a light touch and many winning characters."

—*Kirkus*

"*The* book you need to read before setting your resolutions."

—*The Knot*

"Packed with charm, lovable characters, and a bit of magic... this

—*Woman's World*

"A charmingly sweet time-loop romance about a hard yet hope-filled journey to discovering what truly matters in life, embracing your voice, and standing up for what you believe in."

—Chloe Liese, author of *Two Wrongs Make a Right*

"A sweet, smart, and satisfying rom-com that addresses important issues with grace even as the characters make us laugh and fall in love right along with them."

—Sophie Sullivan, author of *Ten Rules for Faking It*

"A delightful story filled with empowered characters, lovable found family, delicious desserts, and a sweet romance, all sprinkled with a dash of magic. This book warmed my heart like a fresh-out-of-the-oven brownie!"

—Lauren Kung Jessen, author of *Lunar Love*

"The hooky premise drew me in right from the start and kept me turning pages with its hints of magic, found family, and slow-burn yearning for the nerdy dreamboat of a hero."

—Anna E. Collins, author of *Love at First Spite*

"An adorable, swoony, beautifully written romance that is full of warmth, heart, and food. I was completely charmed by Sadie and Jacob and cried all the happy tears. I didn't want it to end!"

—Catherine Walsh, author of *Snowed In*

WISH
I WERE
HERE

Also by Melissa Wiesner

The Second Chance Year

WISH
I WERE
HERE

Melissa Wiesner

FOREVER

NEW YORK BOSTON

Copyright © 2024 by Melissa Wiesner

Reading group guide copyright © 2024 by Melissa Wiesner and Hachette Book Group, Inc.

Cover design and illustration by Sarah Congdon. Cover copyright © 2024 by Hachette Book Group, Inc.

Forever
Hachette Book Group
1290 Avenue of the Americas, New York, NY 10104
read-forever.com
@readforeverpub

First Edition: October 2024

Forever is an imprint of Grand Central Publishing. The Forever name and logo are registered trademarks of Hachette Book Group, Inc.

The publisher is not responsible for websites (or their content) that are not owned by the publisher.

The Hachette Speakers Bureau provides a wide range of authors for speaking events. To find out more, go to hachettespeakersbureau.com or email HachetteSpeakers@hbgusa.com.

Forever books may be purchased in bulk for business, educational, or promotional use. For information, please contact your local bookseller or the Hachette Book Group Special Markets Department at special.markets@hbgusa.com.

Print book interior design by Bart Dawson

Library of Congress Cataloging-in-Publication Data

Names: Wiesner, Melissa, author.

Title: Wish I were here / Melissa Wiesner.

Description: First edition. | New York : Forever, 2024.

Identifiers: LCCN 2024008753 | ISBN 9781538741948 (trade paperback) | ISBN 9781538741962 (ebook)

Subjects: LCGFT: Romance fiction. | Novels.

Classification: LCC PS3623.I396 W57 2024 | DDC 813/.6—dc23/eng/20240226

LC record available at https://lccn.loc.gov/2024008753

ISBNs: 9781538741948 (trade paperback), 9781538741962 (ebook)

Printed in the United States of America

LSC-C

Printing 1, 2024

For my Italian family.

In particular, for my grandma Mary, who—in the one hundred years that she lived—never, ever wavered from the belief that you should get your hair out of your face or take some food with you when you leave.

And for my grandpa Salvatore, who did not hand out butterscotch candies, but who I believe would have… had Grandma Mary let him eat candy.

CHAPTER 1

If only I could have predicted the disaster that would be waiting for me when I stepped off the elevator, I would have taken the stairs. Instead, I rode down to the lobby from my eighth-floor apartment because the last thing I want is to show up to meet my brand-new boss with my blouse sweaty and my hair flying.

My wide-eyed gaze slides to the coffee stain now seeping into my high-waisted herringbone pants. "No!" I balance my dripping travel mug in one hand, lid askew, and fumble in my laptop bag with the other, grabbing a mini pack of Kleenex. From somewhere over my shoulder, the buoyant beat of "Build Me Up Buttercup" drifts into my consciousness.

"Oh...hell," comes a sheepish voice to my right. "I'm sorry, Catherine."

I don't even have to look up to know who is speaking. Luca Morelli. Of course he's responsible for this mocha-colored mess dripping down my thigh. Just like he was responsible for the bike I tripped over in the mail room last week and my dry cleaning that disappeared the week before that.

"It's okay..." I focus on scrubbing at the stain, but it's *not okay*, and those flimsy little squares are no match for the majority of an extra-large latte. The tissue disintegrates, smearing mangled bits of paper into the fabric weave of my pants. "Oh no." I can't meet my new boss like *this*.

"Wait, stop, you're just making it worse." Luca swiftly rounds the lobby's front desk and reaches underneath, pulling out a neatly folded rag and a bottle of water.

I take one last futile swipe. *How could it be worse?*

A moment later, Luca is standing in front of me, holding out the rag. "Try this instead."

I toss the mangled tissue in the trash, and when I reach for the cloth in his outstretched hand, my eyes focus on the burst of vibrant tattoos covering the length of his forearm. I've never noticed them before, and the delicate lines of flora and birds are unexpected and beautiful. He must have rolled up the sleeves of his black doorman uniform when he was doing…*whatever* it was he was doing…when he came crashing into me.

"Why were you…" I wave my hand in the direction of the elevator. "Doing the jitterbug in the middle of the lobby?"

Luca uncaps the water bottle and takes my wrist to pour some into the rag. His hand is warm, his grip firm, and I stare at the etched panels of a monarch butterfly's wings as it lands on an echinacea flower. I'm drawn to those vibrant colors, and with him leaning close like this, I feel a strange pull to the man who displays them, too.

"Technically, it was the Carolina shag," he says, yanking me back to my senses.

Why am I standing here staring at his forearms and not on a bus halfway to the university? I lift my gaze from his tattoos to his face, which hovers a good eight inches above mine. But focusing on those dark eyes and bronze skin isn't helping. So I step away from Luca, swiping at my stained pants. While I manage to dislodge the bits of shredded tissue, the coffee stain doesn't budge.

"Mrs. Goodwin was the 1964 Myrtle Beach Carolina shag champion." Luca hitches his chin at a silver-haired Black lady bopping in the corner. Considering her advanced age, she's pulling off some surprisingly elaborate footwork.

"Hello, honey. Sorry about your pants." Mrs. Goodwin gives me a wave and then steps her left orthopedic shoe over her right to execute a graceful spin across the scuffed tile floor.

"Mrs. Goodwin was teaching me her moves, and I wasn't expecting anyone to step off the elevator right at that moment." Luca holds up his hands in a *who knew?* gesture.

I give up on the coffee stain and drop the wet cloth into his open palm, my frustration growing. When I came to the DeGreco to tour the available apartment, there were at least three other people who were also interested. So I knew I was lucky to be the one to land this affordable rental in a quiet building. The handsome, charming doorman seemed like a huge bonus. I looked forward to the extra security at the front door, especially after growing up in a series of sketchy apartments.

And—I remember a brief flash of attraction that first time we met—*maybe that isn't the only reason I liked having a handsome, charming doorman.*

But it turns out that I'm in greater danger of bodily harm when Luca is around than I am when he's disappeared for hours at a time. I press my palm to the dark splotch on my pants and do my best to be grateful that at least the coffee didn't burn my leg. "Of course," I murmur through gritted teeth. "Why would you expect people in a twelve-story building to be riding the elevator at eight in the morning?"

"Well, to be fair, it must be broken, because the numbers over the door usually light up and the bell dings on each floor, letting me know people are coming." Luca shakes out the rag, and I'm treated to another colorful flash of forearm. "I'll need to get Dante in here to fix it."

"Please do." I cross my arms primly. "And while you're at it, maybe you could brush up on the building's manual of rules and regulations. I am sure that 'no dancing in the lobby' is detailed there."

To be honest, I am *not* sure that "no dancing in the lobby" is detailed in the building's manual of rules and regulations. But I *am* sure that—despite the fact that he's served as the building's doorman for much longer than the month I've lived here—Luca has never actually read the manual of rules and regulations and probably won't go and check it now. I know this because he seems to do whatever he pleases, whenever he pleases. Generally, that boils down to a lot of fraternizing with the building residents and very little manning of the door. Normally, I do my best to ignore his loose interpretation of his job description, except when I can't.

Like today.

"Damn it," I mutter, glancing down at the stain on my pants again. It's really setting in now, and I don't think there's any way to save this outfit. I check the time on my phone, and my heart sloshes like my coffee did moments ago.

I'd carefully timed out my morning to arrive at the bus stop ten minutes before the 54 was scheduled to arrive. That bus would have gotten me to campus thirty minutes before my breakfast meeting with the dean of the mathematics department, which would have allowed me five minutes to walk to the café, five minutes for a stop in the bathroom, and twenty minutes to go over my notes before he arrived. And just in case I forgot—which I won't—I printed out the schedule and tucked it into the front pocket of my bag along with my list of things to accomplish today.

I do some quick calculations in my head. Can I take the elevator back upstairs, change into a clean pair of trousers, and still make it to the bus on time?

My breath hitches. Do I even *have* a clean pair of trousers? The clothes the dry cleaner said they'd left with my doorman—aka Luca—never did turn up, and since my job doesn't officially start for a few more weeks, I had plenty of time to buy new ones. Or so I thought. If I don't figure this out in the next three minutes, I'm going to miss the bus.

I take a deep breath. I don't have a car yet. I'd hoped to be able to afford a car payment after a few paychecks came through from my new job. The job I am currently running late for.

I fumble with my phone for my rideshare app.

Except there's still the issue of the pants.

Hands shaking, I pop the lid back on my half-full mug of coffee and thrust it into Luca's grasp. "Hold this, please." And then I run for the elevator, slamming my finger on the button and pressing it over and over, as if that will somehow make it come faster. I look up. The panel of numbers that usually indicates the elevator's floor remains dark. "What's happening?"

"See?" Luca says, taking a casual sip of what remains of my coffee. "It's broken."

Panic rises up in my throat. "The elevator is going to come, though, right?"

Luca shrugs. "Probably. But it's been a little off lately. I definitely need to call Dante."

"This isn't happening." To my great mortification, I find my control slipping, and my voice breaks.

"Hey." Luca's smirk fades, and he sets my coffee mug down on the front desk. "Are you okay?"

My spine stiffens. "No, I'm not okay." I bang harder on the elevator button. "I need to find a new pair of pants, which I don't have because my dry cleaning is lost somewhere in the ether." *Bang.* "And then I need to get on a bus that is going to drive by here in exactly two and a half minutes." *Bang, bang.* "Or I'll be late for a meeting with my new boss. And I—" My voice shakes with an uncharacteristic tinge of hysteria. "Am never." *Bang.* "Late."

And at that exact moment, the harmonizing voices of "Build Me Up Buttercup" fade, and the music switches over to the Supremes singing "You Can't Hurry Love."

My shoulders droop. I give the button one more hard hit with my palm for good measure and then sink down onto the bench next to the elevator. "I'll never get these pants clean in time to meet my boss at nine o'clock, and I don't have another pair. I'll just have to reschedule." A trickle of sweat drips down the back of my neck, and as I reach up to wipe it away, I can feel my long, wavy blond hair starting to frizz. "I'll look like a complete slacker, but I don't know what else to do."

"Listen, Catherine." Luca rakes a hand through his dark hair. "You won't look like a slacker. These things happen. People understand."

I press my hands to my temples. "They don't happen to me." Not anymore, they don't. Not since I worked like crazy to get straight As in high school, land a full scholarship to college, and finally take charge of my life. Up until that point, I'd had a lifetime of being late, of no-showing altogether, of *we'll remember to pay the bills / buy your school supplies / pick up the groceries another day.* For the last twelve years, I've made it to every single undergraduate *and* graduate school class while also working as a research assistant, and I've planned out every hour of my schedule so I'm *always* early. Always. With this new job, my hard work was supposed to finally pay off. "I've done everything right to land this tenure-track faculty position; I can't start by appearing unreliable."

The Supremes' tambourine jingles, and a piano solo rings out across the lobby, but Mrs. Goodwin's shimmying has ceased, and she's crossing the room to stand next to Luca, sympathy creasing her already wrinkled brow. "You'll be okay, honey."

Luca glances down at the older woman. "Mrs. Goodwin." He takes her by the hand. "Will you please take off your pants?"

My eyebrows shoot up. "Excuse me?" Did he just ask an octogenarian to strip? Right here in the lobby? I am *positive* that the building's manual of rules and regulations would have something to say about that.

But instead of rearing back in shock, Mrs. Goodwin nods. "That's an excellent idea, young man. I think Catherine and I are about the same size."

My gaze flies to Mrs. Goodwin's legs. She's wearing a basic, serviceable pair of black trousers. "I—" This is a ridiculous idea. Except I don't have a better one. And she *does* seem to be about my size. I won't exactly be dressed to impress, but now is not the time to turn into a fashionista. "Are you sure?"

Luca hurries to the opposite wall and swings open the door to a maintenance closet. "You can change in here."

When Mrs. Goodwin and I are ensconced in the closet, I slide behind a shelf, kick off my shoes, and unbutton my waistband. "Thank you for doing this," I call to her over the top of the bleach solutions and other cleaning supplies. "This is a really important meeting." I pull off my pants and am about to pass them around the shelf when a voice rings out from behind me, much closer than I'm expecting.

"My goodness, honey!"

I jump and spin around.

Mrs. Goodwin is standing on my side of the shelf in a pair of pale pink granny panties, holding out her black trousers with one hand and gesturing at me with the other.

"What happened to your underwear? Where's the rest of it?"

My hand automatically flies to my backside and slaps on one cheek. *Oh.* "It's—uh. It's a thong," I mumble, my... *other*...cheeks heating.

"Looks like dental floss to me. I used something like that to get the spinach out of my teeth last night."

"No, it's…it's a standard type of underwear," I stammer. There's nothing really racy about a thong, but being questioned about mine by an eighty-year-old woman makes me feel like I've been caught working as an exotic dancer. "I wanted to have clean lines. Under my trousers."

Mrs. Goodwin raises a silver eyebrow. "I thought you said you were meeting with your boss. Are they going to be looking at your butt? What kind of work are you in?"

"No." I grab the black pants and quickly slide one leg into them. "No, of course not. I'm a mathematician." I step into the other leg and hike the pants up over my hips. "*Nobody* will be looking at my butt. That would be inappropriate."

I remember the calm, quiet math professors I met during my interviews for the faculty position. There didn't seem to be any chaos or drama in the department, just a group of dedicated academics conducting research and shaping young minds. Since there's nothing I dislike more than chaos and drama, I knew I'd fit right in there. Which is why I can't quite understand how I'm spending my first day in a maintenance closet being interrogated about my underwear choices.

"I'm starting a new job." I pause to briefly question why I feel the need to explain myself to Mrs. Goodwin. Except the woman *is* giving me her pants. "I wanted to look nice and put together. To make a good impression."

Mrs. Goodwin looks at me sideways. "And you thought you'd make a good impression by showing off in a pair of sexy underwear?"

I close my eyes. She definitely thinks I'm an exotic dancer. "No. Nobody is going to see my underwear today." I realize as the words are coming out of my mouth that this is a completely inaccurate statement. "Well, nobody *else* is going to see my underwear today...You're the only one." I sigh, shaking my head. *Just give up. Let her think you're an exotic dancer.* There's nothing wrong with that line of work. I'm sure it provides a good income. My dad dated several burlesque dancers during my childhood, and they were all very nice to me.

I zip up Mrs. Goodwin's pants, which thankfully fit perfectly, and hand over my coffee-stained trousers. When we're both fully dressed, I swing open the closet door, but before I can step out, Mrs. Goodwin puts a hand on my arm.

"I was just teasing you about the thong, honey. Just trying to help you lighten up a little. Don't take everything so seriously." And with that, she gives me a wink and brushes past me out into the lobby.

I hesitate in the doorway, turning that familiar phrase over in my head. *Don't take everything so seriously.* I've been hearing that for pretty much my entire life. *It will be fine. Don't worry about it. Rules are meant to be broken.*

Thankfully, I'm pulled from that train of thought by a commotion across the room. Luca is behind the front desk, his fingers tapping on the counter along to the beat of the classic R & B song that he's cranked up on his phone speaker. He belts out the chorus, uncaring that he sounds awful or that Mrs. Goodwin and I have walked right into his less-than-successful attempt at the harmony. In fact, he sings even louder when he spots us, rounding the counter to grab Mrs. Goodwin's hand, pull her into his chest, and then swing her back out into a spin. I have to admit, for someone so tall, he's surprisingly graceful. Except when he's crashing into me and spilling my coffee, of course. And then, like his tattoos, I have to wonder why I'm noticing Luca's height at all. It's hard not to, though, when his long limbs bop in my direction, his palm outstretched. I shake my head and back up slowly.

I don't dance. At least not when anyone is watching anymore. I can't even imagine having the lack of inhibition it would take to gyrate around the lobby, to move with such ease and abandon.

To lighten up a little and not take everything so seriously.

Nor do I have any desire to, I remind myself. Maybe I should be able to laugh off the stain on my pants and show up for my meeting looking like I got into a wrestling match with a Keurig. But what kind of impression would that leave my new boss? Sure, he'd probably be gracious enough to pretend he didn't notice, but every time he was choosing faculty members for a committee, every time I was up for a promotion, he'd remember. People don't forget when you mess up, or when you let them down.

Luca stops in front of me, his eyes drifting down to my feet and then back to my face. For some inexplicable reason, I feel a flush of heat take the same path as Luca's leisurely gaze.

"You look very nice in Mrs. Goodwin's pants." His lips tug into a smile, his dark eyes crinkling in amusement. "Very—uh—clean lines."

So, he overheard my closet conversation with Mrs. Goodwin. Now I have to walk past the front desk every single day wondering if my doorman is thinking about my underwear. Well, it's not like he spends much time at the front desk anyway. He's usually nowhere to be found when I need to pick up my packages or report a maintenance problem.

Or when the dry cleaning is being delivered, I remember, brushing a crease from my borrowed pants.

As if he's intentionally trying to make my point, Luca gestures toward the sidewalk outside. "Come on, my car is out in front. I'll drive you."

I blink up at his face. "No, that's really not necessary. I'll take the bus."

"The 54 just drove past."

Darn it. "Rideshare, then."

"Come on, Catherine. It's my fault you're in this situation. You said your meeting is at nine? I can drive you there in plenty of time." He opens his arms wide, palms splayed, as if to show he's harmless.

I remember his hand on my wrist and the strange desire to trace a finger along his etched butterfly wings. *Harmless* is not a word I'd ever use to describe Luca, and not just because of some spilled coffee.

I pull out my phone and check the rideshare app. The closest driver is twelve minutes away. My heartbeat matches the background song's peppy baseline. If I have to wait, I am definitely going to show up for the meeting with my blouse sweaty and my hair flying.

"This is the least I can do," he insists.

"But—what about your post at the door? You really shouldn't leave. It probably says so in the—"

"Building's manual of rules and regulations." He waves me off, and the flock of birds on his forearm takes flight. "Yeah, yeah."

"Well. It probably does."

"I do get a break, you know." He gives me a wide grin. "And I'm choosing to take it right now so I can drive you to your meeting."

Still, I hesitate.

"Come on," Luca says, drawing out the last syllable as if he can tell I'm wavering.

I don't know why I'm arguing with Luca except exasperation is safer than being drawn into that charming smile. I've spent a lifetime with charming smiles and *come on, it will be fine*s. I'm well acquainted with men who think the rules never apply to them…and the messes they leave in their wake.

Behind me, the music swells, reminding me that the clock is ticking and I'm wasting valuable time. This job was supposed to finally set me free. The first step is making it there. "I'll take that ride." I grab my laptop bag and head for the door with Luca and Mrs. Goodwin trailing after me.

CHAPTER 2

Out on the sidewalk, I head toward a silver Toyota sedan parked in front of the building, but Luca shakes his head and steers me toward a '90s-era Lincoln Town Car.

I come to a stop. "Really?"

His lips curve into a smile, and he gives the black vinyl roof an affectionate pat. "It was my grandpa's." I can't miss the fondness in his voice, and I find myself hoping his grandpa is still around. Maybe he just bought a newer vehicle.

Luca swings the back door open and takes Mrs. Goodwin's hand to help her climb in. For some reason, she's decided to join us on our adventure. Maybe it's better that we have a chaperone. Mrs. Goodwin's presence will keep me from reaching over and wringing Luca's neck for throwing off my schedule in the first place. I calculate that the odds of making it on time if I murder my driver hover somewhere around zero.

I open my own door on the front passenger side, but I can't sit down because there are papers all over the seat and a box on the floor.

"Oops." Luca gathers up the papers, stacks them on top of the box, and carries them around to put them in the trunk while I sit down. "Sorry," he says when he slides into the seat next to me. "I would've cleaned up if I knew I'd be driving a lady around."

"Excuse *me*, young man," Mrs. Goodwin objects from the back seat. "What am I? Chopped liver?"

Luca grins as he flips on the turn signal and pulls the car onto Liberty Avenue. "You're not a lady, Mrs. Goodwin. You have entirely too much fun to be a lady."

"Ha," she barks. "You're probably right about that."

For some reason, this bothers me more than it should. "Are you implying that I don't have any fun?"

Luca's dark eyes dart to mine before he focuses back on the road in front of us. "I don't know you well enough to know if you have any fun."

"So what are you saying?"

The traffic light in front of us turns from green to yellow, and Luca eases the car to a stop. He shifts his torso so he can turn to face me. "I'm saying you seem awfully concerned with following the rules."

This again. "Maybe *you* don't seem concerned enough," I counter. "Rules are there for a reason. To maintain order. To keep things running smoothly and safely."

"Okay. Sure. You're probably right." He nods, and I blink, surprised that he agreed with me so readily.

The light turns green, and Luca shifts his body forward, raising both hands to ten and two on the steering wheel. After a pause, he slowly lifts his foot from the brake and slides it to the gas pedal. But instead of accelerating through the intersection and down the road behind the car in front of us, the Lincoln slowly pokes along like an old man who's feeling every bit of his age. We coast down one block and then another, matching the pace of a mother urging her toddler along on the sidewalk. I glance at the flickering green clock on the dashboard and then to Luca's impassive face.

I thought this ride had bought me back a little of the time I lost thanks to the coffee incident, but we're squandering it at this geriatric pace. Is there something broken in this old car? I'm pretty sure that the mom and baby have lapped us by now.

We putter down another block, and then Luca comes to a full stop at a stop sign. He looks left, right, forward, and then left again before he eases his foot back onto the gas pedal. I shift uncomfortably in my seat as anxiety begins to hum in my chest like a hive of bees. My gaze darts from the clock to Luca and back. He doesn't seem to notice, though, because he's staring straight ahead, his face scrunched in concentration. His shoulders rock gently back and forth, hands sliding on the steering wheel, as if he's an actor in a play pretending to drive a car.

"*Luca*," I yell, and he jumps.

"Yes?" he asks mildly.

"What are you doing?"

He gives an exaggerated wave at the road in front of us, like he's presenting it to me in a game show. "I'm taking you to work."

"Why are you driving like it's Sunday afternoon and Miss Daisy is in the back seat?"

He blinks innocently, and suddenly it comes to me.

"Are we back to that lady thing again? You're trying to make a point?"

"Certainly not. I'm simply following the traffic rules." He cocks his head. "Rules are there for a reason. To maintain order. To keep things running *smoothly* and *safely*." He punctuates the sentence with a series of taps on the dashboard like a preschool teacher reciting the ABCs.

I can't believe he's throwing my words back at me. I can't believe I got into a car with this man. "You know what? I'm good. I can still use a rideshare." I grip the door handle, but Luca has finally accelerated to a normal speed, and I can't very well fling myself out of a moving vehicle. "Stop the car, please."

"You don't need to do that. I'll get you there." He flashes me a grin. "Say the word, and I'll even speed."

He's *still* making a joke of this.

I jiggle the door handle. "Stop. The. Car."

He glances in my direction, his brow furrowed. "Wait. Are you really mad?"

"Of course I'm mad. You're intentionally making me late."

"You said your meeting was at nine o'clock. We left at eight twenty-five. It's a seven-minute drive." He waves a hand at the clock on the dashboard. "You're still going to be at least twenty minutes early."

"Twenty minutes early is *late* in my book."

His face registers genuine surprise. "How was I supposed to know that?" A light turns red ahead, and Luca slows the car to a stop.

"I thought I told you this is an important meeting." My heart picks up speed, and I tuck my hands under me to keep from pulling the printed schedule from my bag and checking it against the clock. Luca would definitely have something to say about that.

"Yeah, but that doesn't mean that you need to arrive—" He abruptly stops talking as his gaze slowly drifts over me. I do my best to let the tension seep from my shoulders and to bend my stick-straight arms into a more natural position. "You know what?" Luca shakes his head. "Never mind. I'm sorry. I didn't realize that you were so..."

I wait for whatever he's about to say. *Picky? Controlling? Fastidious?* I've heard it all before, and it doesn't bother me. I'll take picky, controlling, and fastidious over *unreliable* any day.

"Interested in being early," Luca finally says, looking me over again. "I'm sorry I continue to contribute to your lateness." He lifts his hands, palms up in a gesture that I'll admit does seem apologetic.

I let my shoulders drop another inch. "It's okay. You didn't know."

"I promise I'll drive you safely, yet quickly, to campus so you can be as early as possible to your meeting. How does that sound?"

It sounds like...my best option, to be honest. But I'm not sure how I feel about it. If Luca Morelli is my best option, things might be going downhill quickly. But the clock ticks forward another number. "Yes, great."

The light turns green, and Luca presses the gas. "I'll have you there in five."

I finally give in to the urge and pull out my schedule. The next two lights we hit are green, so we'll probably make it in four minutes. I should be fine to get there with time to spare.

While I look over my printout, Luca tips his chin up to glance in the rearview mirror at the passenger in the back seat. "Mrs. Goodwin, you need to run any errands on our way home?"

I thought he said he was just taking a quick break. Shouldn't he be getting back to his post and figuring out what to do about the broken elevator?

Mrs. Goodwin leans forward in her seat. "I'd love to stop at the pharmacy if it's not too much trouble. And maybe the bank and the grocery store."

"No trouble at all." Luca gives her a grin.

Good thing I'm not expecting any deliveries, because Luca is going to be gone from the front desk all day at this rate. But I can't worry about it now. I turn away from him and watch in relief as the university buildings come into view.

"Thanks for the ride," I say to Luca as I climb out of the Town Car and onto the sidewalk in front of the café. "And for the trousers," I add with considerably more enthusiasm, leaning in to give Mrs. Goodwin in the back seat a wave.

"Good luck with your meeting, honey." She blows me a kiss. "I'll be rooting for you."

That statement cheers me, softening the hard edges of my disaster of a morning. I've been getting by on my own for so long, I had no idea how nice it would feel to have some-one root for me until right at this moment. "Thanks, that means a lot," I say, surprised when my voice comes out a little hoarse. I definitely don't have time to be getting emotional, so I quickly close the door.

I'm just turning to walk into the café when I hear a low hum and a muffled "Hey" come from the direction of the car. When I spin back around, the Town Car's vintage passenger-side window is slowly lowering into the doorframe with approximately zero urgency. It reminds me a little bit of the car's driver. Eventually, it comes to a stop with a high-pitched squeak, and Luca leans across the seat to look up at me.

"How long is your meeting?"

"Um." Why does he care? "About an hour, probably."

"Will you be going to your office afterward?"

"No, my office isn't ready yet. The semester doesn't start for a few weeks. I'll probably do some work at home."

He nods. "Okay, we'll pick you up over there in an hour." Luca waves at a row of benches in front of a wide stretch of lawn where students are lounging on blankets in the morning sun or tossing frisbees around.

It was nice of him to drive me here, but I don't want him to feel obligated to come back. "That's really not necessary."

Luca shrugs. "After ruining your morning, it's the least we can do, right, Mrs. Goodwin?"

Mrs. Goodwin nods. "Absolutely."

"No, really," I argue, but the window is already making its slow ascent back to the closed position. I slowly rise with it, keeping my eyes on Luca through the shrinking crack. "I can take the bus."

"See you at ten," Luca calls, and the window zips shut

completely. Before I can react to what's happened, he puts on the turn signal and pulls the car into a break in the traffic.

I sigh. This will probably further delay him from getting back to the front desk. But then I shrug. Given my experience with Luca, he'll be an hour late or will forget to pick me up entirely. So there's no point in even getting worked up about him driving me home. Glancing at my watch, I realize that despite his antics on the way over here, Luca *did* manage to get me to the café with twenty minutes to spare. Everything worked out in the end, and I can put this whole morning behind me. I square my shoulders, brush a tiny speck of lint from my borrowed trousers, and head into the café to start my new job and my new life.

CHAPTER 3

Well, Catherine," Dr. Gupta says, standing up from the café table and smoothing out a nonexistent wrinkle from his sleeve. "Welcome to the department." Dr. Gupta is a medium-height man of South Asian descent wearing a pair of wire-rimmed glasses. He's about two decades older than me and resembles many other professors here at the university in his pressed Oxford shirt and khakis. You wouldn't know by looking at him that he's one of the most revered scholars in his field.

For the last hour, we spoke about computational science and numerical analysis and then segued into discussing a number of topics for a joint research paper. Though he never even cracked a smile, I can tell I've nailed this meeting and he's impressed with my ideas. And I've earned his esteem. Last night, I stayed up late reviewing research papers and synthesizing my notes into a spreadsheet. I prepared and worked hard for this. Following Dr. Gupta to a stand, I discreetly check that my blouse is still neatly tucked in the waistband of my borrowed pants. I can't imagine how this meeting would have gone if I'd shown up late and out of breath with coffee-stained trousers.

I'll have to ask Luca for Mrs. Goodwin's apartment number so I can drop off her pants once they've been dry-cleaned and thank her again for her help. And since I'm feeling considerably more cheerful about the whole disaster than I was an hour ago, I could also thank Luca for coming up with the idea of switching trousers and getting me to my meeting on time.

Even if he *was* the reason I was late in the first place.

"Your work is very promising," Dr. Gupta says. "I generally choose a junior faculty member to mentor each year, and I'd be very interested in collaborating with you on your research." He holds out a hand, nails neatly trimmed, a sensible leather watch circling his wrist.

A buzz of excitement runs through me, and for a moment, I'm tempted to break out in a Carolina shag right there in the middle of the café. One of the greatest mathematical minds of our generation thinks *my* work is very promising. Of course, on some level I knew that, or he wouldn't have hired me in the first place. Maybe it was growing up with one parent who was absent and another whose head was in the clouds, but finding a mentor who admires and supports my hard work feels like a huge victory.

I don't dance in public, though, and I'm certainly not about to undo all the goodwill this meeting afforded me. So instead of breaking out into a two-step, I calmly shake Dr. Gupta's hand, and we head out of the café onto the sidewalk.

"Your new office should be ready in the next week or so," Dr. Gupta informs me as we cross the street at the crosswalk. "The facilities department is completing a few renovations, but it will be freshly painted with new furniture before the start of the fall semester."

The building that houses the mathematics department is situated right next to the lawn where Luca offered to pick me up, so although the odds that he'll actually show up on time are a million to one, I continue in that direction so Dr. Gupta and I can keep talking.

"I'm sure the office will be very comfortable," I say calmly, though inside I'm doing another little jig. The idea of my brand-new office thrills me in the same way that moving into my new apartment in the DeGreco building did a month ago. Although I'm nearing thirty, this is the first time I'll have any real space of my own.

I've worked and gone to school since I was eighteen, but I've been helping Dad pay the rent for pretty much my whole adult life, so I never had a chance to move out on my own. Not until this new job came along, giving me a taste of calm and order for the first time in my life. The DeGreco building is occupied mostly by quiet older people, so aside from the absentee doorman and coffee mishaps in the lobby, it's perfect for me. I have my very own one-bedroom apartment that I organized exactly as I wanted it, and it's such a thrill to know that when I return home at the end of the day, everything will be just as I left it.

Dr. Gupta stops in front of the building that houses the mathematics department and turns to me. "Human resources should be in touch to have you complete your paperwork and come in for orientation."

I nod, already one step ahead. "I submitted everything in the online portal last week, and they've confirmed they'll be processing the paperwork soon. My orientation is scheduled for Monday in two weeks." It felt amazing to cross off that task and know I was one step closer to my goals. I pat the side of my bag where my to-do list is tucked into a pocket.

Nail my first meeting with the department head? *Check*.

Land myself one of the most accomplished mentors in the field? *Check*.

"Excellent." Dr. Gupta gives a curt nod, a motion I'm beginning to learn means high praise from the reserved mathematician. "I should have known you'd be on top of things."

"Always," I say, aware that I'm sucking up a little now, but I can't help it. Even if I started out this meeting in the wrong pants, I'm determined to go into this new job on the right foot.

"I look forward to seeing your draft of the paper we discussed. Get it to me by mid-October so we can submit to *Studies in Applied Mathematics* in the new year."

I blink at him. "I—" He'd like me to write the draft? By myself? *And by October?* That's less than two months away. I thought this was going to be a collaboration. "Shouldn't we meet to discuss the analysis first?"

"I have faith in your abilities. Feel free to email me if you have questions."

I've been a graduate assistant in the past; I know the junior faculty and graduate students tend to do the bulk of the heavy lifting when it comes to research and peer-reviewed journal articles. But I guess I didn't expect Dr. Gupta to hand it *all* to me. Especially because he'll probably end up being listed as the first author on any papers we—I mean *I*—produce.

But I haven't even started this job yet, and I definitely don't want to rock the boat. Dr. Gupta has made it clear he respects my work, and maybe this is my first big test as a new faculty member. If I complete this paper in record time and impress my new boss, who knows what kind of impact that could have on my career in the department? Besides, it will be an honor to even have my name listed alongside his.

"Sure," I say. "Of course. October is absolutely no problem."

Dr. Gupta gives me his curt nod of approval, but before I have time to feel relieved about that, I hear someone calling me from across the lawn.

"Cat! Cat! Over here."

Oh no.

I'd know that voice anywhere, and it belongs to the last person I want to see right now.

What is he doing here?

And why isn't he at work?

And... I start to sweat. *Is he coming over here?*

I give Dr. Gupta an extra-wide smile. "Thank you again for breakfast," I say, my voice picking up speed with each syllable. "*Itwasnicetoseeyou,*" I blurt in a single breath. Nobody at my new job knows about my nickname, Cat. So, if I hurry this along, maybe I can get out of here before my new boss realizes that the guy in the middle of the lawn is yelling for—

"*Catherine.*"

Dr. Gupta's head lifts at the sound of my full first name, his gaze sliding in the direction of the voice. By the way his eyes widen, I know the moment he spots the middle-aged white man waving at me from across the lawn.

"Excuse me, Catherine." He clears his throat. "Is it possible that...*juggler* over there is calling for *you*?"

My shoulders droop. This patch of lawn is one of "*that juggler's*" favorite places to show off his skills. Usually, a pack of students gather to watch, calling out encouragement and asking to give the juggling clubs a try for themselves. I should have known better than to walk over here. If I'd noticed him on the lawn earlier, I would have turned around and fled in the other direction. But I was so pleased with Dr. Gupta's praise of my work that I let my guard down.

Big mistake.

Because now the juggler is making his way in our direction, colorful clubs flying to the sky and falling back to earth like giant pieces of confetti. His tanned arms move so fast they look out of focus as he deftly plucks each club from the air and then flicks it higher again.

"Is he calling for me?" I stall, knowing full well that he is. "Gosh." I shift my weight, wondering if there's still time to make a run for it.

The juggler is only steps away now, and one by one, he lets the clubs drop into his hands until he's standing in front of me, holding them out like two colorful bouquets of flowers. "Want to give them a go, Kitty Cat?"

I back away as if those juggling clubs are on fire. "What? *No.*" I'm sure in the span of an instant, my face has turned about every color of those clubs—green with nausea, red with mortification, blue with the sad realization that this is actually happening.

The juggler laughs and tucks all six clubs under his arm, reaching out to hug me. "What a wonderful surprise to see you here, Kitty Cat. I'm absolutely delighted." He pulls me against him, and my heart does a tiny flip in my chest. Because I know he's delighted to see me; he's *always* delighted to see me. I just wish that, at this moment, I could feel the same way.

"Hi, Dad," I mumble into his denim overalls as I hug him back. Because what else can I do? Give him a shove and run away? That would only cause even more of a scene in front of my new boss, as if such a thing were possible. My only hope now is that I can somehow make this quick.

When I pull back, the first sight I see is Dr. Gupta blinking over and over, mouth slightly ajar. Maybe it's the nickname my dad has given me that finally broke reserved Dr. Gupta's careful composure. Or it's possibly learning that the circus performer standing in front of us in scuffed green Chuck Taylors peeking out from the rolled cuffs of his overalls, hair tied back in a shaggy man-bun, and, inexplicably, a plastic-flowered lei draped around his neck, provided me with half my genetic material.

"It's, uh, a surprise to see you here, too," I murmur. Despite this being one of his favorite haunts, it *is* a surprise to see Dad here, because I thought he worked the late-morning shift at the grocery store in Shadyside. Why isn't he there now? "But I don't want to keep you if you have to get to work. I can call you later."

Dad shoots me a grin, and the fine lines deepen around his dark eyes and sink into his tanned forehead. "No rush. I don't have to be anywhere but here." He gives Dr. Gupta a wink, miming the motion of tossing his clubs in the air. "This is the best job in the world."

Oh no. That can only mean one thing. My gaze flies to the center of the lawn where Dad was juggling moments ago, and I spot his signature fedora in the grass, lying upside down next to his tote bag. A handwritten sign leans against the hat.

THESE TIPS DON'T LIE

He's out here juggling to make money.

What about his job in the grocery store? My chest burns, and I can hear my pulse pounding in my ears. But I sense my new boss watching me, so I paste on a pleasant smile as if this is all just a bit of fun and not my total nightmare. Dr. Gupta clears his throat, and I realize he expects an introduction. So much for getting this over with quickly.

"Um, Dr. Gupta, this is—my father, Andrew Lipton. Dad, this is Dr. Gupta. He's the dean of the mathematics department where I've *just been hired as a professor.*" I tilt my head in a meaningful gesture that I hope gives him the hint that I'm in the middle of an important meeting, and please let's move things along. But Dad doesn't get hints. He would never imagine that this was anything but a bit of luck that we ran into each other.

"Dr. G., so nice to meet you," Dad says buoyantly. Genuinely delighted, as always. "Call me Andy." He reaches out and pumps Dr. Gupta's hand up and down. "I'm sure you know how lucky you are to have snagged Kitty Cat for your math department."

I press my hands to my temples.

"Of course," Dr. Gupta says, subtly trying to pull his hand from Dad's. When that doesn't work, he screws up his face and gives it a good yank, finally dislodging himself from Dad's overwhelming enthusiasm and stumbling backward. I reach out to keep him from falling in the grass, but luckily, he rights himself before I have to manhandle my new employer.

"Your daughter has a brilliant mathematical mind," Dr. Gupta says when he's finally composed himself. "Her development of methods for solving hyperbolic equations is going to make a huge impact on the field of computational analysis someday. But I'm sure you knew that."

A brilliant mathematical mind! A huge impact! I flush with pride. If we were anywhere else right now, this would be one of the highlights of my career. Instead, I'm just hoping to get out of here before Dr. Gupta changes his mind and takes it all back.

"You don't have to tell *me* that Cat is smart." Dad gives me a wide grin. "I knew that from the moment she figured out how to change her own diaper when she was two. She put the stinky one in the diaper pail and everything."

I close my eyes. Please tell me he didn't. Please tell me none of this is happening. But when I peek through my lashes, Dr. Gupta is still standing next to me, his spine straight, eyebrows raised, and Dad is still talking.

"Cat's always been into math and numbers and calculating the probability of something-something." Dad shakes his head, and a few locks of his silver-streaked brown hair slide out of his man-bun, sticking out by his temples and making him look slightly unhinged. "She didn't get it from me."

I definitely didn't get my mathematical brain from Dad, or my desire for organization, order, or punctuality. I have no idea if I got it from my mom. And just like it always does, my heart gives a tiny lurch at the thought of the parent I've never met. Growing up with Dad's freewheeling, nonchalant attitude toward rules and conventions, I've spent most of my life feeling like a stick-in-the-mud for wanting to be on time to school and pay the bills before they were due. And the more Dad lost job after job, apartment after apartment, the more I dug in. And the more out of place I felt.

But I've always wondered if maybe there's someone else out in the world who gets what it feels like to have her chest squeeze when she walks into a disorganized apartment. Someone who tucks schedules and lists into her bag because they help her to feel in control. Someone who would rather be an hour early than five minutes late.

Dr. Gupta murmurs something noncommittal, and I need to focus because Dad is still talking.

"Yep, definitely didn't get it from me." Dad laughs and gives Dr. Gupta a nudge. "I always thought an *algae-bra* was something a mermaid wears, if you know what I mean."

"*Okay,*" I jump in, mortification finally galvanizing me into action. But I'm sensing it's far too late. There's no coming back from this. "I think Dr. Gupta gets the picture."

"Yes, I—I really should be going." Dr. Gupta's voice is polite but clipped. "Andy, it was very nice to meet you." *Lies. All lies.* The only reason this meeting could have possibly been nice for Dr. Gupta is if he's looking for an amusing anecdote to share with his colleagues while his coffee brews in the department kitchenette. But I'm afraid Dr. Gupta doesn't have enough of a sense of humor to find even this funny. "I have a faculty meeting to prepare for."

"Nice to meet you, Doc," Dad says, reaching out his hand again.

Dr. Gupta pretends he doesn't see it and turns to me instead. "Catherine."

I wonder if there's any way to salvage this. "Thank you again for breakfast. I'm really looking forward to working on that paper we discussed earlier." My eyes search Dr. Gupta's face for signs that he's not as alarmed by this whole interaction as I'm suspecting. "*October*," I add. "I'll have it to you then." He likes my brilliant mind, after all. Surely he won't hold it against me that my father is essentially a clown with no filter.

But even on a good day, Dr. Gupta is impossible to read, and this is not a good day. He silently heads toward the mathematics building.

I turn to my dad. "What are you doing here?" I hiss.

"I told you. I'm working."

"What happened to the Harvest Market?"

Dad waves dismissively. "They were so stuffy. The manager got mad at me for juggling a customer's oranges. Who hates juggling? It's like hating kittens. And he was so rude when I balanced a carrot on my nose." He throws his hands up in the air. "For the record, the customers loved it."

I press my hands to my eyes, a headache coming on. Of course they loved it. The customers always love it.

The truth is that my dad is actually a really talented clown. I don't mean the kind that wears a red nose and big shoes. My dad dresses in fairly normal, if somewhat wacky, attire. But he can do all kinds of tricks, like juggling fire, spinning a half dozen Hula-Hoops on all of his limbs at once, and walking on stilts. He can even perform tricks while balancing on a slackline hovering above the ground or riding on a unicycle. But aside from a few kids' birthday parties, the Renaissance Faire, and Burning Man...oh, and his hat on the ground over there...the clown industry is pretty limited in terms of financial opportunities. And while the customers love it, the managers at Dad's various short-lived jobs tend to object when their employee is tossing burgers and french fries into the air instead of bagging them up and sending them out the drive-through window.

"You promised you'd try at this job. You promised it would stick."

"I know, Kitty Cat. But it's just not me. That grocery store was slowly sucking my soul. Besides"—he brightens—"I have a few things in the works."

He *always* has a few things in the works, and rarely do they pan out. The grocery store job was a steady income and a sure bet. But it sounds like it's too late. That job went up like the flames at the end of Dad's juggling sticks. I gaze out across the lawn at my dad's hat still sitting there. "I guess you should get back to it before someone steals your money," I say with a resigned sigh.

Beyond the hat and the lawn, out on the street bisecting the university's campus, Luca's car pulls up next to the curb. Unbelievable. He actually showed. I check my watch: 10:01 a.m. And only a minute late. Luca climbs out of the car and stands up so he can look at me across the hood. He gives me a sideways grin and a wave. After the morning I've had, I'm strangely happy to see someone smiling at me.

"I should go. That's my ride."

Dad turns around to see who I'm looking at, and when he catches a glimpse of Luca and the Town Car, his eyebrows rise. I get it. Luca looks more like Dad's friends, with his two days of facial scruff, tattoos, and mischievous smile, while I tend to run in the Dr. Gupta crowd.

I reach over to give Dad a hug. "Let's talk more about this at dinner on Sunday." Maybe then I can convince him to get another job.

CHAPTER 4

As I head across the lawn toward the Town Car, Luca jogs around the hood and swings the front passenger-side door open. "Hi," he says with another wide grin.

"Thanks for coming." I lift a foot to climb in and then stop. On the seat is a pile of grocery bags.

"Whoops," Luca says when he notices my hesitation and looks in the car for himself. "Mrs. Goodwin did a little shopping. Let me move these to the trunk."

He's already put a big box in the trunk, and I'm not sure if all these bags will fit, too. "It's fine. I can get in the back."

I pull open the door and slide into the car. Mrs. Goodwin is still sitting there, behind Luca's seat, and they've picked up another passenger, who is now sitting in the middle. He's a short, olive-skinned white man, probably in his eighties, with a shiny bald head encircled by a ring of snow-white hair around the sides.

"Hello," the man says, giving me a smile. "The name's Sal."

"Hi. I'm Catherine."

"We know who you are, dear," Mrs. Goodwin says.

"I know. I was just telling—"

"How did the meeting go?" Luca asks, sliding into his seat and looking at me in the rearview mirror.

"Uh," I stall. The *meeting* went well. It was what happened after that's the problem. But Mrs. Goodwin and Luca have already discussed my underwear today, so I don't think I really want to share any more personal information. And I've just met this Sal person. Although Lord knows what he's heard about me. "It was fine."

"Fine?" Luca's eyebrows furrow, almost like that answer bothers him. I can't imagine why it would. I can't imagine why he cares. "That doesn't sound so promising, especially after all the buildup."

I sigh. "I'm just tired. It's been a long day."

"It's ten in the morning." The furrow deepens.

"You're right." I sit up straighter. "The meeting was good. Really," I reassure him, but maybe I'm also reassuring myself. "It was great. My boss said I have a brilliant mind and he wants to mentor me." It sounds even better when I say it out loud. Dr. Gupta isn't the kind of person to throw around idle compliments.

In the narrow mirror, Luca's eyes connect with mine. They're wide and dark, lined with long lashes and framed by thick eyebrows and high cheekbones. Despite the fact that the rest of his features are hidden, I can tell he's giving me his signature grin by the little lines that crinkle at the corners.

"I'm really glad," he says. His voice lowers a little at the end, as if he's talking only to me despite the other people in the car. An unexpected warmth takes over my limbs. I quickly look away.

As Luca eases the car into traffic, I catch a glimpse of Dad back out on the lawn, juggling colorful balls now. He has at least seven up in the air at once, and a crowd of college students has taken notice, surrounding him, cheering him on. I wonder how many will put a dollar in his hat, though, and I suspect it's not very many.

It all comes back to me in a slow wave. Dr. Gupta in his conservative khakis and Dad in his flower lei. Dad offering me a go with the juggling clubs. I press my hands to my eyes. Surely it wasn't as bad as I'm making it out to be. But then I remember the diaper story.

It was so bad.

And the worst part is, the mortifying run-in with Dad and my boss is only serving as a distraction from the even bigger problem that Dad lost another steady job. He still thinks he's going to support himself with his clown career. It's been thirty years. When is he going to accept reality?

I shake my head. *Dad* and *reality* are not two words that anyone would use in the same sentence. After all this time, I don't know why I keep expecting things to be different. Maybe it's because I hoped this new job was finally going to be my chance to focus on my career and my future. And now, in one toss of a juggling club, it's all in jeopardy.

I'm so distracted by my thoughts that the next thing I know, Luca is pulling the car into the parking lot of a local pharmacy.

"What are we doing?" I ask, my voice slightly high-pitched. After the morning I've had, I really ought to get home and start working on the paper Dr. Gupta and I discussed. But I should have guessed I'm along for the ride on Luca's errands.

He confirms this by opening his car door. "I'm going to grab Mrs. Goodwin's prescriptions. Back in a second."

Mrs. Goodwin wiggles out of her seat belt. "Hold on, young man. I'm coming with you. I need a new shower cap. And some water pills."

Luca peeks over his shoulder into the back seat. "You okay for a few minutes back there?"

"Sure am," Sal confirms.

I sigh. "I'm fine." Looks like we're going to be here awhile.

Luca and Mrs. Goodwin disappear inside the store.

Sal leans back against the seat and reaches into the pocket of his gray trousers. When he pulls his hand out, an old-fashioned hard candy rests on his palm. "Would you like a butterscotch?"

My stomach growls. I was so keyed up about the meeting with Dr. Gupta that I barely picked at my frittata at our breakfast meeting, and now I'm starving. Through the pharmacy window, I spot Mrs. Goodwin standing in the makeup aisle, comparing the labels on two tubes of lipstick. Luca waits patiently behind her, plastic shopping basket hanging from one arm and a mild, unhurried expression on his face. Sort of like the expression he had when he mentioned getting Dante—*whoever that is*—to fix the elevator. As if he could happily wait all day.

And, in turn, he could happily make me wait all day, too.

My stomach growls again. "I'd love a butterscotch. Thank you." I take the candy from Sal, peel away the shiny gold wrapper, and pop it in my mouth. The sweet, buttery flavor bursts on my tongue, momentarily tamping down my hunger, and oddly, soothing a tiny bit of my anxiety, too.

"Here, take another." Sal slips another butterscotch into my hand. "Keep it in your pocket for later."

"Thanks." I wrap my fist around the candy, hoping this doesn't mean Sal knows something I don't. Like the fact that we really *are* going to be here all day. I should hop out of the car and walk to the nearest bus, but I wore heels for the meeting. And the exhaustion of being "on" for the past hour has finally caught up with me. I lean back into the rich leather cushion of the Town Car's back seat, feeling my body relax. They really don't make cars like this anymore. I can see why Luca would want to keep driving it after his grandpa was ready to pass it along.

Sal settles in next to me, and although I'm tempted to close my eyes and take a nap, the older man did just ply me with candy, and I feel like I should at least attempt to make some polite conversation.

"Are you a resident of the DeGreco building, too?" I ask him.

He nods. "The missus and I moved into the DeGreco when our kids were grown. So I've probably lived there for about thirty years."

"Oh, that's wonderful." The idea of that kind of permanence fills me with an unexpected longing. When I was ten, I started writing a list in the front cover of my journal of all the different apartments where Dad and I lived. I've kept it updated ever since, and so far, I've moved fifteen times in twenty years. Dad's chaos came—ironically—like clockwork. He'd lose his job because he was juggling boxes instead of unloading them or because his boss wouldn't give him the time off to go to the Ren Faire. We'd get behind on bills, and then the letter would arrive saying we had thirty days to move out. Dad never minded it. In fact, he thrived on the uncertainty, like it was all some big adventure. And he never seemed to understand how hard it was on me—constantly packing our things in boxes, leaving our home behind, finding a new apartment we could afford on the salary of whatever job I managed to talk him into taking.

And then there were the times we *couldn't* find an apartment we could afford, and we ended up crashing at Dad's friend Ginger's place. Ginger always took us in when Dad and I showed up on her doorstep, and she even fixed up a little closet under the stairs with a reading chair and some fairy lights just for me. Sometimes I thought about begging Ginger to adopt me so I could stop moving and just *stand still* for a little while. But Dad needed me, and I worried about what would happen to him if he were on his own.

But this time around, Dad *swore* he'd work hard at his job, follow the rules, and above all, *not get fired*. I really hoped this was finally my chance to settle down. That the DeGreco would give me the stability I'd longed for my whole life. A real home, one where I could be happy living for a long time, just like Sal. But in light of Dad's latest resistance to gainful employment, I wonder if I'll even make it another month before I end up back in with him because I can't afford the rent on two places.

My heart aches just thinking about having to pack up and move on again. Leaving the DeGreco behind would be a painful blow. I can't imagine finding another place that's so perfect for me.

When I first applied to live in the building, Luca told me that most of the other residents are older people in their eighties and even nineties who've lived there for decades. He mentioned it a couple of times as he gave me the tour of the apartment and showed me around the shared spaces, almost as if he really wanted to make sure I knew what to expect. I guess there aren't too many almost thirty-year-olds clamoring to live among the octogenarian crowd, and maybe he wanted to warn me the building would be a little sleepy. But sleepy is exactly what I love about it. A building full of older people means no loud parties spilling in the halls, no music shaking the walls, nobody shouting at midnight.

Mrs. Goodwin and her Carolina shag notwithstanding.

But I remember her blowing me a kiss earlier—wishing me luck at my meeting—and I look down at the black trousers covering my legs. Mrs. Goodwin is a sweet lady, and I'm lucky to have her as a neighbor. Besides, I can't help but feel like the doorman and his devil-may-care attitude were the real culprits behind the coffee incident this morning. Dancing lessons in the lobby seems like an idea that would come straight from the mind of Luca Morelli.

I really can't fathom how the owner of the building would put a guy with absolutely no regard for rules or order in charge of running the entire complex. But then I remember Luca's gaze in the rearview mirror and the irresistible grin tugging at his lips.

I guess Luca does have his charms.

I peer through the gap in the front seats to see if I can spot him and Mrs. Goodwin inside the store again.

"You seem anxious to get going," Sal observes, leaning back against the seat and crossing his legs with the opposite of urgency. "Are you late for something?"

"Well…not specifically." But my to-do list is a mile long, and I hate wasting time. I have to finish my syllabi for the four different classes I'll be teaching, work on my own research, and should probably start looking for new jobs for my dad, too. Clearly, grocery stores aren't a good fit. All that shiny, round fruit just ripe for juggling. We've already exhausted fast food since french fries are too hard to catch and they tend to end up all over the floor. And clothing retail was a total disaster—it turns out that Gap T-shirts are *not* aerodynamic. "I just need to go home to get some work done for my new job."

"Are you entering the clown industry?" Sal inquires.

My head jerks up. "What? No." *God, no.*

"Your new boss seems to be some sort of juggler."

Sal must have noticed me on the lawn when the Town Car pulled up. "Oh, that wasn't my boss. You probably saw me with my dad." That shaky feeling radiates out to my limbs. "*He's* a clown."

"That sounds like a fun job," Sal says mildly.

I remember Dad holding out the clubs earlier, asking if I wanted to give them a go. It's been years, but I could have juggled at least five of them. With a little practice, I bet I could even get up to six. Juggling is one of those things that comes back to you, kind of like riding a bike. Or, in the case of my family, a unicycle. I used to love juggling and Hula-Hooping and learning all of Dad's tricks.

It *was* fun when I was a little kid who didn't know that

bills needed to be paid, or kids should show up to school on time. Before I missed field trips because Dad never sent in the permission slips, and I failed math tests because Dad decided to take us to a music festival instead. It was fun before I understood that clowning isn't a career, especially if you have a daughter to support entirely on your own. "He seems to enjoy it. But it's not for me. I'm a mathematician."

"Ah, I see." Sal nods, his bald head catches the sunlight slanting in through the side window, and it almost seems to glow. "Well, I'm glad things went well with your boss today, especially after the difficult morning you had." Sal probably heard all about the coffee catastrophe and trouser exchange from Mrs. Goodwin. I hope she didn't tell him about my underwear, too.

"The meeting actually *did* go well," I say. "But then..." Sometimes my life feels like those clubs Dad was juggling. As soon as I manage to grab one thing, the next gets lobbed into the air. I clench my jaw, crunching down on the flat butterscotch disk with extra force. That familiar anxiety rises up, and I try to swallow it along with the bits of candy. They're both sharp going down.

"Sometimes I wish I could just...I don't know. Be someone else." I mumble that last part under my breath.

Through the pharmacy window, Mrs. Goodwin holds up an uncapped tube of hand cream for Luca to smell. He shakes his head and points to a different brand on the shelf. I feel a strange surge of jealousy at Luca's ability to be so utterly unconcerned with his responsibilities. He was supposed to be back at the front desk hours ago. He probably wasn't supposed to leave at all. My dry cleaning is still missing, the elevator is on the fritz, and I'm certain that as we speak, residents are placing illegal flowerpots on the fire escapes and FedEx drivers are roaming around looking for someone to sign for packages. And Luca is calmy choosing lipstick colors and debating the merits of having your hands smell like *lavender and coconut* versus *rose water orange blossom* or whatever they are.

What if instead of always grabbing for the juggling clubs, I just let them drop? And left them where they landed? The classes on my roster, the academic papers I'm on my own to write, my dad's considerable lack of employment. What if, like Luca, I simply wandered off whenever I felt like it?

No, it's not that I want to be *someone else*. It's that, some days, I'd simply like to be...

Nobody.

No commitments. No one expecting anything from me. I can't remember a time when I experienced that kind of freedom, even in childhood. By the time I was six years old, I was the responsible party in our household. While Dad was just *the party*.

"Did you say something?" Sal tugs on his earlobe. "Speak up. My hearing isn't what it used to be."

My gaze jerks to his. Did I just say all of that out loud?

No. It may have been a rough morning, but I haven't quite hit the point where I spill my issues to a stranger in the back of a Lincoln Town Car.

"Never mind," I mumble, crumpling the candy wrapper in my hand. Like I told Luca, it's been a long morning. I force a laugh to show I was joking. "I'm just a little stressed about all the work I have to do. I'll feel better as soon as I get home and get started on it." But as I pull out my carefully ordered list to add the academic paper I'll be writing all by myself between now and October, my desire to hurry home fades.

Nobody, a strange little voice in my head echoes. *Wouldn't it be nice?*

Sal takes another shiny wrapper from his pocket and pulls on it to untwist the ends. He holds it out to me, and I pluck the hard candy off the crinkly paper. "Thanks," I mumble, stuffing it in my mouth.

Luca appears in the doorway of the pharmacy with an overflowing shopping bag under one arm. He holds the door open for Mrs. Goodwin, giving her a wave of his hand and a bow as she walks past—unencumbered by packages—like she's the Queen Mother.

I watch Luca jog gracefully over to us and grab the car door for her, his long limbs gliding like a dancer's. I can see why he'd make an excellent Carolina shag partner for Mrs. Goodwin. And I can also understand why the people in the building want to hang around in the lobby chatting with him, telling a joke, playing a game of cards. He's undeniably attractive—all lean-muscled, dark-eyed, six-foot-something of him. And then there's that charm that he directs with equal abandon at people of every size, age, and gender but that somehow makes you feel like he's directing it only at you.

Maybe riding around in the back seat while Luca and Mrs. Goodwin run errands isn't so terrible after all. I slide the butterscotch from one cheek to the other, savoring its sweetness. The back seat of this Town Car really *is* surprisingly comfortable. And Sal seems like pretty good company. Maybe, just for today, I *can* be nobody.

Tomorrow, I'll face it all again.

"Where to now?" I ask, once Mrs. Goodwin is settled next to Sal and Luca is in the front seat starting up the engine.

Luca catches my eye in the rearview mirror. "Back to the DeGreco."

"Oh." My voice drops at the end. "You don't have more errands?"

"We do, but we'll take you home first."

"I hate to make you go out of the way."

"It's no big deal. I know you're eager to get back. We'll just swing around that way and drop you. We're not in a hurry."

I picture the FedEx driver giving up on obtaining a signature and leaving the packages on the sidewalk in front of the building for someone to steal as they walk by. Of course Luca isn't in a hurry. He never is. But I'm surprised he's concerned about my schedule.

"Great." It comes out more sharply than I intend.

I find Luca's gaze in the rearview mirror, his expression unreadable. I look away.

When we pull up in front of the DeGreco, I say goodbye to Mrs. Goodwin and Sal while Luca hops out of the car to get my door. Before he can get there, I push it open myself and swing my feet out. Too late, I realize I've mistimed my exit, because he's stepped forward to offer me his hand at the exact same moment that my legs propel me upward. My shoulder bumps his chest, and I teeter on my unfamiliar heels. He reaches out to steady me, and through the thin material of my blouse, I can feel the warmth of his hand. My gaze drops to his tattooed forearm, and I have the strangest urge to reach over, push his sleeve higher, and find the end of the vine I can see growing toward his bicep.

Cheeks heating, I lift my chin and meet his eyes with as much composure as I can muster, which to be honest, is not much composure at all. "I appreciate you getting me to work and back safely," I say politely. "And as for the rest, well, hopefully the elevator will be fixed by tomorrow."

"Anytime at all." Luca gives me that charming grin, ignoring my dig about the elevator, of course.

I take a step back, but at the last moment, he tightens his grip around my arm, tugging me closer. His grin slowly fades.

"What—" I stutter. "What are you doing?" My voice wavers, and I clear my throat.

Luca leans in, his face moving closer to mine. He smells like something fresh and citrusy, with a tiny hint of the leather seats of the Town Car. For a wild second, I think he's going to kiss me. And for some completely inexplicable reason, I find myself leaning in, too. My breath catches in my throat. But then, just as his lips are inches from mine, Luca shifts his face to the left, over my shoulder. I feel a tiny brush of his facial stubble against my cheek and the rise of his chest as he takes a breath through his nose like he's trying to smell my perfume.

"What are you *doing*?" I lean sideways to get a look at his face.

"You—" Luca drops back on his heels. I've never seen him look flustered before. He shakes his head as if he's trying to focus. "Sorry. Never mind." And then before I can say another word, he lets go of my arm and backs away.

I watch him head back to the driver's seat. What was that about? And more importantly, *what was I thinking, leaning into him like that?*

Of course, it's not like he was actually trying to kiss me.

But if he was, would I have let him?

This is the weirdest day I've ever had, and that's saying a lot for someone who grew up with a literal clown. It's not even eleven in the morning, and already I've swapped clothes with my neighbor, had my potty training history trotted out for my boss, and come alarmingly close to making out with my doorman.

I need to wrestle this day back under my control. I head for the door to the building, ready to go upstairs, finish my syllabi, and find my dad a new job. But at the last second, I peek over my shoulder just in time to watch Luca sink gracefully back into the Town Car to continue his errands with Mrs. Goodwin and Sal. A strange longing tugs in my chest.

I actually *do* need some new work clothes. Maybe they're going near the mall?

But as I turn around to call out to Luca, my knee bumps something sharp and heavy. I feel it toppling sideways, crashing to the sidewalk, and I slap a hand against the building's wall to keep from ending up on top of the pile. "Ouch," I mutter, clinging to the brick. When I've managed to get my feet under me, I turn around to survey the scene.

You have got to be kidding me.

FedEx boxes litter the sidewalk. I'm sure the driver dumped them here because nobody was at the front desk to open the door and receive them. And now they're scattered almost to the street, where anyone could wander by and take one.

With a heavy sigh, I bend over to pick up as many boxes as I can, balancing them in one hand while I try to fish my key out of my purse with the other. Oblivious, Luca pulls the Town Car out into the road with a loud zoom, not even bothering to put on his turn signal first.

Which clearly goes against the traffic laws.

CHAPTER 5

Today I take the stairs. It's not only because the elevator is on the fritz again, although it is. Or because I'm wearing brand-new work clothes, although I am. And it's not because I'm carrying a travel mug and I've learned my lesson about coffee stains.

Although I have.

It's because today is my orientation for my new job, and I am determined to be one hundred percent in control of this day. This means leaving absolutely nothing to chance, or the whims of bus schedules, or irresponsible doormen.

Especially irresponsible doormen.

With any luck, I won't even have to see him in the lobby. It's a little before seven in the morning, and Luca doesn't start work until eight. I plan to be sitting in the human resources department, calmly waiting for my meeting, before he even parks the Lincoln Town Car in front of the DeGreco building for the day. And just in case anything should go awry, I've built in a comfortable cushion of over two hours before my orientation starts at nine.

As I descend from the eighth floor to the seventh, I hear someone shuffling up the staircase beneath me. I round the bend and come face-to-face with Sal. He's holding on to the railing, hand shaking slightly, and slowly pulling himself upward, step by slow and laborious step.

"Sal!" I exclaim. "Are you okay? You look exhausted." I swear under my breath, damning Luca for not getting the elevator fixed correctly when it broke a few weeks ago. It's gone out twice since then. This is a building full of older people. What was he thinking letting it go on like this?

"You shouldn't have to take the stairs. I'm going to give Luca a call right now and demand he get Dante in here to fix the elevator today." I sigh. "*Again.*" So much for not having to deal with irresponsible doormen this morning. But I'm so angry that I don't even mind that this is disrupting my carefully scheduled morning. This sort of thing is exactly why I built in a cushion in the first place.

But before I can pull out my phone, Sal waves a dismissive hand. "I'm fine. Don't worry about me."

"Of course I'm worried about you. What floor do you live on?"

"The eighth," Sal says, pulling himself up another step. "But I enjoy walking. It keeps me young."

The eighth is my floor, too, a level above the one we're standing on. I turn around, taking Sal's arm and helping him up the next step. "At least let me walk with you."

Sal chuckles. "I'm not going to say no to a pretty girl offering to take me out for a stroll." He gives me a wink. "And lucky me, I get to hold her hand and everything."

We inch our way up the flight of steps, and soon, we're standing in the hallway flanked by a row of apartment doors. "We must be neighbors." I point to my door. "That one's me."

"Yep," Sal says with a nod, like he already knew that. I guess people talk. Or maybe he's seen me around, though he didn't look familiar when I met him a couple weeks ago in Luca's car.

"Let me just make sure you get into your place okay."

Sal waves me off again. "No, no. I'm fine. You've got an important meeting to get to."

I blink. "How did you know that?"

Sal hitches his chin in my direction. "Why else would you be all gussied up this early in the morning?"

I glance down at my outfit. I'm wearing a black-and-white-patterned top tucked into a black pencil skirt with the hopes that if anything should drip, spill, or splatter, it won't show stains. Plus, I have a spare outfit in my bag, just in case. I probably should get going, especially because now I'll need to stop in the lobby to call Luca and give him a piece of my mind about the elevator. "If you're sure you're okay."

Sal reaches into his pocket and pulls out a butterscotch candy. "For luck," he says with a wink.

I can't help but smile. Just like Mrs. Goodwin wishing me luck before my big meeting a few weeks ago, I'm happy to know someone's rooting for me, even just a little bit. I was so busy going to school and working for the past decade that I never had a lot of time to make friends. When the students in my program were going to parties or meeting for coffee after class, I was headed to my job. And I don't have any other family except for Dad. We had dinner two days ago, like we do every week, but we were still brainstorming how to find him a new job, and mine never came up. Or, well, to be more accurate, *I* was brainstorming how to find him a job, and *he* was busy changing the subject. And anyway, mathematics is not really something that interests him.

My face heats at the memory of his *algae-bra* joke.

I take Sal's candy and tuck it into my bag. "Hopefully, I'll see you around, neighbor." And I realize it's not just something you say to be polite. I really *do* hope I'll see him around. Just not while we're climbing the stairs because the elevator is broken.

And with that, I remember I need to have a chat with my doorman.

I head downstairs, pushing open the door to the lobby that's quiet and dark except for the emergency lights over the stairs and the sun just beginning to slant in through the glass transom. Leaning against the front desk, I pull my phone from my bag and search my contacts for Luca's number. He gave it to me when I signed my lease in case I needed to get ahold of him in the event of a building emergency. Well, this elevator situation constitutes a building emergency.

I hit the button to call him, pressing the phone to my ear. Luca's phone rings on the other end, and then strangely, right in tune, the front desk starts buzzing along with it. *What?* I lean over the upper counter to look at the desk beneath and find a phone with my name sliding across the screen. Did Luca leave his phone here?

And then, seemingly out of nowhere, a colorful arm appears, grabs the phone, and disappears into the depths of the desk like some sort of tattooed boa constrictor catching its prey. I jump when a sleepy male voice mumbles "Hello?" from under the desk, and faintly, at a slight delay, through my phone, too. I hit the red button to hang up the phone and charge around the desk. On the floor is Luca, lounging on a nest of blankets, his head propped on a pillow.

"What are you doing?" I demand.

His eyes widen and he sits up abruptly when he spots me towering over him. "Hey, Catherine." He runs a hand through his rumpled hair and gives me a smile like we've just run into each other at the coffee shop down the street instead of over his nap on the floor. "What's going on?"

"Did you *sleep* here?"

"Um." Luca clambers to his feet, and my gaze sweeps from his wrinkled black doorman's uniform to his dark hair sticking up in peaks. "I definitely *laid* here for a while. But this pillow Mrs. Esposito in 6D gave me is pretty lumpy. So I wouldn't call it the best night of sleep of my life."

"Do you sleep here...often?"

"Occasionally." He shrugs and offers no more explanation than that.

"I—" I'm so confused by this that the next thing just pops out of my mouth. "You know that's against the building's rules and regulations, don't you?"

"Eh." He shrugs. "Might be."

"Why don't you go home?" And then something dawns on me, followed by a heavy weight on my chest. "Do you *have* a home?" Maybe Luca is homeless. We live in Pittsburgh, a very affordable city. What kind of poverty wages must they be paying him if he needs to sleep on the floor of the lobby? I'm definitely going to take this up with the building's owners. They can increase my rent if that's what it takes to pay Luca properly.

But then another weight drops on my chest.

Once Dad finds a new job, that is. Otherwise, I might not be able to afford my own rent.

But Luca just grins. "Of course I have a home. I live upstairs."

"Then why are you…" I hold up a hand and remember the clock is ticking and I need to get to the bus. "You know what? I really don't want to know." I square my shoulders. "I'm here to talk to you about the elevator. It's not right that the building's older residents have to walk up the stairs because you can't be bothered to get the elevator fixed."

Luca's eye twitches. *Is that annoyance flickering across his face?* But I must have imagined it because in the next second, he's pulling his stool up to the desk and plopping down on it. "Is the elevator broken again?" He gazes at the spot over the door that's supposed to be lit up with numbers, as unconcerned as ever. "Huh. Guess I need to call Dante again."

"Yes, I guess you do," I say. "I found an older gentleman climbing the stairs near the seventh floor a few minutes ago. I'm sure it took him ages to get there from the lobby, and he had another floor to go."

He squints at me. "An older man came through the lobby and took the stairs? Are you sure?"

"Of course I'm sure."

Luca's face goes back to neutral. "I guess I did fall asleep," he says with a shrug. "I'll have to tell Mrs. Esposito that her pillow isn't so bad after all."

I sigh in exasperation. "Can you just call Dante—whoever that is—to fix the thing once and for all?"

"Sure."

That one word is so maddening and tells me exactly nothing. *When* is Luca going to call Dante? And when will the elevator be fixed? Anxiety fills my chest, and I can feel sweat beading up on my forehead.

Luca reaches under the desk and hands me a rag. "You look like you could use this."

With a slight feeling of déjà vu, I take the rag from his palm. I can't believe I've let Luca hold me up again. Swiping at my forehead with one hand, I stuff my phone in my bag with the other. "I've got to go. I don't want to be late."

"Another big day at work?" Luca asks, his gaze sweeping down to my feet and back up.

"I have my orientation for new faculty members today."

"It's awfully, early, no?" Luca clicks on his phone to check the time and then he looks back up at me. "What time does it start?"

"It starts..." I mumble, knowing he's going to judge me for this. "It starts at nine o'clock."

His dark eyebrows shoot up against his bronze forehead. "You know it's not even seven right now, don't you?"

"Of course I know."

"Of course you do. And you probably also know that the university is eight minutes from here."

"I like to leave early. It gives me plenty of time to get organized." I don't mention that it's *his* fault I'm so afraid to be late because it almost happened last time. I know he won't agree with that assessment. Luca probably thinks that if you show up on the same day as the meeting, you're showing up on time.

"You didn't think leaving at six would be better?" he asks with a smirk. "Just to see the sunrise?"

I cross my arms over my chest.

He cocks his head and gives me a grin so wide it practically reaches all the way to his ears. "You thought about leaving at six, didn't you? Come on. Admit it."

I huff, but don't answer.

"You did."

Fine. I *did* think about it.

"Listen, if you need a ride, I can take you."

"No. That's really not necessary." I narrow my eyes. "Besides, you need to stay here and get the elevator fixed." Has he forgotten about it already?

"It's no trouble. It will actually work out because I can swing by Dante's house on the way back to drag him out of bed."

"Maybe you should stay here and call Dante instead." I shake my head, remembering Sal huffing up the stairs. "I can take the bus. My app says it will be here in five minutes."

Luca shrugs like he doesn't care one way or the other. "Suit yourself." And then he reaches down to fluff the pillow that Mrs. Esposito in 6D gave him. Is he going to take another nap?

I remind myself that I have other things to think about and head out the door.

The bus comes right on time, and in fifteen minutes, I'm sitting in the lobby of the university's human resources building. In order to kill time before my orientation starts, I pull out my laptop and get started on my research paper that I'm collaborating on with Dr. Gupta. Except that Dr. Gupta has yet to really collaborate with me. I emailed him a couple of questions last week, and he directed me to his graduate assistant. So I'm pretty much on my own.

Eventually, a number of other faculty members file into the lobby for the orientation, taking the chairs around me. At precisely eight fifty-five, an attractive middle-aged white woman in a stylish black suit enters the waiting area.

"Hello, all!" she says, her voice projecting around the room. "I'm Helen Hardy, and I'm your human resources representative for today's orientation. Welcome to the university!" Helen has a blend of competence and enthusiasm mixed with a dash of goody-two-shoes-iness that leaves me no doubt she was her high school class president and college dorm resident advisor before she segued seamlessly into human resources. I like her immediately.

A few of the other new faculty members murmur, "Hello," but most just nod and sip their coffees as if they're not up for exclamation points this early in the morning. I guess these are the professors who will be teaching the evening classes.

I sit up straight and give Helen a wave. "Hi, Helen. It's nice to be here." I've been up since five, after all. I hate to leave her hanging.

She directs her wide smile in my direction and keeps talking. "We want to make sure that we stick to our schedule today"—*Yay. I love* sticking to a schedule—"so we'll head into the conference room in a moment. But first, I just want to point out that we have an incredibly diverse group of new faculty members from departments all over the university joining us here today." Helen glances down at her clipboard. "Medicine, social work, biology, English literature, communications, computer science, nursing, chemistry..." She gasps. "My goodness, so much brainpower in one room."

I raise a palm to point out that she accidentally missed mathematics. My department. But I remember the schedule, so I drop my hand back into my lap. I can mention it to her at the break.

Helen begins calling out the names on her clipboard. As each person stands, she checks it off on the paper and directs them into the conference room behind her. Slowly, each faculty member filters out of the waiting area until I'm the only person who remains seated in the chairs.

"And...that's it for today." Helen peeks at her clipboard and then back at me.

"What about me?" I nod at her clipboard. "You didn't call my name."

Her eyebrows knit together, and she stares at the paper now, tapping her pen next to each name. "I believe I got everyone on my list. What's your name?"

I tell her, and she checks the clipboard one more time, muttering under her breath as she scans the page. After a moment she looks up, shaking her head. "I'm sorry, I don't have you listed as an attendee at the orientation today."

My mouth drops open. "But...I signed up weeks ago. I—" Holding up a finger on one hand, I fumble in my bag with the other. "I have the email confirmation right here." I pull out my phone and open my brand-new university email, scrolling past announcements about back-to-school sales at the bookstore and the mathematics faculty luncheon Dr. Gupta is hosting at the University Club later this afternoon. Finally, I find the email confirming that I *did*, in fact, sign up for orientation today and stating that human resources will begin processing my paperwork shortly. "It's right here." I wave the phone at her.

"Hmmmm." Helen taps her lip with her pen. "It does confirm that you signed up. However, that's a form email that's automatically generated when you submit your information in the portal. I wonder if you didn't make the list for the program today because there was a problem with your paperwork."

"A problem? With my paperwork?" My heart stutters because my love for sticking to schedules is only eclipsed in intensity by my hatred for problems with paperwork. "What sort of problem?"

Helen waves her hand. "Oh, it could be anything. Maybe you didn't submit a form that you needed to, for example."

"I'm certain I submitted everything." My words are loud, echoing in the empty room. I clear my throat. "I mean"—I lower my voice—"is there a way to check?" I say it, but deep down I know it's just a formality. As soon as she opens her file, she'll see it's all there. My tax forms, copies of my driver's license and birth certificate, bank information for direct deposit. I'm positive I submitted everything on the day I got the email. Just like I always do.

"Sure. Let's…" She glances at her watch and then into the orientation room. "Let's quickly pop into my office." I feel a surge of empathy for her. It's five after nine, and the program was supposed to start five minutes ago. This delay is throwing off this poor woman's entire schedule. It would leave me flustered. But she gives me a reassuring smile, and I appreciate her kindness.

I follow her down the hallway into a small office, where she leans over the desk and taps on a keyboard. "Catherine Lipton," she mutters, typing something into the field on the top of her screen. "Hmmmm," she says again, with that same ambiguous murmur from earlier that has my nerves buzzing. I lean forward to get a better look, but she's moving too quickly, clicking from form to form, and I can't decipher what I'm seeing.

"It's all there, right? ID? Social Security number? Tax forms?"

"Well," Helen says, clicking between forms again. "I can see you *did* submit the forms on the day you registered for orientation."

Of course I did. I beam at her, grateful we cleared that up. "Wonderful. Should I take my seat in the orientation room?" If we hurry, maybe we can get this meeting back on track. She seems like the type of capable and efficient person who would have built in extra time for contingencies.

"Actually..."

I stand up straighter. "What's the problem now?"

"Well, I can see that you submitted the paperwork, but it appears that the system rejected it."

"*Rejected it?*" Why on earth would the system reject it? I gave them exactly what they asked for.

But then my spine stiffens as I remember standing out on the lawn with Dr. Gupta and Dad a couple of weeks ago. I've gone over and over that day in my head ever since, and

I've managed to convince myself that Dr. Gupta didn't find the interaction as strange as I suspected he did. Maybe he barely even registered it at all. Dr. Gupta meets hundreds of new people every fall: all the new students coming in, visiting professors, support staff. My dad is wacky, but this is a university. There are a lot of unusual characters. In the last few days, I'd managed to put the entire interaction out of my head and focus on all the work I have to do.

But now, as I stand here in this office, paperwork rejected, I can't help but wonder if maybe Dr. Gupta really was more put off by Dad than I imagined. What if he was the one who rejected my paperwork because my family is too strange? What if he thinks I won't be a proper representative of the mathematics department? He did send me to his graduate assistant instead of answering my questions himself.

My heart taps like Helen's fingers on the keyboard.

What if he's decided that he no longer wants me as a member of the mathematics faculty?

Can he do that? Can he simply reject me based on a five-minute conversation with my father on the lawn? My stomach churns. Dad might be wacky, but he was perfectly nice to Dr. Gupta, and I don't deserve this. By now I'm shaking, clutching the desk chair so hard my fingers have gone white. "Does it say the reason for the rejection?"

Oblivious to my distress, Helen clicks around with her mouse, muttering that same "Hmmmm."

The sound is a fire alarm to me now. All it means is that something has gone terribly wrong.

"Will you excuse me a moment?" Helen hurries out into the hall, and I hear her whispering to another person. The person whispers back. I strain to hear what she's saying, but I can't decipher it. A moment later, she's back.

"Ms. Lipton—"

"Doctor." I correct her automatically.

She blinks. "Yes. Of course. *Dr.* Lipton," she agrees, but the warmth in her voice is gone, replaced by a deep skepticism. "You *did* submit your paperwork correctly and on time. However, when we tried to connect it with your government records for tax purposes and to run our standard background checks, it seems there's no evidence of you in the system."

I press my hands to my temples. "Of course there's no evidence of me in the university's system." I say it slowly, as if that might help her to understand. "I've never worked here before." Maybe she's not as competent as I initially thought. After all, isn't it her job to put me in the system?

"No." Helen shakes her head. "Not the university's system. There's no record of you in the *government's* system." Her eyes slide to mine, cold and detached. "There's no record that you exist at all."

CHAPTER 6

—" I stare at Helen with my mouth hanging open. "Of course I *exist*. I'm standing right here in front of you."

Helen's eyebrows rise and lips purse, but ever the professional, she calmly says, "Unfortunately, your physical presence doesn't constitute proof of identity. Your name and Social Security number didn't show up in any of the government records when we ran our checks."

"That doesn't make any sense. I submitted a copy of my official Social Security card."

"Well, at the end of the day, a Social Security card is just a piece of paper. And I'm not saying *you* would do this—" She holds out a manicured hand to reassure me, but something about her tone has a false ring to it. "But Social Security cards can be faked."

Faked? Who does Helen think I am? "Mine wasn't faked."

"Well..." Helen crosses her arms. Underneath her class president exterior, I'm getting a hint of mean girl who puts gum in your hair. "That seems like exactly the sort of thing someone would say if it was faked, doesn't it?"

She has a point.

I grasp for something that makes sense. "But the mathematics department hired me for the position. They have copies of my transcripts and my dissertation. They checked my references. All of that proves I'm a real person."

"Again, I'm not saying *you* would do this, but there are also ways to fake that sort of thing."

I feel the heat rising in my face. It's one thing to suggest I mixed up my paperwork, and entirely another to imply that I didn't write my own dissertation. "Who would have written my dissertation, then? There are only a handful of scholars who understand the nuances of my field of study. How would I fake it?"

"Well..." Helen says, drawing out the word like she hates to be the one who has to break it to me. "Unfortunately, the university *has* discovered the occasional student who relied on artificial intelligence to...enhance...their papers."

My breath hitches and my chest squeezes. "*I did not use artificial intelligence.*" It comes out louder than I intended.

Helen's eyes widen, and she takes a step back from me. One of her hands slides toward the phone, probably to call security, and the other reaches for her desk drawer like she has some sort of weapon stashed in there. Human resources is probably where all the disgruntled employees end up, so I can't completely blame her. Except I'm not a disgruntled employee, and I'm not here to complain about my sick time or lack of dental benefits. My entire career is on the line, and this woman is implying that nothing about me is real.

But even through my panic, I can recognize that throwing a tantrum in this woman's office is *not* going to get me what I want. My control of this situation is slipping, and I need to wrestle it back. I take a deep, cleansing breath, holding my palms up to show I'm harmless. "Look," I say. "I just want to clear this up. I can assure you that I did write my dissertation, my references are real, and I earned every A on my transcript. How can I prove it to you?"

I remember Luca's engaging smile earlier, and how, for just a moment, it almost made me forget about the broken elevator. I try one out for myself, curving my lips upward and flashing my pearly whites. I'm pretty sure I look less like my charming doorman and more like I'm having my teeth checked at the dentist, but it does seem to defuse the situation.

Helen slowly draws her hand away from the phone, curling it into a fist. Just in case I make any sudden movements, I guess. "If you really are who you say you are…there will be some sort of record of you."

"But—where? How do I find a record?" I can hear a little break in my voice at the end. They don't teach you this sort of thing in calculus class: what to do if your identity disappears into thin air. No perfect grades on my transcript or dissertation can help me now. "You said I didn't show up in any of the government systems. I don't even know how that's possible. I've had other jobs before, and they've never had a problem finding me."

Helen sighs deeply, and maybe hovering close to crying is working better for me than a Cheshire cat grin, because her face softens. "It could be some sort of mix-up. A record was moved or deleted. I recommend you take your documents down to the Social Security office and see if they can clear it up for you."

"Really? Do you think that's all it is?"

She nods, maybe humoring me, but hope swells in my chest. Helen is no longer looking at me as if I'm some sort of criminal, and like she said, maybe this is all just a misunderstanding. I'll take a quick trip down to the Social Security office and have this cleared up before the faculty luncheon this afternoon.

Except there's just one little problem. My gaze swings to Helen. "What about the orientation? Will I have to miss it?" I told Dr. Gupta that I would attend today. What if he asks about it over lunch?

But Helen just shrugs. "I think that's the least of your problems at the moment." She brushes off her hands, clearly done with me. "Now, if you'll excuse me, I have an orientation to get to." Helen closes her computer and holds out a hand, gesturing for me to leave the room first. Out in the hall, she pulls the door shut firmly.

As quickly as I can, I head out of the building and make a break for the bus. My personal paperwork is at home, so I'll need to stop there before I can run over and clear this up at the Social Security office.

When I walk into the DeGreco, the first thing I notice is that Luca seems to have cleaned himself up and taken a shower. His thick, dark hair is still wet, waving over his forehead and curling slightly at the nape of his neck. The second thing I notice is that the elevator is still broken.

"Seriously?" I stare up at the dark panel over the elevator door. "Dante didn't come yet?" I bang on the button, though I'm pretty sure I have no hope of it making the elevator appear.

"You're home early," he says, ignoring my question along with my disgruntled expression. "How was your day, dear?"

I don't have time for this. It's one thing to descend eight floors in a pair of heels. It's another entirely to have to climb them. Especially when I'm in a hurry, and my day is falling apart. "What happened to Dante? I thought he was coming to fix the elevator."

"He was here, he fixed it, he left, and now it's broken again." He shakes his head like, *What are you gonna do?* "It's Mr. and Mrs. Hartman's wedding anniversary, so Mrs. Hartman is breaking things all over the building."

"You're saying someone *broke the elevator?*"

"It's a long story." Luca shrugs. "Why the rush anyway?"

"I need to get up to my apartment to get some papers."

"Did you forget something? Otherwise, that was the fastest orientation in the history of orientations."

I'm not sure how he'd know. There's no way Luca underwent any sort of training whatsoever for this job. "No, I did *not* forget something." I can feel that familiar panic pooling in my chest. "I submitted everything I needed to submit on the day I received the email."

Luca nods. "I wouldn't expect any less of you." He pulls out a rag and starts cleaning the counter in front of him. Except I suspect it's a gesture for my benefit—to make it look like he's working—because he just keeps swiping at the same two-square-foot area. "So did you ace the orientation and they sent you home early?"

I press the elevator button again and then give up. "I can't talk now. I have to climb eight flights of stairs to my apartment." And with that, I slip out of my high-heeled shoes and make a run for the stairwell. Once inside, I shuffle up each stair as fast as I can in my fitted pencil skirt, cursing my choice of clothing today. I'd kill for Mrs. Goodwin's black trousers right now.

I manage to keep up a swift, steady pace until I get to the fourth floor, and then my thighs start burning and my steps begin to slow. By the fifth floor, I'm holding on to the railing and starting to breathe hard. Around the seventh floor, I'm panting and cursing. How hard is it to fix an elevator? Maybe Dante should be fired. "Maybe Luca should be fired, too," I mutter.

And then, from behind me on the stairs, I hear the most annoying voice I've ever heard in my life ring out. "You called?"

I spin around as elegantly as I can muster in this cursed skirt while clutching the railing for dear life and find Luca casually ascending the stairs, half a flight behind me, breathing normally, not a hair out of place. "Why are you following me?" I demand.

"I'm not following you. I simply came to ask if you wanted to take the elevator."

I grip the railing harder. "I thought the elevator was broken."

"Oh, it is." Luca nods. "The passenger elevator, anyway. But we could have taken the freight elevator."

I gape at him. "Are you kidding? Why didn't you tell me there was a freight elevator?"

"Maybe I like seeing your nose all scrunched up like that when you're out of breath."

If I had the energy right now, I would push him down these stairs. Instead, I swing around and start my slow shuffle back up.

Luca takes the steps two at a time, and in less than three seconds he's standing on the step above me, looking down. "Actually, I didn't tell you there was a freight elevator because you ran out too quickly and didn't give me a chance."

On equal footing, he's a good eight inches taller than me, so I have to tilt my head back to look at him on the upper stair. "Are you saying I could have been riding the freight elevator all along?"

Luca shakes his head. "It's in the back of the building, and you have to go through the storage closet to get to it. You can't go on your own. I'd have to take you, because you need a key to access it."

My gaze slides past Luca to the door on the landing behind him, lingering on the large number eight painted there. "Well, I guess it's too late now. This is my floor."

I haul myself up the last few steps and push through the door into my hallway. Luca trails after me to my apartment. I consider telling him to go away, but at this point, it would be more trouble to argue with him than to just let him tag along. I do my best to ignore him as I pull out my key, unlock the door, and push it open. It doesn't really surprise me that Luca follows me into my apartment, too. He's never struck me as someone who waits for an invitation. I head directly to the built-in cabinets on the far wall, while Luca stands in the middle of the living room, spinning in a slow circle.

"I like what you've done with the place."

"Thanks." I fling open a cabinet door and pull out a file box full of papers, tossing the lid to the side and kneeling next to it. Inside, I find all my personal paperwork tucked into color-coded files, the contents of each listed on a tab I made with my label maker. The sight of those uniform cardboard shapes lined up in a neat row slows my heart rate a smidge.

Somewhere to my right, Luca is still checking out my apartment. "It doesn't really surprise me that your place is so clean." He takes another turn. "But I admit I didn't expect all this. You've done an amazing job with the decorating." His eyebrows rise, and he sounds impressed. I look up from my box of files and take a second to look around, trying to view my new apartment through Luca's eyes.

I've never had a home, a real home and not just a cheap month-to-month rental that we were in danger of getting kicked out of at any moment. One where Dad's unicycle and stilts leaned against the worn living room couch and his juggling clubs blocked the hallway. So, when I moved into this place, I didn't have a lot of money to spend on furnishings, but I dipped into my savings and splurged on the emerald-green velvet sofa, the cream-colored rug that's as soft as clouds under my feet, and the botanical block prints handmade by a local artist.

I stare at those prints on the wall. The artist carved the delicate lines of each petal and stem into a block of wood that she printed onto a canvas in layers of color. My eyes shift to the vines peeking out of Luca's rolled-up sleeves. Funny that I would choose to decorate my most cherished space, and he would choose to decorate his body, so similarly. My gaze drifts up his shoulder and down to the buttons on his shirt. I've only ever seen the ink on his arms, but he's wearing a V-neck T-shirt under his doorman uniform today and, given the hints of color climbing above the open collar, I'm assuming the tattoos extend down his chest. And maybe...lower? I flush the color of the crimson poppy near Luca's elbow and yank my eyes from his trim thighs. They snap to Luca's, which I now realize have been trained on me this entire time.

I look away. "You expected my apartment to be stark and cold, right? All clean lines and beige surfaces?" From our limited interactions, I imagine how he must think I'm stuffy and uptight, how my desire for rules and order must seem like a curse for someone as carefree as Luca. We've been like positive and negative numbers since we met, always on completely opposite sides of the line.

Luca slips his hands into his pockets. "I never know what to expect with you, honestly. But *stark* and *cold* aren't quite the words that come to mind."

"What words come to mind?" I ask before I can stop myself. Something thrums across the small space between us. I'm reminded that we haven't *always* been like positive and negative numbers.

It was that first day we met. Right here in this apartment, actually. I'd been so thrilled to be moving out on my own, so happy to find this quiet building full of older people and this sunlit apartment full of character. For the first time in my life, I hadn't cared about rules or regulations or what it said in a manual. I'd wanted the apartment, and when Luca said I could have it—I—

Well.

I don't know what came over me.

I kissed him.

My face flushes just thinking about it. I basically threw myself in his direction, and he pulled me against him, mouth meeting mine as if it were the most natural thing in the world. As if I belonged in his arms. It was just a brief brush of lips, but it was like I'd somehow worked out the most complex mathematical equation in my head. The pieces fell into place, and everything added up like I was exactly who and where I was supposed to be.

But I'd pulled away, and he'd made a joke, and that was it. The next time I saw him I was tripping over a bike in the mail room, and the time after that was the lost dry cleaning incident. I realized how unreliable he is, and I'm assuming he decided that I'm—

Well, I don't know what he decided, since I'm still waiting to hear what word comes to mind when he thinks of me. I'm not sure why I'm holding my breath, but I am.

Luca looks me over. "Determined," he finally says. "Passionate."

My heart slams into my chest.

"You never, ever do anything halfway," he says, like he might actually admire that about me.

I could toss these files aside, cross the room, and be in his arms in less than ten seconds. Something about the way he's looking at me makes me think he might welcome it.

Except that Luca kisses everyone, and dances with everyone. And charms everyone.

I spin back around to turn my attention to the file box. What am I doing staring into Luca's eyes and contemplating throwing myself at him when I have the biggest crisis of my life to avert? If I don't get it together, I'm about to lose this apartment and everything else I worked so hard for.

"What are you looking for?" Luca asks, and if it comes out a bit gravelly, it's not because of me.

I pull my neatly labeled files from the red section of the box and fan them on the floor. *Health Insurance, Credit Card, Bank Account.* Here it is... *Personal Identification.*

I reach into the folder and find my Social Security card along with my birth certificate, both stashed in clear plastic envelopes to protect them from water damage. "This. I'm looking for this." I wave the papers in Luca's direction.

Luca's brow furrows. "Why do you need your Social Security card and birth certificate? I thought you said you submitted all the paperwork for your new job already."

"I did! It was all there!"

"Then... what are we doing here?"

I stagger to my feet, clutching the paperwork tightly against my chest. "I don't know what *you're* doing here, but I'm about to go and prove that I exist."

CHAPTER 7

Luca follows me back downstairs to the lobby like an over-eager puppy, lapping at my heels and barking questions. "So wait a minute. The human resources lady really accused you of not existing?"

"She said I made up my dissertation. *My dissertation.* Can you believe it?" Somehow this feels like the worst offense. My dissertation took me three years, about a hundred sleepless nights, and a thousand tears. My back still aches from those uncomfortable library chairs I practically lived in while I was researching and writing it. And Helen just tried to delete it all.

"So where are you going with those?" Luca nods at the paperwork in my hand. "How are you going to prove you really *are* real?"

"I'm going to the Social Security office. I'm sure it's all just some sort of a silly mix-up. I'll give them my paperwork, and they'll find me in the system. By this afternoon, everything will be cleared up, and I'll be on my way to the faculty luncheon like none of this ever happened." My words might sound confident, but this entire day I've felt like I'm trying to solve for x, when y and z are a mystery.

Luca must hear the waver in my voice, because he reaches out a hand and gently touches my forearm. "Listen, Catherine, let me drive you to the Social Security office."

I hesitate. On the one hand, the Social Security office is all the way across town. It will take me two buses and probably an hour to get there. On the other hand...

"What about the elevator?"

Luca sighs. "What if I promised that Dante is on his way over here right now to fix the elevator?"

At that moment, a tall, dark-haired white man pushes open the front door and walks in. "Hey, cuz," he says, crossing the lobby to give Luca some sort of elaborate handshake that ends in a one-armed hug. When he releases Luca's hand and turns to me, I can see the resemblance. He's broader than Luca but has the same dark eyes and almost-black hair swooping over his forehead.

"How's it going?" He hitches his chin at me. "I'm Dante."

"Catherine," I say, giving him a regular handshake. So, it turns out that Dante, the elevator guy, is Luca's cousin? He's wearing coveralls and well-worn work boots, and it looks like that might be his truck with the ladder parked in front of the building. But is he actually a licensed repairman, or did Luca just hire him because he's family?

"Thanks for coming over again," Luca says.

"I can't believe Mrs. Hartman is at it already."

Luca shrugs. "It's their anniversary."

Dante nods like this makes perfect sense.

I look back and forth between them. Someday, I'm going to get to the bottom of this woman who is apparently fiddling with the elevator. Maybe she just needs someone to stop by to tell her to knock it off. I get the feeling Luca is too nice for that. Beyond the front desk, I spot another bike in the mail room. He lets people in this building get away with everything. But today I have my own mess to clean up.

"Thanks again," Luca says to Dante before turning to me. "Let's get you to the Social Security office."

Thirty minutes later, I shift in my hard plastic chair and glance from the backs of the heads lined up in front of me to the paper number in my hand: *150*.

The light-up board above the counter flashes from 111 to 112. Beneath it, several workers calmly type on their keyboards, occasionally glancing at their screens without any sort of urgency.

I am going to be here all day.

Luca wandered off about ten minutes ago, and now he's chatting with a pretty, dark-haired white woman by the vending machine. My frustration grows every time I glance in their direction. I thought he was coming to offer me moral support, but I guess I shouldn't be surprised that Luca is an equal-opportunity flirt who directs his charm at young people at the Social Security office in addition to older ones at the DeGreco.

I turn back to the light-up board. The number flips to 113. I sigh.

From across the room, I hear Luca call my name. "Catherine." He and the woman are making their way over to me. "Over here." He waves me from my seat.

I stand and squeeze past the older man sitting next to me so I can meet them in the aisle.

"This is Ellie." Luca gestures at the woman, and she's even more attractive up close. "My cousin," he adds.

Another cousin. I don't want to think about why I'm relieved to hear they're related. "Hello."

The woman laughs and gives Luca a nudge. "I hope I'm not your cousin, because that time you kissed me would have been highly inappropriate."

"Oh." My spine straightens. Okay, so definitely not related.

"Ellie is my grandpa's brother's second wife's son's kid."

I blink, trying to add all that up. Fractal geometry is easier to understand.

"So not blood-related, but she's basically family." Luca's dark eyes lock on mine. "When we kissed, we were in fifth grade."

I don't know why he felt the need to add that last part. Luca doesn't owe me an explanation. Even more confusing is why I'm stupidly glad to hear he hadn't been kissing Ellie recently. "It sounds like you have a lot of family."

Ellie's laugh is light, sparkling. "When you start paying attention, you'll find Morellis all over the city."

Luca shrugs. "My grandpa had eight siblings and seven children. We're a dynasty."

My eyes widen. "Wow." Growing up, it was always just Dad and me. His parents passed away when I was two. Apparently, they were supportive of Dad and involved in my life, but I don't remember them. And of course, I don't know anything about my mom's side of the family.

"More like the Mafia." Ellie laughs. "*Well* connected." I'm not sure whether to take her seriously or not, but at the next moment, she's waving toward the front counter. "And speaking of, let me hook you up with Tonya in booth two. If anyone can help you sort this out, she can. Come on." Ellie turns and heads across the room.

Luca moves to follow her, but I hesitate, smoothing the crumpled number in my hand and glancing at the rows of people sitting in uncomfortable chairs and waiting for their turn.

"Catherine." I feel Luca's breath on my cheek as he leans over to whisper in my ear. An involuntary shiver runs through me. "You're worrying about the rules, aren't you?"

"It's just that I'm not sure it would be fair to cut the line…"

Luca takes my arm and pulls me toward him, backing up slowly as he goes, and we shuffle a couple of feet toward Tonya's booth. "I promise it's okay to let your hair down this one time. Nobody will ever have to know."

My face is only inches from his chest, and I'm momentarily distracted by his citrusy scent as he shuffles me another couple of feet. "But—"

"Don't you have some sort of faculty something or other to get to?"

At the word *faculty* I snatch my arm from Luca's. "Yes." I check my watch. "Oh my God. The faculty luncheon starts in an hour."

"Then let's get moving, darling."

Unfortunately, Tonya isn't a Morelli, and she seems to be the only woman on earth who is immune to Luca's charms. After Ellie explained my situation and—with a hug for Luca—headed back across the room to her office, Tonya coldly took my Social Security card and has been silently typing numbers and clicking buttons on her screen ever since.

When Luca interrupted her about four minutes ago to flash her a smile and ask how it was going, Tonya grunted at him and kept typing. When he tried again two minutes later, she ignored him altogether.

I rub my sweaty palms on my now-wrinkled pencil skirt. Tonya's eyes narrow, and her mouth twists to the right. She clicks a few more buttons. I shift from one foot to the other. Luca mirrors my movements. Tonya clicks a few more buttons. Her mouth twists to the left. I shift again.

Finally, I can't take it anymore. *"Am I in there?"*

"Nope." She slides the card back across the counter.

"Nope?" I look to Luca, who raises an eyebrow, and then back to Tonya. "But that's impossible." I slide the card back across the counter in her direction. "Can you please check it again?"

Tonya takes my card, types the numbers one by one into her computer, clicks the mouse, and looks back up at me. "Like I said. You're not in here."

I clutch the counter in front of me. "But how is that possible? I have a Social Security card right there in your hand. Someone in this agency issued it to me."

Tonya flips the card over, stares at it for a minute, and then flips it back. "Guess it could be a really good fake."

"It's not a fake." I can hear that hysterical tinge around

the edges of my voice, similar to when I was talking to Helen in HR. But Tonya doesn't look concerned that I might snap. She looks bored.

"Tonya." Luca draws out her name, saying it in that same tone he used to call me *darling* earlier, and that's how I know he's about to really turn on the charm. Not that hearing him call me *darling* charmed me. Absolutely not. But hopefully it will work on Tonya. "My friend is clearly struggling here, so if you could share some of your wisdom and experience and let us know how to prove she exists, we would really appreciate it."

Tonya stares at him for a moment. He smiles. She stares. His grin widens. She finally cracks. "Fine." *Score one for Luca's charm*. She turns to me. "Do you have a government-issued ID?"

I dig through my wallet and slide my driver's license across the desk.

Tonya types some more information into the computer. "Nope. You're not in here."

"That is simply not possible."

Tonya shrugs. "Sorry. According to official government records, you don't exist."

"But—" I stand there in stunned silence, my mouth agape. "How—" I don't even know what to say.

Luca steps forward. "Okay, look. Catherine obviously exists. She's standing right here. She has"—he waves a hand at the cards lined up on Tonya's side of the counter—"these documents."

"Fakes," Tonya mutters under her breath.

I gasp. "*They are not fakes.*"

Luca grabs my hand and gives it a squeeze under the counter. *It's going to be okay*, that squeeze seems to say. "What do you recommend Catherine should do to prove that she really is who she says she is?"

"Well." Tonya considers this, and I hold my breath. "I suppose if you have a birth certificate, you could try to get a new government-issued ID card to prove that you're really who you say you are. From there, we can start the process of tracking down your Social Security information."

"I have one! It's right here." I lay my birth certificate on the counter and wipe a speck of dust from its clear plastic cover.

Tonya picks it up, flips it over, and then quickly flips it back. "This isn't your birth certificate."

"What do you mean it's not my birth certificate? It says my name, and birth date, and place of birth right there on the page." I'm breathing hard now, my heart pounding in my chest.

"This is a very good *copy* of a birth certificate. You'll need the real thing." Tonya taps her finger on the corner of the page where an official-looking seal is stamped. "Your real birth certificate will have an embossed stamp. It will be textured. This one is just a print. It's probably a photocopy."

I stare at that flat, black-and-white seal, and my hands begin to shake. "No. That's not possible."

"Okay." Luca rests a hand on my shoulder. "Can you excuse us for a moment?" Tonya shrugs and goes back to pecking at her keyboard. Luca gently tugs me to the side of the desk. "Do you have your birth certificate at home? The real one?"

"No."

"Okay..." Luca cocks his head. "Where could it be?"

"I don't know."

"You don't know? Are you sure?"

"Of course I'm sure. Why doesn't anyone seem to believe me?"

"It's just...well. Out of everyone I know, you're the most..." He trails off.

"What? I'm the most *what*?"

Luca clears his throat. "*Organized*. You're the most organized person I know."

But I know what he's thinking. He stood in the middle of my apartment earlier today. I know it wasn't lost on him that I line up the spines of my books so none of them stick out farther than the others, I color coordinate the dishes in my display cabinet, and I alphabetize the spices in the rack in my kitchenette. "You weren't going to say organized. You were going to say something like *picky*, or *fussy*, or...*anal retentive*." Luca's apartment is probably complete chaos. Maybe that's why he sleeps on the floor of the lobby. Because he can't find his bed.

Two pink spots appear on his cheeks. "Don't put words in my mouth. I was going to say *capable* and *competent*, actually. But now that you mention it, you *do* have a color-coded filing system with printed labels. So why can't you find your birth certificate?"

"Well," I huff. "My dad didn't have color-coded files. I found that copy of my birth certificate in a box of his papers when I was applying to college, along with my Social Security card." I hold out my hands, palms up. "This was all he had, and I thought it was real. I never needed the embossed stamp, I guess. I just submitted an electronic copy for all the universities and jobs I applied to."

"Do you think your dad has the real thing?"

I remember stumbling on that box containing my most important paperwork. In addition to my Social Security card and copy of my birth certificate, that box held—among other things—a bunch of CDs by bands from the '90s, a single black Converse sneaker, and a rubber chicken. "I suppose it's possible. But good luck finding it in his messy apartment."

"Maybe you can order a new one." He turns to Tonya. "Can she order a new birth certificate?"

"Sure."

I lean into the desk. "Do you know how I'd do that?"

"Not really."

"Can you…look it up?"

Tonya gives me a stare and then slowly lowers her eyes to the keyboard. She pecks out the letters with one finger. "G-O-O-G-L-E." Her eyes flit back up to me. "Ever hear of it?" Then she goes back to typing—presumably my question—and then hits *Enter* with a flourish.

"Okay, let's see here. Uh-huh. Okay…government-issued ID…uh-huh. Got it." She looks up at me. "To get a new birth certificate, you need to apply using a valid government-issued ID." Tonya slides my driver's license across the counter. "Like this one." She pauses, and then says, "Only not a fake."

"For the hundred millionth time, this one is not a fake."

Tonya leans over the counter and waves at the policeman

standing guard by the door. "Bill. Hey, Bill. Come here a second."

Bill strolls over, his thumbs hooked in the pockets of his police uniform right next to the gun strapped to his belt. "What seems to be the problem?"

"Can you look this woman up for me? She claims she's in the system, but I can't find her anywhere in mine." Tonya waves at me to give Bill my ID. "Maybe you'll have better luck with yours." She shrugs. "Or maybe it's a fake."

I open my mouth to object, but Luca squeezes my hand again.

I slide my ID over to Bill, and he takes a look at the front and then flips it over.

"I'll need to run this through in my car. I'll be right back." He heads outside.

I check my university email while we wait, hoping for a note from Helen that says she cleared things up in HR. But the system must be experiencing problems because my messages won't load.

A minute later, Bill returns. "Where did you get this?" he demands, waving my card.

"What do you mean? I got it at the DMV on Smithfield Street."

"That's impossible. There's no record of a ..." He squints at the card and back at me. "Catherine Lipton. This is the best fake I've ever seen. And I used to be a bouncer at a college bar. I've seen it all."

I take a deep breath, but before I can reply, Luca leans in. "It's not a fake."

"If it were real, it would show up in my system."

I wave my hands at my—*admittedly wrinkled*—blouse and skirt. "Do I look like someone who walks around with a fake ID?"

Bill's gaze skates down to my feet and back up. "Criminals come in all shapes and sizes, ma'am."

Criminals? And then things go from bad to worse when he reaches for my arm. "I think we need to go down to the precinct to sort this out."

I stumble backward in my heels to get away from him. I'd kept them on in the hopes that I'd make it back to the university this afternoon. This is an absolute nightmare. How am I going to explain to Dr. Gupta that I missed the faculty luncheon because I was in lockup? My back hits Luca's chest, and he reaches in front of me, wrapping a protective arm across my shoulders as if he's going to wrestle me away from Bill if he has to. I relax against him, just for a second, because I *do* feel protected. And like I'm not entirely on my own.

"Is there a problem here?" comes a deep voice from behind us. "This rascal giving you trouble, Bill?"

Luca and I spin around to face another police officer. Did he really just call me a rascal? I'm honestly not sure if that's better or worse than being called a criminal. But no, I think he must mean Luca, because Luca releases me with a "Hey, man!" directed at the officer, and now they're hugging. I don't even know what to say about that.

Bill nods in my direction. "You know these people, Marco?"

"I know this guy," Marco says, giving Luca's shoulder a shake so hard, I imagine his teeth rattling. "This is my nephew Elbow."

I guess there really are Morellis all over town. But then I register what Uncle Marco said. My gaze flies to Luca, and I mouth, "Elbow?"

Luca shakes his head, mouthing, "Long story," in return. His face flushes crimson, and for all the times he's turned on the charm, it is a hundred times more appealing to see him flustered like this. I look away because the last thing I need is to find Luca appealing.

At that moment, Ellie pops into view, and we're gathering quite a crowd now. "Did we get things sorted out?" Her gaze drifts to the police officers. "Is there a problem?"

Bill holds up my ID. "This woman is walking around with a fake ID."

Uncle Marco's weathered face turns to me, smile gone, eyes narrowed like a movie mob boss who is about to order my disappearance. "Is this true?" he demands.

I am going to jail for sure. And then I remember Ellie joking...or not joking...that Luca's family is the Mafia.

Or maybe I'll end up in the river.

"*No.* It's not true."

"Luca?" he asks.

Luca slides next to me. "This is my friend Catherine. It seems that there's some sort of a glitch in the system, but her ID *isn't* fake. If she were a criminal, she wouldn't be here trying to sort it out. I can personally vouch for her."

A warmth spreads across me at the conviction in Luca's voice. He's certainly under no obligation to stand up for me, but it means a lot that he is. I just hope he doesn't end up a mile downstream in cement boots along with me.

Uncle Marco takes the ID and holds it up to the light. "Well, Bill, it looks real to me. And if my nephew says this girl is on the up-and-up, then she is."

I relax, and my shoulder bumps Luca's. He grabs my hand again, and I hold on.

Bill begins grumbling, and from across the counter, Tonya—my nemesis only moments ago—swoops in. Maybe Luca's charm really did work on her earlier. Or maybe it's the way she's eyeing Uncle Marco like he's a tasty sandwich. "Oh, come on, Bill," she says. "Let the girl go. She doesn't strike me as the sharpest tool in the shed, but she's not a threat to society."

I gasp, opening my mouth to object. *Not the sharpest tool in the shed?* I have a PhD in mathematics, for the love of Pythagoras. But Luca tightens his grip on mine, and my extraordinary computational brain gets the hint that it might be better to keep all that to myself.

"Fine," Bill says, and I get the feeling he doesn't like everyone ganging up on him. Or maybe he's jealous of the way Tonya is fluttering her eyelashes at Uncle Marco. He leans over, gathering the rest of my paperwork off the counter, and shoves it at me. "You can go, but I'll be keeping an eye on you, Catherine Lipton. Now get out of here before I change my mind."

"But—I still don't exist. I need to sort this out."

Bill takes a menacing step toward me. "It's not too late for me to take you into the precinct."

Luca backs up a step, dragging me with him. "Come on, Catherine," he murmurs in my ear, and I can feel his chest vibrate against my shoulder. "You're not going to last ten minutes in jail. Let's go. We'll figure something out."

We will? I'm not quite sure how Luca, of all people, ended up as my partner in crime. Or why I'm so relieved about it.

Outside in the parking lot, I slump against the Town Car. "I can't believe this is happening."

Luca leans next to me. "You really *have* disappeared from the system."

I close my eyes. Sorting this out feels impossible. The bureaucracy of government agencies is a nightmare to wade through even when you actually *have* the right paperwork. Since I don't, people think I'm some sort of catfish or criminal who invented Catherine Lipton for nefarious purposes. "Well," I say, opening my eyes to roll my head in Luca's direction. "At least if I get hauled off to jail, it won't end up on my permanent record...because I don't have one."

He crosses an arm over his flat abdomen as a sharp laugh escapes from his lips. "You should have seen your face when Officer Bill got involved. Was that the first time someone threatened to arrest you?"

It wasn't, actually. Growing up with Dad, there were all sorts of opportunities for run-ins with the law. Like that time we ran out of gas money on the drive home from Burning Man and Dad set up his show on a street corner in Lincoln, Nebraska. He was unaware that it's illegal to loiter in front of the state capitol. And there was that dance party in a warehouse in the South Side. Shocking nobody, the organizers didn't secure a permit, so when Dad juggled fire and almost burned the building down, the firefighters and police had something to say about it. But Luca definitely doesn't need to know about my almost-criminal history. He went to bat for me with his uncle Marco, promising I was an upstanding citizen.

The thought of Uncle Marco reminds me of something important.

I nudge him with my arm. "If I'd been hauled off to the slammer, would you have bailed me out, *Elbow*?"

Luca's cheeks turn pink, and seeing him flustered is as charming as it was the first time around. "I was a skinny kid," he says defensively. "All knees, and—you know."

"*Elbows*," I say, and suddenly, the laughter comes over me like a wave. I press my hand to my mouth to hold it back, but the more I try to stop, the more I lose control of it. I bend forward to suck enough air into my lungs, shoulders shaking. And finally, all the tension I've been holding since Helen told me I wasn't on her list begins to ease.

Luca stands next to me, shaking his head, his expression a cross between amusement and exasperation. Finally, I pull myself together and stand up straight.

"Sorry," I mutter, wiping my eyes as one last chuckle escapes. "Elbow," I can't help sliding in at the end.

Luca sighs. "The dangers of having family all over town," he mutters. "Someone inevitably pops in the moment you're standing next to a woman you're trying to impress and calls you Elbow."

My smile slowly fades. Is he referring to *me* as the woman he's trying to impress? I was the one standing next to him, after all. I suppose it's possible he meant Tonya, but I'm pretty sure she clocks in at about twice his age. My mind flits back to that moment of connection we had in my apartment earlier. *Both* moments in my apartment, actually, because that kiss last month definitely felt like a connection. At least it did for me. But I was never sure about Luca. Is it possible he's attracted to me?

And then I remember that's when Ellie appeared.

"Well," I say primly, pushing off the car and moving away from Luca. "Thank you for defending me back there."

"Of course." His expression says that he's not sure what to make of me. Which is understandable, because I'm not sure what to make of me, either.

"And thank you for the ride over here. I guess I should go home and figure out what to do next." Since I have no idea what that is, I open my purse and dig through it, looking for—I don't know what. Something that will make me feel in control of this situation and of my ragged emotions.

And then Luca is standing in front of me again. "Catherine," he says. "This is a lot. Let me help you. We'll sort this out together."

"Really?" I tilt my head back and meet his eyes. And then I can't help myself. "Why?"

Luca looks at me for a long moment. And then he shrugs. "Why not?"

And that probably sums it up. Luca isn't thinking too deeply about this situation, or about me. It's just something to do. He strikes me as someone who enjoys an adventure. And my lost identity is more interesting than manning the front desk.

But for most of my life, it's been "me" sorting things out. I admit I like the sound of "we." If Luca hadn't been here today, I might have ended up in jail when Bill and Uncle

Marco stepped in. I don't really know what to do next. So, as shaky as I feel about it, I can't bring myself to say no to Luca's offer of help.

"It sounds to me," Luca says, "the first thing you need to do is find the original copy of your birth certificate. You said you weren't sure if your dad has it. Can you ask him?"

I remember the box with the rubber chicken. We moved so many times, packed and unpacked so many boxes, Dad probably doesn't even know what he has. "It's possible, but it could be anywhere."

"Well, at least it's a place to start." Luca pushes away from the car. "Does he live nearby? I can take you there now."

At that moment, my stomach growls so loudly, it could be heard across the parking lot. I slap a hand to my abdomen, and Luca cocks his head. "When was the last time you ate something?"

And that's when I remember the faculty luncheon. "Oh my God, Luca. I'm supposed to be at lunch with my new boss and the other people in my department. It starts in ten minutes. What are they going to think if I'm a no-show?" I make a run for the passenger side of the car and yank the door open. "Can you take me over there?"

Ten minutes later, Luca pulls the Town Car in front of the University Club. I flip down the sun visor and slide open the flap to check my face in the mirror. My makeup wore off hours ago, and after sweating up eight flights of stairs in my apartment building, my hair has gone frizzy. I pull a tube of lipstick and a comb from my bag and clean up as best I can. "Do I look okay? Am I at least passable?"

Luca is silent for a moment as he gazes across the center console at me. "Catherine, you always look..." He hesitates, his gaze roaming over me, lingering on my mouth before sliding to meet my eyes. The air in the car grows heavy. A beat passes, and then another. And behind us, a car honks, reminding me we're blocking the lane.

Luca shifts toward the windshield. "You always look just like a math professor."

I don't know why that disappoints me, because a math professor is exactly what I want to look like. I grab my bag and hop out of the car. "Thanks for the ride."

He nods. "I'll meet you on the lawn over there in an hour?"

"You really don't have to, you know. I mean, you've been driving me around all day. And I'm sure you have other things to do. The elevator..." I trail off.

"You saw for yourself that Dante's taking care of the elevator. And we've got your birth certificate to track down."

There's that *we* again. "Okay. Thanks, Luca."

Inside the University Club, I locate the banquet room where the department is hosting the faculty luncheon. The smell of bland baked ziti and soggy vegetables greets me as I enter—standard fare at these sorts of events—and my stomach growls again. But instead of making my way over to the buffet, I locate Dr. Gupta. He's off to one side, pacing in front of the coatroom, and talking into his phone with uncharacteristic emotion.

"The semester starts next week. How are we just finding out about this now?" he barks at the person on the other end. "We'll have four classes to cover. Not to mention her committee assignments."

He's talking about me. Who else could it be?

Dr. Gupta looks up and spots me standing there. "I have to go. I'll call you back." And without waiting for the other person to reply, he hangs up the phone.

I approach him cautiously. "Hello, sir."

"What are you doing here?"

"I—" I straighten my shoulders. "I'm a member of this faculty."

Dr. Gupta throws his hands in the air. "Apparently, you're not. Apparently, nobody knows who you are."

"I'm Dr. Catherine Lipton. I swear I am." I take another step forward. "This has all been some sort of terrible mix-up. I'm sorting it out right now." Thankfully, my voice sounds much more confident than I'm feeling, but I pull my shoulders back for good measure.

Dr. Gupta just shakes his head. "I'm afraid that's not going to be good enough."

My breath hitches. No. He can't be suggesting that—

"I'm extremely inconvenienced to have to find someone to replace you," he cuts in.

Replace me? Again, I must have heard him wrong.

"You were scheduled to teach four classes. Plus, what about those papers we talked about? Who is going to write them now that you won't be here to do it?"

My mouth drops open. "What do you mean I won't be here to do it? Of course I'll be here. I told you I'm sorting it out now."

"Forgive me if I don't feel a great deal of confidence."

I know I just met Dr. Gupta a few months ago, but I admit I'm shocked by this conversation. A few weeks ago, he was offering to be my mentor, and today he's ready to give up on me. Am I really so expendable? What about my potential? My promising work and *brilliant mathematical mind*?

"Classes are starting soon," he points out.

I release the tension in my shoulders. Dr. Gupta is understandably upset that this identity issue has thrown a wrench in the semester. He's the dean of the department, and he needs to think of the big picture. I'm sure he doesn't mean to come off as cold and unconcerned. But surely, he has some pull at the university. Maybe there's something he could do to help. Or at the very least, he could give me some time to sort it out. "I'm well aware that classes are starting soon. And I'm confident that this will all be behind us by then."

Dr. Gupta makes a vague noise in the back of his throat.

Panic radiates through me. "Please, sir. Give me a few days to sort this out."

He raises an eyebrow. "You have a plan for how to do that?"

I remember Luca out there on the lawn, waiting for me. *The first thing you need to do is find the original copy of your birth certificate.* It's a start. It's a plan. "Yes, of course I do."

"All right." Dr. Gupta's voice drips with skepticism. "I can give you a few days."

My body sags with relief. "Thank you, sir. I promise you won't regret it."

But he's already turned away from me to head across the room where his colleagues sit.

No. Our colleagues.

They're mine, too. Or they will be, just as soon as I prove I'm real.

CHAPTER 8

Out on the lawn, I find Luca juggling.

Or—well—he's trying to anyway. To be honest, he's not very good, but he's laughing as he tosses the clubs in the air and doesn't seem to mind that most of them land on the grass instead of back in his hands. For a moment, I hover out of sight behind a tree and watch him move with that dancer's grace. *How would his lean muscles look wrapped around an aerial silk?*

I shove that ridiculous thought away. This missing identity situation is clearly messing with my head, because not only am I spending way too much time thinking about my doorman, but now I'm thinking about my doorman *doing circus tricks.*

Circus tricks.

Dad, who is of course the owner of the clubs that Luca is dropping, picks them up from the grass and hands them back, making a *go ahead* motion like Luca should keep trying. He does, tossing two from each hand at the same time. They sail into the air, and as gravity takes over and the clubs come careening back down, Luca seems to realize he'll never be able to catch all four at once. He ducks out of the way and wraps an arm over his head to protect himself. Despite myself, a smile tugs at my lips.

I head across the grass and stop to stand in front of him. "Try throwing them one at a time, and a little bit higher in the air next time."

"That's what I've been trying to tell him," Dad says, picking the clubs up again.

Luca's gaze swings to mine. "Hey. You're back early. How did it go?"

Before I can answer, Dad holds out the clubs in my direction. "Here, Kitty Cat. Why don't you show him how it's done?"

Luca's eyes go wide. "Kitty Cat? *Show me how it's done?*" He looks at Dad and back at me. "You two know each other?"

"We sure do." Dad cocks his head at Luca. "How do *you* know Cat?"

Because it completely doesn't surprise me that these two gravitated together, I might as well make introductions. "Luca, meet my dad, Andrew. And, Dad, this is my—uh— friend Luca. He works in my building."

A grin spreads across Luca's face. "You're Catherine's *dad*?"

"Sure am." Dad tucks his clubs under his arm and holds out a hand to Luca. "Any friend of Cat's is a friend of mine. Call me Andy."

"Andy." Luca's eyes shine like he could not be more delighted. "It's *so* nice to meet you."

"Likewise." Dad gives Luca's hand a vigorous shake.

"Andy was teaching me how to juggle while I waited for you," Luca needlessly explains. "I had *no idea* he was your dad." Luca blinks, and something else seems to register. "Wait. Can you do this?" He waves at the clubs. "Can you juggle?"

"Of course she can," Dad says before I can stop him. "Cat can juggle rings, clubs, she used to be a whiz with fire. But it's been a while, hasn't it, Kitty Cat? Do you still remember that partner routine we used to do? Want to give it a go?"

"Wow," Luca says, and then he repeats it. If his eyeballs bug out any farther, they will pop from his head, and Dad will probably juggle them. "I would pay money to see you juggle fire. Seriously, how much money do you want? I'll pay it."

I shake my head. "You could never afford it."

"Oh, come on," Dad says, dumping the clubs into my arms before I can stop him. "At least show your friend a few tricks." He holds up a finger and turns to jog across the lawn to rescue a wayward juggling club.

"Come on." Luca nudges me. "Show me your tricks."

I set the clubs on the ground and press my hands to my temples. "It's not happening."

"Kitty Cat, why didn't you tell me your dad is a circus performer?" Luca's voice has a hint of awe, like he's ten and just found out Dad is an astronaut or Superman.

"When would it have come up, *Elbow*? When you were spilling coffee on my work clothes or when a police officer was threatening to haul me off to the clink?" I sigh. "I guess I was too busy trying to save my job to tell you about my more colorful family members."

Luca's grin fades. "Hey. I guess it didn't go so well with your boss?"

"No, it didn't."

"Shit. I'm sorry."

Dad jogs back with the club and stops in front of us. "What's this about saving your job, Cat?" His forehead wrinkles.

"There's been a little hiccup with my position at the university."

"Does this have to do with your boss I met a couple weeks ago? Maybe he had a bit of a stick up his butt..." Dad turns to Luca and holds his hands about a foot apart to show him the approximate size of the stick. Luca nods like he can believe it. "But he thinks you're pretty smart, so he seemed A-OK to me."

I fondly remember the days when my biggest problem was that Dad had embarrassed me by sharing my mortifying potty training stories with Dr. Gupta. Was that only a couple weeks ago? And was it really only this morning when I learned my identity had disappeared? It feels like ages ago already.

I try to look on the bright side. At least I won't have to track Dad down at his apartment. "Hey, Dad, is there any chance you have the original copy of my birth certificate?"

If I wasn't looking right at him, I probably would have missed the way Dad's shoulders jerk up, just slightly. For a moment, his face goes pale. But then he shakes his head. "Nope."

He answered that awfully quickly. Very decisively. That's so unlike him.

"Are you sure?"

"Yep, I'm sure."

"How do you know? I found a copy in a box when I was in college. Maybe the original is in another box? Maybe it got mixed up in one of the moves?"

"No. It didn't."

I study Dad's face. He's looking down at the juggling clubs in his hand, not making eye contact. Something strange is going on. "What are you not telling me?"

"Nothing." Dad gives an exaggerated shrug, and I remember why his foray into community theater was short-lived. He was always a better circus performer. "It's just that I'm sure I don't have it." Dad is the most noncommittal person I've ever met. He's never *sure* of anything. You could probably talk him out of his own name, and he'd just go along with it and let you call him Doug.

"But how do you *know*?"

It seems that Dad has lost interest in juggling—*also strange*—because he bends over and starts packing the clubs into his tote bag.

"Dad?"

Finally, he stands upright, leaving the bag on the ground. "I know I don't have it, Cat, because your mother has it."

"My—my mother?" My voice wavers, and Luca must pick up on it, because he takes a step closer to me.

Dad doesn't talk about my mother. He's never talked about her. This is the most information he's given me in almost thirty years. Dad isn't just a clown for his job; he's a clown in real life, too. I don't mean that in a disparaging way, I mean he really has the personality of a clown. Fun loving, goofy, perpetually happy. Just about the only time I've seen a break in his demeanor is when I ask about my mother. His face goes dark, and he refuses to talk about her. It's so disorienting to see him shut down that I learned years ago to stop asking. All I know is that she's still alive, and I've never met her. Well, except for the day she gave birth to me, obviously. But then she left me with Dad, and neither of us has seen or talked to her since.

From my birth certificate—ironically—I'm aware that her name is Michelle Jones. My dad was only eighteen when I was born, and I think my mom was young, too. Which means she could be doing anything, living anywhere now.

Here's a fun fact. Michelle was the third most common baby name in the United States in the mid-1970s, around the time I think my mom was born. There are 18,825 people named Michelle Jones living in the United States. When you google *Michelle Jones*, you get 164,000,000 hits. I don't need a PhD in mathematics to know it would take me half a dozen lifetimes to sift through that much data.

I went through a dark phase in my early teens when I wondered if something terrible had happened. Had my mom murdered someone? Had she tried to murder *me*, and Dad had to take me away? He swore up and down it was nothing like that. And then I began to wonder if *he* had murdered someone, and we were on the run. But I quickly realized that if someone wants to hide, they generally don't spend their days juggling in plain sight.

So the sum total of what I know about my mother is her name and that she's probably not a murderer. The fact that Dad just voluntarily shared this little tidbit leaves me stunned.

"How—how do you know she has my birth certificate?" I finally manage to choke out.

Luca is right beside me now, and I can feel the heat of his arm against mine. I lean sideways, just a tiny bit.

"Well, I don't know for sure she has it," Dad admits. "But she used to have it, and it wouldn't surprise me if she still does. Your mother…she was…very organized."

I grasp that information like it's a life preserver and I've spent my life adrift at sea. "She was?" *I knew it.* I knew that's where I got it from. "How can I reach her to get it back?" And then I'm seized with larger possibilities. Is this my chance to finally meet her? To find out the truth about who I am?

To finally—

I yank the steering wheel before I can head down that road. Going there will only lead to heartache. It's been almost thirty years, and she left me. I need to focus on the problem at hand.

Dad turns away from me and picks up his hat and tote. He dumps the tip money into the bag—just mixes it all in with the juggling clubs—and flips his hat onto his head.

"Dad? My birth certificate?"

He sighs and finally looks at me. "Sorry, Kitty Cat. I'm afraid you can't get it back."

"Why not?"

Dad hesitates. "It's complicated."

How complicated could it be? Unless he can't reach her.

My pulse picks up speed. Is it possible I was right about her all along?

Once my dark phase receded and I decided my mother wasn't a murderer, I filtered through a whole host of other scenarios for what might have happened to her, until I settled on the one that was the easiest to swallow. Maybe she *had* to leave. For an important job. Because she's off in far-flung places helping people. Maybe there was some reason she *couldn't* stick around to raise me.

It's embarrassing. I'm an almost thirty-year-old mathematics professor, far too old for these childish fantasies. But I admit that sometimes—when Dad loses another job, when another collection notice comes in—my mind still drifts in this direction. Because it's easier than believing she just didn't care.

"Do you *know* how to reach my mother?"

Dad shrugs again, his shoulders going all the way up to his ears. "Nope."

I take a step closer to him. "If my mother has my birth certificate, and you know how to get it back, you have to tell me. My whole life is falling apart here. My identity has gone missing, I almost got arrested today, I'm about to lose my job, and the only hope I have is that birth certificate."

"I'm sorry. I don't know how to get it back." Dad leans over and pats me on the cheek. "But I'm sure you can solve this without involving your mother. You're the smartest person I know, and you always work things out."

"I can't solve this! It's not a math equation. Math equations have rules. They make sense. Nothing about this situation makes any sense at all."

He slides the tote bag onto his shoulder. I hear the change jingle to the bottom. "I'll see you soon for dinner, Kitty Cat."

"Wait!" I reach out to grab his arm. "You can't just leave. This isn't some kind of joke. At least tell me what you know about her."

Dad pulls away, stumbling in the grass as he backs up. "Let it go, Kitty Cat." His jaw clenches, and he stares over my shoulder instead of meeting my eyes. "Just let it go, okay?" His voice cracks at the end.

I'm so shocked that I drop my hand, my stomach churning with a turmoil that's familiar from my childhood conversations about my mother. I swallow down my protests.

Dad runs a hand through his hair, disrupting his man-bun, and shakes his head as if he's trying to clear it. When he turns to Luca, the tension is gone from his face. "Keep practicing that juggling. You'll get it eventually." He gives a wink, but it lacks the warmth and ease of his earlier smiles.

"Thanks, Andy," Luca says, but his eyes are on me, and his brow creases with something that looks like concern.

"Sorry I've gotta go," Dad says, sounding anything but sorry. He gives me a crooked smile. "I—uh. I've got to see a man about a horse." And with that, he turns and heads in the opposite direction.

I watch him weave across the lawn, waving to a group of older women and making faces at a baby. They all giggle.

"Don't buy a horse!" I yell, just in case he's serious. "Don't even *think* about buying a horse."

CHAPTER 9

So that was my dad." I turn to Luca, who's staring at me with his eyes wide.

"He's..." Luca blinks. "Not what I was expecting."

"Yeah, well..." My mood darkens. "He's never what anyone is expecting. At least not for the father of uptight Catherine Lipton, anyway."

Luca's brow furrows, and he reaches out to touch my arm. "Who said you were uptight?"

Nobody said it, not in a long time, anyway. But for my whole life, I've felt it. Why can't I just loosen up, chill out a little?

Because some people don't have the luxury to loosen up and chill out. But I don't want to talk about it with Luca, who—now that I've seen them together—is even more like Dad than I realized. Fun, unrestrained, always up for a good time. What people don't see is that there's a downside to the guy who's always the life of the party.

He leaves his empty pizza boxes and crushed-up beer cans all over the lawn for someone else to clean up.

I pull my arm away. "It doesn't matter. I need to focus or I'm going to lose this job."

"You said the lunch didn't go well? You were only in there for about five minutes."

I shake my head. "Dr. Gupta is really mad. And I can't blame him. I'm supposed to teach four classes, plus I have three committee assignments and a roster of twenty-eight students to advise. Not to mention the fact that we were going to collaborate on several research papers, the first one due in October. If I can't do the job, who is going to cover all that?"

"If you can't do the job, who cares who's going to write your research papers?" Luca scoffs. "Maybe instead of being mad, this Dr. Gupta could offer a little bit of support."

It's not much of a different sentiment than what crossed my mind just a few minutes ago. But Luca doesn't get it. They chose my application out of hundreds of qualified candidates. I sat through three interviews, conducted a teaching demonstration, and presented my research to select mathematics faculty. It's not easy to go out and find a replacement. If I don't locate that birth certificate, if I can't prove that I exist, I'll be leaving them in the lurch.

And I'll be in the lurch, too. But I can't think about that. I can't think about how everything I've worked for my entire life is about to add up to a big, fat zero. Or the fact that Dad let me down, again. Because if I do, I might just sit down in the grass and cry.

To my great mortification, the tears well up anyway.

"Hey," Luca says, stepping into my line of sight, his face creased with concern. "Hey, it's going to be okay." Once again, he takes my arm, and this time he tugs me over to a bench on the edge of the lawn. "We'll figure this out. We just need a plan."

I give a watery laugh at the irony of Luca lecturing me about plans. I always have a plan, a to-do list, charts and graphs and spreadsheets. But right now, I have absolutely nothing.

Luca sinks down next to me. "It sounds like your mom has your birth certificate. So we just need to find your mom."

"That's impossible."

"Nothing's impossible."

"This is. I don't know anything about her except that she walked away on the day I was born, and she never looked back." I swipe at my wet cheeks.

Luca leans forward, propping his arms on his knees so he can look me in the eye. "What about your dad? What has he told you about her?"

I shrug. "He's never talked about her. He's never said a single thing about who she is, or where she comes from, or why she left. When I ask, he does the same thing you saw him do today. He closes up and walks away."

"And you have no idea why?"

"No. Over the years, I've imagined all sorts of scenarios." I stare at my hands. "Maybe she left us because she has a top-secret government job and had to move overseas to fight terrorists and save the world. Or maybe she's an infectious disease doctor, living in a remote jungle, stopping viruses that could wipe out humanity. Or maybe she's in Antarctica researching the polar ice caps, figuring out how to keep them from melting and turning Kansas into beachfront property."

I realize what I've revealed, and my gaze flies to Luca's. This missing identity really is messing with my head, because I've never told anyone my secret fantasies about my mother.

He's looking at me with an expression I can't quite decipher. It's probably pity.

"But," I continue. "The truth is, she's probably nothing more than a deadbeat. Just an ordinary woman who didn't care enough about her daughter to stick around."

Luca abruptly sits up. "I guess there's only one way to find out."

I look at him sideways. "What are you suggesting?"

"Your dad says she has your birth certificate. You need that birth certificate to save your job. So I'm suggesting we find her."

"Like I said, that's impossible. I know literally nothing about her."

"You know what's on your birth certificate. You know her name and the city where you were born. That's not nothing."

Before I can answer, my stomach growls so loudly I know Luca can hear it. Breakfast was supposed to be served at the orientation this morning, and since I got up so early, I didn't eat before I went. And then, of course, I wasn't invited to sit down at the faculty luncheon. So the only thing in my stomach is the cup of coffee I drank from my travel mug while I waited for orientation to begin.

Luca's eyebrows rise. "Let's get you a snack."

There's a food truck parked next to the lawn that's selling smoothies and bubble tea. He stands, reaching in his pocket and pulling out his wallet. "How about a smoothie? You strike me as a blueberry acai kind of girl. Lots of antioxidants. But if you want chocolate and peanut butter, just say the word."

I wave him off. "Let me get it. You've been driving me all over town."

I approach the food truck counter, and when it's my turn to order, I *do* request a blueberry acai, because antioxidants are good for me. And then I order a chocolate and peanut butter for Luca because...obviously.

The cashier tells me my total, and I slide my bank card into the machine. After a moment, it beeps and the words on the screen tell me to remove my card. But instead of processing my payment, the screen flashes with one more word.

Declined.

What?

"I'm sorry, I don't think that card is working," the girl behind the counter calls down to me.

"Let me just try again." I slide my card back in the machine and repeat the same process. Once again, the screen flashes with *declined*.

"This has *never* happened before." I'll admit I'm one of those people who still balances my bank account. I save my receipts throughout the day and input them in a spreadsheet at night. The word *declined* was such a staple of my childhood, I swore it would never happen once I had control of my own money. So, that's how I know I have exactly $2,541.68 in my bank account as of last night. Enough to pay my rent at the end of the month and cover my bills, food, and other expenses until my first paycheck from the university comes in. "Let me try it one more time."

"Do you have another card?" the girl asks. Clearly, she doesn't have faith in my third attempt.

The bank card should work. I know it should work. I know there's money in my account. But a line is beginning to form behind me, so I pull out my credit card and slide it into the machine. A second later, my heart drops to my knees.

Declined again.

This isn't happening. How can this be happening?

"Everything okay?" Luca has come up behind me just in time to catch the girl behind the counter say, "I'm sorry, but that card isn't working either."

Hands shaking now, I shove the cards back into my wallet and check for cash. "I'm sure it's some sort of mistake. I know I have money in my account, and I barely have a balance on my credit card. I don't know why they're not working." I look up hopefully. "Maybe the system is down." That's the only explanation.

Before the girl can respond, Luca slides a card into the machine. It beeps and processes, and the next thing I know the word *accepted* flashes there. I stare at it, my stomach churning.

"Catherine?" calls the college-aged boy making smoothies in the back of the food truck, sliding two cups onto the counter. Luca grabs them, handing me the purple one, and nudges me out of the way of the line.

I shuffle along next to him, one hand clutching the frigid cup, the other digging in my bag for my phone. "I need to call my bank. And my credit card company. Why aren't my cards working?" My stomach growls again, and I'm suddenly lightheaded. My vision blurs. I come to an abrupt halt and begin to sway. Luca slides an arm around my shoulders and guides me back to the bench. I sink down on the wooden slats and bend forward, breathing hard.

He waves the purple smoothie under my nose. "Drink this."

I take a sip of the blended yogurt and sour fruit, and luckily my stomach is empty or the contents would be all over my shoes. Luca whisks the purple smoothie out of my hand and replaces it with the chocolate and peanut butter one. "Try this instead."

I take a long sip, and as soon as the cold, sweet-and-salty flavor hits my tongue, my nausea recedes. "Thanks," I say, handing it back to him.

"Drink a little more."

I take a few more sips, and before I know what's happened, I've finished the entire smoothie. "Sorry, that was meant for you."

"It's no problem. I love blueberry acai." Luca takes a gulp of the purple smoothie, gags, and lobs the cup into a nearby trash can with a graceful flick of his wrist.

I dial the number for my credit card company and squirm in my seat as I'm directed through menu after menu of options. Finally, the deep, male voice of a customer service representative comes through the phone. I explain my story, and he reassures me it's probably some sort of mix-up. He kindly offers to look into it.

I blow out a breath as I listen to his fingers type on the keys. *This is going to be fine. It's only a mix-up.*

But when he comes back to the phone, his voice is decidedly colder. "It looks like that account was closed due to fraudulent activity. You should have received a letter several weeks ago."

"Fraudulent activity?" I sit up straight. "What sort of

fraudulent activity? I didn't get a letter about fraudulent activity. I *definitely* would remember if I did."

"Hold please."

And before I know what's happening, the low tones of a cello playing Pachelbel's Canon are piped into my ear. "I'm on hold," I mutter to Luca. "How can they put me on hold at a time like this?"

The music fades, and with a click, the representative is back. "Hello? Are you there?"

"Yes! I'm here."

"Well, I've looked into your account, and it seems the reason it was closed is due to the fact that the owner does not seem to exist. The Social Security number associated with this account is a fake."

My shoulders slump. "It's not a fake," I say weakly.

"Our fraudulent activities division says that it is." His voice comes out clipped now. Funny how suddenly everyone's tone changes when you've been accused of faking your own existence.

"Your fraudulent activities division is *wrong*."

"You're welcome to submit a ticket for our team to review."

"How do I do that?" But a little part of me already knows.

"You'll need to fill out a form on our website and upload a photo of your Social Security card and an official letter from the Social Security Administration stating that the number is, in fact, legitimate."

"Right. Okay." I hang up the phone.

"Same story?" Luca asks. "No evidence that you exist?"

I shake my head. "I don't suppose there's any point in calling my bank. I'm sure my account is closed, and my money is . . . " I wave my hands through the air, fingers splayed. *Poof.* I bend forward and wrap my arms around my midsection. "What am I going to do? How am I going to pay my rent?"

"Don't worry about the rent," Luca says.

Easy for him to say. He has the lobby floor as a backup. But I'll be homeless. *Or back with Dad.*

"Do you have any cash to get by?" Luca asks.

"A few hundred dollars for emergencies. That's not going to last me very long." I sit up. "I need a legitimate Social Security card to access my accounts. But in order to get that, I need to show my government-issued ID. In order to prove my government-issued ID is real, I need a birth certificate. And I can't get my birth certificate without my government-issued ID and my Social Security card."

"I'm getting dizzy." Luca turns in his seat to look at me. "But I think what you're saying is that it all comes down to that birth certificate."

"And the birth certificate comes down to my mother." I shake my head. "Dad can't tell me anything. So that's it. It's a good thing I can juggle, because it looks like the professor job is toast. It's clown town for me."

Luca slides off the bench and crouches down in front of me. "Catherine, take a deep breath." His hand slides to my cheek. "Look at me. You are *not* going to end up a clown. We're going to find your mother and get your birth certificate."

"How? How are we possibly going to do that?"

Luca stands, reaching out a hand to me. "Buckle up, Kitty Cat. You're about to meet the Morelli family."

CHAPTER 10

It turns out that Luca's childhood home is only two blocks from the DeGreco building, on a quiet Bloomfield side street lined with mismatched brick and aluminum-siding-covered row homes. Before the developers discovered it, Bloomfield was a predominantly working-class Italian neighborhood, and many of the old families still live here. I'm not surprised that Luca's is among them. Each house has a porch lined up to the next, and if you walk down this street in the morning or evening, you'll probably find them occupied with people reading newspapers, drinking coffee, and gossiping with the neighbors.

From the porch of Luca's family home, he opens the door and leads me into a hallway covered end to end in family photographs. To our left is a living room with a dark wooden coffee table and flowered couch sitting atop beige wall-to-wall carpet. More photos hang on the walls and populate the fireplace mantel. I imagine that this house was passed down to Luca's mother from his grandparents, and maybe the furniture was, too. It's all a bit dated, but in that comfortable and welcoming way of things that are well loved. I can picture this house packed with generations of Morellis at Christmas, the decorations on the mantel, a tree in front of the window. Something about that image fills me with longing. When I was growing up, Dad and I spent most of our holidays at ArtSpace, a warehouse where the circus-performer crowd likes to hang out. Our Christmas tree was an old bicycle someone draped in twinkling lights.

I kick off my shoes and follow Luca straight down the hall past a staircase to the kitchen in the back of the house. A woman in her fifties with dark, curly hair sits at an oak dining table in the middle of the room, and a younger version of her stands at the stove stirring something in a pot. When we enter, the older woman drops her newspaper on the table, stands, and crosses the room to embrace Luca.

"My boy," she says, gripping his shoulders as she stands back to get a good look at him. "It's been so long since I've seen you." She pulls him in for a hug.

Luca tries to extract himself from the woman's hug. "I was just here on Sunday, Ma."

"You know Ma won't be happy until you move back home," the woman at the stove chimes in with a roll of her eyes.

"Is it so terrible that I miss my son?" Luca's mother laments like he's been away at war. She reaches out and brushes a wayward lock of hair off his forehead. "Look at you. When was the last time you got a haircut? You'd be so handsome if you'd get your hair out of your face."

"Stop it." Luca ducks away and guides me into the room. "Ma, Ginny, I'd like you to meet my friend Catherine.

Catherine, this is my mother, Lorraine, and my older sister, Ginny."

"Hi. Nice to meet you," I say, lifting my palm in a wave. Both women turn to look me up and down.

"Is she your friend or your girlfriend?" Lorraine asks with zero subtlety.

"Jesus, Ma," Luca mutters, and two pink spots appear on his cheeks.

"We're just friends," I assure her.

"Catherine lives in the DeGreco," Luca explains.

"Really..." Ginny's eyebrows go up. "Interesting. How do you like it there?"

"I've only been there a month—" I do my best to ignore the pang in my chest when I remember that I might not make it another month. "But so far it's been good." I pause, hesitant to mention the broken elevator or bikes in the mail room in front of Luca's mother. Aside from his hair in his face and too-infrequent visits, I get the feeling she thinks he can do no wrong. "I've met some lovely people."

"You can't be referring to my little brother," Ginny says. "So I assume you mean the older people."

"Yes. They're all very..." I remember Mrs. Goodwin's dance in the lobby and Sal hiking up the stairs. "Colorful." I lift a shoulder. "Although, the doorman is nice, too."

"Interesting," Ginny murmurs again.

Lorraine waves us into the room. "Come in. Sit."

We settle at the table, and she plunks a plate of cookies in front of us. My stomach growls, but I just gulped down an entire chocolate peanut butter smoothie, and I'm not sure a thumbprint cookie should be my next meal.

"So, have you rented out Grandpa's apartment yet?" Ginny calls over her shoulder as she gives the pot on the stove another stir.

"I did," Luca says. "A while ago."

There's something clipped about his tone that has my gaze swinging in his direction. A few weeks ago, he told me that the Lincoln Town Car belonged to his grandpa. I remember the affection in his voice when he mentioned it and how I hoped that his grandpa had just upgraded to a new car. But now he's rented out the older man's apartment, too. Is it too much to hope that it's because his grandpa found a nice condo in Florida? "I didn't know your grandpa used to live in the DeGreco."

"Yeah." Luca lifts a cookie from the plate and then sets it down again. "Until he died last year."

"I'm so sorry." I look around the room. "For all of you."

"Thank you. He was a good man. Luca had a hard time renting out his place after…" Lorraine waves a hand. "They were close, and it's hard to move on."

My gaze settles on Luca. His usually animated eyes have gone dark. I find myself wanting to do or say something to bring that light back. But when I look up, both Lorraine and Ginny are watching me watch him.

After a beat, Lorraine turns back to Luca. "So, you got someone nice in the apartment?"

"Very nice," Luca says in that same clipped tone. "*Anyway*…that's enough about that." He pushes the plate of cookies in my direction. "We're here because Catherine needs to eat something."

"That's not why—" But I stop talking when my stomach

growls again. It's late afternoon, and that smoothie is starting to slosh around. Whatever is on the stove smells delicious. I grab a cookie and stuff it in my mouth.

"Of course you'll eat something," Lorraine says, swinging
open a dark wood cabinet near the sink and taking down
two vintage white bowls with a blue flower print. She hands
them to Ginny, who ladles in whatever is in the pot. Then
Lorraine carries them to the table and sets them in front of
Luca and me. A heavenly garlic and herb scent wafts toward
me. I look down to find white beans and small bits of pasta
floating in tomato broth.

"This looks amazing." I'm already reaching for the
spoon.

"It's just a little pasta fazool," Lorraine says, placing a
hunk of crusty white bread next to each of our bowls.

"Pasta—what?"

Luca's lips curve. "Pasta fazool."

I take a bite and my eyes involuntarily close as I savor it.
"Well, whatever you call it—it's delicious."

Lorraine pats me on the arm in approval.

"What do you do for work, Catherine?" Ginny sits across
from us with her own bowl, pushing a pile of mail, a baseball glove, and a coffee mug off to one side. Normally, this
kind of clutter stresses me out, but it doesn't really bother me
now. Knowing Luca, it wouldn't feel right if his childhood
home were perfectly organized.

"I'm a—" I take a deep breath. "A mathematics professor." At least I hope that's what I am.

"God." Ginny shakes her head. "Good for you. I hate
math."

At that moment a kid wanders into the kitchen. The owner of the baseball glove, I'm assuming. He's about thirteen by the thin line of awkward hair that's popped up on his upper lip and the way his hands and feet look too big for his body. "I hate math, too," the kid agrees, snatching a cookie from the plate on the table.

"No, you don't," Ginny says, swatting at his hand. "Go do your homework."

"I don't have any homework; it's summer vacation." The kid grabs another cookie and makes a break for the door.

"Go mow the grass, then," Ginny calls after him. When he's disappeared around the corner, she turns to me. "Please excuse my son, Angelo."

"Do you two live nearby?" I ask, taking another bite of soup.

"If by 'nearby,' you mean 'upstairs,' then yes. We've lived with Ma ever since my kid's sperm donor stopped paying child support."

Luca grins. "She means her ex-husband. Angelo's dad."

"But sperm is pretty much all he's contributed," Ginny says with a dismissive wave of her hand.

"I'm sorry."

"Don't be. We like it here. Ma can help out with Angelo, and I can help out around the house." She kicks Luca under the table. "Since my deadbeat brother never comes around."

"Hey." Luca kicks her back. "I was here on *Sunday*."

"Leave your brother alone," Lorraine calls from across the kitchen. "He's a good boy."

Ginny rolls her eyes.

"So, speaking of absentee parents," Luca says, standing

up from his chair. "Catherine and I want to get your take on something." He whisks my bowl away, fills it with more soup, and sets it in front of me again. I inhale it while Luca gives them a quick overview of my situation.

"Wow," Ginny says when he's finished talking. She turns to me. "I can't believe that you just don't exist."

"Me neither." I take another bite of my soup for comfort.

"And your dad thinks your mom has your birth certificate?" Lorraine asks. I nod, and she shakes her head. "Why in the world wouldn't he just tell you what he knows? If it were my kid, I'd be knocking down doors if it meant I could help."

"We know you would, Ma," Luca says with an affectionate smile.

Lorraine reaches over to give his shoulder a squeeze. There's something about the unconditional love and fierce protectiveness all wrapped up in that small gesture that has my heart tugging. Is that what it would have been like to have a mother?

I know my dad loves me. But I never really felt that kind of *protection*, like he was looking out for me. It always seemed like I was the one looking out for him. Maybe I'm romanticizing, though. Maybe, in reality, my mother would have been a total nightmare. She left, after all. Who does that?

"And your mother," Lorraine continues, echoing my own thoughts. "I can't imagine what would compel her to leave her own child like that. There *must* be something wrong with her, because you're obviously a lovely girl."

"*Ma*," Luca cuts in. "Maybe Catherine doesn't want to talk about this."

"No, it's okay," I assure him. She's not saying anything I haven't thought about a thousand times. And quite often, I concluded that if my mother left, it meant there was something wrong with *me*. Lorraine doesn't really know me at all, but I'll take any reassurances that it wasn't my fault.

"Maybe you'll think it's sexist of me," Lorraine continues. "But I speak from experience when I say that men take off all the time." She huffs out an indignant breath. "But what kind of mother leaves her kid?"

I glance around the kitchen. Is Lorraine referring to Angelo's sperm donor when she speaks from experience? Or was there a man who left her, too? For the first time, I wonder about Luca's dad. Is he in the picture? I search Luca's face for signs that this conversation upsets him, but when he catches me looking, the corners of his eyes crinkle and his lips curve upward. But this time, it's not that signature grin that lights up a room. This smile is more subtle, and even though we're here with his mom and sister, I know it's just for me. A shakiness radiates out to my limbs. I never noticed the little hazel flecks in his dark eyes before. I want to keep staring, keep searching for what else I can discover about him.

Ginny clears her throat and leans forward, propping her elbows on the table. "So, what do you know about her?"

My cheeks heat, and I tear my eyes from Luca's. What were we talking about?

"Any idea where she might live—or anything?"

Oh, right. My mother.

I shake my head. "My dad won't tell me anything about

her." I glance at Ginny. "I guess you could call her my egg donor. I've never even met her."

Ginny presses her lips together in sympathy, and Lorraine gives me a squeeze on the shoulder. I have the strangest urge to grab her hand and hold on.

"So what do you think?" Luca asks, leaning back in his chair. "How can we find her?"

Ginny and Lorraine share a glance and then in unison say, "Uncle Vito."

Luca nods. "You think he'll help?"

"Of course he'll help," Lorraine says fiercely. "You're family." She turns to me. "Don't worry. If Luca cares enough to go to all this trouble, Vito will look out for you."

"Who's Uncle Vito?" I murmur to Luca. But I already have a pretty good idea. He's a Morelli, of course. I hear they're everywhere. And well connected. And possibly in the Mafia. I'm not sure if that should encourage or terrify me.

"You'll see," Luca whispers.

I think I'm going to go with terrified.

"He'll be at the club tonight," Lorraine says. "Go see him there. Just make sure you arrive before eight so you don't interrupt his card game."

"Okay, we should probably head home, then." Luca pushes his chair back. "Catherine will want to change out of her work clothes before we go to the club."

I set my spoon in my empty bowl and carry it to the sink. "And the elevator," I remind Luca. "Don't forget you'll want to check on the elevator." He hasn't mentioned Dante all day, and I haven't seen him call to check in.

"Yep, and the elevator," Luca agrees.

We head down the hall to put our shoes on, and a moment later, Lorraine meets us there with a Tupperware container. "Take this for later."

"Oh, I couldn't. That's your dinner," I say, but I can't seem to keep my eyes off it.

"We have a whole pot." She slides it into my hand.

"Are you sure?"

"Take it, Catherine," Luca says. "Never argue with an Italian mother who's trying to feed you."

Lorraine smiles, patting Luca's cheek. "I taught my boy well."

"Okay, I'll take it. Thank you." I clutch the container, already thinking of when I can heat it up later.

"I like a girl who can eat." Lorraine turns to give me a pat on the cheek, too. "Apparently, so does Luca."

"Jesus, Ma," Luca mutters, yanking the front door open and stepping out on the porch, but not before I catch a glimpse of his face heating up.

CHAPTER 11

Back at the DeGreco building, the elevator seems to be working properly. I step on and hit the button for the eighth floor. On my way up, it stops at five, and when the door slides open, a tiny gray-haired white woman in a pink housecoat gets on, pushing a walker she's decorated with plastic flowers. Usually when I pass someone in the hall or ride the elevator with them, I give them a smile, or maybe a polite hello. But Luca must be rubbing off on me, because once the older woman has pressed the number for her floor and the door starts to close, I find myself saying, "Hi, I'm Catherine. I live on eight."

The woman shuffles her feet to the left, still clutching her walker, to turn toward me and smile. "Mrs. Hartman on nine. I'm so glad the elevator is working today, aren't you?"

"Yes," I agree. "It seems to be broken a lot, doesn't it?"

"I can't imagine what the issue could be," Mrs. Hartman muses.

The elevator slows at the eighth floor, and I step off. "Have a good day."

"You, too, dearie." Mrs. Hartman waves as the door begins to slide into the frame.

And then it hits me. Mrs. Hartman? *Is this the woman Luca said has been vandalizing the elevator?* "Hey, wait!" I call. But the door is already closed. I give my head a hard shake. That can't be right anyway. That woman has to be in her nineties, and I doubt she can get around without a walker. How would she possibly manage to break an elevator?

I turn around to find Sal standing alone in the hallway.

"Sal," I say, stopping in front of him. "Is everything okay?"

"Oh, everything is fine. I'm just going for a little walk down the hall. Gotta get my steps in."

I unlock my apartment door and then glance at the older man. Luca said Uncle Vito won't be at the club until later tonight, so I've got a little time to kill until we head out later. I should probably get started on my research paper, but I'm feeling too antsy to work, and—as I discovered when I checked my email on the drive over—my access to my university accounts has been suspended anyway. I'll have to figure out how to sort that out tomorrow. "Would you like to come in for a cup of tea?" I ask.

"You know, young lady, I would." Sal hobbles inside and turns left, crashing into my café table.

I rush over and take his arm. "Are you okay?"

"Oh, sure, sure." He waves me off. "I just wasn't expecting that to be there."

I guide him over to the couch. He settles into the velvet with a satisfied sigh. "Ah. Feels good to take a load off." While I move to the kitchenette, he gazes around the room. "I like what you've done with the place."

"Thanks. It's my first apartment that's all my own." A heavy weight settles on me. If I can't get my identity back, I could lose this place. I could lose everything. Right now, all my hopes are pinned on a guy who may or may not be a Mafia boss named Uncle Vito. How did I get here?

I stash my pasta fazool in the fridge and then grab the kettle to fill it with water. "Which one is your apartment?"

Sal waves a hand in the direction of the hallway. "Oh, one of those. Not nearly as fancy as this."

I take two tea bags down from the cabinet. "Is Earl Grey okay?"

"Oh, sure. Whatever you have." Sal slowly lifts one foot as if it takes some real effort and props his black orthopedic sneaker on the opposite knee.

"You said you've been here in the DeGreco for years?" I ask, dropping the tea bags into two mugs.

"That's right. Lived my whole life in Bloomfield. I grew up in a house just down the street and around the corner. Raised my own kids there, too."

I wonder if Sal lived in one of those houses in the same row as Luca's childhood home. My guess is that he did, or on a similar street. I'm starting to see that this neighborhood is a large, interconnected community, at least for the people who've lived here for a long time. Lately, though, it seems like every fourth house on the block has turned into a developer flip. It makes places like the DeGreco even more special with all the lifelong residents.

"So when did you decide to move in here?"

"When the kids started having kids, my wife and I decided to downsize and pass the house on to the younger generation. It's been about thirty years now, and no regrets. We couldn't have handled that big old house as we got older."

"And your wife? Is she from Bloomfield, too?"

"Mary grew up two doors down from me." A shadow passes over his face. "She died a few years back."

"I'm so sorry."

Sal gives me a nod. "I was lucky to have my community in the neighborhood, and here in this building. People look out for each other." He gives me a smile. "A girl like you, though. You must find it kind of sleepy around here."

I pour the hot water in the cups and place them each on a saucer along with a spoon. "No, I love it. I've had plenty of excitement in my life." I carry the tea over to the coffee table and set it on a place mat that I keep there so the cups don't leave water rings on the table.

"Well, that's good to hear. But young people like you need other young people. And we're just a bunch of old folks, mostly." He leans forward, taking a cup. "Except for Luca, of course."

"Yeah, Luca. Luca is…um." And then he flashes in my mind, kneeling on the ground in front of me, his hand on my cheek, promising that everything will be okay. The warmth of his chest against my back as he wrapped an arm around me, ready to wrestle me away from a police officer. I press my hands to my face. What is wrong with me? "He's interesting," I finally say.

Sal chuckles. "He's a character all right. But a really good kid."

A couple of days ago, I would have had my doubts. But

after I've spent this day with him…well, he's surprised me a lot.

"How did your big meeting today go?" Sal asks.

"Not so great. Kind of a mess, actually." My shoulders slump. "Everything with my new job is a disaster all of a sudden."

"I'm sorry to hear that."

"Something kind of unbelievable happened this morning," I confide as I sit in a chair opposite him. "I found out that my identity has disappeared. I'm no longer in any government records, my Social Security card is useless, and my driver's license is a fake."

Sal takes a sip of his tea. "I've never heard of something like that happening."

"Me neither."

"You know, Luca has a friend down in the Social Security office."

I nod. "Ellie. She tried to help, but there's nothing she can do." I give him a brief overview of the Social Security card / driver's license / birth certificate conundrum. "We've figured out that unless I can track down the original copy of my birth certificate, I'll just remain…" I trail off at that familiar tightening in my chest. "I'll just remain nobody."

I pause with my teacup halfway to my lips.

Nobody.

Wasn't there a moment a couple weeks back when I wished for it? *No commitments. No one expecting anything from me.*

But I didn't mean it like this. I just wanted a little break from it all. But is it possible that I somehow put that thought out into the world, like a wish? Did I manifest this identity mix-up? It's the strangest thing that's ever happened to me, and I don't have a rational explanation for it.

"Sal, do you believe in wishes?" I lean forward and set my cup on the place mat. "Like if you send something out into the universe, you can actualize it?" As soon as I hear the words, though, I shake my head. I'm starting to sound like Dad and his friends talking about horoscopes and magic and cosmic intervention. Usually, those conversations take place when they're sitting around a campfire at a music festival, smoking weed and staring up at the stars. I can almost hear the strains of a guitar playing in the distance.

I don't believe in that stuff.

Sal leans back, seriously considering my question. "I believe life is what you make it." He looks at me across the coffee table. "Maybe something seems like a disaster. But if you look deeper, maybe it's an opportunity. It's all about how you look at it."

I turn that over in my head. How could my entire identity disappearing be an opportunity? The faculty job at the university is an opportunity, one I worked my entire life to achieve. One that's about to crumble. Sitting around metaphorically staring at the stars asking what it all means isn't going to fix this.

I need to get that birth certificate back, and I need to get my life back. So it looks like it's in the hands of the Mafia man.

CHAPTER 12

Luca is late.

I sit down on the bench by the elevator to wait, because...of course he's late. I don't know what I expected.

About fifteen minutes after we were supposed to meet, the front door swings open and Luca strolls in from the sidewalk. I open my mouth to comment, but as my gaze slides over him, I realize this is the first time I've seen him wearing something besides his doorman's uniform. He's in fitted black jeans that hug his lean thighs, and a plain white T-shirt that clings to his chest and shows off the lines of his biceps. But when my eyes land on his arms, it's not the lean muscles I'm drawn to, but those tattoos. I've caught only glimpses of them before, flashes on his forearms where he's rolled his sleeves to his elbows. But now I can see that the ink extends all the way up his arms. Flowers and vines and birds winding together to his shoulders. And through the thin fabric of his T-shirt, I catch a couple of dark shadows on his flat stomach, hints of more art concealed there.

When I look up, Luca is watching me with his head cocked, a bemused expression on his face, and I realize I've been caught staring. So I do the only thing I can think of to take the attention off me.

"You're late."

"Sorry. I had a thing, and I couldn't get away."

I wonder if I'm keeping him from a date. That's what normal people would be doing on a night like this, right? Going on a date, hanging out at a bar with friends...anything besides tracking down a guy who may or may not be a Mafia boss to help his prickly tenant get her life back.

"No...don't apologize." I sigh. "I'm sorry I'm keeping you from something. It's just that your mom said we should get to the club to see Uncle Vito before his card game starts at eight." I check my watch. It's 7:47 p.m.

"Shit." Luca jogs over to the bench and pulls me to my feet. "Is it really that late? Come on."

We head out the door and onto the sidewalk, but when I move toward the Town Car, Luca shakes his head, drawing me down the street instead. A few blocks from the DeGreco, he steers me toward a faded black door tucked into a nondescript brick building. I've passed this building and this door probably a dozen or more times since I moved into my apartment, but never in a million years would it have occurred to me to stop here. The windows look like they were bricked over decades ago, and though a marquee hangs overhead, the lights have all burned out and the letters are so faded it's impossible to make out the name of the club. Now that I'm actually stopping to take a look at it, the place looks like the site of a true-crime documentary.

Particularly the spot where the body is found.

"Are you sure this is the place?" I ask, hesitating on the sidewalk.

"Of course I'm sure. Come on." Luca holds open the door, and reluctantly, I walk through it. I've barely made it past the threshold before a man the size of a mountain is towering over me.

He holds up a beefy hand. "Name?" he barks.

"Uh—" Did Luca call ahead? I glance in his direction because I'm pretty sure that Mr. Everest here won't have *Catherine Lipton* on his list.

"Luca Morelli." Luca steps forward, and the guy breaks into a huge grin. It's like watching a pit bull turn into a golden retriever puppy right before my eyes.

"Elbow!" he says, reaching over to wrap a massive arm around Luca and pound him on the back. "Good to see you, kid."

Ah, okay. So, we must have another Morelli here. Is this Uncle Vito?

Luca tugs me over. "This is my friend Catherine. Catherine, this is my cousin Lou."

"Nice to meet you, Catherine." The guy holds out his sirloin steak hand and we shake. He turns back to Luca. "You here to see Vito?"

Luca nods.

"He won't like you interrupting his card game, you know."

"I know. But it's important. Can you let me in?"

Lou pauses, and for a moment I think he's about to turn us away. I can't say I'd be *completely* disappointed if he did. But then he shrugs. "For you, Luca, I'll make an exception. Go ahead."

We continue on into the bar. The place is packed and smoky, but through the crowd and haze, I spot a long bar taking up one side of the room with stained-glass Tiffany lamps hanging overhead and a bartender shaking cocktails on the opposite side. Straight ahead, past a smattering of small, round tables, sits a stage where four musicians play a slow, sad jazz melody. The crowd is older, the men dressed up in sports coats and the women in short, tight dresses and heels.

I push myself up on my tiptoes so Luca can hear me over the din of trumpet tones and ice clinking in glasses. "I thought it was illegal to smoke in bars."

He just laughs and takes my hand, turning to weave through the crowd to the bar. A couple is leaving as we approach, and we grab their seats.

The bartender, a middle-aged white woman with a blond ponytail and deeply lined face—probably from decades of smoke in this place—comes over to take our drink order. When she recognizes Luca, her face lights up. "Hey, kid. I didn't expect to see you here."

Luca hitches his chin in my direction. "This is my friend Catherine. Catherine, this is Barbara. She mixes the best drinks in Bloomfield."

I fully expect Barbara to roll her eyes, but instead she smiles and puts a cocktail napkin in front of each of us. "Just for that, your first drink is on the house. What can I get you?"

Luca's gaze slides over me, and then he turns to Barbara. "Two shots. Whatever you got."

"Be right back."

Barbara heads to the other side of the bar to grab a pair of glasses. Onstage, the woman with the trumpet steps forward for her solo.

I lean in so Luca can hear me. "Is Barbara a Morelli, too?"

"Honorary." Luca bends closer. "She's been working here since I was a kid. Poured me my first shot of whiskey when I was thirteen." His facial stubble brushes my cheek, and a shiver runs down my spine.

I wish Barbara would hurry up with that drink.

"Is that what we're having tonight? Whiskey?"

"I know it's probably not your thing." He shrugs. "But I thought maybe you could use it tonight."

"What do you think *is* my thing? White wine? Spritzer, maybe?" I lean back so I can see his eyes.

He gives me a wry smile. "Something along those lines."

Barbara sets two glasses of amber liquid in front of us. I pick mine up, knock it back, and set the glass back on the bar with a little bit of extra flair.

Luca's eyebrows shoot up. "I stand corrected."

To be honest, he's not wrong. I'm not much of a drinker. I don't like anything that makes me feel out of control, and working full-time while going to school hasn't exactly been conducive for nights out at the bar. But it doesn't mean I'm ordering spritzers. "My dad's friend Ginger Ale poured me my first shot of whiskey when I was thirteen, too."

Luca's mouth drops open. "*Ginger Ale?*"

I shrug. "She's a redhead."

"Is that her real name?"

"Of course not, Elbow. She's a burlesque dancer. It's a stage name."

He's staring at me like he's never been more fascinated by anything in his life. "So, you and...*Ms. Ale*...used to do shots?"

"It was a celebration when I got my first period."

He nods slowly like he's processing this information. "When Ginny got her first period, my mom just took her to the corner drugstore to buy pads."

"My childhood was unconventional."

"I'm starting to see that." He grabs his glass and tosses his drink back.

Barbara appears in front of us. "Another one?"

A warm glow has started to take over my limbs. Maybe Luca is right. I needed that. Maybe we can just stay here doing shots and not thinking about my life falling apart. "Yes, please."

She grabs the bottle and refills our glasses.

"Oh, and one more thing." Luca cocks his head and gives Barbara his charming smile.

Barbara looks at me with a good-natured roll of her eyes. "Here we go..."

"Would you mind terribly if we asked you to call back to Uncle Vito? We need to talk to him."

Barbara makes an exaggerated cringe face. "His card game is about to start."

"I know. Sorry."

"You know he doesn't like anyone to interrupt his card game."

I look nervously at Luca. "Maybe we should come back later?"

Luca shakes his head. "It's important."

Barbara sighs like, *It's your funeral.* I drink my second shot.

"Okay. For *you*, Luca, I'll ask him." She moves across the bar to pick up an old-fashioned phone on the wall. People around here are awfully amenable to doing favors for Luca.

"I guess this card game is really important to your uncle Vito?"

"It's been going on every week since Barbara's been plying me with whiskey."

"What if he says no to meeting with us?"

"Uncle Vito won't say no." Luca bends an arm, resting it on the bar in front of us, and a branch of autumn leaves sways on his bicep. "We're family."

I wish Dad and I had the same understanding when I asked him to help me get my birth certificate back. Then maybe I wouldn't be sitting in a smoky bar contemplating tracing a finger along the lines of my doorman's tattoos.

But then again, I think, as the low tones of the saxophone vibrate in my chest and Luca leans closer so I can hear him over the noise, *maybe this isn't so bad after all.* The warm glow spreads wider.

A moment later, Barbara stands in front of us. "Okay. Vito says make it quick."

"Thanks, Barb." Luca takes her hand and presses a kiss to her knuckles. "You're the best."

We weave back through the crowd and enter an unmarked door on the other side of the room. It swings shut behind us, taking the light from the stage and the noise from the band with it, and when it hits the frame with a loud clang, I jump. Luca reaches out and grabs my hand, and I hold on, staring down a long, narrow hallway. Smoke curls in front of the dim overhead bulb like fog rolling in. At the end of the hall, I can make out the vague shapes of a beaded curtain swaying from a slight breeze. Luca tugs me forward, and the smell of smoke is stronger back here, more pungent than the cigarettes out in the bar. Cigars, maybe. I clutch Luca's hand tighter, stumbling to a stop.

"Luca, are you sure this is a good idea? I know Uncle Vito is family and all, but this looks like the kind of place where people get whacked."

Luca's shoulders shake with laughter, but I stay frozen. The closer we get to meeting this Uncle Vito, the more my nerves are stretching thin. After a moment, my anxiety seems to register with Luca, and his smile fades.

Turning to face me, Luca takes both my shoulders in his hands. He's only inches away, and his eyes find mine in the semidarkness. "Catherine, I promise you, I won't let you get whacked. Can you trust me?"

No.

Luca is the last person I can trust, and not just because he shows up late and loses my dry cleaning and spills coffee on me when I step off the elevator. It's because even in the back labyrinth of this dingy, smoky bar, with something that screams *danger* lurking behind that beaded curtain, I want to lean into him instead of pulling away. I want him to wrap those painted arms around me. And this is so unlike me that I really *don't* know who I am. I've completely lost my identity in ways that have nothing to do with my Social Security number.

"Catherine?" he prompts.

"Okay," I whisper, because the truth is that whatever is behind that curtain seems safer than staying alone in the hall with Luca.

He parts the beads, and I follow him into a room that's dark in the corners and lit by another Tiffany lamp hanging in the middle over a circular table. Around the table sit four middle-aged white men with broad shoulders, wide necks, and—when they look up from their cards—angry expressions on their faces.

The largest and most imposing of the men faces us. He's handsome, with a full head of almost-black hair, sculpted cheekbones, and dark eyes with lashes so long that I can see them all the way across the room, even standing here in the shadows. I immediately note the resemblance to Lorraine, and fifty pounds and thirty years in the future, that could be Luca sitting there.

Except for the scowl. Luca would never have that scowl on his face. I can't picture Luca with anything other than his charming smile.

This must be Uncle Vito. And he's not happy to see us.

Uncle Vito confirms this by carefully setting his cards down on the table and, in a low, threatening voice, demanding, "Why are you interrupting my game, Luca?"

"Sorry." Luca flashes that overexaggerated smile, and I cringe. Is he sure that's the right strategy here? "I know." He holds out his hands, palms up, like, *What can you do?* "I wouldn't interrupt, but this is important."

Uncle Vito's face doesn't crack an inch. "What could be more important than me taking all of Dominic's money?"

Not getting whacked tonight.

But Luca seems unthreatened. "This is my friend Catherine."

Uncle Vito gives me a nod. "How you doin', Catherine?"

"Uh, fine." I hesitate, and then add, "Thank you so much for asking." I notice there aren't just four men in the room. Two more lurk in the shadows, flanking Uncle Vito, their massive shoulders practically wider than the doorway, arms crossed over their colossal chests. They must be bodyguards. I clutch Luca's hand tighter.

"Catherine has a problem," Luca explains.

"We've all got problems, kid. Right now, I have the worst case of indigestion from your aunt Toni's pasta puttanesca."

I know this is crazy, but I think I might be able to help Uncle Vito out with that. I start to reach into my purse, but before I know what's happening, one of the bodyguards rushes toward me. "Freeze!" he barks.

I freeze.

He takes a cautious step forward, holding one hand out like a warning. With the other, he flips open his jacket and reaches for something in the waistband of his pants. "What's in your bag?"

"I—" I keep my eyes trained on the small black object jutting out from beneath his belt. Luca *promised* I wouldn't get whacked tonight. "Uh, well, I have…" Now that I have to say it out loud, this is kind of embarrassing. "I think I might have some Tums. For Uncle Vito's indigestion."

The bodyguard slowly pulls his hand away from his waistband. Whew.

"Can I—?" I point to the bag. The bodyguard gives me a nod. I reach inside, and my hand closes over a roll

WISH I WERE HERE

of antacids. *Thank God*. I hold them up. "They're still in here from when I was stressed out working on my dissertation…" Luca nudges me with his elbow. Right. Uncle Vito doesn't care about my dissertation. But when I glance up at Luca's face, he's not giving me a warning; he looks like he's trying not to laugh.

I take a step forward to deliver the Tums to Uncle Vito, but the bodyguard clears his throat and holds up a hefty palm. I stop short. He steps in front of me, and I hand over the Tums. "Right. Sorry. Here you go."

"So, what is this problem?" Uncle Vito demands, after he's eaten two Tums and washed them down with his glass of red wine. He waves a hand. "Bottom line me."

Luca takes a deep breath. "Okay. Catherine's identity disappeared, and we need to help her get it back. We think we can fix everything if we find the original copy of her birth certificate, but her mom has it. Catherine has never met her mom, and her dad won't tell her anything about her."

Uncle Vito nods like this sort of problem is an everyday affair in his line of work. Which I actually haven't quite worked out what that is, except it sounds like he earns some money from beating Dominic at cards.

"Do you want me to threaten to cut your dad's hand off?" His dark eyes pierce mine. "Squeeze the info out of him?"

"What?" I gasp. My dad is a clown, for God's sake. He's fun loving. He juggles for children. He's not the sort of person you threaten with bodily harm. Plus, he *needs* his hands. "No!"

Uncle Vito nods again. "So, you want me to actually cut off his hand?"

How did this escalate so quickly? "Oh my God. *No.*"

Luca clears his throat. "We just need one of your guys to help us dig up some information on Catherine's mother. Maybe if they could help us track her down, we can take it from there."

Uncle Vito looks a little disappointed. Maybe he was looking forward to cutting off Dad's hand. But he rallies quickly. "What do you know about the mother?"

"Not much, unfortunately," I say.

"We know her name. And Catherine's birth date and place of birth. She was born here in Pittsburgh, but we don't even know what hospital."

It's almost nothing. "Can you work with that?" I ask.

Uncle Vito stares at me. "I can work with anything." He turns to the guy on his left. "What do you think? Start with hospital records?"

Left guy nods. "That's what I'd do."

"Can you hack in?"

"Sure. But—" Left Guy assesses me. "Thirtyish years ago, records weren't kept electronically. Everything's going to be in paper files in a basement somewhere."

Uncle Vito nods. "We need Fabrizio."

"Agreed."

"Okay." Uncle Vito picks up his cards and reclines in his chair. "Text me the info and give me two days."

I lean into Luca, my body heavy with relief. I have no idea who Fabrizio is, or how he's going to dig up what I need. But Uncle Vito seems like the kind of guy who, if he wants information, gets information. "Oh, thank you so much."

"Now let me finish my card game."

"Of course."

"Thanks, Uncle Vito," Luca says, and we turn to head back through the beaded curtain.

"Hey, Luca." Uncle Vito's sharp voice stops us. "Go visit your ma once in a while, will you?"

"Yes, sir," Luca calls behind him. Under his breath, he mutters to me, "I go every Sunday."

Back out in the bar, Barbara shoos a couple away from our stools so we can sit down again. She sets two more shots in front of us, and I quickly swallow mine.

"Do you think Uncle Vito would have really cut off my dad's hand if I'd wanted him to?"

"You know, I don't know." Luca scrunches his brow. "He's offered a couple of times, but I've never taken him up on it." I can't tell if he's joking or not. I decide not to dig deeper.

"And you really think this guy—Fabrizio—will help me find something about my mother?"

Luca nods. "Fab's a good guy. He'll know what to do."

"Another Morelli, I suppose?"

"Second cousin."

I try to imagine what it would be like to be a part of a family who are all willing to help each other out like the Morellis. I've never needed to cut someone's hand off, but maybe it would be comforting to know the option were open to me. To know that people were willing to go to bat for me. My gaze lifts to Luca's. Sort of the way he's going to bat for me.

Why *is* he helping me like this? He keeps introducing me as his friend, but until today, we never spent any time together, and we barely even talked. Is this whole situation just something to amuse him? A distraction from the front desk?

Well, even if I'm just entertainment for him, I'm grateful. "Thanks for your help with this, Luca. You definitely don't have to be doing all this for me."

"Sure I do." He waves a dismissive hand. "It's no big deal. I'm just trying to get you back to solving all the world's numerical problems. Someone needs to do it, and it's certainly not going to be me."

"You're not a fan of math?"

"I have to admit, I can't see the appeal. But I see why *you* like it."

"Really? And why's that?"

"Math adds up and makes sense. You just have to follow the rules, and it will come through for you. You can count on it." He pauses. "Unlike, oh…being a clown."

I sit back on my stool. It's no secret that I'm a rule follower, but I *am* surprised that Luca has put all these pieces together, only having known me for such a short time. Especially because I still can't quite figure him out.

"So what about you?" I fold my cocktail napkin into a rectangle. "Did you always want to do what you're doing? Did you go to college?"

"Nah." He shrugs. "I thought about it. I was into drawing in high school and looked into art schools for college. Even got into a couple. But I realized that once I had deadlines and assignments, it wasn't going to be any fun anymore. It would turn into work, and that's not really for me." He lifts a colorful arm. "I still draw, but just for me and my friends."

My eyes widen and slide from his tattoos to his face. "These are *your* designs?"

"Yep."

"They're beautiful." Again, I'm tempted to trace my finger along the lines of a winding vine, and I even go as far as reaching my hand out. At the last moment, I drop it back into my lap. "I bet you could show your work in a gallery."

I'm surprised to see his eyes darken for just a moment. "I actually had a gallery show booked last year, but…" Luca spins his shot glass in his hand, and I wait for him to say more. Finally, he shrugs. "But it didn't work out."

"I'm sorry." I remember my splurge on those botanical prints on my apartment wall. "I hope you can schedule another one someday. I would buy a drawing of one of these designs. If I ever have any money again, I mean."

The shadows clear from his eyes, and Luca leans in, his lips quirking. "Listen, when you're ready to get your first tattoo, I'll draw it for you. On the house." He looks at me sideways. "If you don't already have a tattoo, that is. A graduation present from Ginger Ale, maybe?"

I laugh. "No tattoos."

"Perfect. I love a blank canvas." He reaches out, and his fingers brush my arm. My head spins in ways that have nothing to do with that third shot of whiskey.

I take a shaky breath, and a completely wild thought comes to me. *I should take Luca to ArtSpace.* They have a gallery, and I bet Ginger Ale would love to show Luca's work there.

I haven't been to ArtSpace in years, but I practically grew up there. Though my living situation was never very stable when I was a kid, ArtSpace was a constant. I did most of my homework and school projects at a paint-spattered table in the corner while Dad practiced tricks with his circus friends. It's where I got to know all the women from the burlesque dance troupe, where I drank shots with Ginger Ale, where a woman named Frenchy Kiss told me everything I needed to know about the birds and the bees.

Dad still spends most of his free time at ArtSpace, but it's not a place that I ever expected to go back to. I'm glad Dad found his people there, but it could never make up for the home I longed for. And Ginger Ale and Frenchy Kiss weren't quite the mom I always dreamed about. To be honest, I have a lot of mixed feelings about ArtSpace. So the fact that my tattooed doorman, whom I found completely maddening just days ago, has me thinking about heading over there might be a bigger mystery than my identity crisis.

Onstage, the trumpet player announces that the band is going to take a short break, and Luca glances at his phone. "Oh, shit. Is it ten already? I should go." He pulls out his wallet. "And you should probably get home to bed."

It doesn't surprise me that Luca has someplace else to be or that he's just getting started for the evening. But he's right, ten is already past my bedtime. The fact that I was just about to take him to a warehouse with strobe lights, loud music, and scantily clad women is completely beside the point. I'm not myself lately. And I'm glad he reminded me of that. I'll get eight hours of sleep and wake up in the morning, well rested and ready to work on my research paper. While he'll probably stumble home and sleep on the floor of the lobby again.

Luca insists on paying our bar bill, and I let him because I have two hundred dollars to my name and no idea when I'll be able to earn more, and that fact is going to keep me up tonight. We step out on the sidewalk, and Luca turns to head toward the DeGreco.

"You don't have to walk me if you have somewhere to be." Bloomfield is a safe neighborhood and I only live a few blocks from here. Most of the bars that would interest Luca are in Lawrenceville, in the opposite direction. "You're already late, so you probably want to get going."

But Luca keeps walking. "I'm going the same direction you're going."

Inside the lobby of the DeGreco, Luca presses the button for the elevator. "You're going upstairs?" I ask. "What floor do you live on?"

"Two." But once we're inside the elevator, he presses eight for my floor, and then eleven.

"You're not going home?"

"Nah, I've got a friend on the eleventh floor. I told her I'd stop by around ten."

Oh. "Anyone I know?"

"I don't think so."

There are a few younger couples in the building, and a family with twin boys, but otherwise, it seems to be mostly older people. I've never seen any single women my age. That doesn't mean there aren't any, though. It wouldn't surprise me that they'd want to hang out with Luca. He *is* outgoing, and fun, and really attractive to look at. I mean, I could see why other women would think so. As long as they don't care that he was supposed to arrive at ten and it's already ten fifteen.

The elevator stops on my floor, and I step off, turning to face him. Luca puts a hand on the door to keep it open. "I'll text you when I hear from Uncle Vito. Could be a day or two."

"Thank you again for your help tonight, Luca. I really appreciate it." And I mean it. Where would I be right now if it weren't for his help?

Completely on my own.

"What are you going to do in the meantime?" He cocks his head to catch my eye. "Are you going to be freaking out?"

"No." *Yes.* "I'll probably try to get some work done. The semester will be starting soon."

"Well, let me know if you need anything." He takes a step back, away from the elevator door, and I'm tempted to shove my hand out to stop it from closing. Because the thought of going back to my apartment, all alone, to dwell on everything that's happened fills me with dread. I don't think solving a math problem or outlining a paper is going to calm me down this time.

I remember Luca standing in my living room earlier today, taking up the small space with his energy. Offering reassurances when I started to panic. For a fleeting moment, I consider telling him I *do* need something and asking him to come over for one more drink. But then I remember the woman on eleven, and I step away from the elevator door.

He has a date, and it's way past my bedtime.

CHAPTER 13

For the first time in as long as I can remember, I wake up to a day where I have nothing I have to do. I could work on my research paper, or develop a computational algorithm, or plan my syllabi. But until Luca hears from Uncle Vito, I'm not sure I'll be able to concentrate. I could clean my apartment, but Sunday mornings are for cleaning, and it's only Tuesday. I haven't been here very much in the past few days, so dust hasn't even had time to settle. Still, I wipe down the counters in the kitchen and run the vacuum over the rug in the living room. Then I sit down on my couch and stare at the walls.

I'm about to jump out of my skin when the phone rings, lighting up with Dad's name. Grateful for the distraction, I answer.

"How's it going, Kitty Cat?" comes Dad's voice through the phone. Like we didn't even talk yesterday.

"What do you mean, *how's it going?*" I snap. "How do you think it's going?"

Dad hesitates and then finally says, "I guess you didn't figure out your dilemma from yesterday."

"No, I didn't. And I can't believe you just walked away."

"I'm sorry I can't tell you about your mother."

Can't? Or won't? I sit up straight. "Don't you care that this is going to ruin my life?"

"I'd care if I believed something like a silly little piece of paper could ruin your life. You're the smartest, most capable person I know. Ever since you were a little kid, you always worked things out."

And with that, I'm filled with a wave of anger. "That's because I never had any choice. *Working things out* shouldn't have always been my job." It should have been Dad's. Or even my mother's. And now, here I am, with a problem that only the two of them can solve, and they've both abandoned me.

For a moment, Dad is silent on the other end of the phone. "I'm sorry you feel that way," he finally says.

I press a hand to my temple. "Please, Dad. All I need to know is how to reach her."

"Kitty Cat..."

I grasp at a fresh idea. "Or maybe you could reach out to her? You could call her and ask her to help?"

"I'm sorry. I can't."

So that's it. But strangely, I'm not as disappointed as I expected to be. Because for the first time in my life, the possibility that I might learn something new about my mother—that I might even *meet* her—is real. She's been nothing but a mystery for thirty years, and the fact that Dad has been so adamant about *not* talking about her makes me want to know even more. So maybe I'll take my chances with Fabrizio.

From somewhere far away, I hear Sal's voice.

Maybe something seems like a disaster. But if you look

deeper, maybe it's an opportunity. If Fabrizio really *can* dig up dirt on anyone, then maybe this is an opportunity to learn about my mom that I'll never have again.

And with that, I find myself reenergized and ready to accomplish something.

"Okay. Thanks anyway, Dad." I hang up the phone.

My dry cleaning bag hangs on the closet door—I wasn't going to take any chances with having it delivered, so I picked it up earlier this week—and Mrs. Goodwin's trousers are inside, cleaned and pressed.

I text Luca. *What is Mrs. Goodwin's apartment number?*

He writes back immediately: *Apartment 1109.* And then less than a minute later: *How are you?*

Me: Fine.

Luca: *You're climbing the walls, aren't you?*

Me: No.

But apparently, Luca knows me well already. *Deep breaths. Uncle Vito will come through for us.*

I stare at those words. *For us.*

Outside Mrs. Goodwin's apartment, I hear the upbeat tones of "Build Me Up Buttercup" pulsing on the other side of the wall. I knock, but the chorus kicks in, and the thumping of the bass and something that sounds like footfalls increase in intensity. I knock louder, and finally, the door swings open. Mrs. Goodwin stands in the threshold, her feet tapping, shoulders shimmying, fingers snapping to the music. "Catherine!"

She backs up, still bopping, and I follow her inside just in time to catch the swell of the music and her elaborate finish complete with a double spin and jazz hands. "Ta-da!"

I clap because she's genuinely good at this and her energy is infectious.

"Thanks." She lowers the music. "It wasn't my best work. I'm really better with a partner."

This, of course, makes me think of Luca. There's no way he's manning the desk, or Mrs. Goodwin would be downstairs dancing with him. So he must be off on an errand somewhere.

I don't know why I care where Luca is.

"You seemed pretty good all by yourself," I say. "Are you practicing for something?"

Mrs. Goodwin blinks in surprise. "It's for the big fundraiser, of course."

"Fundraiser?"

"For the community center. Luca didn't tell you?"

I shake my head. "Luca and I don't really hang out." Although, I guess that's not completely true. I remember his hand squeezing mine. The warmth moving through me after our courage shots at the bar.

"Oh." Mrs. Goodwin lifts a shoulder. "There aren't many in the under-eighty crowd in the building, so I assumed you young people stuck together."

Maybe the other young people stick together. Like Luca and the woman on eleven. I shake my head to dislodge that thought. "So, what is the fundraiser for? You said it's for a community center?"

"Yes, down the street. It's been there for decades, serving

people in Bloomfield. They offer exercise classes, bingo, book club. And they have a full day program for older people to get out of their apartments and have a place to spend their time." Her mouth stretches into a thin line. "A lot of people here in the building have lost their spouses, and their kids are grown and off living their lives. Did you know that research shows loneliness is as bad for your health as smoking?"

I blink in surprise. "As bad as *smoking*?" But it makes sense to me. It must be hard for people living by themselves without any family nearby. Nobody to call, nobody to count on in an emergency. How would that slowly wear on you, day in and day out? What would that eventually do to your heart? "That's so sad," I murmur, and I'm not sure what's happening, but my voice comes out hoarse, and there's a lump in the back of my throat.

I look up to find Mrs. Goodwin watching me, her head cocked.

"Do you have any family nearby, Catherine?" she asks in a gentle tone. "People in your circle?"

"What? Me?" I clear my throat. "I—" Dad and I get together every Sunday for dinner. I mean, I usually spend most of the evening trying not to get impaled by a pair of stilts and rolling my eyes at his math jokes. But I could call Dad in an emergency, couldn't I?

I clutch my phone in my hand as our conversation comes back to me. My voice as I pleaded with him to help me find my mom. How he said no. But I also remember the way his face lights up every time he sees me. Dad loves me. I know he does.

"Oh, I'm fine," I say in a breezy tone.

Mrs. Goodwin's brow furrows, and I'm aware that I didn't really answer her question.

"We were talking about the fundraiser," I prompt.

Mrs. Goodwin sighs. "Yes, the fundraiser. The community center building is up for sale, and developers are swooping in. You know how real estate in Bloomfield is these days."

I nod. This neighborhood is hot property, and developers have bought up dozens of houses like the one Luca grew up in, installed new kitchens, replaced the siding, and put them up for sale for three times the price.

"The nonprofit that runs the community center managed to get a grant to buy the building, but it's not enough. We need to raise ten thousand dollars by next month or that evil Oak Street Capital is going to buy it out from under us and turn it into condos."

"So, you'll be doing your dance at the fundraiser?"

"Yes, and we've got some other performers, too. Hilda Bradley in 307 used to be an opera singer. And Jerome Washington in 902 plays the trumpet. But we need more if we want to attract ticket buyers from all over the city." Her gaze zeroes in on me. "Do *you* have any talents, Catherine?"

"Unfortunately, no." I laugh. "Not unless you need someone to solve for *x*." Just a little math humor. Dad would be proud.

Mrs. Goodwin shakes her head. "No, but thanks for the offer." She gives me an up-and-down look. "But you know what you could do? Help me practice these steps."

"Oh, no." I hold the dry cleaning in front of me as if it will offer some protection. "I really couldn't. I don't dance."

But Mrs. Goodwin waves a dismissive hand. "You'll be fine. I just need a warm body. Put that thing down."

"Really," I say nervously. "I shouldn't. I'll just throw off your rhythm."

Mrs. Goodwin points a not-taking-no-for-an-answer finger at the couch. With a sigh, I drop the bag there. She *did* take off her pants for me, so maybe I owe her this.

"I'll lead," she says, reaching out to take my shoulders and position me in the center of the living room. Her phone is on the kitchen counter, so she leaves me to press play on the music. Then she scurries back over to where I'm standing and takes my hand just in time to catch the last notes of the song's intro.

"Two, three, four..." Mrs. Goodwin tugs me sideways, crossing her left foot over her right and then giving me a gentle shove backward, stepping away from me in the opposite direction. Her hips swish in time with the beat, feet moving in an elaborate kick step before she pulls me back in toward her, repeating the kick step.

I watch her orthopedic shoes flying across the floor and do my best to mirror her movements. Back, kick step, to the center, kick step, back, kick step. I'm concentrating hard, counting to myself, and hoping I don't step forward when Mrs. Goodwin steps back, or trip over my own feet and take us both down. But by the end of the second verse, I've gotten the hang of the rhythm, and my feet are moving automatically.

When the chorus picks up again, Mrs. Goodwin grabs me by the waist, pulling us both around in a circle, and then with a gentle shove to my hip, she sends me spinning out on my own. I follow the beat of the song, turning once, twice, and then I take hold of Mrs. Goodwin's outstretched hand. We settle back into our kick steps, spins, kick steps, and as the notes of the song build, Mrs. Goodwin pulls me toward her. Without even having to think about it now, I twirl under her arm, we both kick backward, hop forward, and stop abruptly in the middle of the room, jazz hands flying for the final piano chords. An exhilarated laugh builds in my throat as I bend to catch my breath and shove my sweaty hair off my forehead.

And then, "Bravo!" calls a voice from across the room.

I jump and look up to find Luca leaning against Mrs. Goodwin's doorframe, clapping wildly. I'm certain my face is turning about ten shades of red, so I spin abruptly and hit pause on the next song that's kicked in through the phone speaker.

"You told me you don't dance," Mrs. Goodwin says, her voice accusing.

"I really don't."

"Well, you could have fooled me. Right, Luca?"

I'm still out of breath, and sweating now, but I don't think it's entirely related to the exercise. I pull my long blond hair off my neck, twisting it into a bun. I usually secure it with a pencil, but since I don't have one, I let it fall down my back. When I look up again, Luca is watching me. Even from all the way across the room, I can feel the heat of his gaze, and something stirs in my chest.

"You looked great to me." His voice is low, with a little rasp at the end. "Where did you learn to dance like that?"

I pick up the dry cleaning bag from the couch, shake it

out, and cross the room. "Mrs. Goodwin must be a good teacher."

"Uh-huh," Luca murmurs, but he doesn't sound convinced.

The truth is, I actually *can* dance. As a little girl, I was fascinated by the burlesque dancers Dad used to hang around with at ArtSpace. The glittering costumes, the glamorous makeup, the grace of their matching kick steps across the floor. I used to sit at my homework table in the corner and watch them practice their routines, memorizing the way their feathered hips shook and their high-heeled feet tapped in time with the music. Later, I'd sneak off to the dressing room and practice in front of the mirror when nobody was looking. One of the dancers, Lola Von Crumpet, found me there, shimmying in a too-large pair of Ginger Ale's vintage patent leather pumps.

Lola took me by the hand and marched me into ArtSpace's rehearsal room. I was sure she was going to report everything to Ginger, and I'd get in trouble. Maybe Ginger wouldn't let Dad and me stay at her house anymore when we got kicked out of our apartment. But instead, she took one look at me teetering in her high heels and declared that she was going to buy me a pair that fit so I could practice the steps properly.

"If you want to learn to dance, we'll teach you," Lola added, pushing a lock of hair off my cheek and tucking it behind my ear. I remember how my heart used to constrict at that maternal gesture. "You've got natural talent. Don't hide away in the corner."

The dancers taught me their kicks and spins, shuffles and hip swings. And I learned all kinds of other things from them, too. How to braid my hair and put on lipstick. How to deal with a man who got too handsy. How to hold my head up high and keep moving, even if I miss a step.

Eventually, though, my homework began piling up from all the school days I'd missed while crisscrossing the country going to music festivals and fairs with Dad. We got kicked out of another apartment, and the reality sank in that someone needed to pay attention to whether the rent was paid. That quiet hum of anxiety—the one that's been with me for decades now—began around that time. I hated to give up dancing with Lola and Ginger and all the others to go back to that homework table in the corner. It was so lonely being the one who had to worry about holding everything together. But I didn't have time to perfect my peacock prance if I ever wanted to go to college, land a good job, and finally find some stability for once in my life.

I haven't danced in years, and I certainly didn't intend to start up again today. Especially with Luca watching.

"What are you doing here, anyway?" I focus my attention on hanging the dry cleaning bag on Mrs. Goodwin's closet door.

"I was just strolling by, and I heard the music."

I look through the doorway, past Luca, at the other apartments along the hallway. It's not lost on me that Mrs. Goodwin lives on the eleventh floor. The same one as Luca's late-night friend. Is he coming from her apartment? My gaze skates to his feet and back up to his face. He's in his doorman uniform, so if he's coming from there, at least he's not doing the walk of shame in that tight T-shirt he wore last night.

Maybe she tore it off him. Maybe it's still on her floor.

I press my hands to my eyes. *For God's sake, Catherine, get a grip. Who cares where Luca's T-shirt is?*

"I'm glad I found you here, though," Luca says. "The eagle flies at midnight. Dress like a crow."

I must be spending way too much time with him, because I think I actually know how to decipher this cryptic message. "Did Uncle Vito call you? Do you have some information?"

He gives me a grin. "Affirmative."

"What?" My spine stiffens. "What did he find out?"

Luca pushes back away from the door. "Meet me in the lobby at the rendezvous time. I'll tell you everything then."

And before I can argue, he turns and heads down the hallway, rounds a corner, and disappears from sight.

CHAPTER 14

At exactly midnight, I'm standing in the lobby wearing a pair of black jeans, a black T-shirt, and a black hoodie over top.

Luca, of course, is not here yet.

He arrives two minutes later, hopping off the elevator that stopped on the eleventh floor right before it went straight to the lobby.

Not that I was watching the numbers light up over the door.

"Hey," he says with a grin when he sees me standing there with my arms crossed over my chest. "Sorry I'm late."

At this point, I'm not even annoyed about the time. I'm dying to know what Uncle Vito uncovered about my mother. Of course, Luca wasn't in the lobby all afternoon when I came looking for him. And he hasn't been answering my text message inquiries.

"Tell me what's going on," I blurt out. "What did Uncle Vito find out?"

Luca looks me over. "Good. You wore black."

"I assumed that's what 'dress like a crow' was supposed to mean."

"Yep, you nailed the uniform."

My gaze shifts from his face, and I realize he's wearing a version of the same outfit as me—black jeans and T-shirt with a black hoodie. I try to close the door on the thought that I prefer him in the white T-shirt with his tattoos showing, but it slips through before I can stop it.

Luca holds up his first and middle fingers, pointing at his eyes and then flipping them in my direction. "I think we're going to make a good team on this."

"A good team on *what*, Luca? What are we doing here at midnight dressed like gravediggers?"

Luca takes me by the hand, pulls me into his chest, and then spins me out again, just like Mrs. Goodwin during our impromptu dance rehearsal. "We, my darling Catherine, are dressed this way because it's the best way to dress when you're about to do a little light breaking and entering."

I plant my feet firmly on the floor. "What? You're joking."

"I'm afraid not."

"Luca." I make my voice firm. "Tell me what's going on right now."

"Fabrizio did some digging."

"And?"

"And since the only information we have is your birth date, place of birth, and your mom's name at the time..."

Her name at the time. I don't know why it didn't occur to me that she might have changed it since I was born. Maybe she got married. Maybe she even has kids. Kids who got to grow up knowing her. My heart aches at the idea of it. Of all the scenarios I imagined, my mom having an ordinary life with another family wasn't one of them.

"So, Uncle Vito and the guys thought the best place to start digging was at the hospitals around here. If they could figure out where you were born, they could access your birth records and maybe find some information that we don't have. Your mom's date of birth. Her address at the time. Things we can use to track her down."

Uncle Vito and the guys really thought this through. I'm grateful they're on my side. "This all makes sense, but none of it explains why I'm dressed like a crow at midnight."

"Fab managed to shake down some people at Pittsburgh General and University Hospitals."

I open my mouth at his use of the phrase *shake down*, but then I quickly close it. I really don't want to know.

"Nobody at either of those hospitals could find any record of your birth. So that leaves St. Anne's. It's the only hospital left that was delivering babies the year you were born. So that must be it."

"Okay. And was Fabrizio able to shake—uh, I mean, question someone at St. Anne's?"

"He was able to confirm what Uncle Vito suspected. The records from thirty years ago are stored in some old file boxes in the basement. They're in the process of moving to electronic records, but they haven't converted anything that far back yet."

It's all starting to come together for me now. "And we're going to—" This is crazy.

"Yep. We're going to break in and find the file."

Twenty minutes later, I'm standing next to Luca's Lincoln Town Car and staring at a broad-shouldered white man named Fabrizio. When we arrived in the hospital parking lot, Luca got out and hugged the guy like they're old friends. Or I guess cousins, in this instance. The Morelli family tree has a lot of branches.

We're in the very back corner of the lot, standing under a dim fluorescent streetlight that's flickering on and off. A red sign with the word *Emergency* glows on the building in the distance.

"Fab, man, thanks for hooking us up," Luca says, pounding him on the back.

"When Vito told me the favor was for you, of course I agreed to it."

There are an awful lot of people in this town who are eager to help Luca. I eye his wide grin suspiciously. Maybe all that good-guy friendliness is a cover. Maybe *he's* the Mafia boss.

But then Fabrizio says, "Thanks again for your help when my grandma was sick," and I start to put the pieces together.

Luca waves him off. "It was nothing." And then, almost like he's trying to change the subject, he turns to me. "Anyway. This is my friend Catherine. She's the one whose mother we're looking for."

Fab holds out a hand, and I shake it.

"I really appreciate your help," I say.

"Sorry your mom took off. That's rough."

"Thanks." I press my lips together, strangely moved by these people who are all willing to help me. Thanks to Luca.

"So, what do you have for us?" Luca's voice cuts into my thoughts.

Fabrizio turns to the car next to us and reaches in the open window, pulling out a bundle of clothes. "This is for you, Catherine." He shoves a pile of blue fabric into my arms. "And you." He hands Luca some sort of coveralls.

I unfold the pants and shirt in my hands and find that I'm holding a pair of scrubs. "What is this for?"

"These are your disguises."

I give the scrubs a shake. "Luca told me to wear black. I imagined us crawling into a broken window or something."

"Luca watches too many movies. To get into the basement, you'll need to blend in." Fabrizio hitches his chin at the clothes in my hand. "Not roll in looking like you're about to rob the place."

"Makes sense," I agree.

"Luca, you are…" Fabrizio pulls a hospital ID badge from his pocket and squints at it. "Janitor Malik Osman."

Fab holds out the badge, and I catch a glimpse of Janitor Osman as the ID changes hands. He looks to be in his midthirties with brown eyes and wavy hair similar to Luca's. Though Malik's skin is slightly darker and his cheekbones more pronounced, Fabrizio has done a pretty good job of finding a match for Luca that won't draw anyone's attention.

Fabrizio hands over my badge. "Catherine, you're Dr. Daphne Dawson."

I take the badge and flip it over. My mouth drops open. "You're kidding."

Dr. Dawson is an older Black woman with short, silver-streaked curly hair. For the record, I'm twenty-nine and have long blond hair and blue eyes. "I'm not going to pass as this woman. She looks nothing like me."

"It's the best I could do on such short notice. Here." He holds out a blue surgical cap that matches the scrubs. "You can wear this on your head. Maybe that will help."

I look back and forth between Dr. Dawson's and Janitor Osman's photos. "Who are these people anyway?"

"They're former hospital employees. Both left their jobs recently, and human resources collected their ID badges. The protocol at the hospital is that when someone leaves their job, they give their badges to my associate in IT to shut off their security access. My associate generously agreed to leave the badges' access on for another twenty-four hours."

I wonder if his associate still has all his limbs. "But if anyone even glances at my badge, they're going to know immediately that I'm not Dr. Dawson. Do I need this to get through security? Show this to a guard?" I clutch the ID in shaking hands, remembering how I handed my driver's license over to Bill at the Social Security office. That ID actually had my own picture, and I still almost got arrested. They'll lock me up and throw away the key if I get caught breaking and entering with Dr. Dawson's badge. And then I'll never get my job back.

"Nobody should be checking badges. All of that is done electronically." Fabrizio gives me a reassuring smile. "The badges just give you access to the parts of the building that aren't open to the public. Like the hospital basement."

Okay, that doesn't sound so bad.

"All you have to do is swipe your badge to ride the elevator down to the basement," Fabrizio continues. "Once you're in the basement, you'll need to locate the file room. There should be a sign. But it will be locked." He thrusts a small piece of paper into my hand. "Your badges won't work for the file room. Access is only granted to certain hospital administrators."

I turn the paper over in my hand. *Donnie*, it reads. And then a phone number. "Who is Donnie?"

"Donnie is my associate, and that's his number. He works in IT and can remotely open the file room door once you're standing outside of it."

"And then what?"

"Then you go inside and find the file from your birth. It should be in there somewhere."

My gaze drifts from the badge in my hand to Luca's face. Can we really pull this off? As if he can read my mind, Luca gives me a nod and a reassuring smile. I guess if we get caught, I can always hope the judge is a Morelli. The odds seem in my favor.

Luca turns to Fabrizio, and they do a hand-slap shoulder-bump handshake. "Thanks again for your help, man."

"Let me know if you need anything else."

Fabrizio gets into his car, and with a wave, he drives off. I clutch the scrubs to my chest and look around for somewhere to change. We're in the farthest row of a dark parking lot with no other vehicles around us. Are there security cameras back here? I guess my only option is to go behind the car and hope for the best.

I turn around to find that Luca doesn't share my concern with public displays of nudity because he's kicked off his shoes and pants and is standing in his black T-shirt and a pair of boxer briefs that hug his muscular legs. Mystery solved about whether his tattoos extend beyond his arms. I clear my throat and look away from the blue jay gliding across his thigh. "You didn't want to go behind the car or something?" I ask, dragging my eyes to his face.

Luca looks down and shrugs. "I wear less than this at the beach." He takes his time stepping into the janitor coveralls and zipping them up. A name tag on the chest reads *Bob*. I guess Fabrizio didn't pilfer Malik's uniform when he stole the badge.

And then I realize I'm still standing there watching Luca, so I quickly spin around and move behind the car to change into my scrubs. I slide out of my jeans, taking another quick glance around for security cameras. When I've pulled on the scrubs and tucked my jeans into Luca's car, I use the side mirror to twist my hair into a tight bun and arrange the surgical cap over it. If anyone actually catches a glimpse of my ID badge in person, I'm done for. But maybe if I keep my hair covered, they won't be able to identify me in a lineup later.

And then I wonder if there's time to grab my to-do list from my bag and add *find a good lawyer* before we head inside. I'm not this person who impersonates strangers and breaks and enters. I eat all my vegetables and go to bed by ten. If I do this, I really *could* be arrested and lose my job.

But if I don't do it, I could lose everything.

"You ready?" Luca asks when I meet him on the other side of the car.

"Not really," I mumble, shaking a little as I pull the security badge over my head.

"You'll be great," Luca says. "Everything will be fine." He reaches out to squeeze my hand, and a warm glow drifts up my arm and settles in my chest. I squeeze his hand back, grateful for his presence. I am deeply skeptical that everything will be fine, but it's nice to know I'll have a companion in the back of the cop car.

I take a shaky breath. "So, what's the plan now?"

"When we get near the hospital entrance, we'll split up. I'll go in the left door, and you go in the right. Just act like you're an ordinary doctor coming back from your break. We'll meet up at the elevator and take it down to the basement together."

"Okay," I say, slightly breathless.

"Whatever you do, just pretend you belong."

He says that like I know what it means.

We head across the parking lot and, like Luca laid out for me, we veer off and go our separate ways, entering the hospital through different doors. I hesitate briefly in the lobby, eyeing the security guard at the desk by the entrance, half expecting him to jump up and arrest me right then and there. But his gaze drifts past me as he casually scans the room, so I keep walking and stop at the elevator.

I sense someone approach from my right, and out of the corner of my eye, I see a flash of blue coveralls. It's Luca, coming from his entrance on the other side of the lobby, but I focus on pressing the elevator button, and I don't meet his eyes. The doors open, and Luca and I step on, still not making eye contact. Instead, I look at the buttons. In addition to floors two through ten, our options are G—the floor where we got on—and B, for basement. The elevator begins to close, and I reach for the B. But just as I'm about to push the button, a hand appears between the doors, and they bounce open again. My shoulders stiffen as a handsome blond man in blue scrubs and a white lab coat steps on.

"Going up or down?" he asks.

I shoot a quick glance at Luca. If I say we're going down, is he going to wonder why a doctor and a janitor are riding down to the basement together? "Uh, up?" I blurt out, slamming my hand on the button with the number ten.

The guy nods and pushes the number seven. Then he looks at Luca. "You?"

Luca gives him a nod. "Also ten."

We settle in, facing the doors as they close, Luca on the right, the blond doctor in the middle, and me on the left. There's a moment of silence as we slowly ascend past floors two and then three. The blond guy looks over at me. "Which department?"

"What?" I look up blankly.

"Which department do you work in?"

I remember Dr. Dawson's badge around my neck. Thankfully, we're all facing the front, so he can't see it. Still, I flip it around and cross my arms over it. "Um. I work in—" My mind whirs. *What should I say?* What if I name a department, and that's where *he* works? "Uhhh."

I start to panic, and suddenly, I can't remember the name of *any* medical department at all. Luca clears his throat as if to nudge me along. I start to sweat.

And then—*thank the Lord*—the blond doctor slaps a hand on his forehead. "Duh, how dumb of me. You're going to the tenth floor. You must be in neurology."

"*Yes!*" I seize on that answer. "I'm in neurology. That's it exactly. Uh—you?"

He puffs up his chest just a little. "I'm in emergency medicine."

I remember the blinking red sign near the entrance. "Isn't emergency on the first floor? Not seven?"

Luca clears his throat again, and I get the message. *Stop engaging, Catherine.* Too late now.

The doctor looks at me sideways. "I'm headed up to the cafeteria. It's on seven?" He says it like I should know that.

"Of course. The cafeteria. I forgot. I'm, uh, I'm new here."

The elevator begins to slow, and the numbers above the door show we're approaching floor seven.

"I could have guessed that," the blond doctor says. The doors slide open, and he steps out but turns to look at me. "I'd definitely remember seeing you around."

Luca gives an awkward cough.

"Oh," I murmur, pressing a hand over Dr. Dawson's ID, just in case. "That's—uh. Thanks?"

The doors start to close, but the doctor shoves his hands between them, and they slide open again. "Since we're here, do you want to grab a coffee?"

My eyes widen. "Gosh. I'd love to, but sorry. I can't. Off to perform an emergency brain surgery." I hold my hands up in an exaggerated shrug. "You know how it is." And then I remember I've left my ID badge exposed and slam my hand back over it.

The doctor nods. "Sure." He takes a step back, and I breathe out a sigh. But my relief is premature, because then he reaches between the closing doors again. "Maybe tomorrow? Same time?"

With a grunt, Luca reaches out and hits the "close door" button. "I really should be going. Emergency spill on ten." He holds his hands up in an exaggerated shrug, a mirror of mine a moment ago. "You know how it is."

"Right. Sorry." I turn to the doctor. "Sure," I blurt out to move this along. "See you tomorrow."

The blond doctor gives me a shiny white grin. "I'll be looking forward to it." With a wink, he pulls his hand from the door, letting it slide closed.

I slump back against the wall. "That was close. I almost forgot to hide my badge."

Luca's sneakered foot is tapping on the floor, and a muscle twitches in his jaw. "I can't believe that guy just hit on you."

"Well, I wouldn't worry about it since Dr. Daphne Dawson is rudely going to be a no-show tomorrow." I adjust my surgical cap, hoping that no blond strands have slipped out.

"Still, it seems presumptuous of him, don't you think?" Luca crosses his arms over his coveralls, and if I didn't know better, I'd think he was—jealous? But that's ridiculous, because Luca definitely doesn't have any reason to be jealous of a guy I met on an elevator when I was in the middle of pulling off a heist.

The elevator rises to the tenth floor, and we stay on it as the doors open and close. Luca hits the B button, waves his ID card to gain access, and we head down to the basement. I begin to worry that someone else might hop on and we'll end up riding up and down on this thing all night, but I don't have to worry. It's close to one in the morning, and we make it to the basement without incident.

Luca and I step out into an empty hallway with dingy pale-blue-painted walls, a scuffed gray tile floor, and a dim fluorescent overhead light that buzzes slightly and flickers just faintly enough to make me wonder if it's my anxiety messing with me. The elevator doors close behind us with a whoosh that sounds louder than it did on the upper floors, and I give a startled jump. Luca glances in my direction.

"You going to be okay?"

"I hope so."

He gives me an encouraging smile.

"How are you so calm?" I ask, eyeing him standing there, seemingly cool and collected. "Have you ever done this before?"

"What? Dress like a janitor? No, but I'm really digging these coveralls."

"*No.*" But despite myself, I laugh. "I mean breaking and entering."

He shrugs. "I used to do a little freelancing for Uncle Vito. But I'm retired now." And then he turns to wander off down the hall.

Dazed, I follow behind with absolutely no idea if he's joking or not.

Ahead of us is a long hallway with nondescript gray doors situated about every twenty feet along the way. "Okay," I say. "I guess we just need to find the one that leads to the file room? Fabrizio said they'd be marked."

We walk past some spare hospital beds lined up against the wall and approach the first door. "This is…" I flinch.

"*The morgue*," I whisper-yell. My gaze slides to those hospital beds, and I stumble backward into Luca. "Fabrizio didn't tell us the morgue would be down here!"

"You've had your head buried in a math book for too long and clearly need to catch up on your crime thrillers," Luca whispers back. "Of course the morgue is down here. It's always in the basement for peak creepiness."

I press my ear to the door. "Do you think anyone is in there?" I whisper.

"I imagine there are a lot of people in there, but none of them will be talking."

A shiver runs through me. "I mean *live* people. Like a coroner."

"Probably not at this time of night." He gives me a light nudge toward the next door. "But we should get moving just in case."

SUPPLY STORAGE the next sign reads. We move to the next. FILE STORAGE.

"This is it!" I try the door, but of course it's locked, just like Fabrizio said it would be. "Let me just text Donnie. He'll let us in." I say it confidently, like Donnie and I are old friends. With the scrap of paper Fabrizio gave me in one hand, I enter the number into my phone with the other. And then I hesitate. Is there some sort of code word I should use? If they subpoena my phone, it probably won't look good if I've texted, *OPEN THE DOOR, DONNIE.*

Finally, I settle on *Here*. Short and to the point.

A thumbs-up emoji appears, and a second later, the door clicks. I push it open and step into the middle of a dark room. The slant of light from the hallway gives me a quick glimpse of file boxes before Luca follows me inside and lets the door swing shut behind us.

We're plunged into pitch darkness.

"Shit," he mutters. And then he crashes into me from behind. His elbow hits my shoulder, jerking my arm forward, and my phone slips from my hand and clatters to the floor.

"Oh no." I crouch down and feel around on the cold tile, trying to locate it, but I come up empty. "We need to find a light switch. Or open the door again."

"Shhhh," he whispers. "I can't open the door."

"Why are you whispering?" I whisper.

"Shhhh!"

"Is someone out there? Can you at least find a light?" I slap my hand on the ground, still searching for my phone.

I hear Luca moving, feel him shuffling directly behind me. Hopefully, he's looking for a wall with a switch on it. But the next thing I know, two bony objects—probably his knees—connect with my back, and Luca trips, falling forward. I go sprawling, and he lands right on top of me.

"Ow," I whisper, struggling to sit up, but his weight presses down on me.

"Shit, are you okay?" Luca asks, and I feel his warm hand slide down my back through the thin material of my scrub shirt. He presses gently, as if he's blindly checking me for injuries.

I do my best to flip over but quickly realize my mistake. Because now, in the complete darkness, his hand is sliding up the front of me. It brushes the side of my breast before finding my shoulder and curling around it. I shiver, though my body is quickly heating up.

"Um, I guess so," I manage. He's still half sprawled on top of me, his breath warm near my ear, our legs tangled together. I still can't see a thing, but I'm aware of every hard plane of his body, and *okay* isn't exactly the word to describe what I'm feeling.

"Why were you crouching on the floor?" he whispers in my ear, and the stubble on his cheek brushes the side of my face.

"I dropped my phone when you ran into me. Where's yours?" I reach out a hand as if I'm looking for his phone. But I'm not going to lie; a little part of me just wants an excuse to run my palm down *his* chest.

His breath hitches, just the tiniest bit. "Uh, I left it in my jeans. In the car."

"Why did you let the door close before we could turn on a light?"

He shifts above me. "I heard another door open down the hall."

"From the *morgue*?" I shudder. "You said nobody would be in the morgue at one in the morning."

"Yeah." Luca breathes out a laugh. "It's probably a ghost."

"*Stop it.*" I reach out in the darkness, and this time I give him a shove. "Don't tell me you believe in ghosts."

"Of course I do."

"Well, not me." I hesitate. "But if I *did*, I'd definitely expect to find one in a creepy hospital basement in the pitch darkness."

Luca laughs again, pushing himself to a seated position and pulling me along with him. I expect him to let go, but his hand stays firmly wrapped around my shoulder. "Cather-ine." His voice is more subdued now.

"Yeah?" For some reason, it comes out breathless.

"I'm really glad to be here with you."

Somehow, I know he doesn't mean he's glad to sit on a cold tile floor being stalked by ghosts in a creepy hospital basement. He's glad to be with *me*, wherever we are. This fills my chest with warmth and makes me feel strangely like crying at the same time.

"I'm really glad to be with you, too," I whisper, reaching for his hand because I can't meet his eyes, and I need to show him what I'm feeling. He laces his fingers with mine.

"I guess we should find your phone and face these files," he says with a sigh.

I reluctantly pull away and feel around on the floor again.

"Found it," Luca says a minute later. He stands, clicking on the light and setting the phone on top of a box so it bathes the room in a soft blue glow.

I do a slow spin in the center of the room, staring at the contents. "Oh my God."

"Oh boy," Luca mutters.

The file boxes that I'd caught a short glimpse of before we were plunged into darkness are piled *everywhere*, one on top of the other, shoved into every available corner, practically towering overhead. It looks like a hoarder lives here. I step toward one of the piles and check out the label on the side. *Da-Dal*, the label reads. Okay, so this box must contain files for people whose name begins with D. But there must be ten or fifteen boxes just for the Ds. And there are twenty-five other letters in the alphabet. Next to the Ds sit the Rs. Nothing is in order.

"I was expecting a filing cabinet or something. We'll be here all night." I turn to Luca, who is staring at the boxes with the same wide-eyed expression that must be stamped on my face. "I'm sorry, Luca. I can't ask you to do this. It's too...disorganized."

His lips quirk.

"What?"

"You're okay with breaking and entering, but you draw the line at disorganization?"

"No." I pause. "Yes." I *do* hate disorganization. What do these people have against filing cabinets?

As if he can read my mind, Luca gives a sharp laugh. "You should have brought your label maker."

"Hey," I protest. "My label maker is actually very useful." I check out the boxes again, and then something occurs to me. "Wait. How did you know I have a label maker?"

"I didn't until right now." His shoulders shake.

I give him a light shove on his shoulder and turn around to survey the room. It really is a complete mess.

"We can do this," Luca says, walking over to a pile of boxes and scanning the labels. "We just need to find the Ls, right? For Lipton?" He shoves two boxes to the side and peers at the ones behind it. "How hard could it be?"

An hour later, we finally locate the Ls, but of course they're in the very back of the room, shoved up against the wall, and with a whole row of other boxes in the way. Luca begins dragging them to the middle of the room, and I move in to help him. My shoulder bumps his, and I feel that same heat zing through me as I did when he took my hand earlier, and when his palm landed on my stomach in the dark.

Luca drags the Le-Ll box to the middle of the room and tosses the lid to the side. I peer in, flipping through the files. Libby...Lily...

And then, there it is. Lipton, Catherine Moonstone.

I pull the file from the box and wave it in the air. "Found it." I sink down on an F box to take a closer look.

Luca sits next to me on H and peers over my shoulder. "Wait." Luca reaches for the file. "Your middle name is Moonstone?"

I yank the file away. "Maybe."

"When were you going to tell me that?"

"Approximately never."

He makes another grab for the file. "I mean, you know my nickname is Elbow, yet you didn't feel the need to share that you have the most amazing middle name ever?"

"You already heard my dad call me Kitty Cat. What more do you want to know about me?"

"Everything, Moonstone." He leans in. "I want to know *everything*." There's something in his voice, a slight edge to it that tells me he's not joking.

I look away and flip the folder open. The first paper is a document listing basic information about newborn Catherine Moonstone Lipton. My name, obviously. Date of birth, birth weight, and height.

Next are my parents' names. I scan past them. But then I stop.

Wait.

I go back.

Parents' names.

My eyes widen. Because my father's name is listed just as I expected. Andrew John Lipton. But where my mother's name is supposed to be...

"Oh my God, Luca."

"What? What is it?" He leans in.

"Look at my mother's name."

Luca's eyes roam across the page and then snap to mine. "Shouldn't it say..."

"Yes."

Except it doesn't.

Luca stares at the page. "Didn't the copy of your birth certificate say your mother's name is Michelle Jones?"

I manage a tiny nod. "It did."

"So, who is Melanie Jankowski?"

"She...she must be my mother."

CHAPTER 15

Are you going to be okay?"

It's three in the morning, and Luca is standing outside my apartment door. I'm still wearing my scrubs, clutching a file folder to my chest. A file folder that reveals that I've been googling the wrong name for decades. That my birth certificate—the copy, anyway—was a lie. In some ways, my whole life has been a lie.

I'm not really sure what "okay" looks like at this point.

I hesitate in the doorway, tempted to invite him in for a drink. I have a bottle of red wine I bought to celebrate when I received the offer from the mathematics department, but I never drank it. Dad was off at the Shanti Festival, and in the end, it seemed kind of depressing to drink alone.

My gaze slides over the janitor coveralls that Luca's unzipped and folded down to reveal his black T-shirt beneath. He's already spent his night breaking and entering on my behalf. I'm sure he wants to get to bed, either his own, or maybe that friend on the eleventh floor's. "I'll be fine," I lie.

"Are you going to try calling your dad again?" Luca asks.

I called Dad twice from Luca's car on the drive home, but he didn't answer. It could be because he's asleep. Or isn't Burning Man this week? I have no idea.

I sigh. "Yes, but to be honest, I don't have high hopes for that conversation." It's not like I can accuse Dad of lying to me, because he's never told me anything about my mom to begin with. Not a single thing. But it's still a shock to find out that my birth certificate was essentially a forgery. I guess that explains why I only ever had a photocopy.

Luca takes a step closer, his gaze locking on to mine. "You know what you need?"

I've spent enough time with Luca to know literally anything could come out of his mouth right now. So I just shake my head.

He reaches for my hand. "You're not afraid of heights, are you?"

I don't know what to say to that, both because I'm trying to work out where he could possibly take me at three in the morning where a fear of heights could be an issue, and because a little zing of electricity shoots through me as his hand closes around mine. "I—no."

"You sure?"

"I once sailed across a warehouse on a trapeze swing, hanging on only by my knees."

Luca opens his mouth to say something and then stops. "Really?" he finally manages.

I admit I enjoy seeing his forehead crease and his head tilt as he tries to work out what to make of this information. "Really."

His grin widens. "I'm going to watch you do that someday."

"You absolutely are not."

"We'll see." He tightens his grip on my hand. "In the meantime, come with me."

I set the file folder inside my apartment and let him tug me back into the hall to a window at the end. As Luca releases the locks and slides it open, I remember making a note of all the ways to get out of the building in the event of a fire, and this window was on my list. Luca grabs the frame and pulls himself out onto the metal slats of a fire escape. I mirror his motion, climbing up next to him.

It's a warm August evening, and the humidity envelops us as soon as we're outside, mingling with the scent of basil and mint growing in pots on the stairs. I should say something to Luca about that, mention that someone could trip over them, but then I remember all the ways I broke the rules today, and I decide to keep it to myself. Besides, I have other things to worry about, like the fact that we're eight stories up and I may have miscalculated my fear of heights. The street looks awfully far below us. We're much higher above the ground than the aerial silks and trapeze swings at ArtSpace. I grab the iron railing for balance. Luca's arm slides around my waist, pulling me sideways against him.

"You okay? It's disorienting the first time you look down."

I nod, leaning into Luca's solid frame. His citrus scent blends with the herbs, making me lightheaded for an entirely different reason.

"Stay on the inside of the steps." Luca angles me toward the stairs, and I guess this means we're going higher. We zigzag back and forth up the rickety iron fire escape, past the windows that open to floors above mine, finally arriving at the platform that leads to the roof. Luca hops gracefully over a low brick wall and lands on the flat, rubbery surface that stretches over the top of the building. Then he turns to help me across. I keep my eyes trained on his so I don't accidentally peer down through the disorienting sliver of space between the fire escape and the wall as I clamber across.

On the other side, I find my footing, but I don't step away from the circle of Luca's arms. I still don't know why he brought me here, but at the moment, I don't really care.

He takes me by the shoulders and gently turns me toward the edge of the rooftop. "Catherine," Luca whispers. "Look around you."

For the first time since my shaky ascent of the fire escape, I focus on the view, letting out a gasp.

The entire neighborhood unfolds before me. To my right, rows upon rows of slanted rooftops form a jumble of angled shapes under the glow of streetlights. To my left, Liberty Avenue stretches in the distance, the arched windows of the old brick buildings lit up by the occasional lamp in a window, the church steeples shadowed against the night sky. And beyond, past one of the city's dozens of bridges, the lights of the university's cathedral sparkle like diamonds on the hillside.

"Oh, Luca." I grab for his arm. "This is amazing."

"Beautiful, right?"

"I had no idea the building had this view. I didn't even know you could come up here." I do a slow spin, taking it all in.

"It's the tallest building in the neighborhood. You can see for miles."

I tilt my head back. The sky is clear tonight, and thousands of lights shimmer overhead. "Living in the middle of the city, I never really think to look up and see the stars."

"Down there, the streetlights block them out. But sometimes you just need to see it from a different angle."

Luca has shown me the world from so many different angles. "Thank you for bringing me to this special place."

"I can't think of anyone I'd rather show it to." He tucks my hand in the crook of his arm and leads me across the roof to a metal lounge chair covered by a durable canvas cushion. "Would you like to sit?" Luca brushes a stray leaf to the ground. "Sorry, there's only one chair. I usually come up here alone, but I'm happy to share if you are."

I slide onto the lounge and move over to make room.

The cushion sinks under his weight as Luca sits beside me. He slips his arm behind my back, and I settle against his chest, my thigh pressed to his. Through the thin cotton of his T-shirt, I feel the warmth of his skin and the beat of his heart beneath my hand. "Do you come here a lot?"

He nods. "I discovered the roof access when I was a kid playing on the fire escape, and I started climbing up here when I needed a little break from my family." He gives me a sideways grin and an eye roll. Since I've met the Morellis... so many Morellis... I smile back. "I kept a bin of sketch pads and an old beach chair up here, and I'd come up and draw for hours."

Just beyond where he sits, I spot a waterproof box on the ground. Through the translucent plastic, I can make out piles of sketchbooks and various drawing implements—charcoal, pencils, pens. It looks like he still comes up here to draw.

"My grandpa found me up here one day, and that's when he discovered I had a talent for drawing."

Though he smiles at the memory, I can sense his sadness. Shifting a little, I reach out to take his hand and weave our fingers together. Luca's thumb strokes against my palm, and it feels like the most natural thing in the world. "I bet your grandpa was so proud of you."

"He was." Luca's chest rises and falls. "There's a little art shop over on Walnut Street, and I think he walked there once a month to buy me new supplies. Every time I showed up at his place, he had a new sketch pad or charcoal pencil for me to try."

My heart aches for Luca's incredible loss.

"When he died last year and we cleaned out his place," Luca continues, "I found piles of my artwork in the cabinet, all organized and labeled by year."

"Where is it now?"

"I put it in my mom's attic." Luca shakes his head. "I just couldn't face it, you know?"

I remember the conversation when Luca said he'd planned to do an art show, but it hadn't worked out. "Is that why your show was canceled last year? Because it was too painful to go ahead with it?"

Luca hesitates and then nods. "He was my biggest fan. It wouldn't have been the same without him. But…" He sighs. "I know he wouldn't have wanted me to keep it packed away forever."

My gaze shifts to the box of art supplies. I'm dying to open it and pore over every one of Luca's sketches. "Would you be willing to show me a few of your drawings?"

A week ago, I never would have imagined asking him to share something so private and important. But now, I can't imagine *not*. Though I've only known Luca for a couple of months and have only *really* known him for a couple of days, this friendship matters to me. *Luca* matters to me. I didn't grow up with a lot of friends, and though I dated in college and grad school, I was too busy to ever get close to anyone. Sitting here with Luca, the buildings lit up in the background, the stars sparkling overhead, I feel a wave of gratitude that this person quite literally stumbled into my life. He's shown up for me again and again, and I want to do the same for him.

He tilts his head to meet my eyes. "Yeah? You really want to?"

I sit up. "Of course I do." These drawings are a window into Luca, and I want to open it and climb inside.

Luca reaches for the box next to him. I slide to the foot of the lounge chair and sit cross-legged so I'm facing him, the box between us. Slowly, he lifts the lid. I hold back, giving him a moment to sort through a couple of the sketchbooks, his brows knitting together nervously. Finally, he chooses one, takes a deep breath, and hands it to me.

I flip the cover open, and the air whooshes from my lungs. On the page in front of me is a delicate drawing of a bird in motion. The lines are sketched in pencil, or charcoal maybe, darker in some places and lighter in others, showing the bird as it descends toward a flat surface on the bottom of the page. Its wings curve back, tail feathers strain forward, and something about the grace of its movement reminds me of Luca.

"It's gorgeous, Luca." I reach out to touch his arm. "The way you've captured the bird's motion. I want to keep watching it settle peacefully before its whir of activity starts up again."

He gives me a smile that tells me I understand exactly what he was going for. "There was a whole summer when I was in high school that that guy kept me company up here on the roof, always flitting around me or landing on the foot of my chair." Luca reaches over to give the page an affectionate pat. "That was the start of my bird-drawing phase. When fall came, I guess he flew south. I still think about him. Sometimes when I climb up here, I still hope to see him hanging out on the wall."

Nothing about this story surprises me. Luca has a way of connecting with just about everyone he comes into contact with, whether that's the older people in the building or three-hundred-pound bouncers at a club. Of course even a bird would be drawn to him.

I tilt my head toward the sketchbook to hide the emotions on my face, flipping the page to the next. And this time, I gasp out loud. It's a drawing of a young woman gazing down at a sleeping baby in her arms. The baby is tiny—a newborn, maybe—and the woman looks tired but captivated. With just a handful of simple lines, Luca has captured all the love and worry and fear that I imagine a new mother must feel.

And then I realize she looks familiar. "Ginny and Angelo?"

Luca nods. "I came up here and drew that one on the day he was born."

"Has Ginny seen this?" My voice grows hoarse. I swipe a palm at the moisture gathering under my eyes.

Luca shakes his head. "I haven't really shared these kinds of drawings with anyone, except my grandpa. And now you."

"No wonder your grandpa was proud of you. These are stunning, Luca. They take my breath away." I look up, and the lights from the distant buildings shimmer in his eyes. I've never been so drawn to someone in my life. He takes my breath away, too. And he's looking at me like I do the same to him.

Luca slowly takes the sketchbook from my hands, setting it back in the bin and sliding the whole thing to the ground. We're facing each other on the chair, our knees just touching in the middle. He reaches out, cupping my cheek in the warmth of his palm. I lean forward, closing the distance between us. Our lips meet, gentle, hesitant. We pull apart, and then Luca gives me that smile. The crooked one that makes me feel like there's nobody else but the two of us, right here in this moment.

He pulls me in again, and I meet him halfway, more urgently now, my palms fisting his shirt to hold on tighter. We fall back against the lounge chair, me leaning against the headrest, Luca propped over me, one hand woven in my hair. With the stars winking overhead, his mouth finds mine, and we stay here, tangled up together until my lips are swollen, cheeks raw from his unshaven face, and the black sky begins to glow on the horizon.

Finally, Luca pulls back, but I can tell he's reluctant. "It's five in the morning." He slides a hand to my cheek. "You've had a long day. I should get you to bed."

"Um," I mumble. *Yes, please.*

He gives me a grin that tells me he knows what I'm thinking. "I meant to *sleep*, Moonstone."

I sigh. As much as I'd love to stay here with Luca on this magical rooftop, or to crawl into bed with him and forget about everything else, I have an identity to save and a dad to track down in a couple of hours.

We climb back down the fire escape to the eighth floor and slip in the window. And then we're standing in front of my door just as we were before, but somehow in the span of a couple of hours, my night has been completely transformed. There's still the shock of finding out about my mother, but it feels less heavy now. I feel less alone. "Thank you, Luca."

"For what?" He cocks his head.

"For sharing your drawings with me. For turning this night into something wonderful."

He presses a gentle kiss to my lips. "You're going to be okay?"

I nod. "I am now." I take a step back and open my door. On the floor is the red file folder, right where I left it before we climbed to the roof. I bend down to pick it up.

Luca eyes it for a second. "You know, that file lists your mom's name. But it also lists an address in Pittsburgh, right?"

I flip open the folder and scan the first page. He's right, there's an address for Melanie Jankowski. In my shock at learning her real name, I forgot about the address. "I think it's a street in Shadyside."

"Maybe we should drive over there and check it out."

I take a shaky breath. The address is so close, we could almost walk. "Do you think someone might still live there?"

"It was thirty years ago, so I know it's a long shot. But worth a try." He leans in and cups a hand against my cheek. "Get some sleep and then meet me in the lobby at five o'clock this evening."

I nod, still staring at the address. "Okay," I whisper.

Luca heads toward the elevator, and I quietly close the door and then lean back against it, still feeling the pressure of his mouth against mine. Though I'm completely exhausted, a thrill runs through me. Whatever this is with Luca feels completely right. And in about twelve hours, I might finally have answers to questions about my mother that I've been carrying for my entire life. It's almost too good to be true.

I push away from the door and head to bed. I have a big day ahead of me.

CHAPTER 16

I sleep for a few hours and wake to find that Dad hasn't responded to any of my texts or voicemail messages about the birth certificate bombshell. I guess I'll have to go find him in person. The elevator appears to be on the fritz again, so I take the stairs. In the lobby, I find Mrs. Goodwin sitting on a bench.

"Hi," I say. "Are you waiting for an elevator? I think it's broken again."

Mrs. Goodwin's eyes widen, and she puts a finger to her lips, indicating that I should be quiet. "You don't want to wake him," she whispers.

"Wake who?" I ask, but in a lowered voice.

She waves at the front desk. I don't see anything unusual, but then it comes to me. Of course. I round the counter and find Luca asleep on the floor. He's still wearing his janitor costume from the night before. Under his head, he's tucked his black hoodie and wrapped one arm protectively around it. His dark hair flops over his forehead, and long eyelashes cast shadows on his cheeks.

I can't help but stare. He usually has that teasing grin on his face, and it's startling to see him looking so peaceful. I'm tempted to pull the blanket up higher and tuck it around him. I'm tempted to climb into his nest next to him.

Instead, I turn to Mrs. Goodwin. "He had a late night," I whisper.

Her eyebrows rise. "Did he, now?"

My cheeks flush. "I didn't mean like that." But then I pause, a little smile tugging at my lips at the memory of his mouth pressing against mine, the warm breeze teasing my hair, the city sparkling in the background. I didn't *not* mean like that, either.

Mrs. Goodwin gives me a knowing look. "Well, let's definitely not disturb him then," she whispers.

I glance back at Luca. "Why does he sleep on the floor? He said he has an apartment upstairs." Is it possible that's not really true? Maybe he really is homeless and doesn't want anyone to know?

But Mrs. Goodwin nods. "He does. On two."

"So why..."

She shushes me again.

"Sorry." I lower my voice to a whisper. "Are you waiting here because the elevator is broken again?"

"No." She nods at a couple of boxes next to the bench. "Luca was going to carry those over to the community center for me. I have some donations for the fundraiser. We're doing an auction. Eleanor up on five donated some of her designer clothes from the sixties. She was a fashionable lady."

"Oh." I glance at Luca again, and his chest rises and falls rhythmically. "I hate to wake him. Maybe I can carry the boxes." I pick them up, and though they're a little bulky, they're not too heavy. With another glance at Luca, who hasn't stirred, I follow Mrs. Goodwin out the door.

The community center is around the corner from the DeGreco in a sprawling redbrick building that looks like it used to be a Catholic school. Large, curved windows reveal high ceilings, and the original brickwork looks to be in great shape. A wooden wheelchair ramp has been added to the front, but otherwise, everything still looks original. I can see why developers want to buy the place and turn it into condos; they'd probably go for a million dollars each. I realize how lucky I am to have found an affordable apartment at the DeGreco since so many people are getting priced out. It must be especially hard for all the families with multiple generations rooted here to see their neighbors unable to afford their homes anymore.

Inside the building, we approach a front desk, and a sixty-something Black woman with graying hair and a purple tracksuit greets us. Mrs. Goodwin introduces her as Mrs. Flowers.

"This is Catherine," Mrs. Goodwin tells her. "She's a special friend of Luca's." Turning toward Mrs. Flowers, she cups a hand around her mouth. "They were out late together last night."

"Ohhhh," Mrs. Flowers says, clapping her hands together. "Any special friend of Luca's is a friend of ours."

I imagine Luca has flirted with everyone at this community center, just like he has with the residents of the DeGreco. Knowing Luca, he's probably made his way down the block, tossing his charm like candy at the Memorial Day parade. Of course they love him. But my heart warms at the way they automatically welcome me just by association.

Mrs. Goodwin gestures at an upholstered chair. "Wait here, Catherine. I'll go get the key to the storage closet."

I set the boxes on a table and sit down near a group of older people in a small sitting area. Someone has moved aside a couple of chairs to accommodate one of the women's wheelchair, and everyone forms a neat circle around a coffee table with teacups and paperbacks scattered on top. I check out the books and realize that all of them match. On each cover, a muscular man in old-fashioned breeches and a flowing white shirt unbuttoned to the waist clutches a long-haired woman in a torn blue gown. His chest glistens in the sunlight, and her bosom heaves.

The Viscount's Secret. I read that one in high school.

"Montague should have told Penelope about his past before he deflowered her," an older Indian woman in a red kurta argues passionately. "She had a right to know."

The plot of the book starts to come back to me.

"He couldn't tell her until he trusted her completely," the white woman in a blue dress argues.

"I didn't like that Montague," the silver-haired white man in the navy sweater says, slapping a mottled hand down on the book cover for emphasis. I realize I'm completely eavesdropping on their conversation now. "He was so in love with that house of his. Always fixing it up and worrying over the renovations. He loved that house more than Penelope."

I can't help but cut in now. "He didn't love it more than her. It was a symbol of his happy childhood from before his mother passed and he had to live with his domineering father." I turn in my chair to look at the group. "He fixed it up to try to re-create the idyllic days of his youth. But what he didn't realize was the house would never fill the hole in his heart. Only Penelope could do that."

"Well, I'll be damned." The older Black man sits up, straightening the hem of his white button-up shirt. "I think she's right."

"The house was a *symbol*," murmurs the woman who had objections to the deflowering.

"Exactly." I point at the book in her hand. "When the house was burning, and the evil Archibald kidnapped Penelope, Montague could only choose one to save: his beloved house or his true love."

"And in the end, he chose Penelope," the first man chimes in.

"Yes. Because she represented love and happiness. He didn't need that house anymore."

The entire book club is staring at me.

My teenage love of romance novels isn't something anyone would have guessed about me with my pile of math books and my seat in the front of the class, hand perpetually raised. But while Dad's friends were certainly comfortable with their nudity—growing up, I saw enough skin at Burning Man to last me a lifetime—I didn't have a mother to answer my questions about sex and love. Luckily, Dad's friend Frenchy Kiss stepped in, making sure I had a firm grasp of the basics and giving me a pile of romance novels to fill in the blanks. The viscount, his virgin bride, and their wealthy, titled friends were a font of information.

"I'm Walt Offerman," the blue-sweatered man says, and then he goes around the circle and introduces the others. He gestures to the woman in the red kurta. "This is

Seema." He points to the woman in the dress. "Dolores. And my husband, Martin," he finishes, referring to the man in the white shirt. "Our book club meets once a week. Next week, we're reading *The Highlander's Baby*. You want to join us?"

I read that one in high school, too, and it's probably still in a box in Dad's apartment. The thought of Dad pulls me back to my current predicament. I need to finish helping Mrs. Goodwin and find Dad to get some answers about my mother. And then, by this time next week, I plan to be back at work, teaching my mathematics classes and immersed in my research papers. I don't have time for *The Highlander's Baby*. But as I stand to pick up the boxes and find Mrs. Goodwin, I wish I did.

"It was so nice talking to you about *The Viscount's Secret*, but I don't think I can," I say with real regret. "I'm about to start a new job at the university, and I've kind of got a lot going on right now."

"Wait a minute," comes a voice from behind me, and I turn around to find Mrs. Flowers approaching. "I overheard you mention your new job, and I just put it together. You're the Catherine who lost her identity."

"I—"

"That's *you*?" Dolores asks, like I'm some sort of celebrity. She smacks Walt on the arm. "Did you hear that? This is Luca's Catherine. The one who's trying to track down her birth certificate."

I'm momentarily distracted by *Luca's Catherine*. But then I focus on the other part. "How—how do you know about me?"

"We heard from Ruth, who runs the bingo games," Walt explains. "I think she heard from Vanessa over at the bank."

My head spins. *Ruth? Vanessa?* I've never met any of these people. But then I remember the front porches on Luca's childhood street, perfect for chatting with neighbors over coffee, and the Morellis stationed all over town. I guess in tight-knit communities, people talk.

"Listen, honey," Dolores says, reaching over to set her teacup on the table. "Don't let it get you down."

"That's right," Walt agrees. "You're in good hands with Vito. But I know a guy at the DMV, if that will help."

I look up. "Actually, it might."

Mrs. Flowers puts a hand on my shoulder. "And I heard that all your money is gone."

I look around the circle. They really know the whole story. "Unfortunately, yes."

"Well, the folks in the Meals on Wheels program have put together a little care package for you. Just to make sure you have enough to eat."

"Oh, that's really not necessary..." But I trail off, because what if it *is* necessary? Two hundred dollars isn't going to get me very far.

Mrs. Flowers raises a palm. "It's already done. They'll drop it off for you at the DeGreco when they do their rounds."

"Wow. Thank you. All of you."

"Nothing to thank us for," Walt says. "We look out for each other."

"You know where to find us," Seema chimes in. "Stop by if you need anything else."

Dazed, I pick up the boxes and head in the direction I saw Mrs. Goodwin go moments before. On my way down the hall, I pass a game room where several long tables are taken up with silver-haired older people stamping bingo cards while a younger woman calls out letters and numbers. *Ruth, I suppose.*

A few doors down, I can't help being drawn to the doorway of a gymnasium where a song by Lady Gaga blasts from the speakers. A woman who can't be much younger than Mrs. Goodwin directs twenty or thirty people—some standing, some sitting on chairs, and a few in wheelchairs—to shimmy their shoulders, get their hearts pumping, and "love yourselves!"

Everyone seems to be having a blast. The song switches from Lady Gaga to Britney Spears, and the exercise instructor switches from a shoulder shimmy to a bop. She spots me in the doorway and waves me inside. "Come on in and join us, honey!"

Juggling the pile of boxes, I shake my head and back up.

I find Mrs. Goodwin standing in a storage room full of what I presume to be donations for the fundraiser. "You can unload those and put the clothes over there." She points to an empty shelf.

I pull a couple of 1960s coats and dresses from the box. They're in good condition, and Mrs. Goodwin said the owner was known for her fashion, so I assume they're by some sort of famous designer. "Do you think all this stuff will fetch good money at your auction?" I ask, surveying the other shelves of donations. There are old watches, a couple of first-edition hardback books, and other stuff that was probably donated by the members of the community center and residents of the DeGreco.

"I think they'll do okay. But only if we can attract enough people to come to the fundraiser in the first place." Mrs. Goodwin pulls a dress out of the box and smooths the wrinkles. "Quite a few people from the neighborhood have bought tickets to support us, but we need a wider reach. Maybe a band or a comedian or someone to draw people in."

I nod, wishing I had something more to offer. But I'm the last person who can help. I have two hundred dollars in cash, and the only jokes I know fall along the lines of "Why is six afraid of seven? Because seven eight nine."

Nobody wants to hear math humor except Dad.

"This place seems to serve a lot of people." I remember Mrs. Goodwin telling me that loneliness is as bad for your health as smoking. If this community center closes down, where will the book club meet each week? And the exercise class? Will all those people just be stuck at home? Alone?

What about their community? What about looking out for each other?

"We serve over three hundred on a typical day. Plus, another hundred and fifty homebound seniors through the Meals on Wheels program. These days, Bloomfield makes the news because of the housing market." Mrs. Goodwin drops her hands to her hips. "But they never talk about the fact that we have one of the largest populations of seniors who are aging in place. If the community center isn't here to serve them, I worry many people will end up having to leave their homes and move to nursing facilities."

I can't imagine that anyone would have an opportunity to dance to Lady Gaga in a nursing facility. Again, I wish I had more to offer, but all I can do is help Mrs. Goodwin unpack the boxes and organize the donations.

And then I head out to grab the bus and find Dad, and hopefully some answers.

CHAPTER 17

When I walk into ArtSpace, the familiar smell of my childhood wafts over me. It's a bit musty, vaguely dank, and mixed with the sharp notes of oil paint and Chanel No. 5. That last scent comes from Ginger Ale, a busty redhead who rushes from her office to throw her arms around me.

"Kitty Cat!" She presses me against her bosom. "It's been ages!"

"Hi, Ginger," I say when she's finally released me from her grasp. "You look gorgeous as usual." I take in the auburn curls spilling over her shoulders, full crimson lips, and low-cut white lace blouse showing off her ample curves. It's the middle of the afternoon, so she's working in the office and not dressed in her burlesque costume. But as she used to tell me, *A woman is always in costume, Kitty Cat.*

"Oh." She waves me off. "You're gorgeous. Look at you all grown up. Andy says you're a math professor now?"

It *has* been ages, so I don't want to get into the whole story about my missing identity. "That's right. Over at the university."

"All the girls and I knew you'd accomplish great things, despite that ne'er-do-well father of yours." She winks a false eyelash at me, and I know she's joking about Dad. Everyone adores him, and he's been a staple of this place since its inception. Ginger opened ArtSpace decades ago—back when you could buy an old warehouse in Homewood practically for pennies—and she turned it into a place for artists and performers to collaborate. Her burlesque group practices here along with an aerial troupe, belly dancers, and, of course, the circus crowd.

"I'm proud of you," Ginger says, tucking my hair behind my ear.

A lump forms in the back of my throat. There was a time when I wished Dad and Ginger would get married so she could be my mom. That was in my elementary school era, when it seemed like every other week we were making Mother's Day crafts in art class or asking our moms to come in for story time or to chaperone field trips. I could have asked Dad, of course. But he would usually start juggling, disrupting the class, or he'd forget.

Ginger was the one who celebrated my first period with a shot of whiskey, and she took me to buy my first bra at the high-end lingerie shop with the leather and lace corset in the window. So I'm not sure she was ever going to be mom material, even if she and Dad had been more than just friends. But back then, my longing cut deep.

I swallow hard. "Is my dad here?"

Ginger gestures at the partition that separates the main warehouse from the lobby. "He's on the stilts today."

"Thanks."

I round the corner and enter a vast room with high ceilings, steel beams, and a concrete floor. Though it's the middle of the day and windows stretch halfway up the walls to the ceiling, they're cloudy and cracked, covered in decades of warehouse grit and plywood panels over broken sections. I blink in the dim light. When my eyes finally adjust, I spot my old homework table in the corner with its same paint-spattered surface and mismatched chairs. Ahead of me, aerial silks hang from the ceiling, and a couple of women in leggings and tank tops are practicing their spins.

Beyond them, I spot a twelve-foot man in a familiar fedora dancing to a song by Ziggy Marley.

Dad.

He spots me as I get closer, giving me a wave and holding up a finger to let me know he'll need a minute. I watch as he totters over to a tall wooden chair, bends down to grab the back, and somehow maneuvers himself to a seated position so he can unstrap the stilts from around his overall-clad thighs. It surprises me that even closing in on fifty, Dad is still this agile, while I have a perpetual pain in my back from hunching over my computer.

"Kitty Cat!" He leans the stilts against the wall and gives me a hug. "I'm the luckiest guy in the world to get to see you so many times this week."

He seems oblivious that anything is wrong. Given that I've been calling and texting him since last night, that could mean any number of things. It's possible he hasn't bothered to look at his phone, or maybe he lost it. It's also possible he's pretending like he didn't get my messages because he doesn't want to talk about this situation with my birth certificate and my mother. Either way, he's not going to feel so lucky to see me when he hears what I have to say.

I take a step back and wave my file folder in Dad's direction. "I just discovered that my birth certificate is a forgery, and the name I thought belonged to my mother is a lie. I need you to explain this."

Dad's eyes widen as they shift from my face to the file. "What is that? How did you find out?"

"It's my hospital birth records."

Dad's face goes pale. "Where—" He blinks rapidly. "Where did you get them?"

I open my mouth but then clamp it shut again. The thing is, Dad would probably be less concerned that I obtained this file by breaking and entering than the fact that I have it at all. He'd probably want to know all the details of how I pulled it off, and I'm not about to let him get distracted. "It doesn't matter where I got them. I need you to tell me the truth."

He tilts his head and rubs the back of his neck like stilt walking might not cause him pain, but *this* does. "I'm sorry, I can't."

I drop the file to my side. "What do you mean, you can't? How can you say that?"

"I'm sorry, Kitty Cat." Dad pulls two balls from his pocket and begins rotating them in his hand. He's done this my whole life. When he's not actually tossing juggling balls in the air, he's fidgeting with them. Right now, his fingers twitch as he spins the blue and green orbs in his palm. He doesn't meet my eyes, staring out across the warehouse as if he might find a way out of this conversation in the dust swirling through the streams of sunlight. Finally, he sighs. "I can't tell you anything. I promised."

"You promised *who*?" But then it comes to me, and my heart pitches. "My mother? You promised my mother?"

He looks away, which basically answers my question.

"But—*why*?" I demand. "Why would you promise that? And why would you still keep it up thirty years later?"

"I can't tell you that, either. But please listen to me, Catherine."

My head jerks up at the sound of my full name. He never, ever calls me Catherine.

"I promise you it's for your own good." Dad shoves the juggling balls back in his pocket and takes me by the shoulders. "Please believe me when I tell you not to contact her."

"Is she a criminal?" I ask, my voice shaking. "A serial killer?" Maybe he really has been protecting me all along.

"No, it's nothing like that." Up close, I can see tiny sunspots on his face, the effects of decades of performing outside in parks and on street corners. When his brow furrows, the lines deepen across his forehead. For the first time, my young, vibrant dad looks older. Tired. That realization tugs at my heart, and the anger seeps from my rigid shoulders.

"Then... why can't you tell me?"

"Look, Kitty Cat," Dad says, his eyes sad. "I know I wasn't a great father to you. I let you down a lot."

"You—did?" I whisper as I'm hit with a wave of emotion. Surprise that he's actually thought this deeply about his ability to parent me. Regret that I've put that shattered look on his face. I open my mouth to argue with him, to tell him he *was* enough, just to see his familiar smile again.

But then a few feet away, his stilts start to slide from their place against the wall. One knocks into the other, and they both crash to the floor. I jump out of the way before they can land on my foot.

"Sorry." He hurries over to pick them up and lean them in the exact same spot where they were when they fell the first time.

I'm reminded of growing up in apartments with all the tricks of his trade: juggling balls and Hula-Hoops, stilts and fire sticks. Pile of hats, suitcases, and other props lying scattered across the couch. My chest squeezes with that familiar anxiety. "I could lose my job. I could lose everything." My voice breaks at the end.

Dad presses his lips together, and for a moment, I think he might be wavering. But then he says, "Look, if all you need is a birth certificate, I know a guy."

My head jerks up. "You *do*?" Fleetingly, I wonder if Dad's guy is named Vito.

Dad nods. "When your mom and I had that copy made, it was thirty years ago. Technology is so much better now. They can make you a perfect dupe of a birth certificate, one with the same information you've been using all this time, but with the stamps and embossed seals and all of that. And then we can put an end to this."

I open the folder and pull out the copy with Michelle Jones's name on it. "Didn't you think anyone would ever notice this was a fake?" Maybe it was only a matter of time before this happened. It's not just the past couple of days that my identity has been missing. It turns out I've been walking around this way for my entire life.

"Well, to be fair," Dad says, "nobody *did* notice. When you went to school and they needed a copy of your birth certificate, I sent a photocopy. Nobody ever asked for the real thing. If it weren't for this weird glitch in the system, nobody would have ever been the wiser."

I stare down at the cut-rate copy of my birth certificate. Maybe Dad's right. If I really want my job back, if I really want to put an end to this, I know a guy, too. I bet Uncle Vito could get me an indistinguishable forgery of a birth certificate before I could even say "Pasta fazool." But it's not just about saving my job anymore.

"*I'm* the wiser," I whisper.

The thick, humid air of the warehouse surrounds me, more oppressive back here away from the door. My skin is clammy, sticky, and with that feeling comes another, equally familiar one. That constant ache in my gut telling me I don't belong. That I never fit. As I stand here in ArtSpace, while my whole life hangs in the balance, it all comes rushing back. Studying on that table in the corner while acrobats sailed overhead and stray juggling balls landed on my textbook. The constant thump of music vibrating in my chest as I tried to focus on my work. How I longed to be a normal kid with a normal kitchen table to do my schoolwork. And for a parent who cared if I actually passed the test.

Maybe it would have been different if I'd had friends at school who understood me. But to the smart, hardworking students, I was the weird clown's kid who was always missing school because I was off at a music festival. And to everyone else, I was the goody-goody sitting at the front of the class.

From somewhere far away, I hear the echo of my earlier conversation with Mrs. Goodwin. And that's when it hits me.

The loneliness.

My eyes burn for that kid just trying to hold it all together and wishing for someone who understood. And for the adult version who's spent most of her life doing pretty much the same. If loneliness is as bad for you as smoking, I feel like I've had a pack a day for three decades.

The stilts on the wall start to slide again, and those fantasies of my mother come back. The wild hope that someday we'll meet, and it will all make sense. She'll understand me, and I'll find where I fit.

Is this my chance? I can't smooth this over with another forgery. I need to know the truth.

My phone buzzes with a text from Luca.

Still on for 5 p.m.?

I wonder if he just woke up on the floor. At some point, I'm going to need to figure out why it is he's been sleeping there. But first I need to figure out my own life.

Yes. See you then.

I feel better after I hit send. Maybe Dad won't give me answers, but I'm not on my own. It turns out I don't just have a guy; I have a bunch of them. I picture Uncle Vito's scowling face, and in this moment, I find it strangely comforting instead of terrifying. And then there's Mrs. Flowers and the book club offering me food and advice. Fabrizio handing me a pair of scrubs in a dark parking lot. I have a whole group of people invested in helping me find my mother.

And it's all thanks to Luca.

"I should go," I tell Dad.

His shoulders slump. "I love you, Kitty Cat."

I sigh, because I know he does, in his own way. It's just not always in the way I need.

"If there's anything else I can do," he says, leaning over to hug me. "Just say the word." He begins absentmindedly tossing one of the juggling balls in the air.

"Sure." I head across the warehouse. When I'm halfway to the door, I pause and turn around. "Actually, maybe there is something else you could do for me."

He nods eagerly.

"Can you and your friends perform at a fundraiser for the Bloomfield Community Center next week?" I wave a hand around the room. "Bring anyone you can find— acrobats, dancers. They need it to be spectacular. And it would be great if everyone could help get the word out. Share it with your networks and help sell some tickets. It's for a good cause."

Dad flashes me a huge grin, the relief evident on his face. "Of course I can do that. And I know lots of people who will help."

CHAPTER 18

The elevator seems to be working again. At 4:55 p.m., I take it down to the lobby, and I'm surprised to find Luca perched at the front desk instead of off on his usual errands. Next to him sits an older woman in a wheelchair holding a hand of playing cards. When Luca deals her another card, she sets her hand face down on the table, shuffles the new one into her stack, and picks it up again, all using only her left arm. She uses her left elbow to nudge another dollar into the pile in the middle.

Luca looks at his cards, raises an eyebrow at the woman, and then tosses them face down on the desk. "You're too rich for my blood."

With a look of glee, the woman fans her cards face up on the table, and from where I'm standing, it looks like a random assortment of numbers and suits.

"Damn, you were bluffing." Luca shakes his head with admiration.

"That's right," she cackles, and her words come out slightly slurred.

Luca looks up and meets my eyes. "Catherine, this is my friend Mrs. Sterling."

She smiles at me, and only the left side of her face curves upward. "Hello," she says. My best guess is that she's had a stroke.

"It's nice to meet you."

"Catherine lives upstairs," Luca tells her.

Mrs. Sterling's smile widens. "Is this the girl you've been telling me about? The pretty one you have a crush on?"

Luca turns in my direction, his lips twitching in a hint of a smile. His eyes meet mine, and for a moment, I'm back on that narrow lounge chair on the roof, his body pressed against mine.

"Well, that answers my question," Mrs. Sterling says with another guffaw.

Luca clears his throat and begins stacking the cards. "You might have won this round, Mrs. S., but I expect a rematch tomorrow." He helps her gather up the dollar bills she's won and tuck them into the side pocket of the wheelchair. Finally, he raises his eyes to me. "I'm just going to get Mrs. Sterling back up to her apartment, and then we'll head out, okay?" Grasping the handles of her wheelchair, he pushes her toward the elevator.

Just as the door closes in front of them, the one to the stairwell swings open, and Sal wanders out.

"Catherine!" he says buoyantly.

"Hi." I gesture to the spot where Luca and Mrs. Sterling disappeared a moment ago. "The elevator is working now, you know. You don't need to take the stairs."

He waves me off. "Gotta get my steps in." He shuffles over to me. "So, how's the identity search going? You figure out who you are yet?" Between the people at the DeGreco, the community center, and apparently the whole neighborhood, I'm surprised he doesn't already know.

I hesitate before answering. I've always known who I am. It's the useless bureaucratic government system that seems confused. But then I remember the forged birth certificate and all of Dad's secrets. Maybe I'm not so sure who I am after all. "I hope I'm getting closer."

"Good, good." He reaches into his pocket and pulls out a butterscotch candy, presenting it to me on the palm of his hand.

"Thanks," I say, sliding it into my pocket.

Sal gives me a wave and heads toward the front door. "See you later."

"Do you want to stay and say hi to Luca? He should be back any minute."

"Nah," Sal says. "I'll see him when I get back. I've got to get to Banjo Night."

I saw a flyer for Banjo Night when I was at the community center earlier. Without a program like that, would Sal just be sitting home, alone? I hope Dad can get a good group of performers together to help out with the fundraiser. It's clear how important that place is to so many people in the neighborhood.

"Okay, have fun." I run over to the front door to open it for Sal.

"You and Luca have fun, too," he says as he walks past. And then he gives me a wink.

I feel my cheeks heat up again. I'm not surprised that everyone in the building knows Luca and I are spending time together. They're all talking about this identity mystery. But we only kissed for the first time twelve hours ago. I don't know how word traveled so fast. "We're just—" But Sal is already shuffling slowly down the block.

I hear the ding from the elevator and turn around just in time to see Luca step off.

"You ready?" He checks the time on his phone. "It's after five o'clock, and I'm officially off duty."

I glance down the sidewalk one more time to make sure Sal is okay, but he's moving faster than I expected and must have already turned the corner. I guess climbing those stairs has kept him spry.

Back in the lobby, Luca yanks off his black button-up shirt, revealing a fitted white T-shirt beneath, but for once, I'm not distracted by the flash of colorful abs that's revealed as the hem slides up. Or at least I'm not as distracted as usual. Because I have my own outfit to worry about.

"Do I look okay?" I run a hand through my hair. When I came home from seeing Dad this afternoon, I washed and blew it dry, and then I tried on every dress in my closet. I opted for the blue to match my eyes. And maybe my mom's eyes.

A shiver runs through me.

Luca cocks his head at me. "You look beautiful. And also like you're about to puke. Are you okay?"

I shake my head slowly. "I have a three-decade history of picturing who my mom might be, and of building her up in my head." I take a heavy breath. "I can't believe I might finally get some answers."

I would never say this part out loud—I can barely even *think* it because it's so irrational—but I'm overwhelmed by how much I want her to be all those things I imagined. How much I want this wild birth certificate quest to lead me to her. And how much I want her...to want me.

"Whatever happens, it will be okay." Luca reaches out a hand to give mine a squeeze. "You're not alone."

My eyes burn and my throat aches. I swallow hard and tighten my grip on his hand.

"Come on," Luca finally says. "Let's go get you your answers."

CHAPTER 19

"The house is so…big." I stare up at the three-story stone structure. Calling it a house is really a stretch. This place is a mansion. I take in the wide front porch, its roof held aloft by imposing marble columns, the mahogany front door flanked by sidelights set into elaborate wooden moldings, and the perfectly pruned topiaries dotting the manicured lawn. "How is it possible my mom ever lived *here*?"

We're parked across the street from the address Luca punched into the GPS when we got in the car. He checks my stolen hospital file and then peers back at the house through the driver's side window. "This is definitely the address listed for your mom thirty years ago. You said your dad was really young when you were born." Luca gazes at the house again. "So she was probably young, too, and this was her parents' house. Or…" He raises his eyebrows. "Your dad was getting it on with a rich older woman."

I breathe out a laugh. "I'm pretty sure he and my mom were just two dumb kids who didn't use protection. But I guess I imagined that maybe my mom gave me up because she was poor and couldn't take care of me. That she was chasing something important, or a better life." I wave my hand at the imposing structure casting a shadow over the car from all the way across the street. "But this is—not poor."

"The good news, though, is that it's not an apartment building, either, which would probably mean she or her family were more transient. It looks like someone owns this place, and maybe they've lived here for decades."

This almost knocks me sideways. Is it possible my mom—or at least her family—lived right here the whole time? That maybe I even passed her on the street? Would I have recognized her if I had?

Luca pulls on his door handle. "I guess there's only one way to find out who lives here." He steps out of the car. "Be right back."

My mouth drops open. "Wait. Luca! Where are you going?"

But Luca has already crossed the street and is standing next to the mailbox on the curb in front of the house. We're in an upscale residential neighborhood in the middle of the city, so while Luca might not be mistaken for someone who lives in one of these houses—especially in his white T-shirt, black trousers, and beat-up black leather sneakers—he could probably pass for a gardener or pool boy.

Luca looks left and then right. A couple of cars swish by on the road, but the sidewalk in either direction is empty. He does a quick spin that reminds me of Mrs. Goodwin, reaches into the mailbox, and grabs a handful of mail.

I watch as he lifts his shirt and tucks the mail into his waistband. And then, instead of returning to the car, he looks left and then right again, and then creeps toward the house.

What is he doing now?

Luca approaches a window on the ground floor, stands up on his tiptoes, and peeks inside the house. We're going to get arrested for sure. He moves to the next window and does the same.

Fifteen seconds later, he's diving back into the car.

"Oh my God, Luca!"

"What?" he pants, out of breath from his sprint across the street.

"You know stealing people's mail is illegal!"

He laughs. "So is breaking and entering, but that didn't stop you."

"Yeah, but this is—" I sputter. "It's a *federal offense*."

"It's fine. I'm just borrowing it." Luca lifts his T-shirt to pull the mail from his waistband and then shuffles through the pile. He flips past a leaflet that's addressed to *Current Resident* and a neighborhood bulletin with no address. I'm relieved to see it's mostly junk mail and we didn't steal anything important. And then—"*Jackpot.*"

I stare at the paper in Luca's hands. It's nothing important, either, just one of those credit card offers. *But the name…*

Victoria Jankowski.

My mom's name is listed in my file as Melanie Jankowski. So Victoria must be a relative. "Her mother, maybe?"

Luca nods. "If Melanie grew up in this monstrosity"—he hitches his chin at the mansion—"then it's possible her parents still own the place. So, that would make Victoria…" He trails off as his eyes shift from the envelope to mine.

"My grandmother."

Luca tosses the junk mail over his shoulder into the back seat of his car. "When I peeked in, I didn't see anyone. And there are no cars in the driveway. But it's only a little after five; a lot of people will still be coming home from work." He reaches under his seat to pull the lever and slide it back. "Might as well settle in and wait."

I continue to stare at the house. "It's just so hard to believe my grandmother might have been here this whole time. Do you think she knew she had a grandchild?"

Luca shrugs. "It's hard to imagine someone having family and not wanting to even know them. But it happens all the time."

Since we're settling in, I lean back in my own seat. "What about you? I met your mom, and she's clearly involved in your life."

He barks out a laugh. "*Too* involved."

"You haven't mentioned your dad." I remember the warmth and chaos of Luca's childhood home. Ginny and Lorraine and Angelo. But there was no sign or mention of Luca's dad. Was he at work?

Luca shrugs. "He's around. I don't see him much."

That startles me. "He lives in Pittsburgh?"

Luca nods. "In Bloomfield, actually."

"But not with your mom?"

"No, they were never married. Like my sister's ex, my dad was more of a sperm donor than a parent. I still see him in the neighborhood, but I gave up on counting on him a long time ago." He says it so calmly, like it's no big deal that his dad hasn't been involved in his life. I glance up at the house where my grandmother may or may not live. I can't imagine being so indifferent.

"Couldn't your mom have asked Uncle Vito to threaten

to cut off your dad's hand to motivate him to come around more?"

He smirks. "I'm sure she thought about it. But it's more fun to let my dad sweat it. Besides, if he doesn't want to be with us, nobody wants to force him."

I reach out a hand. "I'm sorry, Luca." I can't help but feel a rush of anger at this man I've never even met. Luca takes care of everyone around him. He deserves better than a deadbeat sperm donor for a father.

But Luca just shrugs again. "Honestly, it's okay. My dad taught me a lot about the kind of guy I want to be. As in—the opposite of him. And I wasn't hurting for male role models, as you've probably noticed."

"You weren't kidding when you said there are a lot of Morellis."

"You haven't seen the half of it. Someday, I'll bring you to Sunday dinner." He shakes his head slowly as if to warn me to run in the other direction. But I realize how much I'd like that.

"Plus," Luca continues, "I always had my grandpa. He was really more like a dad to me."

I glance around the Town Car. "I'm *so* sorry you lost him."

"Thanks." He meets my eyes, and I can see all the emotion that he lacked when talking about his dad. "He was the best."

"Is your family the reason you took the job at the DeGreco? So you could stay in the neighborhood near them?"

"Yeah, partly. Plus, I just really like older people." His lips quirk. "They're fun, and interesting, and wise."

I think back to my chat with Sal and the interactions at the community center earlier today. I never thought about it before, but maybe it turns out that I like older people, too. "I completely see what you mean."

Luca sits up. "Can I tell you something?"

"Of course."

"I showed the apartment to five different people the day you came to look at it. You're the only one who was actually happy about the building's residents. Everyone else seemed vaguely inconvenienced by them. One guy even asked me if any of the old people might be moving to nursing homes soon so younger people could move in."

"No," I say, appalled. I remember Mrs. Goodwin pushing me into an elaborate twirl while we practiced the Carolina shag. She has more energy than most thirty-year-olds I know. I can't imagine what she'd do in a nursing home. Or why anyone would want to send her to one. "That's terrible."

Luca leans in. "That was the *first* thing I liked about you, and I knew right away that you were the one." His cheeks take on that charming flush. "For the apartment," he clarifies.

But Luca isn't just talking about the apartment. It was that same day on the building tour when I flung myself into his arms, and he yanked me against him like I belonged there. I know now that I didn't imagine that spark between us, or all the ones that followed. This attraction was there in every interaction, even the ones when we were arguing, when I thought he was the most maddening person I'd ever met. I pushed so hard against him. Now I can see that after being on my own for so long, it was hard to let someone in. To disrupt my careful plans.

But there's nowhere else I'd rather be than in this old car, stealing mail and staking out a mansion. Even if it means I'm here because my entire life hangs in the balance. Because it also means I'm here with Luca.

Suddenly, I'm grateful for this vintage Town Car because it doesn't have any of the cup holders and storage receptacles taking up space between the seats. It's just one long bench, and my dress slides easily against the soft leather as I move in his direction.

"Thank you for helping me with this search for my mother, Luca." I shift even closer. "I don't know what I would have done without you this past week. I hope you know how much it means to me."

Luca gazes back, his face serious. "I'm here for you, Catherine. Whenever you need me. I hope *you* know that."

He reaches for me, but an SUV pulls up beside us, slowing to a crawl. I jump back to my side of the car and shift in my seat to watch as it glides past. It slows even more as it approaches the mansion in front of us, and I hold my breath. But it doesn't stop there. Instead, it turns in to a driveway one door down. A teenage boy gets out, pulls some sort of sports equipment from the trunk, and heads into the house.

I sigh. "False alarm. I guess I should have known it wouldn't be so easy."

"It's still early in the evening. We have plenty of time." Luca's grin is back. "Besides, this way we're getting the full stakeout experience." He rubs his flat stomach. "I just wish I thought to bring doughnuts."

I can't help but laugh. "Fabrizio was right. You *do* watch too many movies."

"We might as well settle in." He leans across me to open the glove compartment, his hand brushing my knee. "Do I have any snacks in here?" He comes up empty and clicks it shut.

I check my purse, but with all my nervous energy around tracking down my mother, I didn't think about food. And then I remember the pocket of my dress. I fish out the butterscotch Sal gave me earlier. "It's not quite a doughnut, but you can eat this."

Luca's face registers surprise. "Was that in your seat when you sat down? I still find those things everywhere."

"No, I—" But then I trail off because another SUV is heading toward us, slowing as it approaches. "Luca, look." This time, the car turns off the street into the driveway of the mansion we've been watching. I grab his arm. "Someone's home."

We both peer out the side window as the car comes to a stop next to the house and someone steps out. She's too far away for me to make out her facial features, but she looks to be a tall, slender white woman with silver hair. Something about the way she moves suggests that she's older—maybe approaching eighty.

"She looks like a Victoria," Luca comments. "I bet that's your grandma."

I turn to him with a questioning expression. "What does 'a Victoria' look like?"

Luca shrugs. "Queenlike."

I turn back, and there *is* a grace to the way the woman glides up the stairs to the porch. Her trousers and blouse look expensive, as if they've been tailored just for her and, despite her advanced age, she's wearing heels.

"She reminds me of you." Luca's gaze sweeps over me. "Elegant."

I look back to the woman. "So what do we do now?"

"Now we go and meet her. Are you ready for this?"

I take a shaky breath. "No."

"You can do this." He takes my hand. "I'll be right there with you."

What would I do without him?

We cross the street and head up the path to the front door of the house. I ring the bell, and to the left of us, the sound of organ chimes drifts out an open window. About ten seconds later, we hear footsteps tap past that same window.

The door swings open, and on the threshold stands the same older woman we saw moments ago in the driveway. Up close, she looks a little younger than I predicted—closer to seventy—but that might be because she's put a lot of work into maintaining her appearance. Her shoulder-length silver hair looks professionally styled, her forehead smooth, and her clothes appear just as expensive up close as they did from far away.

Luca commented that she reminds him of me, and as I take her in, I realize the woman *is* wearing a pair of herringbone trousers and a white blouse that are pretty much a carbon copy of the outfit I wore the day Luca spilled my coffee. Is it a complete coincidence, or did I inherit my grandmother's sense of style?

My gaze lifts to her face. Her sense of style, and her blue eyes.

"Can I help you?" she asks. Her voice is cold, detached. Not exactly unfriendly, but not warm and welcoming, either. But then again, we're a couple of strangers standing on her porch. Did I expect her to run outside and fling her arms around me?

"Hi," I say, and it comes out high-pitched and squeaky. I clear my throat. "We're looking for a woman named Melanie Jankowski. Would you happen to know how we can get in contact with her?"

The woman peers at us, eyes slightly narrowed. "What is it that you want with Melanie?"

"Well." I open my mouth, but our entire plan goes out of my head. Because she didn't say no. She didn't say she's never heard of a Melanie Jankowski, or that I must have the wrong house. My gaze darts to Luca. He gives me an encouraging nod. *You can do this.*

"Well, I—the thing is—"

"Yes?" Her voice is clipped. Impatient.

"The thing is my name is Catherine. Catherine Lipton. And I think Melanie might be my mother."

The woman's eyes widen, and she grabs onto the doorframe for support. Her face turns as pale as the white marble floor she's standing on. For a moment, I think she's going to pass out. She's not a young woman, and this could be very bad. Luca's thoughts seem to be going in the same direction, because he takes a step forward, reaching out a hand.

She recoils from him. "No." Her hand fumbles to grasp the door handle. "I'm afraid I'm going to have to ask you to leave." And with that, she staggers backward and swings the door shut in our faces. A distinct click of the lock carries out to the porch.

Luca and I stare at each other.

"Well," I finally say. "That didn't go well."

"Sure it did," Luca counters, ever the optimist.

"How do you figure?"

"Now we know we're in the right place."

I bite my lip. From the open window to our left, I hear the muffled ping of ringing through a cell phone. It sounds like Victoria is making a call and put it on speaker. Is she calling the police?

"Maybe we should talk in the car." I turn to head across the porch. There might be Morellis all over town, but the chances of Uncle Marco showing up to let us off the hook for a second time seem pretty slim. I've avoided arrest more than once this week, and my luck can hold out for only so long. But before I even make it to the steps, Luca reaches out and grabs my shoulder, pulling me back against him. "*What are* you doing?" I demand.

"Shhh." He leans in, his mouth inches from my ear, his solid chest warm against my back. "Listen."

I stop fighting and lean back against him. Instead of letting go, he tightens his arm around me. From the same open window comes a muffled, tinny voice through the phone's speaker. "Hello?"

"Melanie?" The voice of the woman who answered the door drifts out. My pulse picks up speed when I hear the name. *Melanie.* "Where are you?"

"I'm at St. Anne's," says the woman on the other end of the phone. "Where else would I be?"

"*St. Anne's?*" I hiss. We were just there yesterday. I turn to look at Luca, and my cheek brushes his nose.

"Shhh," he whispers again.

"Something's happened," the older woman says. "I need to talk to you right away."

"Are you all right? Do I need to call an ambulance?"

"No, nothing like that."

"What is it, Mother?" Melanie's voice has a hint of impatience. "I'm in the middle of my shift. ER patients can't be kept waiting, and we're short-staffed today."

"Well, I don't want to interrupt. Can you call me when you get off?" the older woman says. "It's important."

"They're paging me right now. I'll call you in a few hours."

They hang up, and I turn in Luca's arms to look at him, eyes wide. He holds a finger to his lips and hitches his chin toward the car. As silently as possible, we creep down the stairs. When we're on the sidewalk, we make a run for it.

"Melanie works at St. Anne's Hospital," Luca says, out of breath, once we're safely back in the car.

"In the emergency room, apparently." I gaze out the front window. "She's a doctor. My mother is *an ER doctor.*" I'm having trouble wrapping my head around this new development. Because if there was one enduring image that I held of my mother growing up, it was that she left me because she was doing something important. Lifesaving. Something bigger than me.

So to find out that this is exactly what she's doing…

The breath whooshes from my lungs.

"Well…" Luca flops back against the seat, one hand pressed to his stomach and the other palm up against his brow. "I think I'm having a terrible case of food poisoning. I need a doctor."

And suddenly, I know where this is going.

Earlier today, I made a wish to find my mother. And now I know exactly where she is.

"Let's get you to the ER right away."

CHAPTER 20

"O hhhh," Luca groans as we burst into the waiting room of the St. Anne's ER. "Ohhhhhhhhh." He staggers around, clutching two hands to his abdomen. "Somebody *help* me."

I run up to the front desk. "My friend needs to see a doctor right away. He's having terrible stomach pain."

Luca moans again, lying down on one of the waiting room couches and curling up in a fetal position. "I never should have eaten that sushi..."

I can feel the whole room staring at us, but instead of flushing with embarrassment, I have the urge to burst out laughing. I meet Luca's eyes, and he gives me a wink before he goes back to rolling around and moaning. As I watch his handsome face screw up in imaginary pain, I can't help but appreciate how completely Luca has committed to doing this for me. He throws himself into everything, whether it's dancing with Mrs. Goodwin or breaking and entering or improvising food poisoning.

And it must be rubbing off on me, because I turn back to the woman at the front desk. "Please, can we get my friend into a room immediately?" I wave in his direction. "Look how much pain he's in. He needs to see the doctor."

The woman types something into her computer. "I'll need his insurance card."

I look to Luca, who rolls his eyes and pulls out his wallet, handing me the card.

"Sorry," I whisper, vowing to pay him back for any medical bills he might incur as a result of this ruse. As soon as I get access to my bank accounts again, that is.

The woman types in Luca's information while he clutches his stomach and moans some more.

"Please can we hurry?" I urge.

She nods and picks up the phone in front of her. "We have an emergency coming back. Dr. Jankowski will need to see him right away."

Hearing that, Luca heaves himself off the couch, and though I know he's trying to look weak and sickly, I can't help admiring his grace. We follow the nurse back to the exam room, and I grab Luca's arm as if to help him hobble through the pain. But, if I'm honest, I'm the one who needs the extra support as I take the long walk down the hall, about to come face-to-face with my mother. As if sensing my apprehension, Luca puts his hand over mine as he shuffles with an exaggerated limp. The nurse waves us into an exam room, and Luca and I go inside. Luca falls face-first onto the bed, and it squeaks under his weight.

"The doctor," he moans. "I need the doctor."

The nurse looks at me sideways. "What did he eat today? We see a lot of cases of food poisoning. In addition to these types of terrible stomach cramps, people often throw up."

My gaze swings from Luca, who hasn't moved from his face-plant position, and then back to the nurse. "Yes, it's definitely something he ate. He had some gas station sushi for dinner. I told him not to, I said this would happen, but he loves a spicy tuna roll."

The nurse glances at Luca and then rolls her eyes, like, *Men.* "My boyfriend eats that stuff, too. I keep telling him he'll regret it, but he won't listen. I mean, it is literally my job to know this stuff."

"I hope he never ends up puking in your car the way Luca puked in mine on the way over here. You should see the front seat. I might need to set fire to it." I throw up my hands. "There's no coming back from that."

The nurse gives me a sympathetic glance.

I hear Luca gasp, and I look over to find his shoulders shaking. I'm pretty sure he's laughing. I cough and move my body between him and the nurse, hoping she won't notice. "Is there any way we could get a doctor in here?"

"Of course. Let me check his vitals, and then the doctor will be in." She approaches the side of the bed. "Come on, let's get you flipped over."

Luca rolls onto his back, keeping an arm thrown across his face to hide his smile. The nurse takes his blood pressure and temperature, then checks his oxygen saturation.

"His vitals are all normal. It does sound like just a bad case of food poisoning, especially given the sushi situation. But I'll send in the doctor to confirm it."

"Thank you so much."

As soon as the nurse is out the door, Luca sits up against the back of the bed. "You ready for this?"

I have the urge to chew on my thumbnail, something I haven't done since I was an anxious kid. "What if they don't send in my mom? What if it's a different doctor?"

"I saw a board on the nurses' station when we came in. It looks like it's only your mom and a resident on duty tonight. Remember she said something to Victoria about being short-staffed."

I bite my lip. "What if we're keeping her from real emergencies?"

"The nurse thinks it was just some bad sushi and that I'm an idiot. So I doubt they're going to prioritize me over anything important."

I rub my sweaty hands on my dress. "I can't believe this is happening. What if she doesn't want to see me?"

"Catherine," Luca says, his voice soothing. "It's going to be okay. I promise."

From behind me, I hear the swish of a curtain moving aside and then a male voice say, "Luca Morelli?"

Luca slinks down in the bed, clutching his stomach, and I turn around and come face-to-face with...

Oh no.

Oh, this really can't be happening.

I quickly turn my body toward the wall.

It's the handsome blond doctor I met in the elevator last night. *The one who told me he works in the emergency room. The one I have a date with tonight.*

I stare up at the laminated sign about handwashing like it's modern art.

What was I thinking? I was so concerned with seeing my mom, I forgot he could be here.

The doctor moves to the sink to wash his hands, and my gaze swings to Luca's. I do my best to get his attention by moving my eyes back and forth and giving subtle nods in the doctor's direction. A moment later, I see it dawn on him, and he makes an exaggerated cringe face.

"Help," I mouth at him.

Luca was in the elevator last night, too, but he stood toward the back, and this guy was really directing his attention at me.

"I'm Luca Morelli," Luca says, his voice conspicuously loud in the small room. "Over here." He waves his arms like he's directing a plane in for a landing.

The doctor nods and approaches the bed. "I'm Dr. Kohler, the resident on call."

Luca clutches his stomach. "Uggghhhhh..." he moans.

"I heard we're dealing with a case of food poisoning?" Dr. Kohler's gaze swings to mine. "The nurse said it was gas station sushi?"

I tilt my head down and press my fingers to my temples, hoping to hide my face from him. "That's right," I murmur into my hands. "Gas station sushi."

"We probably get three cases of it a week in here," Dr. Kohler confirms. "If you could just lie down, please, I'll examine you." Thankfully, he turns away from me to face Luca.

Luca flops back against the pillow, and I shrink against the wall, hoping to blend in with the beige hospital paint. Why did I choose today of all days to wear this blue dress?

While Dr. Kohler lifts Luca's shirt to press on his abdomen, my eyes find Luca's, and I hold up my hands. "What do I do?" I mouth at him.

He gives me a slight shake of his head and discreetly lifts a palm. "Act natural," he mouths in return.

Act natural? How am I supposed to do that?

"Does this hurt?" Dr. Kohler asks, pressing on a dandelion stem growing out of the dip in Luca's hip. I close my eyes and look away.

Luca throws his head back and lets out a low moan. "It huuuuuurts."

Dr. Kohler presses a few more times, listens with his stethoscope, and then flips Luca's shirt down. "I do believe the gas station sushi is the culprit. Some anti-nausea meds and IV fluids will fix you right up. But I'll have Dr. Jankowski come in to examine you and see if she wants to do a scan or any further tests."

"This Dr. Jankowski, she's a skilled practitioner?" I murmur.

"She's the head of our department, actually," he says, turning to me. "Our very best."

I shrink back against the wall. *Damn it.* At the mention of my mother, I forgot I was supposed to be blending in.

Dr. Kohler cocks his head. "Have we met before?"

"No!" If I press my head any farther back against this wall, I'm going to give myself a concussion. "Absolutely not."

"You look familiar." He takes a step closer. "I swear it was just recently . . ."

Behind us, Luca moans loudly and thrashes around on the bed. I brush past Dr. Kohler and hurry to Luca's side. "Can we please get Dr. Jankowski in here?" I keep my back to the doctor, reaching down to fluff Luca's pillow so I have something to do with my hands. "My friend is in a lot of pain."

Behind me, Dr. Kohler hesitates, and I know his eyes are on me. I hold my breath. Finally, he says, "Of course. She'll be right in." He heads out of the room, pulling the curtain behind him.

I turn to Luca. "This was a terrible idea." Pushing away from the hospital bed, I thread my hands in my hair, pacing across the room to the sink. "What were we thinking coming back to this hospital? What if Dr. Kohler puts it together that I was the one in the elevator impersonating a doctor?" I traipse back and forth. "What if my mother has us arrested for faking your illness?"

"Don't worry." Luca shrugs. "Uncle Vito will bail us out."

I stop pacing and look at him. "I suppose Uncle Vito has a powerhouse defense attorney, too?"

Luca nods. "My cousin Bianca."

"Oh my God, how is this my life?"

"Listen," Luca says, grabbing my hand the next time I pace past the bed and tugging me to a stop. "You don't have to go through with this if you don't want to. Fabrizio can send someone to break into your mom's place and steal your birth certificate back. Just say the word."

I admit the idea is appealing, which just goes to show how utterly off the rails my life has gone. But I can't. My mother is down the hall, and after thirty years, this is my chance. "Thanks." I shake my head. "But if I do that, I'll never meet my mom. And I'll always wonder who I really am."

Luca looks at me sideways. "You don't need your mother to tell you who you really are."

At that moment, the curtain rustles, and I turn around to find a middle-aged white woman in a doctor's coat walking into the room.

Dr. Melanie Jankowski.

My mother.

CHAPTER 21

Melanie stops in the doorway with her shoulders back and chin lifted, surveying the room. I stand up straighter, but her eyes sweep past me, and she heads for the table next to Luca, where she sets down the laptop under her arm, flips it open, and scans the screen.

"Okay," she says in a clipped voice. "Let's see what we have here." She slides a pair of glasses on her nose. "Luca Morelli. I'm Dr. Jankowski."

My heart pounds so loudly, I'm surprised she can't hear it. There is no mistaking that I resemble this woman. She has the same blond hair as I do, although hers is shorter. Her blue eyes are the same shape and color as mine. I got Dad's nose, I've always known that, but now I know where my lips came from. Is this what I'll look like in about twenty years?

And more importantly, will Melanie notice?

Luca obviously sees our similarities, because he's looking back and forth between us with his eyebrows raised.

"And you are?" she murmurs, typing something into the form in front of her. Although she still hasn't glanced in my direction, I know she's talking to me.

"I'm, uh—his friend." Can she hear my voice shake?

Melanie keeps typing. Her fingers are long and thin, nails painted the palest pink. "Gas station sushi, Mr. Morelli?"

"That's right," Luca answers.

Finally, Melanie looks up from the screen, and her gaze drifts to Luca stretched out on the bed. "Raw fish is one of the most common carriers of foodborne pathogens. Food poisoning symptoms can include diarrhea, abdominal cramping, vomiting, and fever."

"Ugh," Luca murmurs, sitting up straighter.

Melanie goes back to typing. "Untreated, it can lead to health problems such as meningitis, kidney damage, and hemolytic uremic syndrome." She raises an eyebrow. "You know gas station sushi is not a good idea, right?"

"I know now," Luca says, looking a little green.

"All right," Melanie says, heading over to the sink to wash her hands. Her movements are quick, efficient. There's no hanging around chatting while she scrubs the soap on her hands and rips off a paper towel. I like a person who gets right to work. "Let me examine you." She crosses to the bed, where she presses her stethoscope to Luca's chest and abdomen while he takes deep, slow breaths. "Your vitals are good. Does this hurt?" She pushes gently on Luca's stomach, just like Dr. Kohler did moments ago.

But this time, Luca says, "Nope."

"What about this?" Melanie moves her hand to the right, pressing a few more times, I'm guessing where his appendix might be.

He shrugs. "No, I'm feeling fine now."

Melanie nods. "Sometimes food poisoning can hit you hard, and once you've vomited a few times and gotten the bug out of your system, you'll be on the road to recovery. Still, I'm going to recommend some IV fluids." She moves swiftly back to her laptop and begins typing.

Luca sits up in the bed. "So, Doc. How long have you been doing this doctoring thing?"

Melanie keeps typing. "I've been here at the ER for thirteen years."

Luca lifts a hand to discreetly wave me over, but I'm frozen against the wall.

"Where did you go to school?"

"I went to Harvard for my undergraduate degree, and Johns Hopkins for my medical degree."

"Interesting." Luca gives me another wave, more urgent now, but I'm still not budging. "And do you have any... children?"

Melanie's fingers go still on the keyboard, and her head lifts. But a second later, she says, "No," in that same clipped tone and continues typing.

Did I imagine her reaction?

But then Luca's gaze swings to mine, his eyes wide. He saw it, too. Somehow, that gives me courage to step forward.

"No children?" I ask. "None at all?"

"No," Melanie repeats, but her typing slows.

Luca slides his feet off the bed so he's sitting on the edge. "So the name Catherine doesn't ring a bell?"

Melanie's spine stiffens and her gaze flies to Luca. "What did you say?"

"Catherine." I cross the room and step up to the bed so I'm standing in front of her. "I'm Catherine. Catherine Lipton. And I'm pretty sure I'm your daughter."

CHAPTER 22

"**Y**our father told you everything, I suppose."

I have to hand it to my mother, she recovers quickly. Melanie stood there for only about ten seconds with her mouth hanging open, staring at me before she pulled her shoulders back and regained her poise. I'm jealous of her ability to do that, honestly. I wish I'd inherited a bit more of that self-possession along with her blue eyes. Because right now, my insides are churning, and on the outside, I'm pretty sure I'm shaking.

"No," I say. "Dad didn't tell me *anything*."

"Then how did you find me?"

I glance at Luca, who gives me a reassuring smile.

"A friend helped me figure it out. Does it matter how I found you?"

Melanie takes a deep breath and blows it out slowly. "I suppose at this point, it doesn't." Her gaze slides to Luca. "And you? Who are you?"

"The friend."

Melanie purses her lips. "I'm going to go ahead and assume that you didn't eat gas station sushi, and this food poisoning is all a ruse?"

"That's correct," I say.

"So you lied to get in here and talk to me."

"Yes." I shrug.

"And what is it that you—" She stops and clears her throat. "Why now?"

"I need my birth certificate." I stare in her direction. "My *real* birth certificate. And I believe you have it."

Melanie hesitates, and then she nods.

I lean back against Luca's hospital bed for support, and he inches closer. "Did you really think I would never need the original? That the fake you and Dad gave me would fool me forever?"

Melanie sighs. "We were young when we had the copy made, and probably naive to think nobody would ever notice the forgery. But those were different times." She leans forward. "How did you discover it?"

I search for signs of how she's feeling about the fact that I've suddenly shown up in her life. Is she angry that I'm here? A little bit happy to finally meet me? Did she ever wonder about how I turned out? Her face doesn't give anything away.

"I recently landed my dream job as a mathematics professor," I explain. "But there were some…issues with my paperwork. Dad only had a copy, and when I tried to get the real thing, it turned out that not only do *you* have it, but the one I've been using is a fake." I cross my arms over my chest. "Maybe we lied about a little food poisoning, but you and Dad lied about my entire identity."

Melanie's pale cheeks flush just the smallest hint of pink. "We didn't mean for it to harm you or disrupt your life. Like

I said, we were young, and I suppose we didn't fully consider your future." She leans back in her chair, looking at me from head to toe as if she's really seeing me for the first time.

I straighten my posture, suddenly glad I chose this blue dress.

"You're a math professor now?" Melanie asks after a beat.

"My specialty is computational science and numerical analysis. And I *will* be a professor if I can get this sorted out. It's a tenure-track position, which is hard to come by these days."

Her eyebrows rise. "Very impressive."

"Thank you." I stand a little bit taller. Maybe she expected me to become a clown, like Dad. Or maybe she didn't give it much thought until this very moment. But now she knows, and she's impressed with me. I don't know why I care. I shouldn't care.

"I regret that this birth certificate issue is causing you problems," Melanie admits. "But I do need to get back to work."

Her words cut through me. Is she going to blow me off, just like Dad did? Maybe my parents were young and ill-equipped to have a baby. Maybe they didn't want a child. But they got one, and they owe it to me to help me find my identity. And I don't mean only what it says on some paperwork. This is about so much more than my job now. It's about who I am and where I come from. Melanie doesn't just hold my birth certificate. She holds the answers I've spent my life looking for.

But before I can open my mouth to argue, she says the last thing I'm expecting her to say. "Come over to my apartment tomorrow night. I'll give you your birth certificate and we can talk then."

My mouth drops open, and for a moment, I'm speechless. My gaze swings to Luca and he gives me an encouraging smile.

"What time would you like us to arrive?" I ask.

"Oh." Melanie's gaze lingers on Luca's tattoos before she turns back to me. "Your friend will be coming, too?"

Funny how I automatically assumed he would. He's been with me for all of this, and I realize how much I want him there. How much I don't want to go it alone anymore.

"Catherine and I are a team," Luca says, and I give him a grateful smile.

Melanie stands up, snapping her laptop closed. She pulls a business card from her pocket and writes something on the back. In a smooth gesture, she holds it out to me. I take it, glancing down at the neat script where Melanie has written *7 p.m.* and an address. She moves gracefully toward the door.

I clutch the card in my hand. "It was nice meeting you."

She turns and gives me a hint of a smile. "It was..." She nods. "...nice meeting you, too."

And then she's gone.

CHAPTER 23

just can't believe it," I say as I settle into the soft velvet of my couch cushions. "I can't believe she's..."

An ER doctor.

Smart and efficient and organized.

"Everything you imagined when you were a kid?" Luca fills in the silence with exactly what I'm thinking.

My head jerks up. "Well...yes."

"She's definitely saving lives, just like you thought she'd be." He gives me a sideways grin as he crosses my living room. "For example, I will never eat gas station sushi, or any sushi, ever again."

I can't help but smile.

After the nurse discharged Luca with a printout about the horrors of food poisoning and detailed instructions to never eat sushi from the Sunoco again, we headed back to the DeGreco building. Luca walked me to my apartment, and I invited him in to drink that bottle of red. He took charge of opening it, and now he hands me a glass of wine and sets the bottle on the coffee table without a coaster or a place mat underneath. But at this point, I'm too keyed up to care. Luca takes a small sip from his glass, and I gulp mine down and dump in another splash from the bottle.

"She seemed interested in my career, didn't she?" Her reaction reminds me of something else I longed for in childhood. Someone who cared about my work and encouraged me to be successful. Dad was always proud no matter what I did, but he was much more likely to celebrate if I landed a six-ball juggling trick than he was if I got straight As. Even now, I flush when I remember his *algae-bra* joke to Dr. Gupta.

I pull Melanie's card from my pocket and stare at the neat script on the back. "She wants me to come over. If it was just to give me the birth certificate, she would have asked me to meet her somewhere. But she said she wants to *talk*. That's promising, isn't it?"

"Definitely promising," Luca agrees, his face softening. "You've been imagining this moment for a long time, haven't you?"

I set the card on the coffee table and take another sip of my wine. "When I was a kid, my dad used to take me out of school so we could go to festivals—Burning Man, the Ren Faire—anywhere that he could perform and connect with the circus crowd. I *hated* it. It wasn't the juggling and circus tricks—for a kid, that stuff was fun—it was the complete chaos." I remember the desert dust getting into everything, the pushing and shoving as I waded through crowds, the anxiety about what I was missing in school.

"I never knew where we'd end up sleeping that night. And then, back at home, I'd discover that Dad forgot to buy groceries or worse—pay the bills—so it got to where I didn't really know where I'd end up sleeping, *ever*." I look up to find Luca watching me over his glass of wine.

"Dad could completely go with the flow. He said it didn't matter if I missed tests; life experience was more important than rote memorization. And he wasn't attached to material possessions—like our apartment, for example—so if we had to move out, we'd just find another.

"So, sitting there in the desert, I'd build this whole fantasy about my mom. Not only would she have some sort of really important job, but she'd have her life together. She'd be organized, responsible, and always pay her bills on time. And someday we'd meet, and she'd see how well I turned out. She'd see that I had my life together, and that I was good enough."

Luca sets his glass on the table—no coaster, not that I'm paying attention—and slides closer to me. "Catherine, whatever the reason your mom left, it had nothing to do with whether you were *good enough*. I hope you know that."

"Mmmm," I say faintly. If I was good enough, then why did she leave me? If I was good enough, then how did she live down the road for thirty years and never reach out?

But maybe Sal was right when he talked about opportunities. Maybe this identity crisis is an opportunity, and I just need to grab it. Now that I've found my mom, maybe I have the chance for a relationship with a parent who understands my need for stability, a career, success. Who understands *me*. A tiny thrill runs through me.

"I'm really glad that this all seems to be working out the way you wanted it to," Luca's voice cuts in. "I just—" He hesitates like he wants to say something but isn't sure if he should.

"What is it?"

He runs a hand through his hair. "I hope you'll be cautious tomorrow."

I laugh, reaching over to feign checking his forehead for a fever. "Are you feeling okay, Elbow? After leading me astray with breaking and entering and mail theft and threats of dismemberment, *you're* the one lecturing *me* about being cautious?"

Luca chuckles, pulling my hand from his face. But instead of letting go, he tugs me closer. "I guess you're rubbing off on me, Catherine Moonstone Lipton." His smile fades, and his dark eyes search mine.

My gaze drops to the kaleidoscope of color covering his forearms. And then I reach out to do the thing I've been wanting to since I first spotted those delicate lines disappearing beneath the folds of his uniform. I trace a finger along a sparrow's outstretched wing, over his bicep to a cluster of butterflies, and then to the soft petals of a trumpet vine curling around his shoulder.

Luca raises his hand to my cheek, and his lips find mine. I lean in to press against him, opening my mouth and sliding my tongue against his. His hand snakes around my waist, pulling me closer as he tips back against the arm of the couch. I fall on top of him, our legs tangling together.

My gaze drifts toward the neckline of his shirt. The hint of something blue peeks out from near his collarbone. A bird? A flower? Suddenly, I have to know. I have to explore every inch of the colorful canvas that is this charming, infuriating, irresistible man. I tug his shirt over his head, and my breath catches at the sight of the most beautiful artwork I've ever seen: those delicate illustrations, his hard chest, and those strong arms reaching for me.

And then it hits me with the same intensity as the first day I met him, right here in this apartment, when I threw myself into his embrace. That feeling that I've solved the most impossible equation, that the numbers have finally added up, that I am exactly who and where I am supposed to be.

CHAPTER 24

When I arrive at the community center the next morning, Mrs. Goodwin is on the stage at the far end of the gymnasium, ordering people around through a microphone. "I want the chairs lined up over here." She waves her hand in one direction. "Tables over there." Another wave. "And be sure to leave a wide aisle for the wheelchairs."

I'm here to meet Dad and show him the space for the fundraiser performances. He texted last night to let me know that in addition to agreeing to do a juggling routine, he's reached out to his friends and secured Ginger's burlesque troupe, a group of belly dancers, and possibly an aerial act if the ceiling in the gym is high enough.

As I gaze around the room that hosted the exercise class yesterday and that today is slowly transforming into a cross between a high school prom and a theater production, I realize that half the community is here to pitch in. In addition to Mrs. Goodwin at the microphone, I spot the book club members gluing together felt triangles onto ribbons to make bunting, several of Uncle Vito's security men on ladders fiddling with the lighting, Ginny's son Angelo stacking chairs, and dozens of other people I've passed in the hallways of the

DeGreco or recognize from the shops around the neighborhood. I even see Sal sitting quietly on a bench in the corner, drinking a cup of coffee. I give him a wave, and he smiles in return.

And then I notice Dad is in on the action, wearing a pair of work gloves and pitching in with everyone else. He's chatting with the person opposite him as they slide the tables into perfect rows—leaving enough room for wheelchairs—and I can tell by the way he waves his hands that he's telling the story about the time at the Ren Faire when he was juggling fire on a float in the river, set the whole structure aflame, and had to swim to shore in thirty pounds of chain mail, armor, and a helmet.

The guy moving the other end of the table is laughing so hard he has to stop walking and lean on it for support. Though I can't see his face, I recognize the expanse of lean muscles through his fitted T-shirt. And the tattoos. Of course, the tattoos.

My body heats as I remember pressing my lips to the bird on his shoulder last night. I never expected to be so attracted to a man with tattoos. My last boyfriend, a mathematician I met in my analytic number theory seminar in graduate school, used to wear khakis and a pressed Oxford shirt to class every day. But then again, I never expected to find someone I felt safe enough with to let go of all my careful control the way I did with Luca last night. Or someone who could make me laugh at the same time.

A thrill goes through me at the sight of him—the little lines that crinkle around his eyes when he laughs, the lock of dark hair sliding down his tan forehead. He's so familiar, but this feeling is brand-new. Thrilling. Like I'm jumping from the fire escape to the rooftop, and at any moment, I could fall.

I make my way in Luca's direction, and when Dad spots me, he comes over to give me a hug. "Kitty Cat! What an absolute delight." Though I saw him yesterday, he still greets me like it's been years. I guess it's always been this way, like seeing me is the best part of his day. Sometimes when I was a kid, I'd open the front door after school to find a handmade WELCOME HOME sign, a stack of cupcakes, or Dad unicycling around the living room waiting for me.

Though I've struggled with our relationship, he's still my dad, and I know he loves me. But even if half the time he's in his own world, how could he keep such huge secrets from me? I shake my head, pushing it out of my mind, because maybe I'll finally get those answers from Melanie tonight. Instead, I focus on Luca, who rounds the table to join us.

"Hey," he says, not quite touching me, but standing close enough that I feel the warmth of his body. He gives me a sideways smile, his gaze lingering on mine for a moment. If I lean in, I can smell his citrusy scent. That same scent was on my pillow when I woke up this morning, but Luca was already gone. He left a note, though, using the pad on my desk where I keep my lists.

Off to deal with the broken elevator.

Luca sure knows how to charm me.

I pull my attention back to the present when Dad gives Luca a good-natured slap on the back. "I was happy to run into this guy again."

Luca smiles. "Andy was just telling me about some of the perils of his job."

I *knew* he was sharing the story about the fire juggling and chain mail. It's one of Dad's favorites, now that he's not at the bottom of a lake. "We may want to skip the fire throwing at the fundraiser," I suggest. "Since they're trying to *save* the building, not burn it to the ground."

"I'll stick to juggling balls and the unicycle," Dad promises with a laugh.

"Speaking of that…" I gesture up at the stage, where Mrs. Goodwin is still at it with the microphone. "Do you think this space will work out for your friends' performances?"

Dad gazes around the gymnasium. "The stage will be fine for the dancers and my juggling tricks."

"What about the aerial act?"

"Luca's uncle over there was just helping me figure out how we could hang the silks from the beams on the ceiling." He hitches his chin at Uncle Vito. "Nice guy."

Of course, Dad's only saying that because he doesn't know how close Uncle Vito came to detaching him from his limbs.

"I had no idea there were so many different types of carnival performers in Pittsburgh," Luca muses.

"There's a pretty big community, actually. Tight-knit." Dad looks around the room. "Most of us regularly hang out at ArtSpace, and we all support each other."

"What's ArtSpace?"

"Catherine didn't tell you?"

Luca raises an eyebrow. "No?"

Dad's face lights up. "It's a collaborative space for artists to come together to share their work with each other and the community. Anyone is welcome—performing artists, visual artists, whatever floats your boat. The circus community gets together a few times a week to practice our craft and design our acts, and we do occasional performances for the community."

"Sounds like fun."

Dad reaches out and gives Luca's shoulder a squeeze. "You ought to come down sometime. Everyone is welcome, and I'm happy to show you the ropes."

Luca grins. "I see what you did there."

"Yep, there are literal ropes hanging from the ceiling," I say. There's also an art gallery. I peeked in when I was there the other day and noticed they're between exhibits.

"If you're interested in aerials or acrobatics, it's the best place to learn," Dad adds.

"I'm more of a visual artist, but I'm willing to give it a try," Luca says, up for anything, as usual.

"Really?" A smile stretches across Dad's face. There's nothing he loves more than encountering a fellow artist. "What's your medium?"

"I do illustration, mostly."

"Is any of this yours?" Dad waves a hand at the ink on Luca's arm.

"Most of it, yeah."

"Beautiful. You have a lot of talent, but I'm sure you already know that."

"I mostly do it for fun."

"Nothing wrong with that," Dad says. "ArtSpace supports artists of all levels. Let me know if you ever want to check it out."

"Thanks, Andy. It sounds great. Maybe Catherine can take me over there, and I'll finally convince her to show me a few of her circus tricks." He looks at me. "The unicycle?"

"Nope." I shake my head.

"Acrobatics?"

"Uh-uh."

Luca sighs. "Fine. At least show me how you can juggle."

"That is never, ever happening," I say sweetly. But maybe I *will* take him to ArtSpace. I'd love to show him the gallery. Just in case he ever wants to get those drawings out of his mom's attic.

Mrs. Goodwin shimmies over, doing a two-step to the music playing through the speakers. "Helloooo," she trills. And though she stops in front of us, her shoulders keep bopping. "Now, who is this gentleman?" She looks Dad up and down.

"Andy Lipton, at your service," Dad says with a bow. "Father of the brilliant Catherine. It's an absolute pleasure to meet you." From anyone else, it would be a corny line, but Dad sincerely means everything he says, and Mrs. Goodwin beams.

"Catherine, you didn't tell me your father was so charming." Two pink spots bloom on her cheeks. "Or so handsome."

Dad is only forty-eight, tall, and fit from all the juggling and pedaling and balancing on thin lines of webbing. But it's his charisma that draws people in. He has a way of making everyone want to move in his orbit, and of welcoming them all in. My gaze slides to Luca.

It reminds me of someone else I know.

"My dad is here to talk to you about performing at the fundraiser," I explain to Mrs. Goodwin. "And he has some friends willing to help out, too."

"Oh, that's wonderful." Mrs. Goodwin claps her hands together.

"I can do my clown show—juggling, unicycle, maybe the slackline if we can rig it up." Dad pulls out his phone. "And let me show you some videos of the dance troupes. They'll knock your socks off."

Mrs. Goodwin giggles. "I'm really interested in seeing *your* routine, Andy. Especially if it will knock off more than my socks."

Dad chuckles. "You're going to make me blush."

"Catherine." Luca leans in, his mouth inches from my ear. "Can I see you for a second?" He hitches his head in the direction of a door against the wall. "I need your help with something over here."

I leave Dad to flirt with Mrs. Goodwin and follow Luca across the gym into the supply closet. He closes the door, and we're plunged into darkness. I reach out and grab for him to steady myself, and he pulls me up against his chest.

"How do we keep ending up in dark closets together?" I ask, slightly breathless.

"Excellent planning on my part." Luca slides his arm around my waist.

"So, all of a sudden, you're a planner."

"Like I said, you're rubbing off on me," he murmurs, right before his lips find mine.

And he must be rubbing off on me, too, because never in a million years did I expect to find myself sneaking off to make out in a supply closet. Or that it would leave me feeling so exhilarated.

"I've wanted to do that since you walked in today."

I reluctantly pull away. "I should probably get back to my dad before he notices I'm gone."

Luca kisses me one more time, and I head back out into the gym. Dad has gotten out his bag, handed out the balls, and is demonstrating a basic three-ball cascade for Mrs. Goodwin, the book club, and—*yep*—even Uncle Vito and his guys. Balls are flying everywhere, bouncing off the shiny hardwood floor, but nobody seems to mind. Dad is a good teacher, leaning over to demonstrate an alternative position for Ginny and calling out encouragement to Uncle Vito, who looks frustrated but determined.

Fabrizio and Angelo both show the most natural talent, and Mrs. Goodwin has the most flair. But I spot one of the book club members dropping balls left and right, so I can't help but head over to pitch in. Within about fifteen minutes, everyone in the group has juggled at least two balls, and several of them have managed three.

"Really nice work, everyone," Dad says, clapping his hands as we collect the balls in a pile.

"Now, let's see what you can do, Andy," Mrs. Goodwin calls.

With a smile, Dad grabs a handful of the juggling balls and shows off his skills, tossing seven into the air and keeping them aloft while he does a series of footwork that's reminiscent of Mrs. Goodwin's Carolina shag. The balls speed up as his arms move faster and faster until they're nothing more than a colorful blur. The community center crowd goes wild. He switches to a single-hand throw, then back to double, all the while moving his hips to the music piped through the speakers. Finally, in one graceful motion, he lets the balls drop one by one into his outstretched hands and ends his show with a bow.

"My goodness," Mrs. Goodwin says breathlessly, after the applause has died down. "You have amazing talent, Andy. Have you ever worked for the circus?"

Dad shrugs. "Nah. I work locally, mostly."

"Well, you're wonderful at this. Did you ever think about trying out when you were younger?"

"Sure, I thought about it." Dad bends over to tuck the balls back into his tote bag. "But when I was younger, I had a daughter to raise." He hesitates for a beat, and then straightens, giving me a grin. "That was better than any circus job."

"Catherine is a lucky girl," Mrs. Goodwin gushes, taking Dad's arm and drawing him over to the stage to talk about the sound system for his performance.

I stand in the middle of the gym watching them go. For the first time, it occurs to me that Dad might have actually made a real career of this clown thing.

If it hadn't been for me.

Could he have joined the circus, traveled the country, and had a chance to show off all his best tricks for an appreciative crowd every night if he hadn't had a daughter begging him to get a real job?

I don't have time to think more about it because my phone starts buzzing. I pull it from my pocket, and my body goes cold at the sight of Dr. Gupta's name scrolling across the screen. I haven't actually thought very much about my new job these past few days. I've been too busy breaking and entering, and going on stakeouts, and meeting my mom.

And I've been busy spending time with Luca.

And having more fun than I've ever had in my life.

I quickly swipe to answer. "Hello? Dr. Gupta?"

"Catherine?"

"Yes?"

"Catherine, is that you?" Dr. Gupta sounds annoyed. "Are you at a rodeo? I can barely hear you."

The music is still blaring, people are milling around laughing and talking, and one of Uncle Vito's guys is up on a ladder with a power drill.

"Sorry." I dart across the room to slip into the supply closet. The noise dims into the background. "Is this better?"

"I suppose so."

I clear my throat. "How can I help you, sir?"

"I'm calling to remind you that classes start the week after next."

The bass from the music out in the gym has faded, but now my anxious pulse beats in my ears. I haven't looked at my syllabi in *days*. I'm completely unprepared for the semester to begin. "Of course. I'm aware of that and excited to get started."

"We're coming down to the wire here, Catherine. I'm afraid we're going to have to rescind your offer and hire someone else if this identity snafu doesn't get resolved soon."

"No." I clutch the phone tighter, hoping Dr. Gupta can't hear the quiver in my voice. "Please don't hire someone else. I'm really close. I just need another few days."

"Have you been working on the paper we talked about? Since you can't be here at the university, I would have expected that you'd at least use the time to work on a draft of the paper."

"Yes! Yes, of course! I've been working on it nonstop." Except I haven't been. I've barely been thinking about it at all.

"Well, then maybe we can move the deadline up to September."

"I…" Even without my identity to recover and four classes to plan, churning out an entire research paper by September would be impossible. And it's ridiculous that he'd expect that of me. Nobody can live up to those standards, especially without any departmental support. I open my mouth to point this out but then quickly clamp it shut. Now isn't the time to address this, not when I'm about to lose my job. I can talk to Dr. Gupta about deadlines once my identity has been reinstated. When I'm back at work, he'll be in a better mood. "I'll be in touch with both you and human resources as soon as possible."

"You have until Monday," Dr. Gupta barks. And then he hangs up on me.

I stand in the dark closet, staring at my phone. When I take a deep breath in, my chest squeezes, and I have trouble getting air into my lungs. It's too hot in here, and I'm lightheaded.

I need to focus.

On getting my identity back. On getting my work done.

I spin on my heel and fumble for the door to make my way back out into the gym. But it's even hotter here, and the music is too loud, and the power drill is still whirring over-head. I press my hands to my temples. Luca has joined Dad and Mrs. Goodwin onstage, and they're all practicing the steps to the Carolina shag.

I thought we were here to plan the fundraiser, not to juggle and practice our dance moves. I grab my purse and dig in the side pocket for my to-do list. It's crumpled and torn in one corner. I haven't updated it in days. All the little boxes are still unchecked.

Dad laughs at something Luca says, clapping him on the back like they're old friends. They sure are getting along great. I shouldn't have expected any less. Up there onstage, the similarities are striking. Dad and Luca are both fun and uninhibited, both charming, both the life of the party.

But are they similar in other ways, too? My childhood comes back to me in flashes. The bills that piled up, the schoolwork I abandoned so we could go to Burning Man, Dad's inability to hold down a job. And then I can't help remembering Luca losing my dry cleaning. His naps on the floor of the lobby. The fact that it's eleven in the morning and he's not anywhere near his post at the door.

The elevator was still broken when I left this morning.

Luca sees me watching and gives me that charming smile, and I do my best to muster one in return. He says something to Dad and Mrs. Goodwin and heads over to me.

"You okay?"

"Sure. Why wouldn't I be?" My voice sounds hollow in my ears.

"You're standing in the middle of the gym staring off into space."

"I'm just—" I stuff my to-do list back in my bag. I'll write up a new one when I get home and actually check some things off this time. "I'm just thinking of how much I have to do before the semester starts. I should go and get some work done."

"Seven o'clock at Melanie's, right?" He shoots a quick glance at Dad. "Did you tell Andy that you met her yet?"

I shake my head. "No. I'd like to wait and see what she has to say about the birth certificate first. My dad was so against me contacting her, I don't want him to try to talk me out of it."

Luca wrinkles his brow. "Now that I'm getting to know your dad, it does seem strange that he'd keep this kind of secret from you for all these years."

I turn to study Dad up on the stage. He's standing next to Uncle Vito, waving his arms and telling a story. Maybe it's the flammable boat and chain mail swim again. Inexplicably, Uncle Vito is bent over, clutching his abdomen with his bulging forearms, his shoulders vibrating with laughter. I shake my head. I don't have an explanation. "I just hope Melanie will be able to give me some answers."

I'm about to head out, when I remember the prospect of climbing eight flights of stairs back at the DeGreco. "Did you know the elevator is still broken?"

Luca mutters something under his breath. It sounds like a curse, followed by "*Mrs. Hartman.*" He raises an arm to flag Dante down off a ladder.

"What's up, cuz?" Dante asks after they've done their handshake-hug thing.

"Mrs. Hartman."

Dante lets out a heavy sigh. "She broke it again?"

I picture the older woman I met when she was pushing a walker onto the elevator earlier this week. She seemed so sweet and unassuming. "How is it possible that this woman has broken the elevator half a dozen times, and you haven't evicted her yet?"

"We'd need a séance to evict her," Luca mutters.

"That's not a bad idea." Dante taps his chin. "Hell of a lot easier than dragging my ladder over there again."

Now I'm even more confused. "Can someone please explain what you're talking about?"

Luca and Dante exchange a glance.

"Mrs. Hartman passed away six months ago," Luca finally says.

"So how could she possibly be..." I stand up straighter, his words registering. Six months ago? "Wait a minute. I met Mrs. Hartman on the elevator a few days ago. She was very much alive."

Luca tilts his head. "Are you *sure* about that?"

I stare at him, waiting for his smile to break through. But he just returns my gaze impassively.

"Mrs. Hartman," I say the name slowly. "The short woman with curly white hair? She uses a walker with fake flowers tied to the handlebar?"

"Yep." Dante nods. "That's Mrs. Hartman."

"You're saying that woman passed away six months ago."

"I know it sounds crazy..." Luca begins, but I cut him off.

"You think the building has *ghosts*?" My gaze swings back and forth between the two men. "Ghosts who vandalize the elevator?"

Luca lifts a shoulder. "It's an old building, and lots of people lived there for their whole lives. Some like to hang around for a while. You know…after…"

Dante nods. "Mrs. Hartman caught her husband kissing Judith from 5C on the elevator a couple of months before she died."

"People can *really* hold a grudge," Luca adds.

Mrs. Hartman smiled and called me *dearie*. She seemed as inconvenienced by the broken elevator situation as I was. There was no brush of cold air on the back of my neck, no moment where the older woman suddenly disappeared and then reappeared. Would a ghost really need a walker? Wouldn't she just float along unencumbered?

This whole story is completely preposterous.

But of course it is. I remember Luca's joking tone in the hospital basement when he was trying to convince me there were ghosts in the morgue, his amusement that the idea made me uneasy. Is he teasing me again now? Or is this an excuse because Dante didn't fix the elevator correctly?

Dante and Luca stare back at me, poker-faced.

I sigh. If I don't have time for juggling and dancing, I definitely don't have time for ghosts. Especially made-up ones. "Okay." I turn to head across the gym. "I'll just take the stairs."

CHAPTER 25

My mother lives in a modern downtown condo building complete with tall windows, white leather couches in the lobby, and a doorman. When Luca and I enter, the doorman greets us from his perch at the front desk and calls up to Melanie for approval to let us in. I wring my purse strap in my hands. She could still say no and tell the doorman to send us packing. What would I do about my birth certificate then?

And how would I handle being rejected by my mom again?

Luca must sense my apprehension, because he reaches for my hand.

After a moment, the doorman hangs up the phone and gives us a nod. "You can take elevator two."

We enter the elevator, and Luca pushes the button with his elbow since he's still holding on to me with one hand, and his other is occupied by the flowers he's brought for Melanie. Sometime after I left him at the community center, he picked up a bouquet of brightly colored sunflowers, zinnias, and snapdragons, which is just the most charming, most *Luca* thing to do. Especially because I can't help but notice that the riot of colors matches his arms. He even arranged them in a mason jar so Melanie wouldn't have to deal with finding a vase when we arrived. My heart melts at his thoughtfulness. I was too preoccupied to think of bringing anything but a list of questions.

On Melanie's floor, we turn left down a hallway painted a soothing gray and find the nondescript door to her condo. This isn't the kind of building where people clutter up their entrances with welcome mats or wreaths, like the DeGreco. It's a place that leans into order and clean lines.

Melanie swings the door open, and at the sight of her, my breath catches. Since my dad has dark hair and eyes, I'd always assumed I got my blond hair and blue eyes from my mom, but it's still jarring to see the person I've been picturing for thirty years standing in front of me. She's wearing a wrap dress, eerily similar to the one I'm wearing except hers is black and white and mine is dark green.

We enter the condo into a loftlike main room with tall ceilings. A modern kitchen takes up one side of the room, the crisp lines of shiny white cabinets along the far wall unbroken by appliances. Melanie must have had them covered by the same material as the cabinets so it all matches perfectly. Across from the cabinet, a marble counter stretches the length of the kitchen, completely devoid of fruit baskets, junk mail, or other detritus, like a desert island in the middle of the ocean without the shade of a single palm tree. On the other side of the space is a living room with a sectional, coffee table, and throw rug, all in shades of ivory, cream, and alabaster.

Like the hallway outside, there is not a single hint of clutter or chaos in this condominium, and I immediately feel my heart rate slow like I've stepped into a meditation tent instead of my long-lost mother's home.

"Please, have a seat," Melanie instructs.

As I round the couch into the living area, I pass a desk built into the—also white—living room cabinetry with a single notepad on it. The words *To Do* are printed across the top with boxes down the side. Half the boxes are checked off. I make out the words *Catherine's birth certificate* at the very bottom of the list. Its box sits empty, waiting for someone to pick up the pen and draw a neat X through it.

"These are for you." Luca stops to hand Melanie the flowers.

"Oh." Melanie takes the mason jar and sets it gingerly on the kitchen island. "Thank you." She stares at the bouquet for a long beat, and then reaches out to nudge it to the left and then to the right. But no amount of arranging is going to make a mason jar of wildflowers fit into her modern, lily-white decor, so eventually she picks it up and moves it to the desk, out of the middle of the room.

I feel a little pang for Luca, but he doesn't seem to mind. He crosses the room and drops down on the couch next to me. Melanie's sectional is formal and firm, not really a stretch-out-and-take-a-nap type of couch, so his shoulders rock and he breathes out a little "oof" when he lands a bit too hard.

Melanie pulls open the tallest white cabinet in the kitchen, revealing a hidden refrigerator. From inside, she takes out a plate and a bottle of wine. Back in the living room, she sets the plate in front of us, and I stare down at an equilateral triangle of cheese and a parallelogram of crackers. Fat green olives sit in a bowl next to the cheese, and they're so perfectly oval that they look like polished stones. Even if I had an appetite, I'd hate to disturb the symmetry.

Luca has no such qualms. He pops an olive into his mouth.

Melanie opens the wine—white, of course—and hands us each a glass. "I apologize that I couldn't speak more freely with you yesterday. I knew my colleague, Dr. Kohler, could be stopping in at any moment. I don't like to mix my career and personal life."

"Of course. I completely understand." I remember running into Dad on the university lawn while I was walking with Dr. Gupta. I guess I don't like to mix my career and personal life, either. Some things are too hard to explain to people at work. "I'm sorry we took your time away from your patients. We wouldn't have done that if we'd known another way to track you down."

"That reminds me, you're here for your birth certificate," she says, clasping her hands together. "I have it right here in my files."

Melanie crosses the room to the desk. Pulling open a drawer, she reveals neat rows of documents that I can see from my perch at the edge of the couch are in color-coded files with printed labels. I let out an involuntary sigh of pleasure, and Luca turns to look at me with an amused smile.

Melanie reaches into the green section, pulls out a file, and flips it open. She gives a curt nod, closes the file, and crosses the room to give it to me. "Here it is."

I open it and stare at the single sheet of paper. My original birth certificate. Or at least I think it's the original. I haven't exactly had the best track record with birth certificates this week. It doesn't look thirty years old—the condition is perfect—but it probably hasn't been shuffled from apartment to apartment in damp cardboard boxes like the rest of my things from childhood. An official-looking raised seal is stamped in one corner. And then, beneath it, are the names.

I trace a finger across my father's name, Andrew John Lipton.

"I suppose you're wondering why you were given an altered copy," Melanie says.

My gaze shifts to my mother's name. *Melanie Anne Jankowski.* "I spent my whole life believing your name was Michelle Jones."

"What has your father told you?" Melanie sinks down on the chair across from me.

"Absolutely nothing." I stare at her across the room. "He promised you he wouldn't tell me anything, and he kept that promise. I never would have known any of it, but there was a weird glitch in the government's system when I went to do my employment paperwork."

"The truth is—" Melanie hesitates, as if she's debating what to say. "The truth is, I asked your father to hide my identity because I didn't want anyone to come looking for me."

My breath hitches. By *anyone*, she means *me*.

I don't know what I expected. Of course she didn't want a relationship, or she would have reached out years ago. She would have been there from the beginning. I've probably always known that it was a fantasy to think she wanted to be with me but that for some elaborate reason, she couldn't.

Luca's hand closes over mine.

"The thing is, Catherine," Melanie says, crossing her hands in her lap. "I met your father in high school. He was the popular boy, the class clown, everyone loved him."

I nod, because of course, none of this is a surprise. I saw Dad out there with Mrs. Goodwin and Uncle Vito and the book club today. I understand his gravitational pull.

"On the other hand, I was the teacher's pet sitting in the front of the class," Melanie continues. "The nerd. When your father took an interest in me, well—" She closes her eyes and shakes her head. "I'm afraid I got swept up in it."

Her story isn't completely a surprise, either. I was the teacher's pet, sitting in the front of the class—*the nerd*—too. I remember how lonely it was. How lonely it can still be, sometimes. If the charming, popular guy suddenly wanted to spend time with me, would I be swept up in it, too?

With an ache in my chest, my gaze darts to Luca.

"When I found out I was pregnant, your father and I were seventeen. I had just been accepted to Harvard to start my undergraduate program in biology before applying to medical schools."

I do some quick calculations in my head. I was born in July, which means that my mother gave birth to me a month before she started college. If she'd stuck around, she would have been going to classes with a newborn baby strapped to her back. Or maybe she wouldn't have gone at all.

"For a while, your father and I were idealistic enough to believe we could make it work. But thank goodness, by the time you were born, we came to our senses and went our separate ways."

Luca leans forward in his seat. "'Thank goodness' seems a little…strong, doesn't it?"

Melanie turns her gaze to Luca, her blue eyes cold. "Andy was wrong for me on every level. I was planning to go to Harvard, and Andy…" Melanie raises an eyebrow. "Andy didn't have much of a plan for his life at all. If we'd tried to make it work, we would have failed spectacularly. I might not have made it to Harvard or medical school. I certainly wouldn't have the career that I do."

"But you might have had Catherine in your life," Luca points out.

Melanie turns to me, eyes softening. "I was young, and I made a choice. I hope that a woman with multiple degrees and a successful career like you can understand that."

I nod because I *do* see Melanie's point. She worked hard for her success. Maybe she was smart to not let an ill-fated relationship and a mistake affect the rest of her life.

Even if that mistake was *me*.

Next to me, Luca sighs.

Melanie looks at him for a long moment, her face impassive, but I can sense hostility beneath the surface. I've never seen someone so immune to his charms. Even Tonya at the Social Security office warmed up to him eventually. But then, Luca doesn't seem very interested in charming my mother.

"What is it that you do?" she inquires in a frosty voice.

"I'm a doorman."

"Have you ever made sacrifices for your career?"

Luca shrugs. "I don't make sacrifices for jobs. I make sacrifices for people I care about."

"Well, I suppose that's where we're different. Some of us have careers that require sacrifice." Melanie turns to me. "And I may have missed out on your upbringing, but it seems that for all Andy's flaws, he did an excellent job of raising you." She gives me a smile. "And he even encouraged your intellectual pursuits." There's a hint of surprise in her voice, and part of me understands that, too. If I were her, I would have expected me to become a clown. "I think it's just wonderful that you're a college professor," Melanie adds.

I pull my shoulders back, flushing with pride. "Thank you. That really means a lot."

"I just hope the birth certificate will help you to sort out any of the issues you're having with your new job."

I clutch the file tightly. "I think it will..." But then I realize how indecisive that sounds. I'd hate for her to think I could possibly lose the position. "Actually, I'm *sure* it will. I plan to be back at work by Monday afternoon."

Melanie gives me a nod of approval. "Good. I'm glad we've sorted everything out." There's a note of finality in her voice, as if we've just ended a staff meeting and it's time to file out in the hall.

Is this my cue to leave? I slide to the end of the couch but can't bring myself to stand up.

Melanie stares at me. Luca clears his throat.

I take a deep, nervous breath. "Well, actually, Melanie..." It's the first time I've said her name out loud. It would be awkward to call her Mom.

"Yes?"

"I was wondering if maybe...I know you didn't want... but now..." I flush as I stumble over my words, feeling like a student asking for an extension on her homework. *Get it together, Catherine. This is not how a successful college professor communicates.* "I realize that you had no intention of ever meeting me. But now that you have..." My body tenses. "I wondered if maybe we could get to know each other a little better."

"Oh." She presses her lips together as if she's processing this. Finally, she nods. "I suppose...that would be nice."

My heart leaps. "Maybe we could meet for coffee?"

She gives me a close-lipped smile. "Let me save your phone number in my contacts, and I'll be in touch."

But I'm a planner, and I don't like to wait around. Not when it's something this important. "What about this weekend?" I urge. "Do you work on Sunday?"

Melanie hesitates again. "No," she answers after a beat. "I don't."

The silence stretches.

I'm being too pushy. Of course, Melanie is surprised I asked. Her daughter just appeared in her life after thirty years, and now she wants to see her twice in one weekend. I should back off. But I can't seem to. "So, would that work?"

"Sunday," Melanie repeats slowly. And then finally, "Yes. Sure, I can make that work."

"Oh, good." I can hear the relief in my voice. Luca gives my hand another squeeze.

"I'll text you tomorrow," Melanie says. "We'll set something up."

Melanie and I exchange phone numbers, and then she walks Luca and me to the door, closing it with a quiet click behind us.

"That went really well. Right?" I whisper to Luca as we walk to the elevator, our feet barely making a sound on the muted gray carpeting. "Don't you think it went well?"

"I..." He gives me a smile, but it's different than his usual grin, more restrained. "I'm so glad you got your birth certificate."

I hug the file to my chest. "What a relief. I'll head to the DMV and Social Security office first thing on Monday."

"I bet Tonya will be able to clear your identity right up," Luca assures me. He pushes the elevator button.

"Sure..." The truth is, I *am* relieved by the birth certificate, but for a moment there, I forgot all about it. That scrap of paper isn't what I was talking about when I asked if Luca thought things went well. "But what about Melanie?"

He pauses. And then finally, "What about her?"

"We're going to have coffee on Sunday," I prompt. He knows this. He was there when I asked her. "What do you think?"

"Right," he says. "Great."

Okay, Luca never converses in single syllables. I look at him sideways. "Why do I feel like there's something you're not saying?"

"It's just..." He sighs, his shoulders drooping. "I think you should be careful."

I turn to face him. "You said that the other day, too. Why do I need to be careful?"

He hesitates and then finally says, "Look, I know your mom is all the things you dreamed of...I'm sure she's brilliant, she has an important career, and her condo..." Luca's eyes go wide like he's never seen anything like it. "Is so spotless you could perform brain surgery on her kitchen counters. But..." He waves a hand like he's searching for the right words. "All of that...it's not..."

"It's not what?" I cross my arms over my chest.

"It's not what's important."

The elevator arrives, and Luca waves for me to get on first.

"How can you say that?" I march past him to push the button for the lobby. "A person's *career* is important. Their *success* is important."

"Sure." Luca steps on next to me. "But none of that is who she is. That's just some stuff about her."

"Stuff I *admire* about her," I argue. "I know it's all brand-new, but I think Melanie and I are alike in a lot of ways."

The elevator begins dropping smoothly to the lobby. At each floor, a digital number on the button panel counts down, and a bell dings softly. I bet there aren't any imaginary ghosts breaking Melanie's elevator every other day.

"Maybe you are alike." Luca shrugs. "I don't know her. But I know you, and I'd hate to see you become so... enamored with all that stuff that you end up getting hurt."

"I'm not enamored. She's my *mother*. I think we could have a relationship."

The elevator settles on the ground floor, and we step into the lobby with the white couches. Absently, I wonder if everything in the building is furnished in white, like fresh snow and new pieces of paper. I remember how Luca was surprised when he first walked into my apartment with its emerald couch and colorful botanical prints. He probably expected my place to look like this lobby. Like Melanie's condo. And he probably thought there was something wrong with that.

Luca takes my arm and pulls me back against him. "Catherine, look. I don't mean to discourage you when it comes to your mother."

"Then why *are* you? Why can't you just be happy for me?"

"Because I care about you." His eyes roam over my face. "I care about you a lot. And...I don't know. Your mom just seems a little...cold. The way she talked about your dad... the way she reacted to meeting you."

"Cold?"

Does he think my mother is cold because she's reserved and practical? Because she's organized and maybe a little particular? I get that her cheese was cut into perfect ninety-degree angles, she probably used a ruler to properly space the books on her shelves, and it likely gives her anxiety when someone doesn't use a coaster. But doesn't he see that Melanie is not so different from me? I know I come off as cold, too. That doesn't mean that I am.

Luca shakes his head, pressing his hands to his temples. "You know what? I'm so sorry." I stare at his colorful arm, counting the birds in the flock near his elbow. Seven. No, there's one soaring in from his triceps. That's eight.

Again, it strikes me that I never thought I'd fall for a guy with tattoos. Or a wide, infectious smile. Or charm that draws a crowd. But somehow over the past week, I've developed feelings for him. I go out of my way to pass through the lobby just to see him. My heart gives a little kick when he walks into the room. I've opened myself up in ways I never, ever imagined.

Is this how Melanie felt about Dad, all those years ago?

Right before she ended up pregnant and almost lost out on Harvard and a career in medicine.

Dr. Gupta's words have been hovering on the edge of my consciousness since our call in the supply closet. The old me would never have blown off a research paper for days in a row or forgotten to give my boss a call with an update. Maybe I didn't have any choice about going with Luca into a dark Mafia bar or on a stakeout, but the old me certainly wouldn't have lingered for a drink afterward. Am I putting my career and future in jeopardy for a man who is all wrong for me? Just like my mother did?

"Catherine?" Luca's face slides into my line of vision. "Are you okay?" His hand cups my cheek, and his eyes search mine.

I take a deep breath. This has all been a lot to process in a few short days. But it doesn't mean that Luca and I are wrong for each other. We're not the same as Dad and Melanie. "I'm fine."

Luca leans closer. "I'm sorry I said those things about your mother. I'm sure she's lovely, and I'm looking forward to getting to know her." He cocks his head. "I think I can win her over."

And despite myself, I laugh. Because if anyone can win her over, it's Luca.

"Just like I won you over." With a hint of a smile still tugging at his lips, Luca slides his hand behind my head, tangling it in the hair at the nape of my neck. And then he leans in, his mouth only inches away. I slide a hand up his chest, grabbing a fistful of his T-shirt and tugging him closer.

"Ahem."

I pull away, spinning around to find Melanie's doorman watching us with a look of disapproval. He gives us a sharp shake of his head and hitches his chin at the front door. *Get out*. Like two teenagers who were caught making out under the bleachers, we laugh and make a break for the door, our shoulders bumping as we stumble out onto the sidewalk.

"For the record," Luca says, taking my face in both his hands and planting a kiss on my lips. "The doorman in *your* building is fine with you making out in the lobby anytime you want."

CHAPTER 26

Melanie didn't text me.

And now it's Sunday afternoon, and I'm sitting in the lobby of the DeGreco, staring at my phone. I'd wandered downstairs hoping to find a distraction from the outline of the research paper I'd sent off to Dr. Gupta earlier today. After our phone call on Friday, I'd spent my entire Saturday and most of Sunday working on it to show him that I *am* committed to my job.

Maybe I was hoping to find a distraction from my mother's silence, too.

"Maybe she lost your number," Mrs. Goodwin suggests. She came by earlier to practice the Carolina shag with Luca, but when she caught a look at my face, she shimmied her way onto the bench next to me. And Luca isn't here yet anyway.

"I called her when we were exchanging numbers to make sure she entered it correctly." My shoulders slump. "I watched her add me to her contacts."

"Maybe she lost her phone," Mrs. Goodwin counters.

I shake my head. "Melanie isn't the kind of person who loses things."

"Maybe she got attacked by a murder of crows," Mrs. Goodwin offers. "Maybe she went looking for a pot of gold at the end of the rainbow and fell in. Maybe she ate Magic Chewing Gum, turned into a giant blueberry, and was rolled away by Oompa-Loompas."

I press my lips together trying not to smile. "She doesn't strike me as a gum chewer."

"Well, did you try calling her?"

"I texted yesterday." I stare down at my phone again, willing it to light up. "But I didn't want to appear too eager. She didn't reply."

"Well, honey." Mrs. Goodwin gives my shoulder a firm shake. "You're not playing hard to get. She's your mother. Give her a call."

Before I can decide what to do, the elevator door opens, and Luca strolls off. "Hey," he says when he spots me on the bench. "What time is the big date with Melanie?"

I stare down at my silent phone again. "I don't know yet."

"Her mother hasn't called her," Mrs. Goodwin murmurs.

Luca's eyebrows rise, just a fraction, before he assumes an impassive expression. "I'm sorry, Catherine."

I know what he's thinking. He warned me to be careful. I steal another glance in Luca's direction. He looks like he wants to say something I'm not going to like.

"You know…" I lift my phone. "I think I'll call her."

Melanie's phone rings four times, and then I hear a second of silence before a faint, vaguely distracted "Hello?" comes through the speaker.

I guess a little part of me expected to go to voicemail, and my panicked gaze swings around the room. I didn't plan out what I was going to say first. I always plan out what I'm going to say on important phone calls. And this call is the most important of my life. I give Mrs. Goodwin a bug-eyed look, and she waves a hand at me like, *You've got this.*

I click the phone to speaker and set it on my lap. "Hi. Melanie? It's Catherine. I was calling because we discussed getting coffee today."

"Did we?" Melanie sounds preoccupied, and my heart sinks. Did she forget? But then it rises like the tides when she follows that up with "I'm so sorry. I got called in to work last night and it was a busy night in the ER."

Mrs. Goodwin lifts her hands, palms up, like, *See? I told you there was a reason.* She did. But in my defense, a murder of crows wasn't involved.

"Oh, it's no problem!" I say too loudly, hearing the little girl who just wants her mother's approval. I drop my voice to a normal volume. "Maybe we could still meet today. Whatever time works for you."

Melanie hesitates. "Well, I'm at the hospital again." And there goes my heart back into the sea. "But..." she continues, and my heart grabs for a life raft. "But I'm about to head over to my office at the university to get some paperwork out of the way. I also teach at the medical school."

"Oh. I didn't know." My mother works for the university? Has she ever seen Dad juggling on the lawn? Did she ever see me when I was younger and used to go with him?

How is it possible that we've been moving in the same plane for thirty years, and we've never met?

But I don't have time to dwell on it because the next thing Melanie says is, "I suppose you could meet me at the café on Craig Street. Do you know where that is?"

I clear my throat. "Yes, of course." That's the café where I met with Dr. Gupta. It was only a few weeks ago, but it seems like a lifetime since I lost my identity, met my mother, or...

I glance up at Luca, whose face is twisted into an expression I can't quite decipher. I focus on my mother at the other end of the phone. "I'll be there."

We hang up, and Mrs. Goodwin leans over and gives my shoulder a squeeze. "Oh, honey. That's wonderful. She's just busy. She sounds very important."

"Yep," Luca agrees, back to his monosyllables. He gives me a smile, but for all the hundreds of wide, charming grins I've seen this guy flash at people, he really can't fake it when he's not sincere.

I take in the tight lines around his eyes. "Why do you look so disapproving?"

Luca makes his way around the front desk and pulls out a spray bottle. He spritzes the counter and starts wiping it down with a rag, not looking at me. I know he hasn't suddenly developed the urge to clean, especially on his day off.

"Luca?"

He sets the spray bottle on the counter, and the liquid sloshes inside. "I just don't like that she forgot."

"She got called in to work. Maybe..." I march over to the counter. "Maybe she had her hand in someone's chest and couldn't reach her phone. Maybe she was literally keeping their heart beating."

"And after?" He stares at me. "She was heading to the university."

"She takes her work seriously."

He opens his mouth to say something and then snaps it shut. Finally, he takes a deep breath and blows it out slowly. "I'm worried that she didn't think of you."

I shake my head. Why do I feel like there's more to this? After all, Luca is late all the time. He forgets things *all the time*. And he seems fine with buddying up to Dad, the most irresponsible person I know. Yet, when my mother is busy *literally saving lives*, he has a problem with it. "She got distracted. It happens. You, of all people, should know about how that goes."

Luca's cheeks turn red. "I don't forget people. Ever."

With a huff, I spin away from him. "You and Mrs. Goodwin need to practice your dance, and I have to get to my coffee date."

Luca sighs and rounds the front desk to follow me. "Catherine. We'll drive you."

I give a firm shake of my head. "No, thank you. I'll take the bus."

CHAPTER 27

The bus pulls up just as I get to the stop, and I arrive at the café in record time. Melanie isn't here yet, so I grab a table near the front and sit down to wait. Ten minutes go by, and I check my phone for messages. Melanie said she was heading over from the hospital, and that's only a few minutes from here.

Maybe she's caught in traffic. Or maybe a real patient with food poisoning came into the ER, and she had to explain the dangers of gas station sushi. There could be a million explanations.

The front door jingles, and I turn in my chair. But it's not Melanie who walks into the café; it's Dr. Gupta. This must be his usual spot. I wish I'd thought of that before I'd agreed to meet here. I'm trying to show Melanie that I've got my life together, and a conversation with my angry boss over my lost identity isn't going to help my case. Suddenly, I'm grateful she's running late.

Dr. Gupta makes his way over, and I force a smile and slide out of my chair. "Hello, sir. How are you?"

"Catherine," he says, not bothering to answer the question or return the niceties. "Have you sorted out your identity issues yet?"

"Yes," I answer, picturing my birth certificate tucked into my file box at home. I moved it from Melanie's green folder to a red one so it matches all the others in that section of my personal paperwork. The DMV opens at 9:00 a.m. tomorrow, and I'll be first in line. From there, I'll head over to the Social Security office. "It will be sorted first thing in the morning." I mentally cross my fingers, hoping I'm right.

"I sincerely hope so." Dr. Gupta gives the hostess a wave, indicating he wants a table for one. She nods and sets a menu by the window. He turns to follow her but then stops and looks at me. "I had a chance to look at the outline you sent this morning. I'm intrigued by your thoughts on methods for solving hyperbolic equations." He hesitates and then gives me a curt nod. "Excellent work. I knew there was a reason we hired you."

I let out a relieved sigh.

"I'll send over my notes later today," Dr. Gupta continues. "Make the changes and get it back to me by the end of the week." His gaze slides away from me, distracted by something over my shoulder.

"Excuse me," comes a familiar voice from behind me. "I didn't mean to interrupt."

I turn to find Melanie standing just inside the doorway, and from the way her lips curve upward, I can tell she heard Dr. Gupta's words.

"You're not interrupting," I assure her. And then I have a vision of Dad barreling across the lawn with his juggling clubs and, later, nearly tearing Dr. Gupta's arm off with his vigorous handshake. I appreciate that Melanie thinks about the impression she's making with my boss. "Melanie, this is Dr. Gupta, the dean of the mathematics department. And, Dr. Gupta, this is Melanie Jankowski, my mo—"

"A family friend," Melanie cuts in smoothly, holding out her hand to give Dr. Gupta a quick, appropriate handshake. "Dr. Gupta, I believe we met at a faculty symposium last fall. I teach in the medical school."

"Ah, yes, Dr. Jankowski. I remember your presentation well," Dr. Gupta says, more animated than I've ever seen him, except for maybe that time he was yelling at me for losing my identity. "Brilliant." He turns to me. "You keep very good company, Catherine."

Again, I contrast this moment with Dr. Gupta backing away slowly from Dad. This is all going so well. Or it would be if one little thing weren't nagging at me.

A family friend.

"I'll be presenting again this year," Melanie adds warmly. "Please do stop and say hello."

"Of course." They talk for a moment about her subject area, but I struggle to focus. Did Melanie intentionally cut me off when I was about to call her my mother? I remember her remarking that she doesn't like to mix her career and personal life. I suppose that since we all work at the university, it's easier to keep things compartmentalized. Still, my unease lingers, even when Dr. Gupta gives me another one of his approving nods. "I look forward to hearing from you soon, Catherine." He heads to his table.

"Well," Melanie says, sitting down in her seat across from me. "I'm glad to see you have a strong mentor."

"Oh, yes, I'm very lucky," I agree. Though I'm not sure I'd call Dr. Gupta my mentor quite yet. But I'm sure he'll invest more time once I've sorted out the identity issues.

"He seems to admire your work," she adds. Do I detect a hint of pride in her voice? "Well done. Keep it up."

"I can't imagine it any other way. I've always worked hard, gotten straight As, and had full scholarships to college." But as I say the words, something heavy settles in my chest. *Make the changes and get it back to me by the end of the week.* I know I can do it, I always have, by pulling all-nighters, sleeping at the library, doing whatever it takes.

But even with Dr. Gupta's approval, I can't quite muster the enthusiasm like I used to. All day yesterday, when I was holed up in my apartment working on the paper, I just kept thinking about everyone at the community center. The fundraiser is only a week away, and they need everyone to pitch in.

"It sounds like you take after me." Melanie gives me an appreciative smile.

I sit back in my seat and take in my mother. Even after she spent an entire weekend in the ER, her hair is perfectly styled, makeup light and understated, and she's changed into a pair of dark trousers and a neatly pressed blue blouse. She mentioned on the phone that she was on her way to her office to do paperwork for her faculty position. And then will she be back at the hospital in the morning?

A couple of weeks ago, it wouldn't have sounded very different from my life. But now I can't help but wonder: *What about friends? Or dating?*

"Melanie, can I ask you something? How do you do it all? Don't you sometimes get..." I lift a shoulder. "Tired?"

She tilts her head, thinking it over. "Well, it can be difficult to catch up on sleep after overnight shifts in the ER. I make sure to take power naps in the break room whenever possible."

I trace a finger on the wood pattern on the table. "I don't mean lack of sleep. I mean, don't you get tired of the pace? The workload?"

Melanie shrugs. "I enjoy working hard."

"And what about a social life? Do you—date? I assume you don't have any other children."

"No. When you have children, you give up your whole life." She lifts her hands apologetically. "No offense, of course."

I shrug. She said essentially the same thing the other day.

"I date occasionally. But to be honest, it's hard to meet men who can handle being with a woman like me." Melanie leans her chin on her palm and looks across the table at me. "Women like us. You and I are similar, Catherine. I could see that right away. We're smart, we're driven, and we have the opportunity to make it to the very pinnacle of our respective fields." To my great surprise, she reaches across the table and touches my arm. "We have to be careful of the men we let into our lives. They may seem like fun at first, and you may even think you're in love. But you have to ask yourself if they're truly the kind of person who can help you reach your goals. The wrong person will derail your career if you let him."

I sit back, letting her words sink in. She was in love with Dad once. I can hardly imagine it now. Dad with his buoyant laugh and his juggling clubs and his circus friends. And Melanie off to present at another symposium. They would never have worked out. She would have *hated* ArtSpace. Don't even get me started on Burning Man. And then, I can picture Dad telling embarrassing stories about Melanie at the hospital Christmas party, and Melanie's face growing redder and redder.

It would have been a disaster.

Melanie's voice cuts into my thoughts. "Don't you agree, Catherine? That our careers should come first?"

Oh. She's not just talking about Dad. She's talking about Luca, too. It was clear she was wary of him at her apartment the other night, and now I understand why.

How many times over the past week was I struck by how alike Dad and Luca are? Yes, it's their charm and their ability to connect with people. But it's also their chronic lateness. Their casual attitudes toward work. Their general chaos. Would being with Luca derail my career and my plans? It's not like the thought hasn't crossed my mind. But then he gives me that smile...not the wide, charming one he shares with everyone else. The one that's more subtle, and lifts slightly on the left. The one that's just for me. The smile he flashes right before he's about to say something to make me laugh, or after he kisses me, or when I'm worrying over something and he wants to let me know he's there for me.

But am I just caught up in the fun and excitement of him, like Melanie suggested? Am I flattered that the popular boy likes me? With my mother sitting there like Future Catherine who's come back in time to show me the right path, it's hard not to wonder. And hard to ignore how close I've already come to letting distractions cost me my job.

With an uneasy nod, I change the subject, steering the conversation to Melanie's job at the ER and her presentation topic for the symposium. Then I talk a bit about my work—my research paper, my syllabi—but I haven't started the job yet, so there isn't much to say. When there's a lag in the conversation, I remember that I *do* have something interesting going on in my life.

"I've been helping to plan a fundraiser for our local community center." I wrap my hands around my coffee mug. "Developers are trying to buy the building, so we're working on raising enough money to save it."

"Very interesting. How did you get involved with that?"

"An older woman in my building, Mrs. Goodwin, asked me to help. The center serves hundreds of older adults a day, giving them a place to go and spend time with other people." My voice picks up speed. "Did you know that loneliness is as bad for your health as smoking?"

"Interesting," Melanie repeats. "It sounds like a worthy cause, and perhaps you can use it as community service on your CV."

"Oh, I guess." The thought hadn't crossed my mind. "The fundraiser is next Saturday. Maybe…" I rub my hands on my pants. "Maybe you'd like to come?" I realize how much I want her to say yes. I hope Melanie will be a part of my life, and this fundraiser is important to me.

It occurs to me that Dad will be there, too. But it's been

thirty years. And if this relationship with my mother continues, they'll need to be in the same room together at some
point.

"Sure. Send me the details."

I can't believe how well this is going. "I will."

CHAPTER 28

After coffee with Melanie, I walk into the lobby of the DeGreco to find Luca sitting at the front desk, flipping through his phone. Mrs. Goodwin must have headed over to the community center to order everyone around in preparation for the fundraiser.

Luca's head pops up, and a smile spreads across his face. "Hey, how did it go with Melanie?"

"It went well." I hesitate, remembering my mother's warnings about Luca, and Dr. Gupta's instructions to get another draft of my outline to him by the end of the week. "I'd love to tell you all about it, but I really should get some work done."

"Sure." His shoulders drop.

I press the button to the elevator. "What are you doing here?" I thought he'd be at the community center, too.

"Waiting for you."

"Oh." My heart clatters. I drop my gaze to the vine peeking out of the V-neck of his T-shirt. It's Sunday, and Luca has the day off. Suddenly, the last thing I want to do is work on that research paper.

"I don't want to keep you from your work." Luca gives

me that small, just-for-me smile, and I get the feeling he absolutely wants to keep me from my work. "You have a big week coming up."

That's right. So, what am I doing standing here?

But instead of pushing the button again, I turn away from the elevator. Maybe I can just hang out in the lobby for another minute or two. I'll check the mail. That's something productive to do.

I round the corner to the mail room, and—maybe as a punishment for stalling—I immediately crash into a bike that's parked in front of the mailboxes. The pedal slams into my shin, sending pain up my leg. "Ow!" Knocked off-balance, I reach out for something to hold on to. My hand closes around the bike seat, but instead of steadying me, the bike starts to topple over. The handlebar swings, taking down a pile of mail that hasn't been sorted yet, and the bike, the packages, and I all go sprawling on the floor in a heap.

At the commotion, Luca comes running. "Catherine, are you okay?" He crouches next to me.

"Damn it." I push myself up to a sitting position and shake out my limbs. Nothing is broken, but the bike pedal tore my pants, and my shin is throbbing. A drop of blood trickles down my leg. "Why is this here? Don't we have a room specifically for bikes?"

Luca takes a look at the offending object. "Oh, that's Mr. Winthrop's. He has trouble maneuvering it through the storage room door, so he leaves it for me to do."

"Well, why didn't you?" I snap. "It's dangerous. And against building rules."

Luca sits back on his heels. "Are you hurt?"

"I'll be fine," I mutter, shoving a UPS box off my foot.

He lifts the bike off me and wheels it out into the lobby to stash in the storage area. I limp around the room, picking up the packages scattered across the floor and making two neat piles on the table next to the mailboxes. When I do one last sweep of the room, I find a white corrugated US Mail bin shoved up against the wall, filled with smaller mail items—mostly envelopes and leaflets.

I sigh. These should really go into people's mailboxes. What if there are bills or important papers in here? I pull a stack of envelopes out of the box and begin sliding them into the mailboxes labeled with the corresponding names. I recognize many of them from around the building or the community center, and I'm struck by how many people I've met in just this short time.

There's a small package for Walt Offerman that I'm willing to bet is *The Highlander's Baby*, the next book club pick. He's probably been waiting for that. Next, I set a parcel from a store called Good Vibrations into Mrs. Goodwin's mailbox. I don't want to know what that is. And then, underneath, I find a letter addressed to me.

In the top left-hand corner is the logo for my bank, and in the top right, a postmark dated several weeks ago. I do a double take. Has this been sitting here for weeks?

Scanning my memory, I search for what I was doing on August eighth. I'll have to check my calendar. Nothing specific stands out, though something feels familiar. Important.

Wait, no. The date I'm remembering isn't August eighth, it's the seventh.

That's when I had my first meeting with Dr. Gupta at the café. This letter is postmarked the day after.

I tear into the envelope. And as I begin reading, my stomach churns.

Dear Ms. Lipton,

This letter is to inform you of fraudulent activity within your Charter Bank checking and savings accounts. Our Fraud Services Division has discovered that the Social Security number used to open the account does not exist. Therefore, this account will be closed in two weeks unless further action is taken to register a valid Social Security number. Please call...

Oh my God. This is the letter the person at the bank referenced when I called last week. *The letter I never received.* It's been sitting here in a pile this whole time. I drop the letter on the table and dig through the box until I find a similar envelope, this one with my credit card company's name in the return address area. It's postmarked on August eighth, too.

Dear Ms. Lipton,

This letter is to inform you...

I think I'm going to throw up. I lean back against the mailboxes, taking deep, shaky breaths. The banks *did* send letters letting me know my accounts were about to be shut down. If I'd gotten these letters, I would have called right away, and that would have led me to discover the mix-up at the Social Security office in early August.

Instead, I didn't know anything about it until I showed up for orientation—*weeks later*—and got kicked out by Helen. I didn't know anything about it until my bank accounts had already been shut down, my credit cards closed, my access to my money gone.

I didn't know anything about it until I was dangerously close to losing my job and the life I'd worked so hard for.

Luca strolls back into the mail room. "Catherine, I'm really sorry about the bike. Mr. Winthrop broke his hip a few months ago, and he's just getting back at it..." He stops, probably taking in my pale face and hunched-over posture, and he hurries toward me. "Shit, are you really hurt? I didn't realize that bike was quite so heavy..." He reaches for my arm, but I yank it away.

"Please don't touch me."

He backs away, his gaze roaming over my face, which I'm sure is rapidly going from ghostly pale to bright red. "Is this about the bike?"

"No. It's not the bike." I pick up the letters and hold them out to him. "It's about these."

Keeping his eyes on my face, he reaches out and takes the letters. Turning one over in his hand, he glances at it, and then back up to me. "So you finally got the letter from your bank."

"Finally?" I choke. "Look at the postmark."

He flips over the envelope again. "August eighth. Why does that date ring a bell?"

"I have no idea."

"Wait." He squints. "It's August ninth that I'm remembering."

I press my hands to my face. "It doesn't matter. What matters is that the letter has been here, in the back of the mail room, *for weeks.*"

Luca's gaze slides from the papers in his hand, to the bin on the table, to my face.

"What matters," I continue, my voice strangely calm, when inside I'm screaming, "is that you left it here, in a bin, instead of putting it in my mailbox, where I would see it. When I would still have time to do something about it before my accounts were shut down and my job put in jeopardy."

Luca swears under his breath. "I'm so sorry, Catherine."

"Just like you're sorry about the bike in the mail room? And the lost dry cleaning? And..." I wave my hand. "All the other rules you break and ways you're completely, utterly irresponsible?"

Luca stares down at the envelope. "Look, Catherine. I know what this looks like. But that date—I think I know what happened. This letter arrived on August ninth. I was sorting the mail, and there was an emergency..."

I cut him off. "Why do I feel like everything to you is an emergency if it means not doing your job?"

"Okay." Luca drops his hands to his sides. "This is really unfair. I may not always follow your precious manual of rules and regulations, but I'm good at my job. I'm great at it."

"A doorman's job is to be at *the door.*"

"Only if you look at everything from your narrow view of the world."

I take a step back, away from him. "This"—I wave a finger between us—"is never going to work."

"Catherine, wait. Let's talk about this."

"This is all just a game to you, but this is *my life*." I shake my head slowly, realization dawning. "Melanie was right about you." With that, I turn and push past him, stalking out into the lobby and banging my hand on the elevator button.

Luca trails after me. "What do you mean Melanie was right about me?" He takes my arm, turning me around to face him. And I hate that even now, after all this, my heart tugs in his direction. I hate that his face is creased with worry, and I just want to put the smile back where it belongs. Thankfully, the elevator arrives, and I hop on, quickly hitting the button for my floor. "You're just like my dad." I give the button another push for good measure. "That's what I mean."

The elevator door begins sliding shut. And at the last moment, right before they close completely, I hear Luca call, "I consider that a compliment!"

CHAPTER 29

Upstairs in my apartment, I bury myself in work, pulling books off my shelves, printing out Dr. Gupta's notes and spreading them across the coffee table, and tearing apart my research paper outline so I can put it all back together again. Outside, the sun goes down and the streetlights come on. Down the hall, I hear a door open and close, and footsteps pass by my door. I briefly wonder if it's Sal, but I keep working, stopping only to run to the bathroom and to shove a protein bar in my mouth.

Finally, around midnight, I lean back against the couch cushions and take one last look at the laptop on my knees. My outline for my paper is good. It's better than good. It's great, and when I'm done with the paper, it's going to be accepted to *Studies in Applied Mathematics* on the first try. I'm sure of it. With a sigh, I gaze around my apartment. If I were at Dad's place, I never could have worked like this. There would have been too much clutter to spread out my books and papers, and too many distractions.

I feel a tremor of panic. What if I can't sort out my identity tomorrow? Will I end up living in chaos again? I guess if that's the case, I won't have any research papers to write anyway, and I won't need this clean, organized space. I'll be on a direct route to clown town. At least it's the kind of job you can do without a bank account.

I never thought I'd see the day when that was a silver lining.

I grab for a throw pillow to hug for comfort, and my hand closes around something else instead. A large scrap of black fabric. Luca's hoodie. He must have left it here the other day.

Of course he left it. He also left a glass on the side table without a coaster and a pair of sunglasses on the kitchen counter, and he doodled all over my to-do list. He's like a walking hurricane blowing through and leaving chaos in his wake.

Except…I clutch the sweatshirt to my chest, and Luca's scent drifts over me…When I found those other things lying around, I didn't mind as much as I expected. It was nice to have evidence that someone had been here.

That I wasn't alone.

With a sigh, I haul myself off the couch and clean up my papers and books before heading out the door. I'll leave the sweatshirt in the lobby, where Luca will find it tomorrow. I am *not* secretly hoping he'll be sitting there playing cards with Mrs. Sterling. Or dancing with Mrs. Goodwin.

Nope. Not at all.

I take the stairs because I could use the walk, and arrive to a dark, empty lobby. The elevator appears to be broken again, because all the lights over the door are shut off. I hadn't minded walking down, but I'd planned to ride back up. So much for that.

I drop Luca's sweatshirt on the front desk and am about to head back toward the stairs when I sense movement on the ground below. It's Luca, curled up on a pile of blankets. He stirs for a moment, rolling from his left side to his back, and then he settles into sleep again. I stand above him, taking in the lock of dark hair flopping over his forehead—the one I reached up and ran my fingers through just the other day—his stubbled chin that scraped my cheek when he kissed me, the tattooed arms that wrapped around me, pulling me closer.

How am I going to pass him every day in the lobby without my heart aching at the sight of him?

But then he stirs, and I remember that he's there *on the floor*. I've never gotten to the bottom of why he sleeps there, and I don't care to. *Chaos*, I remind myself. *A hurricane wrapped in a tornado tied up with an earthquake.*

And then my mother's voice: *We have to be careful of the men we let into our lives.*

We both learned that lesson the hard way. I might have gotten this identity mess sorted weeks ago if it weren't for Luca misplacing my mail.

I head back upstairs. About four flights up, I hear a familiar *step-shuffle-shuffle-step* coming from the floor above me. *Sal.* Picking up my pace, I take the stairs two at a time. Around the bend, I find Sal taking slow, deliberate steps.

He glances over his shoulder, flashing me a wide grin, and for just a second, there's something familiar about it. I don't have time to think about it, though, because Sal misses a step and nearly takes a tumble. At the last moment, he grabs the railing for balance.

"Whoops!" he says with a chuckle once he's righted himself.

I run the last few steps and take his arm. "Sal! We've talked about this. You shouldn't be using the stairs."

He shrugs. "Elevator's broken."

"There's a freight elevator, though. You could wake up Luca and ask him to take you on the..." I abruptly stop talking. And it's like the lightbulb over the elevator door comes on in my head. Is that why Luca sometimes sleeps on the floor? Because the elevator is broken, and he wants to be there to take people on the freight elevator?

As if Sal can read my mind, he gives me a wink. "Luca needs his rest, and I need my exercise. Keeps me young."

Still turning this new development over in my head, I keep hold of his arm, and we climb the stairs together.

"How's the identity crisis coming along?" Sal asks as we round the bend from the fifth to the sixth floor.

"It's no longer a crisis, I hope. I found my mother and got my birth certificate. Tonya at the Social Security office seemed to think they could use it to add me back into the system. If all goes well, I'll have my identity back by this time tomorrow."

"And you're sure that's what you want?" Sal asks, setting his left foot on the step above us.

"Of course I'm sure." I shuffle up next to him, imagining the approval on Dr. Gupta's face as he reads my next outline of my research paper, and then again when we're accepted to *Studies in Applied Mathematics*. I visualize coming home every night to my calm, quiet apartment upstairs. "I'll be able to go back to work, and pay the rent on my apartment, and finally get everything I worked so hard for."

"Hmm," Sal murmurs as he takes another step up. "There was a moment there where I thought maybe you wanted something a little different."

I hurry to follow him up to the next step. Did I make that wish out loud that day in the car with Sal? And did he somehow make it come true? My gaze searches his face, looking for a sign that he had something to do with all of this. But his mild expression doesn't waver, and he seems to be concentrating more on getting up the next step than he is on this conversation.

I give my head a shake. How could Sal possibly have something to do with this? Rationally, I know he couldn't have, but just in case, I say in a loud, clear voice, "I don't know what I was thinking, but I was wrong. I want my identity back."

Sal nods. "And you're happy now that everything can go back to the way it was?"

Uncle Vito's gruff face pops into my head, followed by the swish of Mrs. Goodwin's orthopedic shoes as she turns me out into a graceful spin across the floor. Then Fabrizio handing me a pair of scrubs and the book club inviting me to join their group. My chest squeezes, and I hesitate for just a moment. When I opened my door this morning, I found a cooler packed with Lorraine's pasta fazool along with another care package courtesy of Mrs. Flowers and the Meals on Wheels folks at the community center. I would never want to go back to a time when those people weren't a part of my life.

And I'll admit that the idea of writing all those research papers alone in my apartment doesn't have quite the same appeal as it once did. Gaining Dr. Gupta's approval doesn't seem as important, especially if it means he's going to keep piling on more assignments and taking the credit.

But I've worked my entire life for this. And what's the alternative? Going into the clown business with Dad? Becoming a burlesque dancer? No, I want to be a mathematician. I enjoy it, and—like Dr. Gupta said—my work has real promise.

Besides, it's not like things will entirely go back to the way they were before. They'll be better now than they ever were. I picture sitting on Melanie's pristine white couch eating cheese cut into perfect geometric shapes and telling her I'm the youngest woman in the department to make tenure. I'm about to have everything I always wanted.

"Of course I'm happy," I say, hoping my extra enthusiasm masks the tremor at the end. "Of course I am."

"Okay, then." Sal takes another step, and then another. "I'm happy for you." And then he reaches in his pocket and holds out a butterscotch. "I guess I just can't for the life of me figure out why you look so sad."

CHAPTER 30

The next morning, I'm the first person in line at the DMV, but I guess that's how it goes when you arrive at seven and the office opens at nine. I pace in front of the locked glass door, checking over and over to make sure all my paperwork is tucked into the file in my bag. I *know* it's there—I checked a dozen times last night—but it reassures me to run my hand over the embossed seal on my birth certificate.

This one is the real thing.

I finally know who I am, and I'm about to get my life back.

My heart squeezes, not quite believing it. There are still so many ways this could go wrong. What if I go in there, and they still can't find me in the records? What if I'm gone forever? I spent so much time focusing on finding my birth certificate—finding my mother—that I never really let the possibility cross my mind that this wild adventure I've been on this past week could all be for nothing.

I wipe my sweaty palms on my pant legs, pacing back and forth again. This has to work. It just has to. I don't have a plan B, and not even the Morellis can rescue me if my identity is gone for good. My breath hitches, and all of a sudden, I'm unable to suck air into my lungs. Bending forward,

I clutch the red file folder against my chest, panting hard. Is this a panic attack? Do I need to call 911?

A middle-aged white man with a mustache comes to the door, clicking open the lock. His hair is thick and dark, waving over the crown of his head, secured with hair gel. He reminds me a little of Luca's uncles, and that calms me enough to stand up straight and take a gasp of air.

The mustache man squints at me. "You okay, miss?"

I give him a nod. For a moment, I consider asking him if he's a Morelli. But though my heartbeat is slowing, I'm not sure I can squeak out the words just yet. And besides, I don't really want to talk about Luca.

When I slipped out the door of the building earlier, Luca was still sleeping on the floor. On the bus to the DMV, I searched my mind for all the other times I'd seen him lying there. Do those times correlate with the elevator being broken? Does he sleep there to intercept the older people and give them a ride on the freight elevator? I remember Sal slipping on the stairs last night after stubbornly insisting on walking. I know Luca would do whatever he could to keep anyone from falling.

But something about that realization nags at me. I'd automatically jumped to the conclusion that Luca had set up camp on the floor because he was too lazy to go upstairs. Or because his apartment was too much of a mess. Or—*something* that proves he's irresponsible and unreliable. If I was wrong about that, was I wrong about anything else?

"How can I help you, miss?" Mustache Man waves me into an office and settles behind a desk. I sink down into the chair on the other side.

With sweating palms, I pull out my driver's license. "It appears that there's a problem with my ID." I wave my red file. "I brought my birth certificate and other paperwork. Can you please add me to your system and issue a new photo ID?"

"Let me see what you have." He holds out a thick palm.

I slide my license across the desk, and he flips it over, checking the back before he starts typing on his computer. A moment later, he mutters, "Hmmmm."

Oh God, not "Hmmmm" again. I've heard that sound too many times this week, and it only means one thing: not good.

"What?" I clutch the red file in my sweaty hands. "Just break it to me gently."

Mustache Man types a few more things in his computer, looks up at me, and then flips the card over and back. "Well." He slides the driver's license back in my direction. "I won't be needing your birth certificate."

My mouth drops open. "What do you mean, you won't be needing my birth certificate?"

He shrugs. "Don't need it."

My heart pounds in my ears. "Can you please check your records again?"

"Don't need to do that, either." The chair emits a loud creak as he leans back.

I flinch at the sound. Is this really happening? Are my worst fears really coming true?

"Please take it," I insist, my voice shaking. "Please check again."

The man looks at his watch and sighs. "There's already a line forming outside. I'd like to move this along."

My entire body goes cold. "*You're worried about a line?*" I slap the red file on his desk. "Do you know what I went through to get this birth certificate?" When I flip the file open, the birth certificate stares up at me from its embossed seal like a one-eyed monster. "I nearly got arrested. Not once." I hold up a finger for emphasis. "But twice." I flick up another finger. "I realize we just met, and you don't really know me. But if you did, you'd know I *don't* get arrested." I slide the paper across the desk. "I impersonated a doctor, I committed *several* felonies, and I conspired with a mob boss named Vito."

Mustache Man's face lights up. "Vito Morelli?"

"Yes, Vito Morelli." And then, I don't know where this comes from, it's probably a combination of exhaustion and desperation, but the next thing I say is, "And if you want to wake up tomorrow with both your hands, you will take the birth certificate and *check your records again.*"

Mustache Man stares wide-eyed, and then he slowly pulls his elbows off the desk and tucks his hands under his legs. "Um. Miss?"

"What."

"What I'm trying to tell you is that I don't need to check again, because you're in the system, and this ID is legit. Everything seems to be in order."

I open my mouth to keep arguing with him, but then his words register. "I'm—what?"

He hitches his chin at the computer. "I see you right there. Catherine Moonstone Lipton." His mustache twitches. "Moonstone? Really?"

I stare back.

"Anyway..." he mutters awkwardly. "It's all right here." Mustache Man waves at the computer, and then his gaze flies to his hand, and he quickly tucks it back under him. "We—uh—we issued your license back in March of last year. It's valid for another three. I don't know who told you it's not, but I think they were yanking your chain."

"But—" As impossible as it was that my identity disappeared from the system, it seems even more farfetched that it's *back*. Both Tonya and Officer Bill checked their records. Not to mention Helen over in HR. All of them couldn't have been *yanking my chain*.

But it doesn't make a lot of sense to sit here arguing with him. I still need to get to the Social Security office. "Well, thank you so much for your time." I stand and gather my things.

"Uh," Mustache Man mumbles. "Are we good? You know. With the..." With one hand, he makes a chopping motion over his wrist.

"Yes. Of course." I bite my lip. "Sorry about that. It's been a hard week."

He lets out a sigh and sinks back into his chair, which emits another creak, and I make a run for the door.

When I arrive at the Social Security office, Uncle Marco is waiting by the door. For a moment, I wonder if he's there to finally arrest me. But instead, he raises a beefy hand to give me a friendly wave. "Catherine."

I stop in front of him.

"Luca called and told me you were coming."

"He did?"

"He wanted to make sure Tonya saw you right away. She's waiting over here."

I follow Uncle Marco across the Social Security office, my heart in my throat. I insulted Luca, called him irresponsible, and stomped off. And yet he's still rallying the troops to help me?

We approach Tonya's desk, and she gives me a cold stare before turning to Uncle Marco with a wide smile. "Well, hello, Marco."

"Hiya, Tonya. I was wondering if you might help out my friend Catherine."

I hold up my red file again. "I have everything you asked for." I set my driver's license on the counter with a loud *slap*. "Valid government-issued ID, confirmed by the DMV." *Slap*. "Valid original birth certificate, complete with embossed seal." *Slap*. "Original Social Security card. I'd like you to make sure I'm back in the system."

"Hmmmm," Tonya says, gathering my papers together. "We'll just have to see, won't we?"

Tonya turns to her computer and begins typing, occasionally glancing down at my paperwork and then back to her screen. I wipe my sweaty hands on my pant legs. Her brows knit together. I shift my weight from one foot to the other. She mumbles, "Hmmmm," a few more times. I chew on my thumbnail. And then she looks up, her expression softer than I've ever seen it, aside from the times she was mooning at Uncle Marco.

"Well, it seems it's all there."

I freeze. Did she say— "What?" I ask, just to be sure.

Tonya nods at her computer. "You're back in the system."

Uncle Marco lets out a triumphant whoop and pumps his fist in the air.

"Really?" My body sags with relief. "It's really there?"

Tonya nods.

"Thank you so much," I say breathlessly. "I don't know how you made this happen, but I'm grateful."

She shrugs and hands my paperwork back. "I didn't do anything."

"You didn't?"

"Nope. I just typed in your information, and it appeared." She holds up her hands like, *Don't look at* me.

At that moment, my phone rings. I don't recognize the number, but I swipe to answer.

"Dr. Lipton?" comes a feminine voice through the phone. "This is Helen Hardy from human resources. Funny story." She gives a high-pitched laugh. "It turns out that there must have been a computer glitch last week, but it's all been resolved."

"You don't say."

"I'm calling to apologize. When I ran your information just now, everything cleared. We'd love to have you come tomorrow for orientation." Her tone oozes congeniality now that I'm no longer suspected of having faked my identity and plagiarized my dissertation.

For a moment, I consider gloating. But at this point, I'll take the win. "Thank you very much. I'll be there."

We hang up, and dazed, I take my papers and shove them back into my file folder. Uncle Marco gives me a hug, and from somewhere far away, I hear myself thank him and then

Tonya again. I wander out of the building and sink down on a bench to wait for the bus.

How is it possible that a week ago, I didn't exist? My driver's license, my Social Security information...all gone. And now here I am: not just in the flesh, but in the system, too? I'll call my bank and my credit card company later, but I have a feeling that everything will be restored.

Could it be—

Some days, I'd simply like to be...nobody.

Was it as simple as wishing to be me again?

But then I shake my head to dislodge that thought. This isn't the mystical meditation tent at Burning Man. This is my life. It's far more likely that this mix-up can be blamed on a failure of technology—a computer glitch, like Helen said—than on meddling from the universe.

I pull out my phone and send a text to Melanie: *Everything worked out. It's fixed!*

A moment later, she replies, *Sorry, what's fixed?*

I stare at the message. Surely she knows what I'm talking about. My missing identity and the birth certificate were the reason that I reached out to her to begin with. I probably wasn't clear in my message. I try again. *My identity! I'm back in the system, I spoke to HR, and it's all going to be fine.*

A minute goes by, and finally she replies, *Glad to hear it.*

To be honest, it's a little anticlimactic. I guess I didn't expect yelling and fist pumping like Uncle Marco back there. But...

I try again: *Maybe we could meet for dinner to celebrate?*

Another minute goes by, and then: *Okay.*

I guess she's waiting for me to pick a date. *Wednesday? The café by the university? 6 p.m.?*

The bus pulls up, and I pay the fare and make my way to a seat in the back. I check my phone. No answer from Melanie.

I flip over to Mrs. Goodwin's number and send her a text: *Everything worked out. It's fixed!*

Ten seconds later comes her reply: *Yay!*

And then: *Yay! Yay! Yay!*

And one more: *Luca is here, and we're doing the jitterbug!*

I smile, picturing Luca holding out a tattooed arm, offering his hand to Mrs. Goodwin, and the two of them doing an elaborate kick step across the lobby's scuffed tile floor. *Thanks*, I reply.

The bus travels down a block, and then another, and finally Melanie replies to my earlier text. She sends a thumbs-up emoji.

CHAPTER 31

On Wednesday morning, I arrive at the front desk of the mathematics department to begin my brand-new position as a tenure-track professor. The orientation went off without a hitch yesterday, and today is finally—*finally*—my new beginning.

"Hello, I'm Catherine Lipton," I say to the middle-aged white woman in a cream-colored blouse and high bun sitting at the front desk. "I believe you were expecting me?"

"Yes, Dr. Lipton. We were actually expecting you last week."

I hesitate, taken aback. "I suppose you heard there was a little mix-up with the paperwork, but it's all cleared up now."

"Of course." The woman stands to greet me, holding out a hand to shake mine. "I'm Georgia Ronstadt, the administrative assistant for the department. I actually have your paperwork right here."

I take a look at the file in her hand. "Just keep it away from me," I joke. "I'm still a little sensitive about paperwork."

She gives me a blank stare and then marches around the desk. "Let me give you the tour."

Okay, so that joke fell flat. Maybe they're still sensitive about paperwork around here, too. After all, they would have been scrambling to replace me if I hadn't worked this out.

Georgia heads down the hall. I trail behind her as she leads me around the newly renovated building, knocking on office doors with a sharp tap and introducing me to the faculty members inside. I met a few of them when I came for my interviews, and I meet several more now.

My impression of the mathematics faculty is the same now as it was then. Everyone seems quiet and a bit reserved as they calmly do their work in their respective offices. I notice they all keep their doors closed, and nobody bothers to make small talk.

It feels a little...cold.

It's not just the people; the entire place feels that way. The mathematics department is housed in an old brick building from around the same era as the DeGreco. When I came this spring for my interviews, the interior still had all the original charm. Dark moldings framed the entrance to the classrooms, stained glass transoms hung over each doorway, and the offices were furnished with vintage wooden desks and built-in shelving. Now it seems that much of the charm has been renovated away: the wood floors replaced by tile, the walls painted white, and the furniture sleek and modern in tasteful shades of gray and alabaster.

It reminds me a little of Melanie's condominium building. I didn't realize until this moment how soulless it felt. But then, everything would feel soulless if you compared it to the hallways of the DeGreco, where the residents' personalities are displayed by their choice of door decor. The floor mat across the hall from my apartment reads *Knock if you want to meet a cat*, and I'll be honest, I've been tempted to knock.

But then I remember that during my interviews, I *liked* that people in the department kept to themselves, the lack of drama, the focus on work. So why am I feeling more down-hearted with each click of Georgia's no-nonsense heels on these stark tile floors?

Why am I wishing for warm colors and open doors and... community?

We round the bend, and my mood lifts. Ahead of us, between the somber line of closed white doors, one stands open. And in front of it, the resident of the office has placed a colorful welcome mat.

"Ah," Georgia says. "Dr. Sharma must be in." She gives a little sigh like she's sorry about that, and then forges ahead toward the door. Though we can see inside, Georgia still gives the same sharp rap on the frame, and the woman inside looks up. She looks to be of South Asian descent and a little older than me. Though she's dressed conservatively in black trousers and a white blouse, her office is decorated as brightly as her floor mat, with a vase of flowers, colorful throw pillows, and vibrant art prints on the walls.

"It's nice to meet you," I repeat for the tenth time up and down these hallways. But instead of a polite nod or half smile like I received at the other nine, Dr. Sharma stands and gives me a hug. "Please call me Radhika. Welcome to the math department."

"Thank you," I say, more warmly now.

"You had everyone in quite a state last week with your lost identity." Radhika gives me a grin.

"I'm so sorry about that."

She squeezes my arm. "I'm just glad to see you've been found."

I can't help but laugh. "Me, too."

Radhika taps her finger to her lips. "Now, I remember from when they hired you that your research is in computational science and numerical analysis. But remind me what you're teaching this semester."

"I believe I'm teaching the freshman seminars—geometry, calculus, and algebra."

Radhika smiles. "Ah, yes. They always stick the new faculty with the freshmen. I taught those courses my first year, too. I know you're getting started a bit later than expected, so I'm happy to share my syllabi with you."

It's a generous offer, one I appreciate more than she knows after the week I've had. "That's really kind of you. It's been a while since I spent much time on the core subjects." I give her a sideways smile, and her grin in return is so infectious that before I can stop myself, I say, "At this point, all I remember about *algae-bra* is that it's something a mermaid wears."

Georgia rolls her eyes, but Radhika lets out a startled laugh and throws an arm around me. "Let's get lunch later this week, Catherine. I think we'll be friends."

Georgia and I head back down the hall to my office. It's everything I always dreamed—*my own space to work!*—except I can't help but think it looks like the "before" photo to Radhika's "after." Once I'm settled in, I'll have to do some decorating, maybe pick up a couple more of those botanical prints once I get my first paycheck.

At the thought of those prints, my mind drifts to Luca's colorful limbs, and my heart aches.

Maybe not the botanical prints, after all.

I spend the morning checking my university email—there's quite a backlog since I couldn't access it for a week. And then I find the syllabi that Radhika sent over, so I spend the afternoon planning for my classes. At five forty-five that evening, I pick up my phone and send a text to Melanie.

Heading over to the café. See you at six.

Less than thirty seconds later, my phone beeps with a reply.

Sorry, hung up at work. Can't make it.

I'm disappointed, but I know I'll see her at the fundraiser.

And speaking of the fundraiser, I remember that Mrs. Goodwin said they'd be hanging the decorations this evening. Maybe I can make it over there in time to help.

I'm packing up my bag when there's a knock at the door. Since I left it open, all I have to do is look up to find Dr. Gupta standing there.

"I see you're finally one of our faculty members, Catherine," he says dryly.

"I am, sir. And very happy to be here."

"I read the new outline of our paper last night." He pauses and then...

He gives me the approving nod. But for some reason, I just can't get excited about it.

"Excellent work, again," Dr. Gupta adds. "I think it's almost ready for you to write it up." He steps back from the doorway, turning to head down the hall. "Then we can start talking about the next one."

Before he can disappear from the doorway, something comes over me, and I blurt out, "Wait!"

He swings back around, eyebrows raised.

And I almost take it back. I almost say, *Never mind*, and buckle down and write the next paper. Except...I can't. I can't be the rule follower or people pleaser that I was a week ago. Something's changed in me, and I can't change it back. I don't *want* to change it back.

While I do want this job, somehow in the past week, I've discovered that success doesn't only mean getting ahead at work. It's also having a coworker whom you can laugh with at math jokes. And it's having the time to join the book club, and plan the community center fundraiser, and to stop to chat with Sal in the stairwell, too.

It's about the people you surround yourself with and the community you build. Luca tried to tell me that, and I was too wrapped up in my narrow view of the world to listen. But maybe it's not too late.

I clear my throat. "Thank you for pushing me so hard on this paper."

Dr. Gupta gives me a nod like, *Of course*.

"It's turning out better than I imagined," I continue. "And I look forward to submitting it to *Studies in Applied Mathematics* with you."

"Of course," Dr. Gupta says, turning to leave. "You're welcome."

"But the thing is..." I raise my voice.

He slowly spins back around.

"My name will have to appear as first author."

Dr. Gupta raises an eyebrow. "Is that right?"

I give him a shaky nod. "There's one more thing. We're going to have to ease up on the deadlines. I *just* got here."

His mouth drops open.

Well, that's it. I've definitely done it this time. All that work to get my identity back, and I'm going to end up a clown after all. But still, I don't take it back. I can't.

Dr. Gupta stares at me for a moment, almost like he's calculating something in his head. "All right," he finally says, backing away from the doorway. I hold my breath. "I look forward to being listed as the second author on this paper and collaborating with you on many in the future. On more reasonable deadlines, of course." He gives me one more approving nod, eyebrows raised, like this time I've really impressed him. "Like I've always said. You have a bright future ahead of you."

CHAPTER 32

On the night of the fundraiser, I wade through the crowd at the community center, checking out the silent auction, the food table, and the stage where Dad and his friends will perform later. The entire neighborhood must be here, spilling out of the gymnasium and down the hall to the lobby where the front desk had been transformed into a bar.

"Catherine." Mrs. Flowers waves from behind the counter. "Over here!" I make my way over, and she gives me a hug. "Don't you look gorgeous? Luca isn't going to be able to keep his eyes off you."

"Well, actually . . ." I begin, but she's already moved on.

"Make sure you try the wine." She slips a plastic cup of red into my hand. "It's Vito Morelli's special blend."

"Uncle Vito is a winemaker?"

"Of course." She flashes me the bottle. *Morelli Winery*, it reads. Of course. "He makes it right here in Bloomfield, beneath the club." Her eyes skate to someone behind me, and she waves frantically. "Darlene! Over here! Try the wine!"

I take a sip, and it's surprisingly good for a Merlot made in a Mafia man's Pittsburgh basement. But at this point, it doesn't surprise me that Uncle Vito has hidden talents. I toss a few bills into the collection jar and keep moving. Next, I mill around, chatting with Lorraine and Ginny and then checking out the book club's contribution to the silent auction: a giant box full of romance novels, one for every week they've been meeting for over a decade. I can't help myself, and I put in a bid.

An hour passes and then another, and I circle again, keeping an eye out for Melanie, who seems to be nowhere, and Luca, who seems to be everywhere. He's making the rounds, chatting with all the guests, pulling them into his orbit. I look for an opportunity to talk to him, but I'm not surprised that he's constantly surrounded by people. A few times, he glances up and sees me watching, but he immediately looks away, going back to his conversations.

After my realization at work, I want to tell him that he was right. And that I'm sorry. But I don't know if he'll want to hear it. And maybe this isn't the right time. I'm still expecting my mother any minute.

I wander back to the front desk / bar. "Mrs. Flowers, have you seen a middle-aged blond woman?" I know it's a long shot, but I expected Melanie to be here hours ago. "She's about forty-eight, looks a little like an older version of me, but her hair is cut into a bob?"

Mrs. Flowers shakes her head. "Doesn't ring a bell, honey, but I'll keep an eye out."

"Thanks. If you see her, could you tell her I'm in the gym?"

They're taking a break between performances, and I think Dad's act is first after the intermission. I'd hoped I could get the two of them together for a moment before he went on, but they may just have to talk after. I check my phone again to see if she responded to my text, but nothing shows up.

In the gym, I find the burlesque dance troupe all decked out in their sequined leotards and feather hats, and Dad in the center of it all. He, of course, is in his element, surrounded by a flock of bejeweled women and pulling Morellis into the mix to introduce them around. Uncle Vito seems especially pleased when Dad nudges him in Ginger Ale's direction.

When the dancers see me approaching, they push Dad and Vito aside to fawn over me, fussing with my hair and calling me Kitty Cat. Frenchy Kiss, my romance novel benefactor, pulls me into her arms, and I'm reminded that I want to introduce her to the book club later. Ginger grabs me by the shoulders, looking me over, and declares that I'm "perfection" in my emerald-green dress.

I take a step back to take in the group of women. "Thank you so much for coming to perform at this fundraiser. It really means a lot to me."

Frenchy reaches over to give my arm a squeeze. "Of course we came."

"Absolutely." Ginger's feathers bob along with her nod. "We were never going to be able to help you out with all those math problems of yours," she says. "So, when your dad said how important this is to you, we jumped at the chance."

An ache builds in the back of my throat. My gaze slides from Ginger and Frenchy to Betty Butterfly—who taught me how to drive—and then to Lola Von Crumpet, who found me dancing in front of the mirror all those years ago. "I don't think I've ever told you how much I appreciate everything you did for me as a kid."

"Don't be silly, Kitty Cat," Lola says, adjusting her bustier. "You've always been like a daughter to us."

"We're so proud of what you're doing to help this community," Betty chimes in.

The other women nod, their crystal headpieces glittering in the overhead lights, feathers waving. Beyond them, across the gymnasium and out into the hall, the crowd mingles. There's still no sign of Melanie.

And then it hits me.

Melanie isn't coming.

Melanie never wanted a daughter, and she still doesn't. It's fine to meet up for coffee when she can fit it in her schedule, but she's not going to go out of her way to come to the fundraiser because it's important to me. She's not going to make me a priority. Not like these women did. And still do.

How did I miss this? How did I miss that all along, I've had this slightly eccentric but deeply loving group of bedazzled godmothers who helped raise me? Who understood what I needed more than I understood it myself? These women, they weren't just teaching me how to shimmy and jazz walk. They were teaching me about life, just like any parent would do.

My eyes burn, and a lump forms in my throat. How did I ever think I was alone, that I was *on my own*, when all this time, ArtSpace wasn't just Dad's community, but mine, too? And the dancers, artists, and performers there had my back; they took me in; they were my family. A slightly eccentric family, maybe. But—I gaze around the community center gym at all the Morellis gathered there—*isn't that the best kind?*

I give another round of hugs so nobody will notice my eyes growing wet.

Eventually, Uncle Vito manages to reclaim his space next to Ginger, and Lorraine sidles up to Lola. I glance over at Dad, who was watching my exchange with the burlesque dancers, and his eyes look a little red.

"Hey," Dad says, pulling me into his chest. "I haven't had a chance to hug my girl yet."

I give him a squeeze, breathing in the faint, familiar scent of weed and sandalwood that's lingered on him since my childhood. "When do you go on?"

"In about ten minutes, I think."

It's now or never. I step back, bracing myself. "Dad, I have something to tell you."

"Tell me anything, Kitty Cat."

"The thing is…" The crowd mills around us, laughing and talking. Music blasts from the speakers. "I know you said I shouldn't. But—I found Melanie. I went to her condo, and I got my birth certificate back."

Dad takes it well. Better than I was expecting, honestly, and instead of reacting at all, he just kind of stands there silently for a moment, nodding and processing the whole thing. Finally, he meets my eyes. And then he says, "I know."

He knows?

"Wait." I hold up a hand. "How do you know?"

He pushes his hands into his overall pockets. The left one won't quite fit inside, and when he pulls it out, he's holding a yellow juggling ball. "She reached out last week. I guess it was the day after you and Luca met her at the hospital.

Excellent work on the food poisoning ruse, by the way. I'd honestly pay money to see you and Luca pull that off."

"You don't have any money," I point out. But then I focus on the other part of the conversation. "You're saying you knew I met her a week ago, and you didn't tell me?"

Dad shrugs. "It wasn't my place. I figured you'd tell me when you were ready." Which is just such a very *Dad* thing to say. For most of my life, I might have been annoyed by that and taken it as a sign of his complacency.

Whatever you want to do. Whatever makes you happy, Kitty Cat. When I told him about studying math in school, and getting my PhD, and moving to the DeGreco. *Whatever makes you happy, Kitty Cat.*

But maybe—like so many other parts of my life lately—I was looking at it all wrong.

He's never told me what to do or injected his opinions. He just let me be me in his own quirky way, even if that meant I turned out to be a rule-following mathematician instead of a happy-go-lucky juggler.

Which reminds me of Melanie.

"What did she say when she called you?"

He gives the juggling ball a couple of short tosses into the air. "Well, first, she had a really hard time believing *I'd* raised you." His amused expression fades. "And then she said…" His voice drops, and his words are cut off by the music and noise from the crowd.

"What?"

"Some other things."

"What other things?"

"It doesn't matter."

I huff out an indignant breath. "Why are you still covering for her? I mean, I get it that she didn't want a kid knocking on her door. But that doesn't mean that you had to go along and agree to change the birth certificate so she could be nothing but an egg donor. It takes two to—" I wave across the room, where Mrs. Goodwin is warming up with a kick step double spin combo. "You know. To Carolina shag, so to speak."

"She didn't want to be involved, and I didn't want to force her."

Whatever you want to do. Whatever makes you happy.

I sigh.

"Besides…" Dad starts tossing the ball higher. I don't think he even realizes he's doing it. "She wasn't *completely* just an egg donor."

I grab the bright yellow orb from the air. "What does *that* mean?"

"Well…" He shoves a hand back into his pocket. "We had an agreement."

"What kind of agreement?" This is the first I'm hearing of this. Melanie certainly didn't mention an agreement.

"Melanie's family is rich. Very, very rich."

I nod, remembering the expansive front porch and stately columns on the mansion where Luca and I had our stakeout. The well-dressed older woman. "I think I met my grandmother once." The door slamming in our faces. "Very briefly."

"Yes, Victoria." Dad sighs. "She was angry that Melanie got pregnant at the age of seventeen, especially with *my* baby. Even though I was just a kid myself. So—" From the depths of his pocket, Dad unearths another ball—blue, this time—and starts tossing it into the air. "She wrote me a very generous check."

"She—" I blink. "How generous?" We never had any money when I was growing up. "How much money could it have been?"

"Enough to put you through college and graduate school."

That's not possible. "I got scholarships."

"You did." Dad cocks his head. "But for an absolutely brilliant girl, I wondered that you never looked into the Cirque Foundation."

The music swells around us. From somewhere over my shoulder, I hear Uncle Vito's booming voice and Lorraine's buoyant laughter. But my gaze is focused on Dad. "You're saying Victoria's money paid for me to go to college, and you never told me?"

"I couldn't. It would have broken the terms of our agreement."

I give the bright yellow orb a squeeze over and over, like one of those stress balls people keep on their desks. Dad had money all along, and he'd saved it for me. He'd saved it so I could go on to become a rule-following mathematician.

"And now that we've broken the agreement, Victoria wants her money back?" I ask.

"Pretty sure she wouldn't have a leg to stand on." Dad lifts one leg high in the air, holds his arms out wide, and wobbles around like he's about to fall over. Classic clown move.

"How would we possibly pay her anyway? In juggling clubs?"

"Hey!" Dad presses a hand to his heart like I've wounded him. "Those clubs have real value."

"Sentimental value, maybe."

"Sentimental value is all I care about." He shrugs. "But no, she doesn't expect her money back. She wanted Melanie to tell me that we wouldn't be getting any more."

My mouth drops open. It's loud in here, but I'm pretty sure he said— "*More?*"

"She was going to write another check on your thirtieth birthday. That's why I couldn't tell you how to find her. Not until you turned thirty." His shoulders slump. "I'm sorry, Kitty Cat. I know how you worry, and I hoped that money would finally give you the security you always needed." Dad shoves his hands in his overalls, produces an orange ball this time, and starts passing it back and forth with the blue.

He can't *not* be juggling. It's just who he is.

"Can I ask you something, Dad?"

"Sure thing, Kitty Cat."

"Did you give up your dreams to raise me? You really could have gone into the circus, but you were stuck with a kid."

Dad lets both balls drop into his hands. "I didn't give up a single thing. You were the best thing to ever happen to me."

But I know he did. I see how much he loves performing. How the jobs I've been pushing him to take at the grocery store and the fast-food restaurants slowly wear away at his spirit. He could have used Melanie's money to fund his own career aspirations. Instead, he saved it for me.

I grab his arm. "Dad. I don't need my apartment at the DeGreco. I can move back in with you to save money and to support you to pursue your clown dreams full-time."

"Nah." Dad waves me off. "It's time you stopped worrying about me altogether. Besides, Vito hooked me up. Turns out he owns a bunch of nightclubs, and he needs regular performers to open for the national acts. He's booked me and the girls"—Dad nods at the burlesque troupe—"five nights a week."

I can't believe Vito came through for me again.

But that's the Morellis for you.

I gaze around the room at all the people who've come together to support the community center. To combat loneliness and make sure everyone has a place to go. I don't need my estranged grandmother's money for security, not when I have *this*. This community of people who care about each other.

And who care about *me*, who stepped up to help me when I needed it most. The aerial troupe is in front of the stage, testing out the silks that Uncle Vito's guys secured from the ceiling. The burlesque dancers are warming up in the back of the room. I can hear the belly dancers' tassels jingling. All of these people showed up because I needed them. My gaze slides to Mrs. Goodwin, and Fabrizio, and the book club. To all the people who jumped in to offer advice, or a pair of pants, or their help in breaking and entering. What would I have done without them?

I wish there were a way to thank them. But I have no idea how to say what's in my heart.

At that moment, Mrs. Goodwin climbs the stage and steps up to the microphone. "Ahem." The speaker gives a high peal of feedback, and Mrs. Goodwin leans back slightly. "Testing? Testing? Okay." She looks out at the crowd and spreads her arms wide. "I hope you all made sure to try some of Vito's tasty wine during the intermission. And remember that you can place your silent bids on all our wonderful auction items laid out in the game room." She clears her throat. "And now, we're going to resume the entertainment portion of the evening with a very special treat."

And then it comes to me. I turn to Dad. "Remember how you asked if I still remember that partner juggling routine?"

Mrs. Goodwin continues her introductions. "Not only is this performer incredibly handsome..." She fans herself with her hands. "But his balls are huge!" The crowd gasps. "Juggling balls, people. Get your minds out of the gutter!"

The crowd roars with laughter.

Dad's eyes sparkle. "*Do* you remember the partner juggling routine, Kitty Cat?"

"Of course I do."

"Without further ado..." Mrs. Goodwin says.

Dad takes my hand and tugs me toward the stage. "Come on."

"I present to you..."

We climb the stairs.

"Andy Lipton...oh!" Mrs. Goodwin's hand flutters to her lips as she spots me.

Dad picks up the juggling clubs and hands half to me. Then he takes his place on one side of the stage, and I cross to the other side.

Mrs. Goodwin turns back to the microphone. "Actually, I present to you the father-daughter juggling duo of..."

She pauses for dramatic effect. Down on the floor, someone beats on a table in a makeshift drumroll. *"Andy and Kitty Cat!"*

And Dad and I are off. He tosses a club in my direction at the same moment that I toss one in his. We mirror each other's movements, reaching out to catch the club coming our way in one hand while we throw the next club with the other. Soon, we have four clubs flying back and forth across the stage, then six. The crowd cheers, and the bass from the music thumps through the speakers. Dad gives me the nod, and we each do a spin, landing back in our original formation in time to catch the next club. The movements come back to me, the steady rhythm of throw-catch-throw-catch like a song that's been playing in the back of my head for all my life.

The crowd begins clapping along. Dad goes left and I go right, keeping the clubs flying as we switch places on the stage. The crowd stomps its feet. We execute another spin, flip the clubs under our legs, and turn around to throw them backward over our heads with perfect precision. Finally, we each do a double spin, toss the clubs as high as possible, and seamlessly catch them, ending in a bow.

The crowd goes wild.

Laughing, Dad wraps me in a hug, and I squeeze him back.

And then I spot Luca in the crowd. He's staring back, and when he sees me looking, he gives me that smile. Not the wide, charming grin, but the smaller, more subtle smile. The one that he saves just for me.

The crowd screams for an encore.

Keeping my eyes trained on Luca, I lean over to Dad. "I have to go."

He nods and gives me a light shove in the direction of the stairs. "Go get him."

I hold out my hand, letting the crowd know that Dad will take over from here—he's the real star, after all—and then I jog off the stage and wade into the crowd in the direction I saw Luca. I catch a flash of his white T-shirt and colorful limbs, but the audience surges around me. I talk to Lorraine and Ginny, Fabrizio, and Walt and Martin from the book club, and then a whole bunch of people I've never met before but who want to give me hugs and rave about my performance.

By the time I manage to slip away, Luca is onstage with Mrs. Goodwin, and the opening notes of "Build Me Up Buttercup" are blaring through the speakers. He reaches out a painted hand, and she takes it with her age-spotted one. I stop in the middle of the gym and watch as Luca pulls Mrs. Goodwin into his chest and then spins her back out. He matches her, kick step for kick step with his dancer's grace, that familiar grin flashing with each turn toward the audience. I can't help but smile and clap along, as charmed as the rest of the crowd.

When the dance is over, Mrs. Goodwin and Luca take bow after bow while the audience cheers. Finally, Luca gives the crowd a wave and jogs offstage, disappearing in the wings. Mrs. Goodwin steps up to introduce the aerial troupe on the floor below, and I make my way across the gym to sneak up the steps and duck behind the curtain. I find several of Uncle Vito's guys moving props and sets, but no Luca. I ask around, but nobody's seen him.

A moment later, Mrs. Goodwin joins me. "Wonderful show, Catherine. Everything is going beautifully."

"You and Luca were perfect, Mrs. Goodwin." I lean over to give her a hug, but I just can't linger any longer. "Do you know where he went?"

She checks her watch. "Oh, it's ten o'clock. He had to go put Mrs. Sterling to bed."

I blink. "He had to what?"

"Mrs. Sterling, who lives on the eleventh floor? She had a stroke about three weeks ago? Wait..." Mrs. Goodwin trails off, looking up at the ceiling and counting on her hands. "Maybe it was four weeks ago...?"

Mrs. Sterling, the older woman who won Luca's money playing poker. I remember her movements with only one hand, and I'd wondered if she'd had a stroke.

"It doesn't matter how many weeks," Mrs. Goodwin continues, brushing it off. "At any rate, her stroke was in early August."

"And Luca...puts her to bed?"

Mrs. Goodwin nods. "They wanted her to go to a nursing home, but you know, those places are where old people go to die." She waves a hand like, *Forget it.* "Mrs. Sterling has a nurse who comes by each day, but Luca checks in on her every night."

Mrs. Sterling is Luca's mystery woman on the eleventh floor? When he was running late to meet me, he was helping the older woman? "I didn't know anything about this..."

Mrs. Goodwin looks surprised. "He didn't tell you about finding Mrs. Sterling in the mail room?"

The mail room? My head jerks back. Did she say early August? The pieces begin to slide together. "No—" I stutter. "He didn't."

"I guess I'm not surprised Luca didn't say anything." Mrs. Goodwin sighs. "He doesn't like to accept praise. But he was a real hero that day, picking the poor woman up and rushing her to the hospital. Doctors say she wouldn't have made it if it weren't for Luca's quick thinking." She presses a hand to her heart. "But that's Luca for you. Always taking care of us."

I picture Luca trailing after Mrs. Goodwin in the pharmacy aisle, patiently waiting for her to choose a lipstick color and hand cream. "Like taking you to run errands or stop at the pharmacy."

Mrs. Goodwin nods. "You have no idea how hard it is to give up driving. It's like someone's stolen your freedom. But my eyesight isn't what it used to be, so I had no choice. I could get my water pills delivered, but I like to get out and pick things out for myself. It makes me feel like I'm still in charge of my life."

I'd been annoyed that day when I was along for the ride—that Luca was wasting my time, that he wasn't doing his job at the front desk. "So Luca helps you." I gaze around the community center at all the people milling about. "He helps *all* of you."

"The truth is..." Mrs. Goodwin leans in, like she's about to tell me a secret. "The DeGreco doesn't really need a doorman. We never had one before Luca started coming by every day to look in on his grandpa when he was sick. He came so often and helped us all out so much, Vito insisted on putting him on the payroll."

"Uncle Vito?"

Mrs. Goodwin nods. "He owns the building. Someday it will go to Luca. And good thing, too. It will never get into the hands of those nasty developers that way."

I feel my body flush with shame at the memory of how I'd hounded him about shirking his responsibilities, complaining that he wasn't following the rules.

A doorman's job is to be at the door, I'd insisted.

Only if you look at everything from your narrow view of the world, was his reply.

My view of the world *had* been as narrow as the cold, soulless hallways of Melanie's apartment building. But thanks to Luca, it's stretched and expanded and grown to include older people and Mafia men and burlesque dancers and…*Dad*. And a doorman who reminds me of my dad in all the best possible ways, with his charm and generosity and openness.

I throw my arms around Mrs. Goodwin and plant a giant kiss on her weathered cheek. "Thank you, Mrs. Goodwin."

She pats me on the back. "Of course, dear. You go get him."

CHAPTER 33

I yank open the door to the DeGreco's lobby and run inside. It's dark, all the lights are off except for the emergency ones by the stairs, and my footfalls echo across the tile. Luca's not here. Maybe he's still upstairs with Mrs. Sterling, or maybe he went to bed. I check the elevator to see if I can tell which floor it's on, but the numbers are burned out.

It's broken again.

"Damn it, Mrs. Hartman," I mutter. I don't believe in ghosts, but if my identity can disappear and then magically reappear, I'm not ruling them out, either.

At that moment, I hear a muted shuffle from behind the front desk. *Of course.* The elevator is broken. I sprint around to the other side and stop short. And then the back of my throat aches with emotion. Because there on the floor is Luca. He's lounging on the pillow that Mrs. Esposito in 6D gave him, feet crossed and tattooed arms propped behind his head.

I tower over him, and he looks up at me. "Hi." His lips curve into a hint of a smile. Just enough to make me want more.

"Hi," I repeat. My heart pounds, but it has nothing to do with my run over here. "How's Mrs. Sterling?"

"She's fine. Beat me at poker again."

"I think you're letting her win."

He shrugs, and I know he'd never admit it.

I take a step back to lean against the wall opposite him and slowly slide down until I'm sitting on the floor. He pulls himself to a cross-legged position, and in the semidarkness, our eyes meet.

I grab a corner of his blanket and twist it in my hands. "I know Mrs. Sterling had her stroke the day you were sorting the mail. That's how my letters got lost."

He nods slowly.

"That must have been so scary for you."

Luca blows out a breath and runs a hand through his hair. "I'm just glad I was there."

"I'm sorry I doubted you." I stare past him, at the underside of the front desk. "I'm sorry I was so wrapped up in following the rules that I missed the fact that you're the most caring, thoughtful, good-hearted person I've ever met."

His mouth curves upward. "I forgive you. You had a bad couple of weeks."

"See, that's what I mean." Suddenly, these few feet between us are too many. I push away from the wall and crawl over to the blanket nest. "You take care of everyone. Your family, the people in this building…and me." I inch closer. "I don't know what I would have done without you these past few weeks."

"You're the most capable person I've ever met," Luca says. "You would have figured it out on your own."

"I think I'm done with being on my own."

And then Luca gives me that crooked smile, the one that's

just for me, and he reaches out a hand to pull me against him. "Well, it's a good thing, because you have a lot of people who care about you."

And then he kisses me.

I inch closer, sliding onto his lap and pushing him back against the blankets. His arms wrap around me, gently shifting me sideways so I'm lying next to him on the pillow, and then he kisses me again. When we finally break apart, Luca props himself up on his colorful arm, bending it under his head so he can look me in the eye. "Moonstone," he murmurs.

"Yes, Elbow?"

"Watching you juggle tonight was amazing."

"That was a onetime thing," I warn. "So, don't expect it to happen again."

"You keep saying that, but..." He draws out the words like he doesn't believe me one bit. "Mrs. Goodwin told me earlier tonight that the community center made so much money just on ticket sales alone that they can cover the last 10k they needed to buy the building. So anything they make on the auction can go toward funding new programs."

I close my eyes. "Don't tell me."

"The community is very interested in juggling lessons."

"I wonder whose idea that was."

"We've got one guy on board to teach the class. But do you know anyone who might be able to assist him? Maybe someone with teaching experience..." He cocks his head. "Like a professor, for example?"

I lean back to look in his eyes. "I am never going to escape my clown destiny, am I?"

"Why would you want to?"

I think back to an hour ago when Dad and I were up on that stage together. Matching each other step for step, throw for throw. I can still hear the hoots and cheers from the crowd. Dad's shows bring real joy to people. And then there was that day in the gym when Dad taught the whole group how to juggle. You couldn't miss the pride and sense of accomplishment on their faces when they landed a catch. "You're right," I admit. "Why would I want to?"

Luca's smile widens. And in that moment, I know that not only will he coax me to juggle again, but I might as well give up on coasters, and someday, I'll probably end up with a tattoo.

But I don't mind one bit. I reach up and run my fingers down Luca's shoulder to the edge of his T-shirt and then across his colorful arm. "Sal was right. Something might seem like a disaster and turn out to be a beautiful, wonderful opportunity."

Luca's eyes widen. "What did you say?" He springs upright like a jack-in-the-box. "*Who?*"

I stare up at him. "Sal. You know. That sweet older man with the butterscotch candies. He gave me some advice about my identity disappearance. And he was right."

Luca blinks at me over and over. It goes on for so long that I begin to worry. Finally, he chokes out, "That's impossible."

I push myself up to a seated position next to him. "What's going on? Did something happen to Sal?" My heart squeezes. "Now that I think about it, I didn't see him at the party."

Luca slowly shakes his head back and forth. "Sal wasn't

at the party, Catherine...because he died last year. Sal was my grandpa."

Now my mouth drops open. "That's—*no*." But I know Luca would never make a joke about something like this. "Then who was the guy I met in your car? That day you picked me up from my meeting with Dr. Gupta? We chatted while you went in the pharmacy."

"The day we went to the pharmacy, it was just me and Mrs. Goodwin. You waited in the car alone."

"No, I'm sure he was there. You introduced me." Except... the memory hovers at the edge of my consciousness... *I'd* introduced myself when I got in the car, and Mrs. Goodwin had remarked that she already knew who I was. Is it possible Mrs. Goodwin and Luca didn't know Sal was there? Is it possible Sal *wasn't* there?

"Luca, I've seen him half a dozen times in the stairwell. He gave me butterscotch candies, and I ate them. They..."

"Made me think of my grandpa." Luca looks as dazed as I feel. "That day when you got out of the car. You smelled like butterscotch."

That moment when Luca leaned in, and I thought he was going to kiss me.

Luca's gaze drifts to mine. "How did Grandpa look? How..." His voice breaks. "How was he?"

I grab his hand and squeeze. "He was wonderful." I slide closer. "I'm so grateful I got to know him."

"I bet it was Grandpa who meddled with your identity." He gives a stunned laugh and shakes his head. "It had to be."

And then it comes back to me, too. *Some days, I'd simply like to be...nobody.* Sal was there. Even if I didn't say it out loud, he heard me. And somehow, he knew I needed this. I needed an opportunity disguised as a disaster. And maybe he knew I needed Luca, too.

Luca's eyes soften. "Your apartment used to be my grandpa's. It took me ages to rent it out. But then you came along, and…I knew you were the one." He pulls me against his chest. "Maybe Grandpa knew you were the one, too."

We drift back down to the floor into our nest of blankets. I lay my head on Luca's chest, and he tucks his arm around me, settling his hand on my hip.

"You know," I muse. "This strange nest on the floor is actually pretty comfortable."

"The elevator is out…"

I nod. "It's been a hard couple of weeks for Mrs. Hartman."

Luca raises an eyebrow like *finally* I'm getting it. "Half the building will be heading home from the fundraiser soon. So I'm going to need to stay here to make sure I'm available to take them on the freight elevator."

"Would you like some company?" I glance up to meet his eyes.

Luca cocks his head, squinting at me like he can't quite decide. "Well…technically, sleeping on the floor isn't permitted. It's all laid out in the building's manual of rules and regulations."

"That's fine with me." I lean in and press a kiss to his lips. "Don't you know that these days, I'm breaking all the rules?"

EPILOGUE

One year later

When I step into the vast warehouse of ArtSpace, the first thing that hits me is the scent. It's a bit musty, vaguely dank, and mixed with the sharp notes of oil paint and Chanel No. 5. But instead of leaving me disconcerted with memories of my childhood, it's pleasant, comforting. I've spent more time in ArtSpace in the past year than I have since I was a kid. I usually come here about once a week now—to visit with Dad, but also to share a bottle of wine with Ginger Ale and to talk romance novels with Frenchy.

We all spent Christmas Eve at the Morellis' last year, but Ginger still puts our presents under the bike that she'd dressed up in twinkling lights, and we came by on Christmas Day to keep traditions alive. And today, I'm here to celebrate ArtSpace's thirtieth anniversary.

My gaze skates across the crowd of people, and I absently wonder if Melanie made it this time. Though she RSVPed, my mother actually shows up about fifty percent of the time that she says she will. But I think she's trying as best she can.

It's funny that I ever thought she was the reliable one, when actually, that title has to go to Luca. He's still always late for things, but it's usually because he's driving someone to the pharmacy, helping out at the community center, or putting an older lady to bed.

I search for him in the crowd, and I find him standing with Dad. They're talking and laughing—probably rehashing one of their adventures at Burning Man earlier this month. They had a blast.

I opted to stay home.

When Luca spots me across the crowd, his face lights up with that smile that's just for me. He says something to Dad and heads in my direction. I greet him with a kiss.

"I thought you'd never get here, Moonstone," he says with a raise of his eyebrows, and I laugh because this time, *I'm* the one who's late.

"Radhika and I just found out that our paper was accepted to *Studies in Applied Mathematics*."

Luca gives a yell and picks me up off my feet in a hug. "I knew it would." He takes my hand. "Come on, let's get some champagne to celebrate."

As we cross the warehouse, I can't help but notice that ArtSpace is sparkling like one giant burlesque costume come to life tonight. Uncle Vito sent his guys over earlier this week to get up on ladders, clean the windows, and install brand-new lighting. The aerialists spin on their overhead silks, the acrobats do flips, Mrs. Goodwin is leading the Macarena, and the community center's juggling club tosses colorful balls in the air.

Luca and I pass by the gallery space, and he nudges me inside. It's empty—I guess everyone is in the main room enjoying the performances—and I'm glad they're otherwise occupied when he kisses me again.

"Catherine," Luca murmurs against my mouth.

"Yes, Elbow?"

"I have something to show you." He sounds nervous. Unsure.

I pull back. "What is it?"

He presses his lips together, looking in my eyes for just a moment, and then he steps back and waves a hand around the room. I look up and gasp.

On the walls are the most beautiful illustrations I've ever seen. Blue birds, and red flowers, and green vines, and butterflies with wings of every color of the rainbow skate across canvases hanging on the wall.

"Oh my God, Luca." My wide-eyed gaze darts to his, and then to his painted arms, and then back to the walls. "These are *yours*?" I knew he was spending more time at ArtSpace working on his illustrations, but I had no idea he was doing all of this.

"Ginger asked me to display them." Luca smiles. "I wanted to surprise you."

"I'm surprised." I gape at the walls again. "And I'm so proud of you."

"I'm still just doing it for fun," he says. "If Ginger sells any, I'm going to donate the money to the community center." And that part doesn't surprise me one bit. Because Luca is the most caring, thoughtful person I know, and of course he wants to use his art to help the people in his community. And then I remember that I'm meeting with the book club tomorrow, and I have to get the keys to the Town Car so I can take Mrs. Sterling to her doctor's appointment the following day, and next week Mrs.

Flowers wants me to stop by to look over her accounting spreadsheet.

Actually, it's *our* community.

And that's when I sense movement across the room. I look up, and my heart leaps into my throat. Next to me, I hear a gasp from Luca, and my hand reaches out to grab his. Because there in the doorway stands Sal, gazing around the gallery at Luca's drawings. His face shines with pride as he slowly takes in each one.

Luca's hand tightens on mine. "Grandpa?" he whispers.

Sal looks over at us, flashing a wide smile that so exactly matches Luca's that I can't believe I didn't see the resemblance last year. He gives Luca a nod and a wave. And then he turns and shuffles back out into the main room, disappearing into the crowd.

We stand there for a moment, too stunned to speak. Finally, Luca's gaze flickers to mine. "You saw him, right?"

"Yes," I say breathlessly, turning to wrap my arms around Luca's waist. He pulls me against him, his heart beating fast.

I never saw Sal after I got my identity back last year. I always hoped he'd show up again for Luca's sake, but it never happened. Until now. Of course he came back now. Because nothing would mean more to Luca than knowing his grandpa approved of his art, that he was proud of him.

"Are you okay?" I take his face in my hands.

"Yes." Luca sucks in a deep breath and blows it out slowly. "I'm a little sad. But he'll be here whenever I need him."

I know he will. That's where his grandson gets it from.

"And in the meantime, I'm pretty sure he's telling me to keep doing my art."

I nod. "That's definitely what he's telling you."

Luca cocks his head, the corner of his mouth twitching. "I'm actually really glad to hear you say that, Moonstone." His hand slides up my back, and he taps a spot above my shoulder blade. "I'm thinking a hummingbird right here."

His lips curve into that charming smile, and I find myself wavering. By this time next year, I'm pretty sure I'll have a hummingbird on my shoulder. Because somehow, Luca can talk me into anything.

ACKNOWLEDGMENTS

I am so grateful to the entire team at Forever who made this book possible. In particular, thank you to Estelle Hallick and Alli Rosenthal for everything you do to support authors and to share our books with the world. To Sabrina Flemming, thank you for your fantastic insights. And my enormous gratitude to my editor Junessa Viloria for always knowing exactly how to make a story better. It's been such a joy and honor to work with you.

To Jill Marsal, thank you for always delivering the perfect combination of wise and thoughtful advice with a side of realistic expectations. I am so grateful to have you as my agent.

To Sarah Congdon, you did it again. Thank you for (another!) book cover that I absolutely love. It captures my story perfectly.

With each book, I am more grateful for my wonderful and supportive writing community, and I truly don't know what I'd do without you. In particular, thank you to Sharon Peterson, Anna Collins, Lauren Kung Jessen, Meredith Schorr, Dylan Newton, Lainey Davis, and Elizabeth Perry.

Thank you to Riverstone Bookstore in Pittsburgh, Pennsylvania, for all that you do to champion my books. And to all the Bookstagrammers, bloggers, reviewers, book clubs, and so many others who dedicate their time to sharing their love of books, I am so grateful for you.

Thank you to my amazing family for all of your support. And finally, my enormous love and gratitude to my husband, Sid. I couldn't write a better husband, father, or best friend.

YOUR
BOOK
CLUB
RESOURCE

Visit **GCPClubCar.com** to
sign up for the GCP Club Car
newsletter, featuring exclusive
promotions, info on other
Club Car titles, and more.

Find us on
social media: **@ReadForeverPub**

READING GROUP GUIDE

Dear Reader,

Thank you so much for choosing *Wish I Were Here*! I hope you enjoyed it.

This book was inspired by a true story...sort of. A few years ago, I clicked on a news article about a woman in France whose identity had gone missing. In that woman's case, she was declared dead through a mix-up of paperwork and had to fight for years to prove she was still alive. The story was actually quite tragic, and the error ruined her life.

So how did a sad story like that one inspire me to write a romantic comedy? While I was reading about that woman in France, I couldn't help but wonder: What if the story *wasn't* tragic? What if a similar mix-up became an opportunity for someone to change their life, or to view the world in a new way? What if stepping out of their normal routine leads to new beginnings, friendships, and love?

Essentially, I asked myself: Could I turn that sad story into one that's magical, uplifting, and hopeful? I hope so! I'd love to hear more about your book club discussion, so please reach out over social media! And thank you again for reading!

Best wishes,
Melissa

DISCUSSION QUESTIONS

1. When we meet Catherine and Luca, their opposite natures immediately become clear. Catherine is a reserved, perpetually early rule follower, whose life is organized by calendars and lists and label makers. Luca is a charming free spirit, who rarely shows up on time and has probably never made a list in his life. Which character do you relate to? In what ways are you more like Catherine or Luca?

2. Like Luca, Catherine's dad, Andy, is more of a free spirit. Catherine is delighted to learn that her mother is reserved, organized, and focused on her career, just like Catherine is. Do you think she inherited those traits from her mother, or did her need for order and her desire to be responsible form as a response to the instability at home when she was growing up? How much of Catherine's personality is nature vs. nurture?

3. Mrs. Goodwin and many of her friends challenge the stereotype of the grumpy, frail older adult by living full, vibrant lives. What are your goals for growing older, and what sorts of things will you do to ensure that your life, like Mrs. Goodwin's, stays full of friends, activities, and fun?

4. There is a moment when Catherine wishes to be "nobody." Have you ever felt this way? What would you do if your identity disappeared like Catherine's?

5. "Found family" is an important theme in this book: the idea that you may be born or adopted into a family, but it doesn't end there. There is a whole world of people who you can *choose* as your family—and they can choose you. Do you have a found family? Who are those people for you, and how did you come together?

6. Luca and Mrs. Goodwin understand the importance of community and found family from the beginning of the book, but it takes Catherine a while to realize that she's had a large and loving, if somewhat unconventional, family all along. What are some factors that contributed to Catherine's inability to see all the people who love her?

7. Catherine asks Luca, "Do you think Uncle Vito would have really cut off my dad's hand if I'd wanted him to?" Luca's answer is vague. Do *you* think Uncle Vito would have cut off Andy's hand...or anyone's? What is your impression of him?

8. In addition to the older residents, the DeGreco is populated by a couple of (mostly) harmless ghosts, who meddle and cause mischief. Luca comments, "It's an old building, and lots of people lived there for their whole lives. Some like to hang around for a while...after." Do

you believe that people might stay in a place after they die? Have you ever had a ghostly encounter?

9. Catherine says that she knows her dad loves her in his own way, but it's not always in the way that she needs. What was your impression of Andy as a father?

10. Luca's mother, Lorraine, asks, "What kind of mother leaves her kid?" While Catherine is hurt by her mother's abandonment, there are moments when she understands why Melanie didn't want to be a part of her life. How did you feel about Melanie leaving her daughter and never looking back? Do you blame her, or is there a part of you, like Catherine, who understands why she did it?

ABOUT THE AUTHOR

Melissa Wiesner's mother didn't allow her to watch much TV as a child and, instead, made her play with paint, colorful pipe cleaners, random bits of fabric, and all manner of other crafty things. This set Melissa up for a lifetime of creative pursuits, and it was only a matter of time before things took a bookish turn.

A night owl, Melissa began writing novels when her early-to-bed family retired for the evening. She is the award-winning author of contemporary romantic comedies and emotional women's fiction. Her work has earned praise from *Kirkus*, *Booklist*, *Library Journal*, and *Publishers Weekly* and has been featured in *Woman's World*, *First for Women*, and *The Knot*. Her novels will soon be translated into a dozen languages.

Along with her charming husband and two adorable children, Melissa splits her time between the big city of Pittsburgh, Pennsylvania, and rural West Virginia.

You can learn more at:
MelissaWiesner.com
Instagram @MelissaWiesnerAuthor
Facebook.com/MelissaWiesnerAuthor

YOUR
BOOK
CLUB
RESOURCE

VISIT
GCPClubCar.com

to sign up for the **GCP Club Car** newsletter, featuring exclusive promotions, info on other **Club Car** titles, and more.